BOOK I

KW-177-988

RELUCTANT GODS

by

Paul Hutchens

authorHOUSE®

AuthorHouse™ UK Ltd.
500 Avebury Boulevard
Central Milton Keynes, MK9 2BE
www.authorhouse.co.uk
Phone: 08001974150

First published by AuthorHouse 7/28/2008

ISBN: 978-1-4343-9726-3 (sc)

Printed in the United States of America
Bloomington, Indiana

This book is printed on acid-free paper.

1
AN EXPERIMENT

Mark carefully arranged his notepad, pen and elbows on the desk in front of him, drew a deep breath and slowly exhaled as he looked around the state-of-the-art auditorium. At twenty-four, he was still a student, a very shy and retiring student, and yet here he was in the Eurasian Space Agency's control centre in Geneva with some of the world's finest scientists. He felt like an interloper, especially on this potentially momentous day, but excitement and curiosity overcame much of his usual self-consciousness. Sitting at the back of the auditorium also helped a lot.

He had not received an invitation from the Space Agency, nor had he ever expected to, but chance intervened. One of Mark's two PhD supervisors was Professor Edward Banks, an eminent particle physicist whose face was moderately familiar to people who watched science programmes. Professor Banks, accompanied by a research assistant, would have been the only representative of any British university to go to Geneva, but he had suffered a minor stroke two weeks earlier and could not travel. It was agreed that Dr. Rebecca Marchant, Mark's other supervisor, should take Bank's place. Rebecca's Doctorate was in particle physics but she now also specialised in the philosophy and ethics of science. Because Mark's research was closely related to Rebecca's interests, she asked him if he would like to accompany her as her research assistant. He said he would love to go, but there were plenty of people who were more qualified than he was. 'No worries,' she said in her softly spoken Australian accent, 'I don't really need an assistant. It'll be useful experience for you, and you can tell me what you think.'

Unlike Professor Banks, who was a rather distant figure to his many research students, Rebecca's only postgraduate student was Mark and she was not distant at all. In fact, during their frequent supervisory meetings, he was all too aware of her presence. She was more than ten years older than him, married, and had never spoken or acted in an overtly flirtatious manner. She did, however, have a disturbing way of leaning over his shoulder to look at his computer screen. Her warm hand on his shoulder would have been enough to make him feel a bit awkward, but the closeness of her face and her warm breath curling around his face made his cheeks burn with a mixture of involuntary desire and intense embarrassment. For as long as he could remember he had felt that other people could read his thoughts and feelings like a book, and he did not want any 'improper' thoughts or feelings intruding into his relationship with his supervisor, no matter how involuntary they were.

Mark was shy in virtually all social situations and painfully shy with women. Had it not been for a short fumbling relationship soon after leaving school, he would still have been a virgin. He had hated most aspects of school, but did at least find sanctuary in the school library. When he left school he spent two years working in poorly paid jobs and making occasional fruitless attempts to find a social niche to slot into. These two years were worse than school and he missed the gentle friendships of those who, like himself, sought out quiet corners to escape the daily cruelties and minor indignities inflicted upon them by their physically competitive schoolmates.

The disappointments of post-school life soon prompted him to re-immerse himself in academia, partly to get a foothold on a decent career ladder and partly because reading, any kind of reading, had the power to dispel his sense of social isolation without challenging it. In addition to his interest in science, he kept up a long-standing fascination for all aspects of ancient Roman history, and sometimes wondered whether he should have studied ancient history rather than science. In terms of fiction, his all-time favourite book was Tolkien's *Lord of the Rings* and he enjoyed comparing Tolkien's characters and story lines with characters and situations in the real world. As he graduated towards doctoral level he liked to think of himself as a wizard's apprentice, but the scent of Rebecca at such close quarters made him feel more like a slightly sordid hobbit in the presence of a great elf queen.

He was nervous about flying to Geneva and checking into the same hotel as Rebecca, although he need not have worried. She was friendly enough, but mostly absorbed with her work during the journey, and within ten minutes of checking-in she had disappeared completely for the entire thirty hours or so before they were due at the Space Agency building. Being a largely solitary individual, Mark spent most of this time sleeping, reading and eating in his hotel room and did not engage in conversation with anyone before reporting to the Space Agency's reception.

An uncommunicative security guard swiped Mark's plastic pass over the reception's scanner, led him along two corridors and through three sets of doors to an area reserved for invited correspondents and observers at the back of the auditorium. After vaguely gesturing towards an empty desk with his hand, the security guard left without speaking. There were six other people in this area, all of whom appeared to know each other and seemed to be utterly unaware of Mark's existence. Their desks were set slightly above and behind forty-five people sitting at workstations arranged in three curved ranks. These in turn were set slightly above and behind a large central workstation which was occupied by two women and one man. Everyone in the room faced a wall that was completely filled with computer screens, including a big screen at its centre. With all of the seats occupied, it took Mark a couple of minutes to spot Rebecca sitting near the middle of the room.

All the screens were showing images, graphs or information of some kind. The big central screen was split into two images. The left-hand half of the screen showed a portion of an enormous space station, called *Achilles*, in geostationary orbit three hundred and fifty thousand kilometres above their heads. The right-hand half showed a real-time representation of a small device, named *Molly*, that was aboard *Achilles* but could not be filmed in its perfectly sealed chamber. Mark had taken his seat about three hours before *Achilles* was due to launch *Molly* into the antimatter universe.

At just over three centimeters in diameter, *Molly* looked liked a metallic-green miniature rugby ball. Although small, *Molly* contained a huge array of cutting-edge micro- and nano-technologies. Eleven years had passed since a similar device had sent back what information it could in the incredibly short space of time that it took to pass into the antimatter universe. A few photons of light had apparently been detected in what otherwise seemed to be an empty bit of 'anti-space'. Scientific opinion among those involved in this field tended to regard the experiment's findings as evidence that our universe had an antimatter equivalent that operates on much the same principles as our own universe, although most other scientists and commentators remained unconvinced by the fuzzy images. Subsequent experiments merely served to reinforce the initial views of enthusiasts and skeptics alike.

This time, *Achilles* carried a beefed-up particle accelerator that produced a bombardment of subatomic particles in a carefully choreographed arrangement referred to as 'the rifle'. An initial burst of super-accelerated particles would open a 'window' to the antimatter universe, followed by a tubular stream of heavily concentrated particles that would attempt to hold the window open. Within the rifle, much lower concentrations of particles would undulate in spiraling waves that were designed to sweep antimatter particles past *Molly's* flanks as she hurtled through the window and beyond. It was hoped that *Molly* could survive and transmit information back down the centre of the rifle for as long as the window into the antimatter universe could be kept open. No one knew how long that would be, but anything approaching one full second of uninterrupted information transfer would represent a major advance on anything that had been achieved so far.

Everyone watched in silence as the digital clock above the big split-screen marked the final countdown. When the countdown ended, a green light directly above the clock turned red. Nothing changed on the left of the big screen, but the real-time representation of *Molly* on the right vanished. At the same instant, some of the smaller screens started scrolling streams of digits and symbols at a dizzying rate, while others showed coloured bars going up and down as if they were synchronised with an orchestral climax, or traced lines as though indicating someone's vital signs during a heart attack. Breaths were held in anticipation of an extremely short burst of information that might be analysed at leisure when the light went green again. But the connection held and *Molly* continued to send colossal amounts of information back down the rifle for second after second.

Ten seconds passed in silence, then twenty. At thirty seconds someone breathed out the words, 'whoa, what the hell!' and another said, 'no shit!' and laughed nervously. Still the light stayed red as the clock passed forty seconds, fifty, then sixty seconds. At this point there were a few restrained cheers and claps, but several people seemed to be getting restless and began to give voice to their uncertainty with comments like 'what's going on here?' and 'this can't be right, can it?' At around one hundred seconds, someone called 'is something stuck? should we give something a kick?' Then the red light went back to green, the digital clock stopped at 108.34964362 seconds, some of the more frenetic activity on the screens settled down a bit, and silence returned. The split central screen remained as it was, but six smaller screens on either side of it went dark for a moment, then begun to show points of light that steadily crystallised into high-resolution images of what Mark soon recognised as different sections of the night sky.

Being quite familiar with star patterns, it did not take him long to figure that the twelve images together represented all areas of the sky that surrounded the Earth. However, he was just beginning to think that something was missing when the woman sitting in the middle seat of the central workstation cleared her throat and said, 'well, there you have it. *Molly* tells us that the anti-universe looks like that.'

The nameplate on the desk in front of the woman who had spoken read: *Kimie Yamamoto – Project Coordinator*, although Mark overheard whispered comments that referred to her as Kim.

'It *seems*,' Kim continued in a very cautious tone, 'that the anti-universe does not just operate on similar principles to our own universe, it looks very much like a copy of our universe, but, err, with some fairly obvious exceptions.' As she spoke, Mark suddenly realised that the sun and the moon were missing.

A few people worked intently at their consoles or exchanged hushed comments with their neighbours, but most just stared at the screens on the wall, or at Kim as she tapped a ballpoint pen against her teeth. After some quiet consultations with the two people sitting either side of her, Kim used her console to replace the two images on the big central screen with two new images. Both sides of the screen now showed pristine three-dimensional views of very similar-looking sections of the night sky, except that the one on the right included a tiny image of Saturn. On closer inspection, there were some other differences too.

'That,' said Kim, pointing to the image on the left, 'according to *Molly*, is a section of the anti-universe. On the right is the corresponding section of our universe, as seen from

Achilles.' Then she used her cursor to drag the right-hand image and superimpose it on the left-hand image. Most of the stars matched more or less exactly, but some were visibly out of sync and a few were well out or missing completely.

'Our solar system is not replicated here at all,' she continued, 'otherwise, the stars that are most out of line with our own universe are those that are closest to us in our bit of the galaxy. Beyond them, our closest star systems seem to be a little out of place, but distant stars and galaxies are in identical or virtually identical positions.'

As she spoke, Mark wondered if they were looking at star systems and galaxies in the ordinary universe, but from a different angle than they were used to. On the basis of this thought, he began to suspect that *Molly* had not been sent into another universe at all, but had somehow popped out a long way from where she was launched; far enough to make our own sun look like just another star. Other people were evidently having similar thoughts, for a lively debate was developing in the middle of the room about whether *Achilles* could have opened up a wormhole to another part of the known universe.

'Wormhole my back-passage,' boomed the baritone voice of a venerable and very well-known American scientist called Jack Richardson, who was seated directly behind the central workstation, 'wormholes are pure fantasy.'

'Jack!' Kim called over the rising hubbub, 'please don't refer to wormholes and your back-passage in the same sentence: that's certainly not one of my fantasies!'

Caught off-guard, Mark had to suppress a convulsive laugh with such force that a snot bubble blossomed from one of his nostrils. He immediately ducked under his desk and wiped the bubble off, but the loss of composure broke his concentration. After a quick scan to make sure he had not drawn anyone's attention, he spent a little while gazing at Kim and marveling at her huge presence and faultless composure among such an august gathering of quarrelsome scientists. She was in fact very small, looked to be in her early thirties, and her guileless almond eyes gave her a look of innocent wonder when her face was in repose. But she spoke with an unmistakable air of easy leadership and a cool, sharp mind. Mark could not imagine anyone acting more unlike he would act in her position. He watched her in fascination for a few more moments before his focus returned to what she was saying.

Kim's intervention had had the desired effect throughout the room. Silence quickly returned and she directed everyone's full attention back to the images in front of her. She separated the images again, and said, 'Luka,' to the woman sitting on her right, 'could you get a fix on where we would need to be in the anti-universe, or vice versa, if these images were to match up?'

'Yes, already on it,' said Luka nodding at the big screen. 'There, middle of the box.' A white square frame outlined a small portion of the antimatter universe. 'Zoom?' she asked.

'Yes, please.'

The area featured inside the box enlarged to fill the left side of the big split-screen, and another small box appeared in the middle of that, then this box enlarged too. The process was repeated until a star near the centre of the frame became a yellowish sun at the edge of the frame. The sun did not appear in the next frame, just another bit of skyscape where Luka's computer said the Earth should be if the images of the two universes were to match up.

'Nothing there,' said Kim.

'No, but that sun looked very like our own. Can I have a minute or two?'

'Sure.'

Luka took several minutes adjusting the zoom to scan sections of space that lay ninety-three million miles from the yellowish sun. Eventually, a tiny crescent-shaped object appeared at the upper left of the screen, and another zoom put the crescent in the middle. The image was then enlarged to fill most of the screen. The next enlargement did not sharpen the image, so Luka zoomed back out a little to give optimal resolution. The image was grainy but clear enough to show that the crescent was blue with swirls of white. The three-quarters that lay in darkness could be faintly discerned if one looked hard enough, as indeed could the shapes of what looked like the Iberian peninsula and northwestern Africa on the edge of the dark areas, and what could have been part of Brazil on the horizon.

Kim broke the deepening silence, 'hmm, that's interesting.'

'Huh, ever the master of understatement,' said Jack, which drew a sharp 'shh' from two or three others.

'Are we looking back at Earth?' asked a doubtful voice from near the back of the room.

Kim gestured towards the dark portions of the planet with an upturned palm. 'There are no lights. If we were looking back at ourselves, there would be thousands of patches of light marking towns and cities.'

'Excuse me,' a new female voice interrupted from the middle of the room, 'but there do appear to be lights.'

'Where, Sunita?' asked Kim.

'I've found three possible sources so far, but I'm fairly certain of one of them.'

'Just a moment,' said Kim, tapping a few keys at her console, 'it's yours now if you want it.'

Sunita maneuvered the cursor over the left-hand image. A box appeared over a dark and grainy section of what looked like the Mediterranean, which was then enlarged to fill the whole screen. No lights were immediately apparent, but then another box appeared around one spot and was enlarged, and enlarged again until it was pixilated. A cluster of pixels at the centre of the screen was now clearly lighter than the rest. 'This frame corresponds to a part of western Italy. Or more precisely, to that of Rome.'

There was complete silence as Sunita repeated the process. Another cluster of pixels were seen to be somewhat lighter than those that surrounded them. 'The lighter pixels in this frame correspond to part of Greece, specifically Athens.' She went through the process a third time. 'Here, the lighter patch corresponds to a part of Tunisia, but it does not actually match Tunis or any other city or town as far as I can tell. I'm not totally sure, but . . .'

'Don't tell me,' Kim interjected, 'could that be the site of ancient Carthage, by any chance?'

'Yes, I think so.'

'The ancient world!' someone said in awe.

Jack's voice boomed out again. 'Are you sure all this comes from *Molly*?'

'Yes,' said Kim quietly.

'And you are quite sure of that?'

'Yes.'

'Then could we be looking back in time?'

'No, I don't think so. Or at least no further back than the time that light takes to travel from the planet we are looking at'.

'It's just under nine light-years from us,' Luka added.

'Then what do you suppose we are looking at?' asked Jack.

'Well, I . . .' Kim hesitated. 'I think it's a bit soon for that.'

'I've got something interesting,' said the man sitting to the left of Kim.

'Okay, Sanjay, let's see what you have, please.'

The big screen went back to the earlier images of the night sky, then panned outwards so that Saturn receded further into the distance and the sun entered the right-hand frame. Then the sun also receded until it became a yellowish star at the centre of the frame. A box appeared round the sun, and another box appeared round a similar-looking star on the periphery of the left-hand image.

'That', said Sanjay, pointing to the left, 'is the sun Luka mentioned.' He dragged a copy of the right-hand image over that on the left. 'The superimposed image is a simulation of our universe. As Kim said, a few stars are well out of place and a few are a little out of place, but the vast majority match, more or less. Now look what happens when the simulation goes back in time.'

Some of the simulated stars started to move slightly, and then accelerated. Two very faint points of light whirled round the simulated sun while the sun itself wobbled round in an elliptical orbit.

A digital date at the top of the image ticked off the centuries until it had gone below 500 AD, then started to slow down. By now the simulated sun had traced a meandering path until it was quite close to its antimatter counterpart, and some of the stars that were slightly out of sync were merging with their counterparts. Eventually, all but the two fast moving points of light had more or less merged.

'The two still visibly moving are Jupiter and Saturn,' said Sanjay as they also slowed to a crawl and merged with their counterparts. The date stopped changing at 10/9/166 BC. 'I think everything matches now.'

'That's why I had trouble locating Earth,' said Luka as the merged stars were again replaced by the crescent-shaped Earth in anti-space. 'It's late winter here, in Switzerland, but it would be autumn in, err, the other Switzerland.'

'166 BC,' Kim mused, 'or 157 BC if one accounts for it being nine light-years away. That's shortly before Carthage was destroyed by Rome, if I remember correctly'.

'Do you still maintain that we are not looking back in time?' asked Jack.

'Until I have some reason to suspect that everything *Molly* is telling us is false, yes, I do.'

'What then? A parallel universe that is running a bit slow?'

'Something like that, perhaps.'

'Wouldn't that imply that a slight temporal disparity is the only thing holding the two universes apart?' asked Jack. 'I mean, two universes created at the moment of the last Big Bang, both of which perfectly mirror each other right down to the last subatomic particle, except that the progress of time in the two universes is fractionally different.'

'Possibly,' said Kim, tapping her teeth with her pen again while she stared at the image of another Earth in the days of the Roman Republic. 'If the two universes were truly identical in *every* other respect, it would only take a very small time differential since the Big Bang to account for what we are looking at.'

'In which case,' said Jack, 'what's to stop us from going there?'

'To the other Earth?'

'Why not? *Molly* seemed to be unharmed while the connection remained open, and we have no reason to think she isn't still speeding her way through anti-space.'

'Well, if it turns out that the only thing holding the two universes apart is a slight temporal disparity, then it might be possible one day, I really don't know. I almost hope not.'

'Why?'

'There are fourteen billion people on Earth, this Earth, how would it be for another Earth, a pre-modern Earth, if large numbers of sightseers and settlers go there? Or pilgrims?'

'Pilgrims?' Jack asked.

'If it really is a parallel Earth, parallel in *every* respect, except for it being 157 BC and running slightly slower, then it might be possible for people from our Earth to get there in time to say hello to Jesus Christ.'

'Ah!' was all Jack found to say, and no one else said a word for a minute or so.

Finally, Kim stood up and turned to face her colleagues. 'Right, I don't know about anyone else, but I could do with a break. Back in one hour.' With that she turned on her heel and matched off through an exit at the front of the room, followed by Luka and Sanjay.

When Kim and the others were gone, about half of those left behind started talking at once, while the other half, including Mark, sat in silence. Gradually, people started making their way through the control centre's rear entrance. Rebecca joined the slow exodus and Mark got up and walked beside her in silence. They found themselves entering a small café bar before either said a word.

'So,' Rebecca said, 'what do you think?'

'I think I need a coffee,' he replied.

'Me too, my brain hurts.'

They got their coffees and sat at the last empty table. 'So,' Rebecca said again, 'What *do* you think?'

'I think she's amazing!'

'What? Who?'

'Kim. She's so young, not much older than me! But the way she handled that! Amazing!'

'Young!? She was born at the beginning of the last century.'

Mark just gawped at her.

'Don't you read the papers, or science journals?'

'Yes, of course, I must have missed . . .'

'Silly boy!' Rebecca interrupted, 'Kim has been regenerated.'

'Oh, yes, of course! I wasn't thinking. What about cancers?'

'She's bound to have plenty, but they're obviously under control, for now.'

The trouble with regeneration, apart from being horribly expensive, was that the procedure triggered multiple cancers in many parts of the patient's body. Cancers were now easily treated, but the sheer number of cancers brought misery to the regenerated, and quite a few fatalities. This was mainly why

13

the costs remained so high. The cost of the actual regeneration process had been coming down since it first became available to the fabulously rich and well-connected thirty-odd years earlier, but the levels of aftercare treatment required, much of which was very invasive, remained firmly beyond the budgets of all but the very wealthy. Even very old billionaires tended to go for the cryogenic solution of total suspended animation while better methods of rejuvenation were being worked on. According to much of the popular media, ageing celebrities were the mainstay of regeneration clinics while the science was still in its infancy. Retro-ageing implants and drugs were said by some to be the next big thing, but for the time being they were only effective at rejuvenating specific organs. This was very useful in its own right and now rivaled the use of newly grown organs using stem cells, but did not yet provide an overall solution to ageing.

'Why the interest in Kim?' Rebecca asked. 'I would have thought you'd be more interested in what you've just seen and heard about the anti-universe.'

'I am, of course I am. I guess I'm just having trouble coping with all the big stuff right now. I mean, it's a lot to take in all of a sudden.'

'Yeah, fair enough.'

As they lapsed back into silence, Mark tried to think about the 'big stuff', but his train of thought was soon interrupted again, this time by the familiar scent of Rebecca's breath as it wafted across the table. He did not doubt that her breath was chemically enhanced, but that did not prevent him feeling the even more familiar tingle in his lower abdomen, or the inevitable colouring of his cheeks that always accompanied such feelings when he was in her company. He should have been used to this sort of thing by now. After all, virtually everyone popped pills to block, create or enhance various body odours, and had been doing so for decades before he was born. He did it himself; not primarily out of vanity or to attract a mate, but mostly because it was considered the thing to do. As he sat opposite Rebecca, his mind wandered to a boy in his class at school who did not take any odour blockers or enhancers for some months. The boy eventually succumbed to peer pressure, but he could not shake the nickname 'Smelly Crotch Bill' as long as he remained at school. 'I won't forget that lesson in a hurry,' he thought absently.

Rebecca caught his gaze and locked it with a gaze of her own. 'Right!' she said, 'we haven't got much time before we go back, so let's get on with it!'

'Sorry?'

'I want to know what you're thinking.'

He gawped at her again.

'For God's sake, Mark, wake up! The anti-universe and all that!'

'Oh, right, yes, umm, I'm not sure, exactly. Err, which bit?'

Rebecca heaved a theatrical sigh of weary resignation, and succeeded in wrapping him in her scented breath again. 'Well,' she began, 'how about the ethics of it? What if we have found an exact duplicate of Earth, except that it's still in one hundred and whatever BC? Should we broadcast it? Won't a lot of people want to go there to see Jesus or whatever? Would that be a good thing or a bad thing?'

'Well, we don't know if that's possible, or how long it would take,' he replied. Then several thoughts that had lurked at the back of his mind when he heard Kim and Jack speak of the ancient world lurched to the front of his mind and threatened to logjam if he didn't get some of them out of his mouth quickly.

'The way things are progressing,' he went on, 'I wouldn't be surprised if it happened a lot sooner than people might think. 157 BC, wasn't it? If the technology came together within the next twenty or thirty years, people could probably get there before Caesar conquers Gaul. There are already spacecraft around, helium-3 shuttles and such like, that might be adapted. Then, once we're there, we would find it very difficult not to intervene with high-tech solutions to the mass exterminations of the time, or slavery.' As he warmed to these subjects, of which he was quite well read, he thought of one of his all-time favourite films: *Spartacus*.

'In the Third Servile War, Spartacus and his slave army were eventually defeated and crucified en masse by Rome in 71 BC, I think. That's eighty-six years from now, as far as the other Earth is concerned. Imagine what a temptation it would be to stop that kind of massacre! And then, having intervened and irreversibly altered the future of an entire planet, why stop at that, why not end slavery? But where would it stop? Would Jesus ever be born? If he was, how would anyone be able to tell if he was the genuine article or just another nutcase? Would we shape the world in our own image and swamp it under an ever increasing tide of migration from our over-populated planet?'

At that moment, Kim and Luka bustled into the café bar. Brushing past Mark and Rebecca with the smell of stale cigarette smoke trailing in their wake, they marched up to a table where Sunita was sitting and Kim whispered in her ear. Sunita got up and the trio marched back towards the café's exit. When they got to the door, Kim hesitated and then came back and whispered quietly in Rebecca's ear, too quietly for Mark to hear. Rebecca said 'excuse me' to Mark, and she also joined the group and marched off.

'That reminds me,' he thought, still musing over the things he might have said to Rebecca if she had not been whisked away, 'regeneration, or perhaps retro-ageing. Imagine the population pressures that perpetual youth would bring, and a nice juicy sparsely-populated second Earth just there for the taking!' Then he thought of these things in terms of his own future: 'I wonder if they'll have it all worked out by the time I get old. If they can do regeneration or retro-ageing affordably and without cancers or whatever, then I could live indefinitely. What would I do then, especially if I got the chance to go to another Earth in something-or-other BC? I would like to meet Spartacus! I wouldn't let him or his slave army get crucified, not if I could help it!' The absurdity of such an idea suddenly struck him. 'Now I really am being silly. If I'm going to have fantasies, they might as well be credible enough to enjoy. I'm too timid even to think of speaking to the likes of Spartacus. Like I'm going to save his army, ha bloody ha!'

Then it occurred to him that he had very little idea how long it would take spaceships to travel nine light-years. He knew it would have to take quite a few decades, otherwise the acceleration on the first half of the journey and deceleration on the second half would squash people into sticky red smears, but he had no idea how many decades. 'Fancy not thinking of that before gabbling on in front of Rebecca,' he thought, 'what an arse I am!'

As he got into the swing of ridiculing himself, a paranoid thought came to him: perhaps Kim had fetched Rebecca as an afterthought simply to rescue her from the idiot she overheard spouting nonsense about Caesar, Gaul and Spartacus. They could be laughing at him now, saying what an arse he was. Feeling more than ever like an interloper, he made to down the last of his coffee and return to the control centre, but his cup was nearly full and he choked on the cold coffee. Coughing, spluttering and eyes streaming, he retreated out of the café bar and made his way as fast as he could stumble to recover in the privacy of the nearest men's toilets.

When he got back to the control centre a few people were gathered outside talking and a few more were milling around inside the room, but Rebecca was nowhere to be seen, and all the screens were blank. Overhearing snippets of conversations around him, he realised that some kind of announcement had been made postponing all further proceedings until further notice.

Mark left the control centre and aimlessly wandered down a corridor. Passing through an open exit, he found himself walking across the lawn of a walled garden. It was night, but the garden was lit by tasteful background lights that silhouetted people helping themselves to finger-buffets and drinks or chatting in small groups. Pouring himself a large glass of wine, he stood on an empty patch of lawn and looked around. Another figure, a tall gangling man who looked to be about thirty years old, came out of the exit and stood still for a few moments scanning the inhabitants of the garden. When he spotted Mark his faced seemed to lighten as if in recognition and he moved purposefully towards him, although Mark did not have a clue who he was.

After four or five long loping strides, the man held out his hand for Mark to shake while he introduced himself. 'Hi, I'm Peter Ingham, *Science Today*, very pleased to meet you!' As he shook Peter's hand and tried to drag his eyes away from his extraordinarily mobile Adam's apple, which bobbed up and down at about Mark's eye-level, he returned the introduction.

'Mark Goodwin, pleased to meet you.'

'I gather it's been quite a day, Mark.'

'It has. Weren't you in there?'

'No, couldn't wangle an invitation. Forced to wander around the periphery of things until they give a press briefing. What do you make of it all?'

'Err, should I be talking to a reporter before a press briefing?'

'Feature-writer. Well, general gofer, really. But don't worry, I am absolutely not here to report what people say, unless they explicitly invite me to do so. I'm interested in the science and what it means to the world at large. Or should I say *worlds* at large?' he said with a broad smile.

Mark already felt that he liked this gawky-looking character. He was not sure why he had been singled out; probably because he looked like he would welcome the company. Well he did welcome the company, so that was fine by him.

'You've heard the gist of it then?' Mark asked.

'Oh yes! A parallel universe with a parallel Earth nine light-years away, in, what was it, 157 BC? Incredible! I've been following the development of *Achilles* and *Molly* in any case, but this! Unbelievable! But true, or so I'm led to believe. Amazing! And worrying too.'

'Worrying?'

'Certainly. Population pressures here, especially if regeneration takes off, a few hundred million there, at most. Settlers, demagogues, bible-bashers bent on converting a whole new world. There will all kinds of opportunities and problems if we can get there.'

'Do you think that's possible?'

'I don't know, but if a slight temporal disparity really is the only thing keeping the two universes apart, then I don't know why not. *Molly* survived for one hundred and eight seconds and counting, so I don't see why spaceships can't survive indefinitely.

'Mm, nor do I.'

'Sorry if I'm being impertinent, but you do look young to be the kind of scientist I'd expect to see here today.'

'Oh, yes, I'm still a research student and I'm kind of here by accident.'

'Really? PhD?'

'Yes.'

'What's your thesis on?'

'It's to do with scientific breakthroughs and initial resistance to them from parts of the scientific community.'

'Really? How appropriate! Here by accident you say? Seems to me like you're in the right place at the right time. I wonder,' Peter mused as if to himself, 'could be that you're in the right place at the right time on a range of fronts.'

'Why?'

'Well, today's events are likely to cause quite a stir. For a start, there's bound to be a heck of a row about whether the whole thing is one big illusion, or whether it all points to there being two universes or an infinite number of them. Then there's the question of whether it's ethical to meddle with . . .'

'Peter!' interrupted a man who strode towards them and clapped Peter on the back, 'there you are, old chap. There's some people I want you to meet.'

'Hi Scott. This is Mark, he's . . .'

Scott did not wait for Peter to finished his introduction. Instead, he simply said 'hi, Mark' as he turned Peter away with an assertive pull on his elbow and shepherded him towards three people standing a few metres away. Peter gave Mark an apologetic smile, but he went nonetheless. Mark watched them go with regret. He very much wanted to hear Peter's ideas and views, especially about the ethical issues involved in meddling with a parallel but pre-modern Earth. He considered following them but decided that that would look needy. So he finished his wine and left the garden. Seeing no one else he recognised back in the building, he set off back to his hotel room replaying the events of the past few hours in his mind as he went.

He sat on his hotel bed with his mobile (cell phone) and spent about two hours on the Net reading about slavery in ancient Rome and the slave rebellion that Spartacus led in the so-called Third Servile War. He found a great deal of speculative material but surprisingly few undisputed 'hard facts', although what there was left him feeling despondent about the slaves' ultimate defeat. Putting his mobile aside, he lay on his bed and stared at the ceiling while he tried to take his mind off slavery and think of something sensible to discuss with Rebecca the following day, although it seemed to help his train of thought if he pictured himself talking things over with Peter Ingham. Sleep took him unawares.

He dreamed he was looking at a blue and white planet, not crescent-shaped like the other-Earth he had seen earlier on the big screen, but he knew it was the same planet. A kind of space-fighter slid into view, flying towards the planet, and he materialised inside its cockpit. His leather-gloved hands gripped two joysticks that controlled the craft, and each of his thumbs hovered over a button at the top of the joysticks. With a whoosh, he tore into the planet's atmosphere. He felt his thumbs apply a little pressure to the buttons as if to ready himself for something.

Descending rapidly towards rolling hills, he maneuvered the craft so that it rushed over the ground at a little over treetop level. He approached a fairly large hill with an army arranged along its long sloping crest. The army, which he knew to be Spartacus' slave army, was facing away from him. He glided over the slave army and saw huge numbers of Roman soldiers marching in checkerboard squares down the slopes of another hill towards them. As he came closer he felt his hands tightened around the joysticks and his thumbs begin to increase their pressure on the buttons. They were firing buttons, he now realised, and he was about to rip the Roman army to shreds. 'No need to kill them,' he thought, 'just scare them away', but when he tried to lift his thumbs off the buttons they merely pressed a little harder.

His space-fighter was going much slower now. He could just about make out individual Roman soldiers as he closed in for the kill. He tried to resist what he was about to do but seemed unable to stop himself. His thumbs jerked downwards and rockets flew from his craft in flights of four at a time; two rockets per Roman square. The rockets plunged into the Romans and explosions erupted and spewed lethal sprays of white-hot shards through the survivors. The first rank of Roman squares were ripped apart. Most of the soldiers in these squares now lay crumpled or broken into pieces strewn over the hillside. There was no blood, probably for the same reason that Mark avoided gory films when he was awake: he was terribly squeamish. Instead, the soldiers simply came apart like porcelain figurines that had fallen onto a concrete floor.

The survivors tried to flee back up the hill, but they could not make much progress. He could sense the effort they made to run, but it was as if they were struggling through syrup. As he closed upon them, he willed a message to pass through his arms to his hands: 'no, stop, don't kill them, let them run, let them run!' His fingers lessened their grip a little, as though they were not quite sure what to do; but his thumbs were having none of it. They willed an uncompromising message straight back into his brain: 'they're Roman soldiers, trained killers, kill them or they'll be back.' With that, his thumbs stabbed down again and white-hot heavy-caliber machinegun bullets swept methodically through the soldiers trying to run away.

Now hovering, the space-fighter tilted up to face the second rank of Roman squares. He was close enough to see the faces of individuals as they stared in horror at his craft. He knew they wanted to run but some force held them rooted to the spot. He was battling frantically to regain control of his hands as more flights of rockets flared out and smashed into the squares. His craft moved closer to machinegun the survivors. In a supreme effort, he willed his hands not to fire and they hesitated, although his space-fighter gradually edged closer. He was now so close that a few soldiers completely filled his cockpit window. They toppled backwards as they watched the craft nose towards them and lay on their backs staring up at him with terrified faces. 'No', he pleaded, 'they're people, just people! Don't kill them!' His craft moved closer still and his thumbs readied themselves again. The features of one soldier's face came into sharp focus – it was the face of Peter Ingham. Peter's eyes bulged and his Adam's apple bobbed violently as he tried to draw in the oxygen he needed to keep screaming. 'No, please no,' Mark whimpered, 'they're people, only people', but he felt his will draining away. Crosshairs appeared on the bridge of Peter's nose and Mark's thumbs tensed. 'NO, FOR GOD's SAKE, NO!' Mark cried out, but his thumbs stabbed down viciously and he felt the recoil of the craft's guns. 'NO!

NO! NO!, they're people,' he implored a wall light in his hotel room as he sat bolt-upright on his bed, 'just people.'

It took him a few seconds to convince himself that it really was only a dream. He got up and closed the curtains against the misty predawn light. He took a miniature whisky from the room's mini-bar, but then thought better of it and went back to bed without fully recovering his wits.

He slept fitfully for a while, having unformed fragments of dreams, until he found himself on a long paved road lined on either side with tall wooden crucifixes. Roman soldiers were herding people along the road while more soldiers used ropes to haul them onto empty crucifixes as they went. Mark looked around in panic, scared they were going to crucify him too, but the soldiers looked straight through him as though he were invisible. Feeling afraid but somehow sure it was all his fault, he made an ineffectual effort to untie the feet of a crucified man. He split a fingernail on the rope and stopped to suck his stinging finger. Looking up, he realised he was at the feet of Spartacus (with Kirk Douglas' face). 'Oh God', Mark whined miserably, 'I should have stopped this, why didn't I stop this?'

Spartacus turned his head, opened his eyes and looked down at Mark. He felt pathetic, sucking at a little sore spot on his finger while Spartacus was dying in front of him. With obvious effort, Spartacus opened his mouth to speak. Mark knew he was about to hear his last words.

'You,' Spartacus struggled to say.

'Yes, Spartacus, yes?'

'Are'

'Yes?'

'A'

'A?'

'Arse,' said Spartacus, and died.

Mark woke up again, confused and perplexed, and thought, 'Spartacus called me an arse. With his dying breath, one of my greatest all-time heroes called me an arse!'

He heaved himself out of bed and tried to shake off a feeling of despondency. As he was brushing his teeth he stopped and stared at himself in the mirror. 'Spartacus said I was *a* arse. I am not *a* arse, I am *an* arse!' Then he laughed, spraying the mirror with toothpaste.

Despite the dreams, his spirits were rising fast in anticipation of the day ahead. He found an email from Rebecca saying to meet her at a press briefing at the Space Centre that afternoon. He was looking forward to it, even though large gatherings of people always made him feel self-conscious. He also hoped he would bump into Peter again and get a chance to discuss the other Earth.

When he approached the Space Centre he spotted Peter sitting on a bench beside the building's big front doors. Peter had a look of intense concentration as he stared at a cigarette he was holding. When he drew on it he did so in an awkward manner that suggested he hadn't quite got the hang of it. 'Ah, there you are!' he said, looking up.

'Do you normally smoke?' asked Mark.

Peter looked at the cigarette in his hand as if it were an unpleasant apparition, flicked it into some bushes and crinkled his brow as he breathed out smoke. 'Me, smoke? No, never!' he replied emphatically, standing up and beaming one of his big smiles. He did not offer any explanation and Mark did not ask him to. Instead, he said, 'I think you are going to find this briefing especially interesting, given your academic interests.'

'Have you heard something, then?'

Peter just beamed another of his big smiles.

'A case of being in the right place at the right time, is it?' Mark asked.

Peter's smile grew bigger, almost comical, but he did not elaborate. Gesturing towards the doors, he said, 'shall we?' They walked into the building and along a couple of corridors in the kind of companionable silence felt by people who have accepted each other's foibles. As he stepped into a big hall bustling with journalists beside his gawky new friend with the dancing Adam's apple and the big soppy smile, Mark completely forgot to feel self-conscious.

2
RIGHT TIME, RIGHT PLACE

Mark and Peter sat in a large cafeteria a few hundred metres from the Space Centre, toying with their coffees in silence.

'So,' said Peter, 'what do you think?'

'What is there to say? I mean, you were there, they made it pretty plain that it was one big illusion'.

'Yup.'

After quite a long pause, Peter said, 'they used the word "exciting" a lot, didn't they?'

'Yes, I suppose they did, and maybe they're right, but I can't help feeling deflated, and a bit foolish.'

'So you bought all that about mirages of the past being etched into antimatter, did you?'

'Well, why shouldn't I? Not that it's my field, exactly.'

There was another pause before Peter asked, 'what was your thesis about again?'

Mark was surprised and slightly disappointed that his new friend needed to ask, so he repeated his earlier mini-explanation verbatim. 'It's to do with scientific breakthroughs and initial resistance to them from parts of the scientific community.'

'Right,' said Peter. After a short pause, he directed an exaggeratedly quizzical look at Mark. 'Would you mind running that by me again?'

Beginning to feel irritated, Mark said, 'it's to do with scientific breakthroughs and initial resistance to them from .

. .' he hesitated, and then returned a pretty good imitation of Peter's quizzical expression. 'What are you getting at?'

'Oh, probably nothing.'

'Tell me!'

'Why do you suppose Kim wasn't at the briefing?'

'They said why. She was the Project Coordinator. The project was coordinated, now it's about analysis, and Kim's having a well-earned rest.'

'Can you think of anyone more qualified to analyse *Molly's* journey into the other universe than Kim?'

'Well, no . . .'

'The ladies and gentlemen of the press were itching to ask Kim questions. She must have known that. She knows the project intimately and could handle a press briefing standing on her head. And if she wasn't well enough, I expect Luka or Sanjay could have done just as well.'

'So . . .'

'Did you see her at all after she called a halt to yesterday's proceedings?'

'Yes, briefly, but it was only meant to be for an hour.'

'I watched her gathering her entourage, her favourites. She looked worried, Mark, worried about the implications of what they were doing, I would say.'

'Perhaps she was worried because she didn't know if any of it was real.'

'That's not what she said at the time, is it?'

'No, but she might of thought differently during the break.'

'True, I suppose, but that briefing reminded me of gardening programmes.'

'Gardening programmes?'

'The sort of gardening programmes where they keep saying how exciting it all is, as though the excitement of it all might escape people's notice if they're not repeatedly told how truly exciting it really is.'

'You've lost me now,' said Mark.

'How can I put it? That pompous little turd they wheeled out to front it, Dr. Bernard Verhagen, how dry was he?'

'Very.'

'He kept going on about how exciting he thought it was without actually explaining why anyone else should find it exciting at all.'

'Well, it would have seemed quite exciting if the experiment hadn't raised everyone's expectations.'

'Exactly!' exclaimed Peter, 'but now it can quietly recede into the background, not as a complete failure that's not worth anyone's while to fund, but as an esoteric backwater that's alright if you like that kind of thing.'

'Like gardening?'

'Yes, in a sense.'

'But why? No, don't answer that; because they're worried about the implications.'

'Yes, well, maybe. Or perhaps something like the kind of resistance to scientific breakthroughs that you're looking at. Or a bit of both, I don't know, but that briefing just didn't ring true to me. You'd have thought they'd put the best possible spin on it for the sake of the enormous budgets they've been running, but no, they wheel out Bernard the bore to send everyone to sleep. They might have told it how they saw it, but then again, if they wanted to put a lid on it without actually losing their jobs, I would say it was a damn fine performance.'

'My thesis is also about resistance on ethical grounds, as well as resistance to new ideas because they're new,' said Mark.

'Is it? Sorry, we haven't really discussed that, have we?

'We only met yesterday evening.'

'So we did!' said Peter, giving Mark another of his broad smiles. We must have a good chat about it sometime soon, if you're up for that.'

'I'd like that.'

'Good. In the meantime, have a think about today and yesterday, and then tell me I'm just being paranoid.'

'You're not paranoid, just disappointed, like I am. But yeah, I'll certainly think about it.'

They lapsed back into silence and Mark began thinking about it then and there. As was his way when he tried to think about something, his initial thoughts wandered around the edge of the issue at hand. Casting his mind back to the briefing, there were some things that he thought were slightly odd. For one thing, Rebecca said she would meet him there, but she didn't. He saw her, near the front among a knot of other people who were in the control center the day before. He hadn't noticed her leave, although he had noticed that she and a few others were nowhere to be seen by the end of the briefing. Quite a few people came and went during the briefing. Whether they went to call their editors, or go to the toilet or simply because they were bored, he could not tell, but the hall had perceptibly thinned by the time the briefing ended.

Rebecca had not shown up afterwards either, and her absence had added to his sense of anticlimax. Now that he thought about it, it was not just a sense of anticlimax, it was also irritation at the short space of time allowed for questions and the way that the most interesting questions, from Mark's point of view, never seemed to be properly answered. Luka and Sanjay had sat either side of Bernard the bore, but they seemed guarded in what they said and allowed Bernard to dominate the proceedings. As he presided over the briefing, Bernard had looked and sounded like a dry bureaucrat, and his answers to the more probing questions were as vague and evasive as those of an annoying career politician.

Mark's train of thought was interrupted by a rapid tapping on his shin under the table. Looking up, he saw Peter indicating to his left with his head, eyes and eyebrows. Turning in that direction, he saw that Kim, Rebecca, Sanjay, Luka and Sunita had entered the cafeteria. Apparently unnoticed, he watched

29

as they organised seating for the five of them around a table set for four at the other side of the cafeteria from where he and Peter sat.

'I wonder if I should wave to Rebecca, or something,' Mark said, half to himself.

'Who?'

'Rebecca's one of my PhD supervisors, the one with the red hair.'

'No kidding?'

'No, why?'

'Well, for one thing, just look at the company she's keeping!'

'Yeah, I've been wondering about that.'

'She knows Kim, then?'

'As far as I know, she didn't know Kim personally until yesterday, shortly after she called that break. Like you said, Kim was collecting her entourage, or favourites or whatever. Then she spoke to Rebecca, as an afterthought, I think, and Rebecca joined Kim's group and they marched off together.'

'Why? What did she say?'

'I don't know, I didn't hear.'

'Well! The plot, as they say, thickens!'

'Perhaps I was a bit hasty, saying that you're not paranoid.'

'Never mind me, Mark, get yourself over there and say hello!'

'I can't, I haven't been invited.'

'Doesn't matter now, we've been spotted.'

Mark saw Rebecca saying something to her companions as she stood up, and then she turned towards him and Peter, followed shortly after by Kim.

'Right place at the right time, old chap,' Peter whispered at Mark and gave him a conspiratorial wink, 'right place right time.'

Mark half expected Peter to do most of the talking, asking journalistic questions and the like, but he did not say much at all. After everyone had been introduced, Peter offered to get them all drinks, and returned a little later with the two mineral waters that Rebecca and Kim had asked for. Kim was very friendly and polite for the few minutes that she stayed at their table. When she made her apologies for leaving, and confirmed something with Rebecca about six o'clock, which Mark took to be when she and Rebecca would next meet up, he thought that Kim looked and acted quite humble. When she had gone, he entertained passing fantasies of her concealing super-human ninja skills, or that she might one day reveal herself as the heir to a resurgent Japanese empire.

Rebecca was all smiles as she made pleasant small talk. Peter responded in kind at the right moments, but he too made his apologies and left a few minutes after Kim had gone, handing a card to Mark as he went.

When they were alone, Rebecca said, 'so, what do you think?'

He didn't really know what he thought. He did, however, feel under some obligation to come up with something at least halfway interesting, if only to show that he had been paying attention and that the expense his university had gone to sending him to Geneva was not totally wasted. He found himself giving an embellished version of what Peter had just said, with the emphasis firmly upon ethical considerations in respect of a vulnerable other-Earth heaving under the impact of future migration from a technologically advanced Earth.

'So you think it was real, do you?' Rebecca asked noncommittally, 'rather than a freak recording of our own past caught in antimatter?'

This question put him in a bit of a spot. He was not at all sure of the answer. To say that he thought it was real was too much of a commitment, while saying it was not real might sound like he was calling Kim and others delusional. He opted to leave his options open as far as he could by saying: 'it's not really my field, but Kim certainly seemed to think it was real when the data started coming in.'

'And how would you deal with that in your thesis?'

He felt he was in danger of digging himself a hole with no easy way out, but had to play the hand he had dealt himself. As fast as he could, he thought about Kim and the ethical dilemmas she might face if she still thought that the other Earth was real. Suddenly, gaining his doctorate seemed utterly trivial, and to write about people hiding the existence of another universe might have incalculable implications if his thesis got into the public domain and was taken seriously. So he said, 'I couldn't possibly do the thesis if it meant messing with the work going on here, much less so if it meant messing with a whole planet as well.'

'What about your career?'

'I'd have to find another one.'

Rebecca gave the barest hint of a smile.

'My God,' he thought, 'I do believe I said something right!' Then he thought, 'perhaps Rebecca knows exactly what's going on. If she does, and approves of what I just said, then does that mean that Peter was right?'

They talked for a while longer, not about a possible antimatter universe, but about the people they had met or seen in 'action' in the control room or at the briefing. Rebecca was particularly interested in Peter, possibly because Mark had hardly talked to anyone else. She said she had read some of Peter's work, which she described as 'insightful', and had seen him at one or two conferences.

'Now I come to think of it,' Rebecca said, 'I've seen him at quite a few conferences, or at gatherings after conferences. I can't say I've paid him much attention, but I seem to remember him now, standing still and smiling innocuously.

Mark wondered if that was how Peter got a lot of his information. He pictured him now, still as a heron waiting for a fish to pass by. Peter stood several inches above most people's heads, but Mark felt that he could remain largely unnoticed by those around him. Or if he did speak there was every chance that people's attention might be drawn to his bobbing Adam's apple or to his open and thoroughly unthreatening smile rather than wondering why he had attached himself to their particular sub-group.

'Seems like a nice chap,' Rebecca said.

'Yes,' he agreed. 'What about Kim?'

'What about her?'

'I didn't know you knew her personally.'

'I didn't, not as such. I've seen her at conferences too, and spoken to her. She said she had read some of my work, and I've read hers. Kind of similar take on things.'

Rebecca had written a book on the philosophy and ethics of science called: *Science Limited?* Mark had read it and thought it was good; a very thoughtful look at some of the moral issues that confront scientists and others at the cutting edge. He thought the ideas in this book would probably be of interest to Kim if she were struggling with the ethical issues of finding a parallel but pre-modern Earth, and wondered if that might have had something to do with Kim whisking Rebecca away from the café bar the day before.

'Has she read *Science Limited?*' Mark asked.

Rebecca smiled, 'yes, she has.'

A few silent seconds later, she said, 'I've got to be off. I'll be in touch later today, or tomorrow morning before the flight. In the meantime, can I suggest that you, err, practice some discretion about what you say and who you say it to.'

He felt that was a little unkind and unfair, but he took her point. He was sure that she was referring to Peter, who worked for a media outlet, albeit a highly respected one. On the other hand, he now thought guiltily, he had done little more than pass Peter's thoughts on to Rebecca and allowed her to think they were Mark's thoughts. She seemed to have reacted well to these thoughts, and this made him feel that he owed Peter something.

When he got back to his hotel room, he sat on his bed and toyed with Peter's card, wondering whether he should give him a call and what he would say if he did. Undecided, he checked his emails and found one from Peter. It read: 'I'm going to try that Greek restaurant next to where we had coffee today. If you fancy joining me, I'll be there at 8pm.'

'Well, no harm in that,' he said aloud to himself while vaguely wondering how Peter had got hold of his email address, and replied with: 'See you at 8pm.'

They caught sight of each other a couple of hundred metres either side of the Greek restaurant at almost exactly 8pm. Peter smiled broadly and stuck out his elbows as part of an exaggerated impression of speed-walking. Mark followed suit. Gathering speed as they went, they arrived outside the restaurant together, veered sharply towards the entrance and started barging each other away from the doors. Eventually they squeezed through a single door together and tumbled into the restaurant laughing.

Mark was not sure whether they were both waiting for each other to broach the subject of the anti-universe, but neither of them mentioned it at all while they ate. Instead, they discussed the feminine charms of 'the girls' they had seen at the cafeteria. They thought Luka was probably in her late forties and had slightly stern features that were more than offset by her lively hazel eyes and smoky Russian accent. Sunita looked to be in her late twenties and they wondered if she had been regenerated, but thought it was unlikely given that so few people could afford to. Peter pronounced Sunita as 'sweetly raunchy,' Kim as 'a bit scary, but I bet she knows everything worth knowing about sex,' and Rebecca as 'pure *phoore*!' Mark agreed wholeheartedly with

Peter's opinions, although he offered no comment on Rebecca's womanly charms.

After the meal, they sauntered along the road, passed two bars that looked too crowded for them, then decided to go into one which was slightly less busy. Mark was ordering their drinks when he got a call.

'Where are you?' Rebecca asked.

He told her where he was.

'Anyone with you?'

'Peter's here.'

'Good! I'll join you, if I may?'

Mark did not want her to join them. He was relaxed and enjoying his last evening in Geneva just fine without her unsettling presence, but he felt he had no choice but to say 'yes, of course.'

He told Peter that Rebecca was coming, and Peter just shrugged and smiled.

Finding a high circular wooden table with four high stools, they sat and looked around without saying very much. A few minutes later, Mark saw Peter's eyes widen. Looking over his shoulder, he saw Rebecca and Kim coming towards them. Dressed in clothes that were far more feminine than he would have expected either of them to own, they seemed to be in very high spirits and looked like they were doing their best to recover their poise after a bout of laughing. Taken aback, he thought, 'Jesus! Anyone would think it was a double date.'

Peter stood up to welcome them and offered them drinks. When Peter made for the bar, Mark thought, 'coward,' for leaving him to it, but he knew he was being irrational. He managed to say 'so . . .' before he realised he had nothing else to say. Rebecca and Kim looked at him for a moment, then at each other, back at him, at each other again, and burst out laughing.

Mark's cheeks were on fire. They tried to stop themselves laughing, but went into fits of giggles whenever they looked at each other, which they did several times. He thought they must be drunk, or at least very tipsy.

They were just getting over a fresh fit when Peter returned with the drinks. 'Well,' said Peter, beaming, 'I see Mark's been keeping you girls entertained,' which just set them off again.

'Oh, sorry, sorry,' said Kim, recovering as best she could, 'I think we're a bit hysterical at the moment. We've had lots of things to think about.'

'And a bottle of wine,' added Rebecca, also recovering.

'We're not drunk, though,' said Kim, 'just unwinding.'

'Ah,' said Peter, 'laughing for heart's ease rather than from jest.'

'Exactly!' said Kim.

'Well here's to unwinding,' said Peter, raising his glass to all three in turn.

'To unwinding,' they all replied, whether unwound or not, and raised their glasses.

'So,' Kim said to Mark, almost setting herself off again, 'I gather you are doing a thesis on resistance to scientific breakthroughs?'

'Yes, sort of.'

'I hope you don't mind my coming along,' she said earnestly, 'but I was fascinated by what Rebecca told me about what you're doing!'

'Really?' he said doubtfully.

'Absolutely! I do hope you don't mind if I ask you about it.'

'Err, no, no, not at all,' he lied, trying to fight off a sulky mood.

And she did ask him about it, at length and in surprising detail. After a while, Mark found he was almost enjoying himself again, partly because fresh drinks kept appearing in front of him – Peter had opened a tab and told the barman to 'keep them coming' – and partly because Kim was extremely attentive and seemed unwilling to let him move on from any point until he had told her his opinion, which she generally greeted with enthusiastic nods.

While he and Kim were talking, Rebecca and Peter also seemed to be getting on well. Eventually their two separate conversations merged and ranged freely, although Mark was later unable to recall much of what was said. By the time they left the bar they were all behaving like firm friends. Mark found himself walking beside Rebecca, mimicking Bernard the bore's drearily evasive performance at the press briefing, with Peter and Kim trailing behind. Then he said, 'you know, I really enjoyed this evening.'

'Me too.'

'How did you and Kim get to be such good friends so quickly?'

'She needed friends and allies.'

Something at the back of his mind told him that she was speaking incautiously, probably because she was now drunk, even if she hadn't been earlier.

'That's a bit like me and Peter, I think.'

'Yeah, yeah, it's important to have friends who are on your side.'

'Side?' Mark asked; but an involuntary jerk of her head and her sidelong glance let him know that she had caught herself being incautious, and the moment of candour was over.

Rebecca stopped and turned to look at the other two, now thirty or forty metres behind. Mark turned too. Kim was chatting merrily as she looked up at Peter's soppy smiling face. She was scarcely more than half his height. In the semi-darkness, they looked very much like father and child, and like a child, Kim suddenly grabbed Peter's hand and made him trot alongside her as she ran to catch up with Rebecca and Mark.

'I can't believe she's over a hundred and twenty years old,' said Mark, 'she doesn't look a day over a hundred.'

Rebecca laughed. As Kim and Peter caught up, they also started laughing, without knowing or caring what the joke was.

A few more paces took them nearly opposite a small hotel; 'that's mine,' Kim said, and led the group jaywalking across the road to the hotel steps.

Kim stopped them at the bottom of the steps. 'Well, we've still got some talking to do, haven't we, Becky?'

'Yes, we have,' Rebecca replied.

Standing on her toes, Kim kissed Mark on one cheek as he lowered his head. Then she turned to Peter, who suddenly looked to be the shyer of the two men, and air-kissed him about half a metre below each of his cheeks. She giggled at their obvious shyness, grabbed Rebecca's hand and they both ran up the steps. When they reached the hotel door, they turned again and waved merrily. Mark and Peter both waved back and continued to wave after the door had closed again. A few seconds later, still waving, they turned to look at each other. Knowing how silly they must have looked waving at a closed door, they laughed, but carried on waving for a bit, just for the fun of it.

Rebecca was not very talkative when they flew home the next day, which suited Mark because he had a serious hangover. After waving goodbye to the two 'girls', Mark and Peter had not been quite ready to call it a night. Besides, they had some talking of their own to do, especially as it was Mark's last night in Geneva. They had spotted a fairly quiet bar where they could talk things over. Before going in, they sensibly decided to drink coffee, but then made the age-old mistake of delaying that decision until after they had just one glass of wine, and then another, and another. They agreed that Kim and Rebecca were definitely up to something. Other than that, the only firm decision they made was that they would be keep in touch after they went their separate ways.

Over the next few weeks they kept their promises to keep in touch by email (neither of them enjoyed video calls), but they both seemed guarded about discussing what had happened in

Geneva. Mark had in any case entertained doubts as to whether he should talk about it at all, especially to someone working in the media, even someone working for a publication like *Science Today*. He felt somewhat relieved to find that Peter's article on *Achilles* and *Molly* had soberly toed the line given by Bernard Verhagen, and by the complete lack of questions on the matter in the emails that Peter sent as he hopped around the world covering various scientific events and conferences.

Mark wanted to talk about the possibility of an antimatter universe to someone, but he didn't know who. Rebecca had mysteriously disappeared again shortly after getting home. He had managed to worm his way out of taking some of her undergraduate classes on the grounds that it filled him with such stage fright that he could barely think about anything else. However, even spared this task, he had still not been able to concentrate on his thesis since returning from Geneva. The weeks dragged by, the gaps between emails from Peter became longer, and Geneva began to feel like a half-forgotten dream. Then, without having heard that Rebecca had got back from wherever she had been, he got a call from her summoning him to her office the following morning.

He arrived at her office a little early and was told to take a seat while she finished what she was doing on her computer. He was mentally rehearsing his prepared excuses for not doing very much of anything during the five months or so since they had last met, when she turned to him and asked: 'what do you want to do with your life, Mark?'

This was not the kind of question he expected her to open a supervisory meeting with, and it caused him to drop his guard.

'I've no idea,' he said, more or less truthfully.

'Don't you want your PhD, or a career in academia?'

'I did do, but I'm not sure now.'

'You must have some idea of what you'd like to do.'

'Not really.'

'Are you in a relationship?'

'No.'

'Is there anyone who depends on you being around?'

'No.'

'Have you any particular preference about where you would like to live?'

'Not really.'

'Would you like to work for the Eurasian Space Agency?'

'Huh?'

'Would you like to work for the Eurasian Space Agency? It pays well.'

'Err, yes, but . . .'

'Could you be in Geneva this time next week?'

'Well, yes, of course, but . . .'

'Okay, leave it to me. I'll call you in the next day or two.'

Mark sat in silence as Rebecca returned to her computer screen. A few minutes later, she turned to him and said, 'oh, I'm sorry, Mark, I didn't realise you were still here. Was there something else?'

'No, no, not really, not that I can think of right now.'

'Okay, bye for now, then.'

'Bye,' he said, getting up and sidling towards the door, 'bye,' but Rebecca had already returned to her work.

He walked slowly and dazedly out of her office and down the corridor. He could not think about what just happened in any direct way, he was still too stunned. His first coherent thought was: 'I really ought to be excited,' and his second was: 'didn't know I was still there, indeed! Is she a bloody ice queen, or what? I bet nothing ever excites her, unless she's drunk.'

When Mark had gone, Rebecca poked her head out of her office door, looked up and down the corridor, withdrew her head and quietly locked the door behind her. She then paged Kim so that she could give Rebecca a video call over the Space

Agency's secure line if she was available. Kim's face appeared on Rebecca's screen within seconds.

'Hi Becky.'

'Hi Kim.'

'How did it go?'

'Fine, of course. How about your end?'

'No problem.'

'God, Kim, I can't tell you how excited I am!'

'Yeah, I know, but it's a long road, too long to stay excited all the time. And it could all go horribly wrong.'

'Yes, I know, but I can't help it!

'I know.'

'And I'm really looking forward to seeing their faces when we tell them.'

'Yeah, me too.' said Kim. 'But we don't want to tell them too much too soon. Not that we'll need to, not if they're worth their pay, they should be able to work it out for themselves soon enough.'

'Well, then, speak to you later,' said Rebecca, seeing Kim's hand move to cut the link.

But Kim hesitated, and said, 'Becky?'

'Yes?'

'I'm excited too!'

With that, they both did something that would have surprised Mark as he wandered off thinking what an ice queen Rebecca was. Still sitting, they pummeled their feet on the floors, pummeled the air in front of their desks with their fists, shook their heads from side to side like they were 'headbangers' at a rock concert, and squealed excitedly.

Mark barely glanced at the contract of employment before signing it. Professor Bank's Personal Assistant then gave him his air ticket, a permit and some printed instructions, which he stared at for a while but could not focus on. While he waited outside for his taxi, he called Rebecca.

'Hi, Mark, what is it?'

'I just thought I'd let you know I've got everything.'

'Good. So you're on your way?'

'Yes,' he said, and paused.

'Go on, what is it?'

'Well, what will I do when I get there?'

'I told you. You're a research assistant, like it says on your contract. When you arrive, just find your office, settle in and wait to be given instructions. If you run out of things to do, find out where the stationery is kept and make a list of what's there.'

'How can you be sure I'm what they're looking for? Will I be any good?'

'I have every confidence in you, Mark, as far as stationery is concerned.'

'Oh, thanks a lot, that's very reassuring!'

'For goodness sake, relax!'

'Okay, I'll try.'

'Right. Well off you go then. I'll be in touch.'

'Right,' he said after the line went dead.

His taxi arrived late, but not too late. His flight was uneventful and he had two or three hours to freshen up in the same hotel he stayed in five months earlier.

'Five months,' he thought as he stared at his reflection, 'it seems like five years in some ways and five days in others.' He looked quite smart in the mirror. His new suit, the best he could afford, needed no cleaning or ironing: its particle-repelling smart-fibres had seen to that. He had no need to check for untucked shirttails or open buttons either: discreet vibrations would let him know if and where anything was amiss (the vibration warning him that his fly-buttons were open would be felt on his upper arm – it was not *that* kind of suit). His briefcase was quite old but showed virtually no signs of wear. He was shaved and showered, had taken his odour-blockers and his hair was in place. If only he could be sure that his nerves would not cause his bowels to make overdue demands upon him, he would be as ready as he was ever likely to be. Time to go.

When he presented himself at the Space Centre's reception he was pointed towards a corridor off the main foyer. DNA scanners let him through two sets of double doors to another, much smaller, reception. A security guard checked his credentials and pressed a button to open another set of doors. After consulting his printed instructions again, he looked for room 14. He was just registering faint surprise at there being no room 13 in such an august scientific institution when he heard a familiar voice coming from the partially open door of room 14. It was the voice of Peter Ingham.

'Peter?' Mark said as he gingerly pushed the door further open and took a step or two inside.

'Mark? What the devil . . ?' said Peter, getting up from his chair with a smile growing on his face. They shook hands vigorously, although Mark was very aware that they were not alone.

There were four other people seated at a rectangular table. Mark recognized them all immediately. Kim and Luka were seated opposite Peter's chair, Rebecca sat at one end and Bernard Verhagen at the other. The three women were all smiling; only Bernard looked noncommittal.

'Hello,' said Mark diffidently.

'Hello Mark,' said Kim. 'Peter has only just arrived, so we can fill you both in at the same time. Please take a seat.'

Mark and Peter looked at each other in renewed surprise, then Peter resumed his seat and Mark took the only other empty chair, next to Peter.

'We realise this is a bit of a surprise for both of you, so we will keep it brief and let you get reacquainted with each other. Luka, would you care to do the honours?'

'Certainly,' Luka replied. 'Firstly, we would like to welcome you both and thank you for being punctual on your first day as employees of the Eurasian Space Agency. We have got you both here today because you will be working quite closely together.'

Peter and Mark now positively beamed at each other.

'Peter is to be our public relations man and will be attending events and conferences on our behalf. We have put together an initial itinerary,' she said, handing Peter a sealed brown envelope, 'but it is not set in stone. You may take Mark with you as and when you and he think it would be appropriate; although Kim, myself and Sanjay, who is away at the moment, reserve the right to veto any decisions that either of you make and to re-direct your efforts as we see appropriate.

'Mark, your main task will be to analyse materials gathered by Peter and to conduct related research in accordance with the priorities we have laid out,' Luka said, handing Mark an identical envelope. 'This is not set in stone either, although you are subject to the same provisos that apply to Peter. Do you have any questions?'

They remained silent.

'Okay. The two of you will share this office. You have no specific duties for the next couple of days, so I suggest you use this time to go over your itineraries and settle in.

When the others left the room, Peter sat down again and opened his envelope, but Mark just stood for a while staring in silence at the door that had just closed in front of him.

'Mmm,' said Peter, 'looks pretty damn demanding. What have you got?'

'Sorry?'

'Don't worry about it, catch your breath if you need to.'

Mark sat down, looked at his envelope, turned it round in his hands, shook it slightly to see if it rattled or anything, and opened it. Inside, there was a plastic nameplate with his name on it, which he guessed was to be attached to the office door, and a sheaf of papers. In the middle of the top sheet, bold letters read: 'Eurasian Space Agency', and above that was the Agency's logo: a minimalist sketch of a space rocket with its pointy end nearly touching an equally minimalist sketch of a star.

Leafing through four or five sheets of closely typed text, he came to one with the heading: 'Priorities for Research and Analysis'. Below the heading there were three bullet points. Beside the first bullet point, a sentence read: 'Find out who is doing what about antimatter, why they are doing it and how far they have got.' Beside the second bullet point, it read: 'Do the same in respect of regeneration, retro-ageing and related matters.' Beside the third, it read: 'Do not discuss your research or findings with anyone other than Peter or members of the Team.' Below that, a smaller heading read: 'The Team: Kim. Eddie. Sanjay. Luka.' There were no surnames and nothing else was written on the sheet. Mark leafed through the few remaining sheets, which consisted of information about the Space Centre, some travel and tourist information about Geneva and a large-scale map of Switzerland. The last sheet was blank except for: 'Happy hunting, TT (The Team).'

'No mention of Rebecca,' thought Mark, 'or Bernard; and who is this Eddie? The only Eddie or Edward I know is Professor Edward Banks, my other PhD supervisor. Could they mean him?'

'There's a definite pattern here, Mark,' said Peter, reading through his lengthier instructions, 'no doubt about it, not now'.

'Go on.'

'Well, for a while I wasn't sure if the other universe was as real as *Molly* told us it was, and thought that Kim was probably hedging her bets. On the one hand, she could make a fool of herself if she proclaimed the existence of a parallel Earth in 157 BC and it turned out to be a mirage. On the other, if it was real, there would be all kind of things to think about before releasing that kind of information to a technologically sophisticated and ever more populated planet. She came close to saying as much the day after you left Geneva, and I sympathised with her

45

dilemma and decided to toe the line they wanted, for now. But I quite naturally wanted to know whether the other Earth was for real, and spent quite a bit of time looking into it while most other media types just accepted what they were told. Despite being repeatedly told it was all an illusion, I began to think that it was in fact quite real and that Kim and others knew it to be real. Then Kim contacted me and offered me this job because she would prefer me, as she put it, "to be inside the tent pissing out rather than outside the tent pissing in". So then I pretty much knew it was real, and that employing me was their way of keeping me on side. I took the job partly because they made me an offer I couldn't refuse and partly because I wanted to be involved in such a fantastic project. If that meant losing a degree of journalistic freedom, well it seemed to be for the best of ethical reasons.

'But looking at this itinerary, it seems to me that this team of theirs wants to know all they can about the anti-universe and how people might travel into it. And not just that, according to this, I'm booked into just about every anti-ageing conference going, and there's a lot more of them than I realised. Research into antimatter might come under the remit of a space agency, but I wouldn't have thought that anti-ageing did. If I had to put money on it, I'd say Kim's planning to be around until the anti-universe can be visited. I'm only guessing, of course, but I wouldn't put it past her to go along for the ride.'

'What, to the other Earth?'

'Why not?'

'I've just had a thought,' said Mark, 'what if we could go as well?'

'I doubt if that's the intention, but you never know,' Peter pondered as he looked around their new office, 'if it does turn out to be possible, we might have just washed up in the right place at the right time.'

3
THE RACE IS ON

Peter and Mark had been kept extremely busy since they joined the Space Agency, nearly three years earlier. They had spent about half this time traveling around the world together, with Peter very much in the lead and Mark happily following in his wake. Virtually all international conferences were now conducted in the host countries' own languages, which made the verbal language translation function on Mark's mobile his most treasured aid.

Throughout this time, anti-ageing techniques and developments were the most popular and controversial topics of the day across most of the globe. Conversely, antimatter and anti-space had languished in the public consciousness. Funding for research into antimatter had also languished. Only in parts of Europe had spending on such research actually increased, mostly because the Indian Government had opted to cut its expenditure and pool the remainder with the Eurasian Space Agency, which was predominantly based in Europe. The Indo-European alliance was further cemented by changing the name of the Eurasian Space Agency to that of the (Mahatma) Gandhi Institute for Space Exploration; partly in return for Indian co-operation and partly to emphasise the alliance's purported ideals of non-violent, non-exploitative ethical development.

It was only in the past few months that signs of increased funding for experiments into antimatter had become apparent in China and the USA, but these two space-giants were now increasing their spending at a phenomenal rate.

One of Mark's earlier reports to the Team had argued that the quiet patch in relation to antimatter owed a good deal to the way that the achievements of *Achilles* and *Molly* had been reported and received by members of the scientific community who were predisposed towards skepticism. Peter published several articles on antimatter that used the word 'exciting' a lot, but also hinted that the 'sunk costs' of earlier investments had kept the Gandhi Institute especially active in this field despite its limited long-term value. The effects of such articles were difficult to quantify, but no one was denying that the Gandhi Institute had got their noses ahead in this 'scientific sub-field', as Peter chose to publicly describe it. Now, however, the 'race', as Peter and Mark privately spoke of it, was on again in earnest. Although the Indo-European alliance had got slightly ahead in terms of the science, their main weaknesses lay in their relative lack of hardware in space and their inability to ramp up funding without protracted international negotiations. China and the USA had the hardware and now they were ready and willing to turn the financial taps full on.

There was only one credible explanation for this change: influential scientists and others in China and the USA had come to realise that the other Earth was real, that it was still in antiquity, and that if they did not get there first then someone else would. Peter also felt that the period of relative quiet elsewhere had not been long enough to give the Gandhi Institute a sustainable lead. They were, in short, heading for third place in any race for the other Earth.

'So,' Peter said after discussing these points with Mark, 'what do you think will happen if the Chinese or Americans get there first?'

'Well, they're both making non-interventionist noises, saying they just want to observe the other Earth. They might even mean it, but I don't believe it will happen like that.'

'No, nor do I. Is that what you're writing in your latest report?'

'Yes, it is,' Mark replied, 'among other things.'

'Like what?'

'Like how I figure things could develop if the Chinese and Americans get there more or less simultaneously.'

'Go on.'

'Well, I think they will be competing with each other. I'm not saying it would be like an old-style Western gold rush, where Native Americans get clobbered in the stampede, I think the Americans and the Chinese would behave much better than that now. But I am concerned that the competition between them might end up driving them to spread their influence over the other Earth in a much more radical way than they would if either one of them got there alone. I also think they are aware of this and would like to stop each other from getting there, not just to be the only ones there, but also out of ethical considerations for the fate of the other Earth.'

'You're not saying they'd be willing to fight over it, are you?'

'I doubt if it'll come to that, but I do think they will both go all out to get there ahead of each other by the biggest time margin possible, so as to put themselves in the strongest possible position to negotiate limits to the spread of each other's influence and possible future settlements. Negotiations might break down, I don't know, but I feel fairly certain they could agree on at least one thing.'

'What?' Peter asked.

'They won't want a third player involved.'

'So you reckon they'll cut us out altogether?'

'If they can, yes.'

'I think you're safe in assuming they can, if they put their minds to it. Nine light-years is a long way away. Even allowing for new developments to come off the drawing board, a one-way journey to the other Earth would take at least seventy-five years after entering anti-space. If the Chinese or American expeditions decide to arrange some nasty surprise for our people when they get there, then I don't see what anyone on this world could do about it.'

'So the Institute's best hope of being a player is to get there first.'

'Yes,' said Peter, 'but we can't do that. I've just had a chat with Sanjay. He says the Indian Government are beginning to think they're spending their resources on the losing side. In the meantime, China and the USA have been making fortunes on helium-3 imports from the Moon and have an almost infinite supply of energy generated by helium-3 to open big windows to the antimatter universe, and they have the industrial muscle to convert or build new spacecraft for the voyage to the other Earth much sooner than we originally thought possible. If we get left behind and the Indian Government pulls out of the race, then we'll have to follow suit. Kim and the others will be very disappointed, but I think that's the way it will go.'

'Umm, that's not quite what I'm writing in my report.'

'Oh?'

'I'm not disputing what you're saying about the relatively short timeframe for China and America to send expeditions, I just wonder if their massive resources and competitive instincts might be to our advantage.'

'How so?'

'Because we needn't compete on their terms. As you say, nine light-years is a long way away, but the competition between them when they get there will probably be won by an aggressive power with tons of high-tech equipment rather than the first power to plant their flag on the other Earth's soil. We can't hope to match either of them for resources or even long-term technologies, but we still have a technological edge in terms of sending small probes, like *Molly*, into the anti-antimatter universe. What I was wondering was whether we could concentrate all our energies on sending a small expedition with very little equipment or supplies; just enough to get by and to play the honest broker between the two space Goliaths without posing a threat to either of them.'

'No good, I'm afraid, Mark. I don't think you fully appreciate how quickly the Chinese and Americans can swing into gear when they have a mind to. They're bound to send what they can as soon as they can, as well as following up with bigger ships. So, sorry, but they'll be ready to launch small expeditions before us as well as bigger ones later on.'

'Perhaps, but I wasn't necessarily thinking of a Euro-Indian craft launching first.'

'You weren't?'

'It would obviously be better if we could launch first, but if that's not going to happen, perhaps we should be thinking in terms of focusing our resources on where we already have an edge and on speed of travel rather than on speed of launch. That way, I mean, I'm probably talking out of my backside, but I pictured us wishing the two Goliaths bon voyage and sending out a little David that could overtake them en route.'

Peter had got used to being ahead of Mark in terms of ideas. However, as they sat together now in silence, he had to admit to himself that Mark had beat him to this David idea. It was strikingly simple, would certainly be thought of by the Chinese and the Americans, and yet it was just possible that the psychology of competition between the two space Goliaths would lead them to spread their resources to match or surpass everything that each other were working on, including large-scale expeditions with tons of equipment. If that was the case, then focusing the lesser but far from inconsiderable resources available to the Gandhi Institute on making a fast, albeit belated, dash to the other Earth in a small ship with minimal equipment might just come off. They were still sitting together silently thinking about these things when they both got calls, simultaneously.

'Hello, you two,' said Kim.

'Hello,' they replied in unison.

'I think it's time we had a little chat.'

'Now?' Peter asked.

'Yes please. Bernard knows where I am, he'll be with you shortly. Okay?'

'Okay,' they both said, and their lines went dead.

'Funny, that,' said Peter.

'What?'

'I just had a distinct feeling that she's been listening to our little conversation.'

'Me too,' said Mark, looking around their office as if he might spot a listening device or camera.

Bernard drove them to a very exclusive and highly security conscious clinic on the outskirts of Geneva where Kim was receiving some kind of treatment. After showing them the door to her room, Bernard left without entering. Kim was sitting at a desk in front of three screens. Beside her stood a wheeled contraption that was connected to her arm by two thin tubes.

Rising to welcome them, she said, 'apologies for calling you away from your work like this, but I think the time has come for some straight talking.'

'You've been spying on us, haven't you?' Peter asked.

'Yes, I have. I'm really sorry about that, but I had to know what you were doing and be able to react to events as they happen. The issues you were discussing are simply too sensitive to risk being talked about casually. Do you forgive me?'

'Not yet,' Peter replied.

'You have good reason to be annoyed, I accept that. What can I do to make amends?'

'Tell us everything you haven't told us already, and tell us now.'

'Okay, I will, as far as I'm able. For one thing, things are indeed moving much faster than we ever imagined. For another, you were right to suspect that I and others have entertained thoughts of going into the anti-universe, but it now looks highly unlikely that I will be fit enough to do so until well after others have gone through. You should also know that our reasons for wanting to go are *not* exploitative, but stem from our concerns about what an influx of emigrants from this planet might do to the other Earth if they are less interested in the impact they have than we are. We, the Team, that is, have devised a very simple plan that we think may help mitigate some of the worst effects of any such migration.'

'How?' Peter asked.

'By reporting what goes on. Communication between the two Earths will be based on digitised optical pulses relayed by a string of *Molly*-like devices. If everything goes according to plan, our expedition will be able to send footage back to this Earth at the speed of light, which means that we can show the viewing public what happens on the other Earth about nine years after it happens. Our hope is that such media attention will help to constrain any undue interference from the Chinese or the Americans or anyone else. However, you need to understand that this plan could be blocked unless we get to the other Earth before anyone else does.'

'How?' Peter asked again.

'Actually, very much like the David verses the Goliaths idea that Mark spoke of just before I called,' she said, smiling at Mark. 'In fact, we initially talked in terms of the same David and Goliath analogy and would have called our craft David had it not been considered too obvious. In the event, we decided to keep our craft's original name: *Iskra*, which is Russian for *spark*.'

'You mean it already exists?' Peter asked in surprise.

'It's still some way from being operational, but yes, it exists. It was designed as a helium-3 carrier and lunar resupply shuttle, but it was declared obsolete before the Russians finished building it. It has never seen service in space, and we managed to buy it on the cheap for experimental purposes less than a year after the first probe went into antimatter; a decade before *Molly* was launched. I'm sure Bernard would be happy to take you to it now and show you round, if you wish, it's not far from here.'

'I would like that,' said Mark.

'I'm afraid you will not get much information out of Bernard, and I have to ask you not to speak to anyone working there, or anyone else other than Bernard or Team members for the present: for security reasons, I'm sure you understand.'

'Yes, of course we do!' said Mark.

'I suppose so,' said Peter.

'Now, if you will excuse me, I have a nurse coming to do some unpleasant things for my benefit. If you would like to come back later, I would enjoy another chat and I will answer any other questions you have, as far as I'm able.'

Bernard was not very informative during the forty-minute drive, although he was able to answer some technical questions when they arrived at the uninspiring aircraft hanger that housed the *Iskra*, except where these questions touched on anything to do with antimatter.

The helium-3 carrier did not look very impressive. It looked a bit like a small old fashioned railway carriage; except that it was cylindrical, rounded at each end, had no windows, no wheels, and its colour was a dark metallic green on the outside and battleship grey on the inside. Only about half of the interior was accessible. There were no seats as such, although there was space for two people to sit on what looked like a large toolbox in front of a control panel. The remaining space was taken up by shelving and a complex arrangement of clamps, straps and variously shaped mouldings fixed to the craft's rounded floors, walls and ceilings. It did not look at all like something that one would want to travel in, even between two nearby railway stations; much less so for a journey of several decades through anti-space.

The nearest Bernard got to saying anything relevant to such a long journey was that the nine largest shelves were 'designed as bunks for the crew or to accommodate biodegradable items that are frozen and pre-packed into coffin-sized containers.' Mark and Peter both felt a slight shudder at Bernard's words, despite knowing that passengers in deep suspended animation would not feel any discomfort nor, indeed, have any awareness of any time passing, no matter how long the journey took. They had both been wondering how human bodies could possibly survive the passage between the two universes, or could tolerate the acceleration and deceleration generated by progressively faster generations of spacecraft. They both supposed that being frozen had to be part of the solution to these problems, and to the chronic lack of space available for equipment and supplies aboard the *Iskra*.

They put these suppositions to Kim when they went back to her room at the clinic later that same day, and got them confirmed regarding supplies and partially confirmed in relation to acceleration and deceleration. In terms of initially entering the anti-universe, she said:

'When we had time to take a good look at how the rifle kept a window into anti-space open for one hundred and eight seconds, the Team soon realised that the less dense core of the rifle was doing most of the work after Molly had passed through the window. It was effectively sychronising the temporal mismatch between the two universes at their interface; just as Eddie, Mark's old PhD supervisor, said it would when he designed it. Put simply, the prospect of widening the window then became enormously less energy consuming, and the wider the window was the longer it would take to close. The longer it takes to close, the less speed is needed to pass delicate objects like human beings through it.'

Then Peter asked one of the two questions that had been playing on both their minds since their earlier meeting with her.

'Who do you propose to send on this journey?'

'Eight people, all told. Not me, unfortunately, I will not be up to this trip, but maybe I could join one later on. In the meantime, it has been agreed that Rebecca will take my place.'

'Rebecca?' asked Mark. 'What about her husband?'

'Her husband is now living in the US with his lover; a plumber called Tony.'

'Oh! I see.'

'Luka, Sanjay and Bernard have long wanted to go, and that has been agreed. Eddie wanted to go too, but the rest of the Team vetoed that, also on grounds of health. Then there is Sunita and Tarak, who I do not believe either of you have met.'

'Sunita was with you that time at the cafeteria,' said Peter, 'just after the post-Molly press briefing.'

'Yes, she was, perhaps I should have introduced you. She is a communications specialist, and Tarak is one of the most accomplished of India's new generation of astronauts. That's about as far as we've got so far.'

'Are you deliberately teasing us?' said Peter. 'That's six places, and you have allowed us to wonder whether we stand a chance of going.'

'Would you want to?'

'Of course,' Peter said irritably, 'you've been listening to our conversations long enough to know that!'

'I have not been constantly listening to you, but I take your point. How about you, Mark, would you still want to go now that you have seen the *Iskra*?'

'Err, yeah, why not?' Mark replied, not wishing to let Peter down but also hoping that Kim would come up with some very good reasons why they need not entrust their lives to that ugly and untried spacecraft that the Russians had deemed obsolete.

'There is no guarantee that you will survive it. Even if you do, there are currently no plans to bring anyone back.'

'Hey ho,' Mark replied in what he hoped was an heroic tone, 'if Peter's up for it, I'd hate to miss out.'

'Well then, if you are both volunteering, I shall put it to the rest of the Team and see what they say. Any other questions?'

'Just the obvious one, for now.' said Peter. 'When do you think the *Iskra* will set off on this little epic?'

'We had thought it would be many years away, but we have been under pressure and, as it turns out, we already had most of the technology and hardware required before *Molly* was launched.'

'How long?' Peter pressed.

'I cannot say exactly, but if it is agreed that you should go, then you would be wise not to start working on any projects that you cannot finish by the end of the year.'

'What!? Seven months? That's ridiculous! We wouldn't be overtaking the Chinese or the Americans, we would be leaving well before them!'

'I know! Isn't that just sweet? You were right to think they'd guess what we're up to, Peter, and would go all out to beat us to it. So we have had to make a few changes. We are already working on the design of a supply craft that we hope will be able to overtake the *Iskra* en route, but it should be ready quicker and travel considerably faster for having no one on board to crush by the force of its acceleration. When, or should I say *if* those aboard the *Iskra* get into orbit around the other Earth, they should find the essential supplies and equipment they need, *if* such a supply craft has managed to overtake the *Iskra* en route, including a re-entry vehicle waiting to take them to the surface; *if* they manage to board it and *if* it still functions properly. Whether it all works out like that, and whether they arrive before or after the Chinese or Americans, I cannot say for sure, but it's our best hope.'

Peter and Mark were stunned into silence; not just by the speed with which things were moving, but also by the number of 'hopes', 'shoulds' and especially the 'ifs' of such a plan. They both began to feel a clammy sense of fear and claustrophobia at the thought of defrosting in a nasty little spacecraft only to find that a re-entry vehicle had not arrived and there was no way of getting home.

'So,' Kim said brightly over the deepening silence, 'would you like to think a little longer about volunteering?'

'Perhaps we should,' Peter muttered, 'perhaps we should.'

Mark stared at his own feet and said nothing.

When Bernard dropped them off outside the Gandhi Institute building, Peter and Mark decided to take a walk in a nearby public park where they could talk. But then Peter had second thoughts about this too as he considered their buttons, belts, shoes and so on; suspecting listening devices everywhere. Instead, he called Luka and Sanjay and asked if he and Mark could meet them. They agreed to a meeting the following day and said they would ask Eddie to come along as well.

As they left the park and walked back to their office, they did at least feel comfortable enough to discuss the basics of the issues troubling them. It was going to difficult for either of them to decide what to do. Kim clearly thought there was a possibility of them joining the expedition if they wanted to, otherwise she would have killed off the idea as soon as Peter had asked her about it. They did want to go to the other Earth, provided they felt reasonably sure they would get there alive, which they were not sure of at all. There was also the question as to why the Team might want them to go, but they decided to wait until the meeting before discussing it any further.

After the following day's meeting, Mark was left with a much more upbeat impression of their chances of survival, partly because the Team had obviously spent a considerable amount of time analysing the colossal amount of information that *Molly* had sent back. Every available piece of evidence that could possibly confirm that the other Earth was an exact parallel of their own had confirmed it; except, of course, in respect of the time differential. Eddie also gave a very enthusiastic and reassuring presentation on the modifications being made to the *Iskra* and on the development of a proposed follow-up craft. When Peter asked what his and Mark's roles would be and how the Team could possibly consider that it might be worth allocating them two of the *Iskra*'s eight berths, Eddie smiled and said:

'In many ways your roles would be similar to the roles you play now, not least in terms of your combined research and analysis of how the other players are likely to behave when they get there and how the locals might react to them and to us. Mark's extensive knowledge of ancient Roman history has not gone unnoticed, and this may prove invaluable to us in ways that we haven't even thought of as yet. However, the most important reason why we would consider the possibility of you joining the expedition is this: in the three years that you have been working for us you have shown yourselves to be an exceptionally hard working and conceptually sharp double-act that can be counted on to take a similar ethical stance to that of the Team in this venture's non-interventionist raison d'être.'

Such flattery worked wonders on Mark, but Peter only smiled weakly.

And so it went on; an uplifting meeting of enthusiasts dedicated to their task, wedded to noninterventionism as far as practicable under the circumstances, and flatteringly keen to welcome Peter and Mark into their inner circle. Their upbeat confidence was infectious, at least as far as Mark was concerned. When the meeting was over he felt a renewed sense of excitement and purpose, although Peter had looked ill at ease throughout the meeting and his expression darkened perceptibly as soon as they left the room.

'So,' Mark began what he had come to think of as a mantra of the Institute's personnel, 'what do you think?'

But Peter would not talk until they had walked out of the building, driven to a deserted patch of woodland on the shores of Lake Geneva, signaled that they should take off their jackets and shoes, empty their pocket of anything that might harbour listening devices, and walked to the tip of a tiny spit of land. Then he said, 'I think we are about to join one of three powers making a headlong dash to a thoroughly pre-modern Earth to be the first thoroughly noninterventionist batch to arrive there just so that we can *report on each other*!? Like hell! As far as I can see, we are just being given the same bullshit served up by the Americans and Chinese.'

'That's a bit harsh, don't you think?'

'Is it? Well you tell me what the difference is, will you?'

'Okay, I'll try, if you want me to. For one thing, the two of us would constitute a quarter of the personnel aboard the *Iskra*. If we don't like what's going on, we stand a fairly reasonable chance of influencing it. For another, right from the outset we have heard members of the Team and those close to them speak of ethical considerations. If it was their intention to fool us, then they got their act together damn fast and have kept it up ever since. Do you really think that's credible?'

Peter offered no answer.

'Then there's Rebecca,' Mark continued. 'I knew her before I'd even heard of *Molly*. I've read her work; her whole way of thinking is geared to *limiting* any harmful effects of scientific breakthroughs, and she constitutes another eighth of the crew. Kim might be a bit of a dark horse, but she's not coming with us. Bernard definitely is a dark horse, but we have both got to know Luka and Sanjay quite well and come to like them. I can't believe that they would stand by and let this expedition turn bad if they could help it. That gives us at least five eighths of the crew who I believe can be counted on, and I have no reason to suspect the others . . .'

'Okay, okay,' Peter interrupted, 'I get the point.'

'So what's really bothering you, Peter? Is it that it's suddenly become a reality instead of a distant dream that would probably never come true? Is it the risk of dying, or leaving behind everything that we know and feel comfortable with? Because I can assure you that these things bother me plenty. Or is it that we might inadvertently do more harm than good?' he asked, half hoping that he had supplied Peter, and himself, with enough good reasons to bow out gracefully.

'I am frightened, *very* frightened. I'm daunted by the whole thing for all sorts of reasons. But the thing that's bothering me most right now is what we're turning into.'

'How do you mean?'

'Take a good hard look at yourself, Mark. Don't you think you've changed at all? Well you have. You've become a lot more sure of yourself, which is a good thing, but why are you assuming that you can do any good at all on the other Earth? I'm amazed at how little has been said about the kinds of things we'll do when we get there. Alright, we're told that we're to report what the Chinese and Americans get up to, but we have no idea what effect we ourselves might have. I don't mean just by being there, but by stirring up a media frenzy and stimulating the kind of mass migration that we suspect the Chinese and Americans will open up. Can you imagine how much media companies would be willing to pay for sole rights to cover the birth of the other Earth's Jesus Christ? Or the lengths that many devout Christians would go to to stop the birth being desecrated by a media circus? We could be the first wave of countless others who go to the other Earth, some with the intention of making a fortune out of it and others with the intention of saving it, but all of them taking a piece of it for their own purposes.'

'Isn't that the point of you and me going along,' Mark said, but with dwindling conviction, 'to analyse the effects of this and other expeditions?'

'This is big stuff we're messing with, Mark, and a potentially multi-trillion dollar industry. I'm worried that we're getting sucked into a corporate sense of who we are. Look at the way we've been talking about the Institute as *us* and the Americans and Chinese as *them*, about how they might cut us out as *players*, as if we were involved in some great game. You've changed alright, Mark, and so have I. We talk about global matters and interplanetary expeditions like some people talk about inter-corporate rivalries. Who the hell do we think we are? And this Team of theirs, who do they think they are? Gods? And if we don't like what they're doing, do you seriously think that we could usurp their plans without acting like gods ourselves? I tell you, Mark, this is beginning to really freak me out.'

They did not say any more just then, or do anything other than stare at the lake until they realised they were cold. Then they drove back to their own hotel rooms lost in their own thoughts.

'Stupid, stupid, stupid, how could I be so stupid?' Mark asked himself as he sat on his bed with a bottle of wine and slipped back into his old self-ridiculing ways. It was not much more than twenty-four hours since he had felt a surge of self-esteem on the back of Peter and Kim's reactions to his David and the Goliaths hunch. This was quickly followed by a mixture of fear and self-importance when he found he might well be able to go to the other Earth. But so soon! And in that horrible coffin-ship called the *Iskra*! He felt sure that fear would have won out if it had not been for that flattering meeting. He remembered listening to the Team members and toying with the idea that he might not be quite so junior in his partnership with Peter, but it had been Peter who had kept his critical faculties while Mark's went flying out the window.

He felt he needed to think about the issues that Peter had raised rather than his own fear or tender ego, or even about his friendship with Peter, and yet he could not do so in any sustained way without worrying about their personal friendship above all else. Over the past three years they had become so accustomed and secure in each other's company that they had taken their friendship for granted as a constant rock in their working and social lives. Then Peter told him a few home truths and that rock had suddenly begun to feel brittle and set on uncertain foundations.

Downing the last of the wine in his glass, Mark lay on his bed and tried to make a major effort to think through the things that Peter had said by Lake Geneva. 'Right,' he thought, 'let me get this into some logical order. Firstly, should I volunteer?' As soon as he asked himself this question he knew that he had already decided to volunteer if Peter did. So, assuming it all panned out, what would happen when they got there? This he did not know and could not focus on properly, so he just lay on his bed and let his mind wander until it got some kind of fix on the issues. Sleep took him unawares.

He found himself looking at a blue and white planet. A kind of space-fighter slid into view, flying towards the planet. He materialised inside its cockpit. His leather-gloved hands gripped two joysticks that controlled the craft, and each of his thumbs hovered over a button at the top of the joysticks . . . 'Hold on, I've been here before,' he thought as his consciousness nudged at the margins of sleep and wakefulness, 'and my thumbs wouldn't do what I told them to do.' He tried moving his thumbs off the buttons and they readily responded. 'Well, at least that's not the same as last time,' he thought in relief as he slid further from wakefulness. Then he began to notice other differences. For one thing, he appeared to be sitting on a large cold toolbox. In fact, the whole spaceship felt cold. He sensed the presence of frozen sleepers behind him and realised it was not a space-fighter after all, it was the *Iskra*, and he seemed to remember that he was the only one of eight people aboard who was not in suspended animation.

Still in space, he tentatively tried pressing the button on his right-hand joystick while it could do no harm. There were no rockets or machinegun bullets. Instead, a screen on the control panel came on and showed an image of the planet before him. He tried the left-hand button, and the image zoomed in towards some clouds. 'At least I'm not going to kill anyone with a camera!'

With a whoosh, he tore into the planet's atmosphere, passed high over low hills, high over Spartacus' slave army and towards Roman soldiers marching in checkerboard squares towards them. Preparing to film the impending battle, he found that the *Iskra* had dropped lower than he had meant it to. Roman soldiers started pointing at him and then began to flee; 'Oh, shit!' he thought, 'I wasn't supposed to interfere.' Passing right over them, he banked and flew back as Roman officers were forming their men back into squares; but he was again flying too low and again the Roman soldiers started to take flight. 'Shit, I've done it again! I'd better get out of here.' Now passing low over the slave army, he saw that they were waving madly and seemed to be cheering him. 'Damn, what am I supposed to do now? Leave the Romans to reform again and wipe out Spartacus' army?'

'You'll have to work that out for yourself,' Peter said from behind him.

'Peter!' Mark called as he twisted round. 'Oh, thank God you're here! What should I do? I can't just film them getting slaughtered or crucified?' Then he realised that Peter was covered with frost.

'Sorry, Mark, I'm too cold to think about it now, I have to get back in the freezer.'

'Please don't go, Peter, not yet, I don't know what to do!'

'Sorry, can't help, got to get back in the freezer.'

'No, no please don't go, not yet, I don't know what to do!' he pleaded again as he flew further from the battlefield. Against his will, his hands suddenly applied pressure to the joysticks. The craft banked round sharply and headed back to the battlefield just as crosshairs materialised on the screen in front of him. Becoming really afraid of what he might do next, he found himself shouting: 'no Peter, don't go, I don't know what to do!' at a light fitting in his hotel room.

In an effort to gather his wits, he got up from his bed, drew the curtains and decided to have another glass of wine. The open bottle beside his bed was empty, but it was still before 11pm, so he decided to open another one and watch some mindless television. About two hours later, this bottle was also empty and he went back to bed. As far as he could remember, the rest of his night was not disturbed by any more dreams, although it was disturbed by a parched throat and acid indigestion.

He went to work the following day wondering why he had been inflicting so many hangovers on himself of late. When he got there, he and Peter got on with their own work and hardly said a word to each other all day.

On his way back to his room that evening, he decided that his friendship with Peter could not be separated from his decision about volunteering for the proposed expedition. It was not just that he valued their friendship for its own sake, which he most certainly did, but he also felt that he needed Peter to be his mentor if he was to be mentally strong enough to deal with all the 'big stuff' that they might end up messing with. He called Peter.

'Hi Mark, what is it?'

'I need to talk.'

'Now?'

'Please.'

'Okay, meet me at that spot by the lake at eight.'

'Yeah, okay.'

They parked next to each other, shed the garments and possessions most likely to conceal listening devices and walked onto the spit of land.

'What do you want?' Peter asked curtly.

'I want to know if we're still friends.'

Peter regarded Mark thoughtfully. 'I think you're being a bit paranoid, I wasn't aware that much had changed in that respect.'

'You said I've changed.'

'You have changed, so have I. Change happens.'

'Perhaps, but couldn't we change together, not in ways that diverge?'

'That's part of what's worrying me.'

'How do you mean?'

'I don't think we are changing in ways that diverge, I think we're changing in ways that converge.'

'I don't understand, weren't you annoyed with me?

'I was a bit annoyed by your reaction to their flattery, yes. But I was more annoyed at them for their flattery and deceit. Exactly who they were trying hardest to deceive, us or themselves, I'm not entirely sure, but they are intelligent people who must know damn well that the raison d'être for the expedition cannot possibly be non-intervention. That's patently ridiculous when you consider the likely effects of showing billions of people on this crowded planet just how empty the other Earth is. I was annoyed about that and annoyed to find that they expected us to buy into such an idea. I was also annoyed with all this cloak and dagger stuff that Kim and whoever's been doing, and I still am annoyed to be skulking out here just so that we can talk freely to each other. But most of all, I'm annoyed with myself.'

'Why?'

'Because I've lied to myself and everyone around me. I'm going on this expedition, Mark, if they'll let me, and I'm selfish enough to want you to come as well, despite the danger we'll be in. I've tried telling myself it's because we might be able to stop people wilfully interfering with the other Earth, but I know that's at least three-quarters bullshit, probably total bullshit. The truth is, I want to interfere. I want to do big things. I want to cure pestilence and hunger, stop massacres, end slavery, do all kinds of things that dewy-eyed teenagers dream of doing when they grow up to rule the world. Well, there is a world out there where doing such things might really be possible, and I want to do them.'

'I see.'

'Are you disappointed?'

'No, I don't think so. To be honest, I've had kind of similar thoughts myself, from time to time.'

'I know, I've seen it in your eyes, heard it in some of the things you've said, especially when you've had a few drinks. Like I say, we're not changing in ways that diverge, we're thinking more and more alike.'

'Right, I see. So, what do you think I should do?'

'You could volunteer to go as well, if you still want to.'

'I still want to.'

'Don't you want to pick up the threads of your PhD again before you go?'

'No, not a chance, not with all this going on.'

'Are you sure?'

'Positive.'

Okay then, but if we are going to do this, we must be fully committed to each other, not just as friends, but also as partners in whatever lies ahead. Do you understand that? Do you agree with it?' Peter asked as he studied his friend's face.

'Yes, I do understand that! Yes, I do agree with it!' Mark earnestly intoned back in the manner of one who makes a sacred oath of allegiance.

'Well, if that is to be the way of it,' Peter said gravely, 'if we really decide to stick together in this, then we must never – *never ever* – have this sort of conversation again on this world, not even if we feel sure that no one is listening. When, I should say *if*, we get to the other Earth, we must keep reminding each other to keep our feet on the ground, and do so in utter frankness. But until then, we *must* keep our thoughts to ourselves and swallow all the shit they're feeding us about non-intervention; *not* buy into it, just swallow it. Understood?'

'Understood.'

They gazed at the lake in silence for a minute or two. Mark turned to face Peter again, offered his hand for Peter to shake, and said, 'partners?'

Peter scrutinised his face intently. Mark wondered if he were looking for some sign of duplicity where none existed, but then a smile grew on Peter's face as he took and shook his hand. 'Partners!' he said back with enthusiasm, and his smile broadened into one of those big smiles that Mark had not seen for a while. A deal had been done, or so it seemed to Mark, that could not be easily undone.

4
TOUCHDOWN

Six months had passed since Mark and Peter voiced their allegiance on the banks of Lake Geneva. They had asked to go on the expedition and their request was granted. Aside from a few hints and cryptic comments that they alone were likely to understand, they stuck to their promises not to broach the subjects that their pact made taboo. Now they sat together in a large and comfortable lounge with the other six members of the expedition, counting down the final hours before they went into suspended animation.

The preparations had gone smoothly, and everyone involved had been heartened by a preliminary experiment in which Tarak and another very well paid 'volunteer' were sent into the antimatter universe in a tiny spacecraft launched from the enlarged and re-equipped *Achilles* space station and returned alive and well four days later. The *Iskra* was then given a piggyback ride into space and Tarak manoeuvred it to dock with *Achilles*. He and seventeen technicians worked on the station for five days before he returned to Earth to join the expeditionary crew while they waited.

The crew now had eighteen hours of consciousness left, plus a further nineteen days in suspended animation before they and the *Iskra* were propelled into the antimatter universe to begin their long journey through anti-space. They wouldn't know anything about the last nineteen days wait, of course, or about anything else until they were revived in orbit around the other

Earth an estimated seventy-nine years later. It was hard for any of them to accept that they would not have any sense of the passage of time throughout these seventy-nine years, and hard for some of them to suppress feelings of panic that something might go terribly wrong while they 'slept'. Nonetheless, they all did manage to suppress such feelings, or at least to remain outwardly in control of them.

Then the Chinese Government announced that they had sent two men and two women into the antimatter universe earlier that day. Kim hastily convened a meeting of the crew and several others who were closely involved in the project to discuss the implications of this new development.

'They have beaten us to it,' said Kim, opening the meeting. 'The Chinese Government say that theirs is a long-range civilian reconnaissance mission into the anti-universe, but we know they are building at least one unmanned backup craft designed to overtake their manned journey to the other Earth. A twenty-day head start may seem small over the course of a seventy-nine-year journey, but given that we appear to be using much the same technology and expect to be travelling at much the same speeds, I see no reason why we should not work under the assumption that they will arrive ahead of us.

'This has taken all of us by surprise. I applaud their achievement, and I cannot help but marvel at their ability to keep their readiness to go so soon a secret. I also cannot help but wonder at the lengths they must have gone to in order to overturn our lead in this field and hope they have not felt obliged to make dangerous shortcuts to achieve this. Our latest reports also suggest that the Americans are close to launching, and they are clearly thinking big, so their arrival may well usher in a period of American dominance on the other Earth.

'There is a good deal more I would like to say about all of this, but there is not much we can do about any of it for the time being. I am sure that all of you are in any case aware of the potential implications of our not being securely in situ when other expeditions plant their flags on the other Earth. The reason I have called this meeting is not primarily to discuss these matters, but to ask you, the crew, to take some things into consideration that we have not discussed at any length together before; things that I feel sure none of you would wish to consider but nonetheless may need to bear in mind.

'While I do not feel that our position need be significantly weakened in the short-term by the Chinese move, we do not know what kind of equipment they have aboard their craft or what they intend to put aboard their follow-up craft. On the other hand, we do have some information regarding the proposed American multiple launches and Chinese allegations regarding their purposes.

'It seems that a significant portion of the funding for the American effort has been raised through religious groups who are of a somewhat fundamentalist persuasion, in return for some members of these religious groups to be included in the crews. Whether there is any truth in Chinese claims that the religiosity of the American expeditions necessarily makes them expansionist and aggressive in nature is not for me to judge. However, it seems likely that the Chinese will see the involvement of American Christian fundamentalists as justification for taking measures for their own defence over and above that which they would otherwise need to defend themselves in a pre-modern world. This, in turn, may well be seen as a justification for the Americans to do likewise. Whilst I would hate to contribute to any such self-fulfilling prophecy, those of us who remain behind will need to monitor these developments and perhaps review arrangements when equipping your supply vessel.

'I realise this is not the kind of mini-lecture that you would want to be listening to right now, but it is important to be clear about this. You will be a long way from home, and assuming our optical relay system functions properly, any news you receive from us when you arrive will be nine years old. When you get into orbit, it is critically important that you review the situation on the surface and take sensible measures to protect yourselves before landing. This does not mean that we are asking you to descend to the surface armed to the teeth. However, I would like to take this opportunity to reinforce our earlier requests that you study your supply vessel's inventory *very* carefully, that you get acquainted with any unfamiliar items, and that you keep an open mind as to what you might need to take with you to the surface.

'It grieves me to think that I may be casting a militaristic shadow over your adventure, but we cannot altogether guarantee that all the individuals involved in current or future expeditions will act according to the highest ethical standards, even if the motives of the governments or organisations that are sending them are above reproach. Indeed, were we not concerned about ethical standards of behaviour there would be considerably less need to mount this expedition in the first place.'

Mark and Peter could not resist giving each other sidelong glances during this very un-Ghandi-like lecture, but they said nothing.

'Okay, unless there are any questions on this difficult issue, I would like to throw this meeting open, hopefully to discuss more pleasant matters.'

There were no questions on this difficult issue, Kim did throw the meeting open and more pleasant matters were discussed; chiefly concerning the cultivation of kitchen gardens on the other Earth. Mark felt a pinch of ironic amusement at the apparent excitement with which this kind of gardening was debated, and wondered whether the introduction of such an uncontroversial subject at this point might have been pre-planned, although it did make perfect sense for the crew to think about future food supplies. Pre-planned or not, the horticultural debate seemed to have a calming effect, not least because talk of growing cabbages implicitly assumed that they would survive to grow anything at all. Nonetheless, Kim's opening address had left the crew in no doubt that they were expected to defend themselves if they came under attack from people from their own world as well as from any dangers that might already exist on the other Earth.

When the meeting broke up, the crew were left to pass the remaining hours as they wished. They spent much of this time talking in pairs or brooding on their thoughts alone, and taking turns to be beaten at chess by Bernard. The main collective activity consisted of listening to Tarak and Sunita playing amazingly professional duos on various stringed instruments. As well as listening to these performances and losing games of chess to Bernard, Peter and Mark spent several hours playing table tennis and computer games in the hope of distracting themselves from their intense anxiety.

The moment they had all been waiting for finally arrived. Everyone took turns to hug each other or shake each other's hands according to their habit, and then all eight of them went into individual cubicles, swallowed several pills handed to them by a nurse, lay on hospital beds and tried to relax as breathing masks were put over their faces.

'That's fine, Mark,' his nurse said, 'just relax and count to ten.' He counted in silence, 'one, two, three, f, f . . .'

'. . . f, f, f, ferr, ferr, five, f, f, fer, four, f, fer, five, s, s, six, s, seven, eight, nine, ten.' Mark felt disorientated and terribly tired, but not quite asleep. He thought he was supposed to be asleep before he got to ten. This didn't seem quite right. If he was supposed to be properly asleep when they started to put him in suspended animation, could it be dangerous if he was still awake? He didn't know, but he thought he must make an effort to let the nurse know he was still awake. Lying still for a few more moments, he gathered what inner strength he could and opened his eyes for half a second. No good; his eyes seemed to be immersed in misty stinging liquid. Then he heard his name called. 'That didn't sound like the nurse,' he thought, 'it sounded a bit like Rebecca.' He heard it again, and this time it sounded more like Rebecca. 'W, w, what's wrong?' he managed to croak, but his eyes remained closed.

'Nothing's wrong Mark, your fine, it's time to wake up now,' Rebecca said gently.

'W, wake up? Why, w, what's happened?'

'We've landed.'

'Landed?'

'Yes. We have landed on the other Earth. Everything is fine. Everyone is well. Take your time, Mark, I just wanted you to know that you've made it, that everyone made it. You are on the other Earth now.'

'Made it?'

'Yes, to the other Earth.'

'Other Earth?'

'Yes,'

'What year is it?'

'What, here? Umm, I think it's seventy-four BC.'

'Seventy-four BC? That's still quite early, isn't it?'

'Err, yes, if you say so.'

'Time for a bit more sleep then?'

Rebecca laughed softly, wafting her scented breath over him. 'Of course there is, Mark, you have a nice lie in.'

When he woke up again, he soon remembered what Rebecca had said about having landed on the other Earth and about it being seventy-four BC. In fact, it was seventy-three BC, the very year that Spartacus' slave revolt was due to break out, but Rebecca had been feeling a bit fuzzy from her awakening from suspended animation, and Mark was not in the habit of questioning what she told him.

He instinctively made to get up but stopped himself, partly because he was very tired and achy, and partly because he realised he had a full erection. 'Not the best entrance to make on another planet, waving that around!' he muttered to himself as he manoeuvred his erection to minimise the impression it made on the thin blanket that covered him. Carrying out this manoeuvre distracted him enough to overlook the presence of another person sitting directly behind his head. Then his mind registered the sound of suppressed laughter just as it ceased to be suppressed and was released into unrestrained peals of laughter.

Mark tried to whip his head around and immediately regretted it. Pain seared up the left side of his neck, smote deep inside his left ear, behind both eyes and spread across his brain.

'Steady, now,' Peter said, containing his laughter, 'just take your time.'

Hearing his friend's voice had cured most of his embarrassment, and the pains in his head were quickly reducing his erection. His curiosity was now the most aroused thing about him. Gingerly looking around, he saw that he was in a small domed tent-like structure. It had a triangular entrance that was partially open. Mellow sunshine slanted in through the opening, suggesting dawn or the beginnings of a sunset. He could see some long grasses beyond the entrance, and heard the pleasant murmur of contented voices and frequent gentle laughs that reminded him of summer holidays. It was warm. 'Sunset,' he thought.

'Weren't we were supposed to be revived in orbit?' he asked.

'Yes, but there were a few problems. Nothing to worry about now, though,' said Peter, yawning.

'How long have you been awake?' Mark asked

'They woke me the same time as you, I think, but I managed to get up. That would be, err, about five or six hours ago.'

'Have you been sitting there all that time?'

'Yeah, more or less, but mostly sleeping where I sat.'

'What kind of problems?'

'When Tarak was revived automatically, the supply vessel hadn't turned up and it didn't turn up for another two months.

He had to wake Sunita up to sort out the communications with home to see if it was on its way, but not the rest of us because they had to spin out the supplies until it did arrive.'

'God, imagine that! Hanging around that thing for two months! They must have been terrified in case it didn't come at all.'

'Yeah.'

'Where are we?'

'An island near Madera. Can't remember its name now.'

'What's it like? Are there any people?'

'From what little I've seen it looks like a great place for a holiday. Luka said it's uninhabited, but I don't know much else. I plonked myself down here shortly after waking up and haven't moved or spoken much to anyone since. I thought we might have a look round together, when you feel up to it.'

'In a minute. Did you have any feeling of time passing?'

'No, not as such, although I do feel a bit different somehow.'

'Yeah, me too,' Mark said, still puzzled that so many years could have passed while he was in the middle of counting to ten. 'Okay, I'm feeling a bit better now, I want to see if I can move alright. And I badly need a pee.'

After some experimental movements, Mark tentatively got up. By the time he had peed in what he hoped was a toilet basin, he felt reasonably secure on his feet, so he and Peter went for a little explorative foray. They were four or five hundred metres from an idyllic beach, but Mark's bunged up nostrils had prevented him from smelling the sea. He blew his nose and very nearly toppled over from the dizzying exertion. Recovering his balance, he stood beside Peter and surveyed their encampment. The voices and laughter seemed to have come mostly from Sunita and Tarak, who looked to be very happily working together as they shuttled a pile of plastic racking into a transparent dome. There were four of these transparent domes, four similar-sized non-transparent domes and ten of the smaller kind that Mark had woken up in. There was also a super-light beach buggy with four seats, two single-seat motorbikes and, about two hundred metres outside the encampment, a large sleek craft that caused Mark to breathe in sharply the second he saw it. It looked to him like a kind of space-fighter: not quite as sleek as the space-fighter that he had dreamt of wielding to such lethal effect in aid of Spartacus' slave army, but not far off.

When he dragged his eyes from this ominous-looking craft, he saw Sunita smiling brightly and waving at him. Then Tarak, who strolled in and out of the transparent dome with the kind of rolling gait that suggests a body packed with powerful muscles, smiled and nodded to them while he carried on working.

'They don't seem to be any the worse for their ordeal, do they?' said Peter, waving back. 'I guess they must have got along together quite well up there.'

Mark felt a slight pang of envy as he waved at the couple. Everything about their body language seemed to suggest a loving relationship that was still new enough to thrill yet secure enough for them to feel fully at ease.

Rebecca came out of one of the larger domes and walked towards them, waving and smiling at Sunita and Tarak as she went. 'Ah, aren't they wonderful!' she said when she joined Mark and Peter. 'We'll all be sorry to see them go.'

'Go?' said Peter, 'go where?'

'Oh, yes, hasn't anyone said?'

'Said what?'

'Well, to begin with, they'll be helping the Chinese expedition to set up a base in the western Pacific.'

'What? How come? When?' Peter asked in confusion.

'Their supply vessel still hasn't turned up. Tarak brought one of them back here and he's still recovering from his ordeal. The poor man was in a terrible state. He spent over four months cooped up in a tiny spacecraft without knowing whether help was on its way. He would have died of thirst before Tarak rescued him if he hadn't had the foresight to start bottling his own urine as soon as he emerged from suspended animation. The other three are still in orbit and still in suspended animation. The idea is to bring them down when their base can accommodate them. Then we will be setting up another base of our own, in the Indian Ocean. All this should go ahead a few weeks from now: shortly after Kim gets here.'

On the afternoon of their second day of consciousness on 'New Earth', Mark and Peter sat on the sand staring out to sea with the sun on their bare backs and a refreshing breeze on their faces. Mark felt that the taboo they had put on certain subjects was about to be lifted, but he waited for Peter to break the silence. While he waited, he cast his mind back over a meeting of all the expedition members held the evening before, although he had felt too tired and bewildered by the possible implications of what he heard to take in every detail.

He and Peter had been the last to be revived, which he presumed was a reflection of their junior status. Their revival had obviously been delayed by quite a few months, but he had not kept track of how many. In the meantime, Sunita had managed to cure some glitches to download four years of information that had pursued them through the chain of communication devices that the *Iskra* had dropped off en route, but then all the information traffic had abruptly and mysteriously ceased, effectively cutting off the expedition from their home planet.

Sunita then established a communication link with the Chinese craft in deeper orbit (further out in space), and discovered an unmanned American probe in still deeper orbit and traced its communication link to an unmanned communication module on a small island off the western coast of Mexico. With Sunita's help, Tarak had rescued the conscious but much distressed Chinese crewmember, then offloaded dozens of tiny spy satellites from the Gandhi Institute's supply ship and set them in orbits that would cover every square metre of the planet's surface.

When Sunita and Tarak had selected a suitable uninhabited island to set up a base camp in the northern hemisphere, this intrepid duo landed and begun reviving the others. After that, they selected another uninhabited island, in the Indian Ocean, where they proposed to base themselves along with Luka and Sanjay to monitor developments in the southern hemisphere.

This would leave Rebecca, Bernard, Peter and Mark at their current location, waiting to be joined in a few weeks time by Kim and three other crew members aboard her spacecraft. Kim had apparently set out just a few weeks before the point at which all information had ceased to be sent, or at least ceased to arrive, from their home planet, but she was on a slightly faster ship than the *Iskra*. It was not made clear what Kim's role would be when she arrived, although Mark assumed she would take overall command. The three crewmembers coming with her, two women and one man, were described as communications specialists, but the roles they would play or where they were to be based was not mentioned, as far as Mark could recall.

In respect of Mark and Peter, Luka explained their main role for the present was to analyse data from the spy satellites to see whether there was any indication that their various activities had been noticed or were having any appreciable effect upon the behaviour of local populations. In other words, whether their presence had caused the course of this Earth's future to shear away from the history of their own planet Earth. In so doing, their primary area of analysis was to be the Mediterranean and surrounding lands.

That was all that Mark could remember for the moment, probably because he had stopped concentrating on what people were saying to mull over some of the possible implications of what had already been said. In particular, the Third Servile War was, he thought, due to begin in about a year, with six thousand survivors of Spartacus' defeated slave army being crucified by the Romans about two years after that; and it was all going to happen on his and Peter's 'patch'.

Now, the thing that was making him think that Peter was about to end their taboo over certain subjects was that Peter had turned up at Mark's sleeping dome wearing only shorts and suggested that they go for a walk whilst conspiratorially indicating that Mark should also wear only shorts. With less chance of being bugged, they set off in silence until they were about a kilometre from the encampment. Then they stopped, looked around a bit, and sat down, still in silence. Eventually, Peter said, 'so, what do you think?'

'I think it's funny that we might end up with Kim and Rebecca again.'

'Ah, yes, just us and the girls again, eh?' Peter said with a not very convincing look of lecherous intent. 'And Bernard,' he added, 'we mustn't forget our esteemed colleague, Bernard the bore.'

'Oh, yes, I do keep forgetting him.'

'It seems to me that that has always been his role, Mark, to be where Kim is not and then to be forgotten.'

'Yes. You'd have thought we would have got to know him better by now, but other than that press briefing he fronted, and beating everyone at chess, he's always just been there, part of things but never in the middle of them.'

'Then there are Kim's three new crewmates,' said Peter, 'we don't know what they'll be doing or where they will be doing it.'

'True, but no one seems to be paying much attention to the Americas, which I would have thought the Americans would have got their eye on, especially given that that's where they chose to land their communication module.'

'So you think Kim's bringing a new team to keep an eye in that direction, do you?'

'Could be,' said Mark, 'although the more religious Americans are likely to take a keen interest in the Holy Lands as well, which seem to be part of our patch.'

'Sounds sensible, although I do wish we weren't spreading ourselves so thinly, especially now that our communications with home appear to be cut.'

'Yeah, me too!' Mark said with feeling.

'Anyway,' Peter began after another period of reflective silence, 'we're here now, so what do you think our game plan should be, just lie back and enjoy it while we can?'

'I'm still too scared of everything to enjoy any of it.'

'Me too, but perhaps we should try. Unless you have something else on your mind?'

'Are we really going to just observe what goes on, Peter? I mean, if our communications with home are cut, doesn't that mean that the whole idea of reporting what goes on here is nonsense?'

'If they stay cut, then yes, of course it does. But what would you propose we do, assuming our communications don't get switched back on again anytime soon?'

'I'm not sure, but I wouldn't want to sit on my arse while terrible things were going on in front of my nose, would you?'

'No, I don't think I would. Did you have any particular terrible things in mind?'

'Well, according to my reckoning, there's going to be mass crucifixions in about three years time, thousands of them. That's pretty terrible, wouldn't you say?'

'Aha, I was wondering when you'd get round to Spartacus!'

'You know about that?'

'You drink too much, Mark. Can't you remember going on about it to me? I already knew a little about Spartacus and the slave revolt, and then you started to talk about it from time to time, when you had a few drinks, but not since we had that little chat beside Lake Geneva.'

'Oh, yes, I suppose I did, but I didn't think you took much notice.'

'I might not have done if I hadn't been thinking similar sorts of things. Not so much about wars and rebellions, I've

81

always been more interested in how famines and epidemics can be averted or tackled. But then all this suddenly became so real and we both clammed up, and quite rightly so. But now, here you are, with your uncanny knack of being in the right place at the right time!'

'Same goes for you, doesn't it?'

'Of course.'

'Do you think Kim has any idea of the kinds of things we've been thinking?'

'Probably, Mark, probably, but she might be thinking the same kind of things herself.'

'Can you read her at all? Because I certainly can't!'

'I wish I could, Mark, I wish I could, but she's so deep I don't know where she stops.'

'She might tell us when she gets here, so I suppose we'll just have to wait 'til then.'

'Maybe, but in the meantime we can keep an eye on developments, just like we've been asked to, and have a few more of these little walks, if you're up for it.'

'I'm up for it.'

'Good. But for now,' Peter said smiling, 'let's see if we can't enjoy ourselves a bit, shall we?'

'Yeah! Why not? That beach-buggy looked like fun, so did the bikes, I wonder if anyone would mind if we had a training session with 'em.'

'Good idea! After all, Kim did say we should get acquainted with any unfamiliar items, didn't she? So let's go and do what we've been told to do!'

By the time they got back to the encampment, Tarak and Sunita had also decided to do what they had been told to do, so Mark and Peter took turns with them on the buggy and then with the motorbikes. Rebecca, Luka and Sanjay soon joined in and they all raced on the beach, five at a time on the four-seat buggy or one precariously perched behind another on the single-seat bikes. After a while, Bernard and Tsang, the rescued Chinese crewmember, came out to watch and laugh at their antics. After two or three hours getting acquainted with these unfamiliar items, Mark asked Tarak if he could have a look at the 'space-fighter'. Tarak chuckled at Mark's description of the Institute's near-space shuttle, but agreed to give him and Peter a guided tour the following morning.

They turned up for their guided tour fully dressed and wincing from sunburned shoulders and backs. Tarak was very helpful and informative. He not only showed them around the shuttle, he let them see and handle any and every piece of equipment they showed an interest in and gave brief explanations of what everything was for and how it worked. The only major piece of equipment he did not show them was a small nuclear generator that Tarak said he and Sunita had placed in an underground chamber that they had dug out before reviving the others. Their tour was fascinating and occasionally disturbing. It was fascinating in that most of the equipment consisted of user-friendly aids to self-sufficiency, and both fascinating and disturbing in that some of the equipment consisted of user-friendly aids to self-defence.

In terms of self-sufficiency, two of the four transparent domes that Sunita and Tarak had now finished setting up were to be used as propagation nurseries for crops grown outside, and the other two as hothouses for crops such as tomatoes, tropical fruits and herbs and spices. In addition, a long plastic tunnel had been erected to serve as a fungi factory. Various types of fungi were to be blended into variously flavoured pastes and used as a base for a potentially huge range of foods. Sunita, who had now joined the tour, said that the fungi from this one tunnel could provide sufficient sustenance for the whole expedition to survive indefinitely if all else failed. Among many other items, there was also a two-metre-long inflatable powerboat with a built-in water desalinater and a fish-stunning nodule on its hull. In all but the most sterile parts of the world's seas, one person aboard this boat could easily stun enough fish in one afternoon to feed the expedition for a week.

In terms of defence, the near-space shuttle had a laser weapon that Tarak said could 'burn' most types of missiles or other targets in space, in the air or on the ground; provided they were unmanned, so that their destruction did not altogether violate the Gandhi Institute's principles of non-violence. Tarak also spoke freely about the hand-held weapons that were stored in one of the four larger non-transparent domes, although none of these weapons were designed to kill people. They included various types of stun guns, tranquilising guns, deafening sirens and cylinders that sprayed a debilitating but non-lethal gas. There were also force-field suits that could defend the wearer from light and medium calibre projectiles, and which offered almost complete protection from any weapons that already existed on New Earth. With small generators in their backpacks running on helium-3, the suits could be worn for many months without any loss of power; 'even large rocks thrown from Roman ballistae would only bruise someone wearing one of these,' Tarak said as he proudly held one of the suits up for inspection.

Sunita then showed them to one of the larger domes that contained two workstations and would serve as their joint office. Finally, Tarak fetched them bowls of Chinese food that Tsang had somehow conjured up, and he and Sunita left them to it.

When they were alone they watched real-time footage of people on New Earth going about their business, via the expedition's tiny spy satellites. The images gave optimum resolution when the viewer seemed to be hovering about twenty metres above the ground. Peter spent most of the afternoon hopping from one centre of civilisation to another while Mark stayed with Rome and other Roman cities, towns and villages. Neither of them were able to positively identify individuals but, among other things, Mark found what he believed were Roman senators and their entourages coming and going from Rome's

Senate House, military units on parade, shoppers haggling, and slaves and overseers repairing roads and working the fields. He even found a group of gladiators training in an arena near the city of Capua and spent over an hour watching them and wondering if one of them could be Spartacus.

As far as either of them could see, no New Earthers were behaving as if they were aware that any 'visitors' had landed on their world.

A gong was struck at seven in the evening, local time. Mark and Peter joined the others for a communal meal under a newly erected awning. When they had eaten, Sunita, Tarak and Tsang struck up a mini concert with an improvised guitar, sitar and mandolin that they had cobbled together using strings that Tarak had brought from the home planet. After that, everyone except Bernard went down to the beach and helped kindle a small fire, for homeliness rather than warmth, and talked or played their instruments. So ended Mark and Peter's third day of consciousness on New Earth. Had it not been for the anxieties and fears that still lurked in the back of his mind, the sadness that their company would soon be divided, and the lack of alcohol, Mark would have thought it had been a perfect end to a fascinating day.

On their fourth day, Mark and Peter's guided tour and private lunch were replaced with about three hours of communal work on the settlement's production of food followed by a long communal lunch break. The rest of the day and evening was spent much as the day before and set a pattern for several weeks to come. However, as fascinating as Mark and Peter's observations via the spy satellites were, they had nothing untoward to report and they began to feel they were not contributing much to their mission. Thinking that enjoying themselves was a good antidote to the fears and anxieties that still lingered around the camp, they decided to spend more of their time devising communal games on the beach and in the surf. The others joined in when they were not working, but 'the lads', as Mark and Peter became known as, excelled in the fun stakes.

For the most part, everyone else remained as intensely engaged in their activities as ever. This even applied to Tsang, who seemed determined to restrict his movements to one small corner of the camp so as not to arouse any suspicion of spying, and he was ferociously keen to earn his keep by dint of hard work in the encampment's small farmlands and cooking Chinese meals for his rescuers. Nonetheless, Tsang, Sunita and Tarak found almost as much time for having fun as the 'lads'. These five seemed to become firm friends. Rebecca, Luka and Sanjay also joined in, albeit to a lesser extent. Only Bernard became more aloof, absenting himself from most communal activities and eating alone while he worked on some undisclosed project. Then Kim arrived in near orbit, already wide awake and in a hurry, and everything changed forever.

Bernard gathered all the members of the expedition to the dining table below the awning and told them some of what Kim had told him. Apparently, the three-way competition to get to New Earth had turned ugly in the years immediately after the Chinese expedition and the *Iskra* left the home planet. The Chinese, Americans and the Gandhi Institute all claimed that they were the victims of sabotage and high-tech interference with their communications between the two universes. No one had actually been killed in these activities before Kim set out, but the Chinese and Americans now appeared to be set on an arms race in space and anti-space while the Indo-European alliance was feeling intimidated and squeezed out.

Bernard turned on a computer screen that he had set on the dining table and Kim's face appeared. After some hurried greetings and congratulations on what they had achieved so far, Kim's image said:

'I am truly sorry to break up your little community, but I'm afraid that is exactly what I must do. Immediately. I want everyone except Peter and Mark to get ready to leave the base this evening. Tarak will take everyone else to the supply vessel, where we will rendezvous. Tarak, Sunita, Luka and Sanjay will be setting up their new base in the Indian Ocean, so they will need to pack all their things as soon as this meeting is over. I will answer any questions you may have when you join me, as far as I am able. As for Peter and Mark, if you could just sit tight and keep an eye on things I will join you when I can, and call you beforehand; so keep your mobiles switched on. I apologise to all of you for disturbing you like this at such short notice, but things have been moving quickly and we need to be in a position to cover whatever the future may hold for this world as soon as can.'

When she had parried a few questions that she said she would answer later, Kim closed the meeting and vanished from the screen. After about half a minute of silence, Bernard cleared his throat loudly to draw everyone's attention, and said, 'okay, I suggest we all get moving.' Everyone got moving, except Peter and Mark, who sat for a while in silence and then wandered around offering help. No one needed their help, so they retreated into their office dome, but left the flap open in case anyone wanted to speak to them.

Sunita and Tarak were the first to be ready and they joined Peter and Mark in their dome for an hour or so. They expressed their sorrow to be leaving, spoke of keeping in touch and of meeting up again as soon as they could, and then hugged them both and bid their fond farewells. They were followed by Luka and Sanjay who said and did similar things and departed twenty minutes later. Then Bernard popped in, gave them both a handshake and promised to see them soon. Rebecca came in last and hugged them both more tightly than either of them would have expected for a brief parting, and she too left. Finally, when they heard the shuttle's engine start up, they went outside, shook Tsang's hand vigorously, and then waved them all off.

When the white dot that was the shuttle could no longer be seen, Peter and Mark wandered off towards the beach and sat for a while in silence round the dead fire that they had all gathered around listening to the little stringed concerts.

They spent the following day in a similar routine as before, even lighting a fire on the beach in the evening to lighten their mood, although they could not dispel the feeling of being very alone and vulnerable. They thought their role was essentially that of caretakers for the base, but in the absence of any local inhabitants or instructions of what they should do if anyone else turned up, they felt as though they had been left behind like unwanted baggage.

Early on their third day alone on the island, Peter said he was not in the mood for work, and nor was Mark. Instead, they put the inflatable boat in the beach buggy and drove to the beach, then sat and stared at the sea and periodically checked their mobiles. They had both been receiving messages from Kim at twelve-hour intervals, saying that all was well, but no calls. Neither of them were in the mood for talking; and neither of them had any idea that Spartacus' slave revolt had erupted the evening before.

After a while, Peter inflated the boat and took it beyond the surf while Mark drove the buggy up and down the beach. An hour or so later, they changed places. Mark was three or four hundred metres from the beach and thinking of going back when he thought he saw something in the sky with his peripheral vision. He turned his head and saw what appeared to be a bright star, except that it was broad daylight. As he watched, the star grew bigger and seemed to fragment. Puzzled, he looked harder and became alarmed when he saw that the fragmenting parts had vapour trails and were beginning to resolve themselves into tumbling pieces. Mark's alarm was not caused by concern for his own safety, for the falling pieces were clearly coming down many miles from him, but by the only explanation he could think of for what he was witnessing: he thought it must be the wreckage of a spaceship that was burning up in the atmosphere.

He turned to look back at the beach and saw Peter sitting still on the beach buggy near the top of the beach, also staring at the crashing object. A second or so later, there was a brilliant flash behind Peter. Mark blinked once and then squinted against the subsiding glare as a cloud of sand raced towards Peter and started to pass him before the beach buggy and Peter were lifted up, somersaulted several metres in Mark's direction and crashed among some rocks near the water's edge. A moment later, Mark felt as though his entire body was slapped by a huge rug. His boat heeled over and pitched him overboard. He felt the impact of the water, but then bounced off the sea's surface as the boat rolled over him and found himself tumbling back aboard when the boat righted itself. Feeling totally bemused, he lay on his back until he absorbed the fact that he had somehow escaped a dunking and was not even wet.

Looking up, he saw droplets of water run down across the surface of a clear dome that had appeared over him. He had not known that the boat carried such a dome and he briefly marvelled at the speed at which it must have formed in order to save him from going overboard. Then the horror of seeing what had happened to Peter hit him. 'Peter!' he cried out as he got to his feet and bumped his head against the transparent membrane that completely sealed him inside the boat.

Pressing his face against the dome, he could see the buggy and just about make out Peter's inert form. He struggled to open the dome but could find no way of doing so. Frustrated in this, he started the boat's motor and guided it towards Peter until it bumped against an underwater object. He made frantic attempts to get the dome open but could not make any impression on it. Frustration, rage and despair were overwhelming his increasingly hysterical but vain efforts to come to Peter's aid. Sobbing violently as he dashed himself against the clear membrane, he became exhausted and slid to his knees while trying to see if there were any signs of life in Peter. No movement was visible. Mark felt trapped, useless, and judging from the wreckage he had seen tumbling through the sky, he guessed he was now utterly alone.

Then his mobile rang.

5
ALONE

'Mark? Is that you?' said Rebecca.

'Rebecca?'

'Oh, thank God! Are you alright, Mark? Where are you?'

'Yes, I'm okay. I'm in the boat.'

'Is Peter with you?'

'No, well, sort of, he's just outside.'

'In the sea?'

'No, on the rocks. He's injured, badly, I think.'

'Is he breathing?'

'I don't know, I can't get out of the bubble!' he whined bitterly.

'What? What do you mean? What bubble?'

'Mark!' Tarak's voice intervened, 'there's a flap at the back of the boat.'

'Where? Oh yes, I see it.'

'Lift the flap and pull the orange toggle.'

He pulled the toggle and the dome obediently parted above him and started packing itself away while he leapt out towards Peter. Both of Peter's legs seemed to be lying at unnatural angles, his heat-shrivelled hair was matted with blood and blood was flowing from his head into a pool of water. 'There's blood flowing: that means life, doesn't it?' he asked Tarak as his panic gave way to a more focused concern for his friend's life. Tarak said that it probably did mean that

Peter was still alive, and he began instructing Mark on what to do to keep him alive.

As instructed, he checked Peter's airways and fetched a medical kit from the boat. He took an electronic bracelet from the kit and fastened it around one of Peter's wrists so that his condition could be monitored from space. Taking three little syringes from the kit, he pressed their needle-less tips onto the skin of Peter's bare arm and pressed their plungers with his thumb until there was a small click. Then he carefully applied synthetic skin patches over his external wounds and covered him with a thermal sheet that looked like a shroud. Tarak said that Peter was alive but very badly injured and in need of more extensive treatment than Mark could give him. He promised to do his best to arrange what help he could, but warned Mark that the rest of the expedition had major problems of their own. Mark could do little else but wait for help to arrive. In the meantime, Rebecca came back on the line and, in a very shaky voice, she tried to explain what had happened.

The first thing she told him was that the spacecraft he had seen disintegrating could have been the one that Kim had just arrived in, or the *Iskra*, or Tsang's craft, but that Kim and the three Chinese 'sleepers' had not been harmed. This was not making any sense at all to Mark, so Rebecca gathered herself and started to tell him the whole story from when she and the others had left the base, or as much of it as she knew and understood.

Tarak had taken everyone aboard the shuttle to the supply vessel, which was in geostationary orbit above their island base, for their rendezvous with Kim and her three traveling companions. After a meeting and discussion, they divided into two groups. One group, which consisted of Luka, Sanjay, Bernard and the three new arrivals, headed southwest in the shuttle towards the proposed new base in the Indian Ocean. The other group, which consisted of Kim, Tarak, Sunita, Rebecca and Tsang, stayed in the supply vessel while it docked with Tsang's craft to transfer his cryogenically frozen crew prior to delivering them to the proposed Chinese base in the western Pacific. Then, as the first group passed over the Americas, someone, Rebecca did not know who or why, used the shuttle's lazar weapon to destroy the unmanned American communications module on its island near Mexico.

This attack triggered a counter-attack from the unmanned American spacecraft in deep orbit. Several large missiles were launched. When these missiles drew close to New Earth they spewed out dozens of small missiles programmed to orbit the globe until they detected and attacked any electronic equipment that they found operating in space or on the ground. There were no intercept weapons available to destroy these missiles. However, Sunita managed to relay signals to all of the Institute's tiny spy satellites to switch on all their electronic systems so as to attract the American missiles, and then all the supply vessel's electronics were switched off. In addition, Tsang and Tarak had programmed the now empty Chinese craft, the *Iskra* and the craft that Kim had just vacated to act as electronically active decoys to shield the helpless supply vessel. After that, they just waited and prayed that all of the missiles found active targets before any selected their electronically inert vessel as a secondary target. Fortunately, these measures proved to be effective and the supply vessel escaped attack.

Unfortunately, the other group tried to defend themselves with the shuttle's lazar weapon, but it was useless against the attacking missiles' reflective surfaces. Rather than defending them, activating the lazar weapon merely served to attract more missiles. Attempting to flee, the shuttle was caught and obliterated as it was reentering the atmosphere above India. In addition to this and the destruction of the three craft used as decoys, most of the Institute's spy satellites and their only base on the planet had also been destroyed.

Mark sat for a long miserable time beside his friend trying to absorb the enormity of this catastrophe. Not only had Luka,

Sanjay, Bernard and the three new arrivals apparently been killed, the destruction of the shuttle also meant that there was no longer any ship that could travel between space and New Earth. Other than Peter, who Mark sensed was mortally injured, he realised that he was now the only person from the home planet left on New Earth and that he was stuck on a tiny devastated island. The other four survivors from the Gandhi Institute's expedition and the four members of the Chinese expedition were all left stranded in the supply vessel.

After a while he wondered if he should switch off his mobile in case it attracted a missile from any follow-up attack, but then he thought that the electronic bracelet he had put around Peter's wrist might also attract a missile, so he did nothing until he got a call from Kim.

'Mark, are you okay?'

'Yes, I suppose, but I think Peter is dying.'

'Yes, Mark, he is. But we have come to a decision that might help him. We are preparing our only escape pod to carry a suspended animation module for Peter, but we have no way of bringing it back again. Before we send it, we must know whether you have a consistent source of power to run it. You will only have such a source of power if the nuclear generator has survived intact in its underground chamber. Tarak will tell you how to open the chamber and then you can show the generator to him on your mobile.'

He did as he was told. He had little difficulty finding the generator's chamber among the sparse debris of the base. He opened the chamber with the codes that Tarak provided and let him examine it via his mobile. Tarak deemed it to be unharmed and Kim authorized the suspended animation module to be sent to Mark with as many supplies as could be squeezed into the small escape pod.

Five weeks later, Mark went down to the beach in the early evening and laid out the equipment that Tarak had sent in case he had to leave the island and needed to defend himself. There was a force-field suit, a pistol containing two hundred supposedly instant tranquilising pellets, a needle-less syringe with an antidote to the tranquilising serum, a canister that sprayed non-lethal gas, a thermometer-sized poison tester, a siren, a small but extremely powerful torch, a knife that was easily sharp enough to shave with, and, in apparently contradiction of the Gandhi Institute's non-violent philosophy, four silver bomblets.

He had spoken to Tarak earlier about these bomblets and was told that they were not designed to kill people or destroy anyone else's property, but to vaporize any equipment or materials that they had to leave behind if they abandoned any of their bases in a hurry. Given that they had only got round to establishing one base, and that had been completely destroyed by the American missile, the bomblets appeared to be quite useless. However, they were only about the size of large chicken eggs, so they did not take up much space, and Tarak had sent them on the off-chance that they might be useful. Tarak had not actually seen one of the bomblets go off, but he warned Mark that they were far more powerful than they looked and emailed an alarming list of safety precautions with instructions for their use.

Mark thought the force-field suit was easily the most reassuring piece of equipment. He switched on its backpack and placed it over one of his last remaining packages of food and stabbed at it as hard as he could with his razor sharp knife. The package was undamaged. He got into the suit, which automatically adjusted itself to fit comfortably over his body and clothes, and stabbed the point of the knife at his leg, tentatively at first and then with increasing violence until he was using both hands and all his strength. He did not feel any pain at all. The suit made him look a bit like Spiderman in an over-sized beige outfit, except for its backpack and a clear face shield, but it protected every part of his body. Satisfied with his test, he sat on a rock and looked through the suit's face shield at a magnificent sunset.

Feeling momentarily inspired to rise above his immediate woes, he thought about the catastrophic collapse of the expedition and dreamed of how he alone might make it all worthwhile. After all, if he really was the only person from the home planet left standing on New Earth, no one could stop him from doing whatever he had the ability and the will to do.

Saving Spartacus' slave army from their ultimate defeat and mass crucifixion had long been one of his fantasies. Thinking the outbreak of the revolt was not due for another year, he could still enjoy unrealistic fantasies about his part in it. He pictured himself now, strutting up to the Roman army before the final battle, scratching a line on the ground and grandly announcing: 'in the name of the goddess Kim, none shall pass this line!' Roman spears and arrows would bounce harmlessly off his force-field suit. A detachment of Roman soldiers would come forward to seize him, but they would drop to the ground when Mark shot them with his instant tranquilising gun. Having sown fear and doubt in their minds, he would walk boldly through their ranks heedless of all blows. Coming to their general, he would demand obedience to the One True Goddess. If the general refused, Mark would shoot him with the tranquilising gun along with any others who dared to defy the goddess' will. Finally, the awed and leaderless Romans would obey him and he would march them all back to Rome.

However, as much as he enjoyed toying with such fantasies, he felt he would ultimately do as Kim had 'asked' him to do, if for no other reason than that her will seemed so much stronger than his. Part of him felt like the only pawn she had left to move on New Earth, and another part of him thought she was simply trying to make the best of things in extremely difficult circumstances. The first stage of her new plan was for him to take the boat and head for the European mainland before he completely ran out of supplies. That much of the plan had sounded sensible, but the rest of it seemed to him like pure desperation.

Kim told him that an automated signal from the shuttle's escape pod had been detected through the canopy of a forest in eastern India, although there was no indication that anyone had used it to save themselves before the shuttle was destroyed. Her idea was for him to take the boat and travel by 'easy stages' to the east coast of India and then work his way about four hundred kilometres inland to find this escape pod and see if anyone had used it to survive the missile attack or if any useful items could be found aboard. Mark thought this was a terrible idea.

For one thing, he had spent a large portion of the past five weeks wondering who was responsible for provoking the counter-attack by destroying the American communication module. He had more or less persuaded himself that Bernard was the prime suspect, and that if anyone had survived it would probably be Bernard. 'If Bernard caused all this mess and survived,' he thought, 'then I don't want anything to do with him!' For another, sailing a little boat from an island in the middle of the Atlantic Ocean to eastern India in the faint hope of his doing anything useful when he got there sounded like a ridiculously dangerous and quixotic enterprise. Nonetheless, he would go along with the first stage of Kim's plan while he thought about what he should do after reaching Europe.

He was scared of going anywhere on his own, but he was no Robinson Crusoe either. He would have preferred to be a Friday character to Peter's Crusoe, but he had frozen Peter and buried him in his suspended animation module in the hope that someone would one day come to revive him and fix his broken legs, fractured skull, broken ribs and all his other injuries.

'There's nothing useful I can do here anymore,' he said aloud at the sunset as if he were talking to Peter. 'In fact, we never actually did anything useful at all, did we? And now I'm going away on my own, probably just to be useless somewhere else.'

He knew the bit about being alone was not yet wholly accurate. He was in contact with those aboard the supply vessel as they made their way back from the American deep-orbit craft after ripping it apart with explosives charges to make sure that it could never fire any missiles again. Of the five conscious survivors in space, four of them would soon be going into suspended animation in order to eke out their remaining supplies while they waited for someone from the home planet to turn up and rescue them. Only Kim would be left to guide him, and even she would have to go into suspended animation eventually if no one showed up. He thought how ironic it was that the only surviving ship was a supply vessel, and yet it had become the least well supplied ship after offloading most of its contents to the other ships. The only things it had enough of were power and the suspended animation modules that it carried in case the whole expedition needed to make the long journey home.

As for his position, apart from the buried nuclear generator, the base had been utterly destroyed. The meager supplies of food and clothing that came in the escape pod were certainly useful, although most of the pod's capacity had been taken by Peter's suspended animation module and the equipment needed to move his broken body without killing him and to rig his module to the nuclear generator. In addition to the two or three days supply of pre-packed food he had left, he had squirreled away about half a kilogram of edible grains that he had finger-plucked from hollows and crevices in and around the blasted ruins of the base. Other than this, his best aids to survival were the boat's water desalinater and its fish-stunner, although he had not entirely conquered his revulsion at gutting fish.

With plenty of protein from fish and enough vitamins and minerals available from seaweed and other edible vegetation, it was theoretically possible for him to survive on the island indefinitely. But he was already beginning to feel weak, listless and troubled by a lack of appetite and diarrhoea; all of which he blamed on his efforts to conserve his supplies by forcing down some repulsive meals made from local produce. If he did not leave soon it seemed likely that his strength and his will to fend for himself would leach away to nothing. Getting out of the force-field suit and packing it into one of the two plastic sacks that now held all his possessions, he could think of nothing else that he could usefully do on the island. He decided he must leave in the morning.

The morning arrived fresh and bright. There was a bit of a swell, but the weather report Kim sent him seemed promising for the next week or so, which Mark hoped would be enough to take him to Europe.

He sat beside Peter's 'grave' in his shorts while he ate as much as he could of a fried fish and oat-mush breakfast and dispiritedly chewed on some bitter and leathery boiled seaweed. He wondered if he should say a few words before leaving his friend. Peter had not regained consciousness after the attack, so Mark had had no opportunity to say goodbye or to ask his friend's advice on what he should do. He decided he would speak his thoughts out loud and try to imagine what Peter would want to say to him in reply. Standing up, he cleared his throat and begun to speak as frankly as he could.

'Peter, I have to leave the island now, while I still have the strength to get anywhere. Kim wants me to head for India and find the shuttle's escape pod. For what it's worth, I think it's a fool's errand that will probably achieve nothing and very likely mean my own death. I think I should go to Italy and try to do something to help Spartacus and his slave army. I would like to make some kind of sense out of all this mess by doing something worthwhile, something that I think you would agree with. But I suppose I will just end up doing what Kim tells me to do.'

In his mind's eye, he pictured Peter raising himself to his full height and saying: 'to hell with that! Kim isn't in a position to *make* you do anything, no one is. It's up to you now, so you should do what *you* think is right!'

He felt ashamed of himself. He was sure that Peter would have thought his attempt at a parting address had sounded incredibly feeble. He did not want to sound feeble. He did not want to *be* feeble. So he stood up straighter, rethought what he wanted to say and said it in a stronger voice: 'sod it, Peter, I *am* going to help Spartacus, one way or another, and as many slaves as I can! If someone comes and fixes you up, then you might join me. If not, I will do everything in my power to find people who can fix you up and bring them here myself!' Goodbye for now, my friend, until we meet again.' With his promises to Peter still echoing in his mind, he bowed his head in a moment of silent respect for his friend and then turned on his heel and marched resolutely towards his boat.

If there had been one major event in Mark's life that had gone smoothly, it was his journey to New Earth. Now his journey to the European mainland seemed to be going almost as smoothly. His boat was behaving impeccably. Once he had tapped in his destination and pressed the 'GO' button on the little onboard computer, it sailed itself until he instructed it not to. The safely encased twin propellers turned silently and the boat slid effortlessly through the surf into deeper water. Two large solar panels unfurled from the stern and pivoted themselves so as to strike the optimum balance between capturing sunshine and using the wind for extra propulsion. The two halves of the transparent dome came out like beetle's wings and maneuvered themselves to catch more wind or to counter any tilt to the boat. The use of sun and wind power was so efficient that the motor's battery was fully charged at the end of the first day and continued to power the propellers throughout the night.

Despite his fear and sadness, Mark felt exhilarated as his boat skipped over waves and became momentarily airborne before landing with the grace and control of a humming bird.

The speed it moved at was quite remarkable, and yet he lost all sense of threat posed by even the largest waves or storm clouds looming on the horizon. Tarak also informed him that the boat was programmed to detect and respond to the DNA of all expedition members, so if he fell overboard the boat would automatically stop and gently nose towards him until he climbed back aboard. He thought that there must be some dangers involved in sailing this little craft halfway across an ocean but, short of a major malfunction, he found it almost impossible to imagine any sea conditions that it would not make light of. Every new situation encountered merely allowed the boat to show another set of superb design features; and he was not even troubled by seasickness.

In the evenings, he watched films on the onboard computer or played games on it with Tarak, Sunita and Tsang. When he wanted to sleep, he pressed a button to close the dome and used the computer to select the opacity of the dome and how much light would emanate from the glow-in-the-dark panels inside the boat and along the seals of the dome. When he wanted to cook some food, mostly fish caught after being stunned and scooped from the surface of the sea with the boat's telescopic keep-net, he pulled down flaps on either side of the boat, used the electrically heated surface on one of them to cook with, ate from the molded surface of another and drank desalinated water supplied from a plastic tap in the stern. If there were any obstacles on or under the water, the computer would let him know about them if he wanted it to, or he could simply leave the boat to give all obstacles a wide berth. In his mind he christened the boat the *Ladybird*, and he loved it.

In the late afternoon on the fourth day of his voyage he spotted a distant smudge that was the Iberian peninsula. Kim called and instructed him to make his way to a small coastal village in an area equivalent to the Portuguese Algarve on his home planet, but ruled by Rome on New Earth. She told him that she had watched people from this village via one of the surviving spy satellites and seen them store a substantial quantity of goods in a cave by the beach. Whether they were trying to avoid paying taxes to their Roman overlords, she did not know, but the cave did not appear to be guarded. He was to get close to the village under cover of darkness, don his force-field suit and raid this cave.

Kim said he must take care not to be seen or heard and only to take as much food as he needed to help sustain him on his long voyage. The Gandhi Institute's 'guiding principle', she reminded him, was still one of nonintervention, which meant that he must minimise any impact that his presence might have on any populations he encountered.

Mark tried to do as he was told. He stepped ashore as soon as the bow of the *Ladybird* slid through the gentle surf onto the wet sand in front of the cave, but then he heard a dog give an uncertain bark close by. In an ill-thought-out move, he tried to placate the dog by saying 'here boy' in a hushed but friendly tone.

The dog came as bidden, but it also let out a wailing barking yowl that was quickly taken up by the rest of its pack three or four hundred metres from the shoreline. Mark saw several of them loping towards him in the pale moonlight, yammering aggressively. He knew they could not hurt him in his force-field suit, but he panicked anyway.

He turned the boat around and started to push it back out to sea without realising how quickly the beach shelved. Suddenly there was no sand below his feet and he pitched forward and plunged below the water. When he surfaced, he was only waist-deep in water but he had lost his hold on the boat. The *Ladybird* made a sedate turn and gently moved back within his reach. By then, however, three of the maddened dogs had leapt into the water and fastened their teeth onto his suit; two on his right arm and one on his suit's backpack, and he heard human voices adding to the din the dogs made.

There was no chance of the dogs' teeth penetrating his suit, so he did his best to ignore them. Even so, their weight made it impossible for him to climb back aboard the boat. Not knowing what else to do, he simply held onto the boat with his left hand and fearfully waited to see what would happen next.

What happened next was this. When the vanguard of the villagers arrived at the bit of beach closest to Mark, the dogs let him go and made for the shore, allowing him enough time to climb aboard the boat while his human pursuers waded into the sea. They were not quick enough to grab him, so they grabbed his boat and held it fast. He rummaged through his plastic sacks as quickly as he could and pulled out the siren that Tarak had sent in the pod, but which Mark had not thought to test. He pointed the siren at the people holding his boat and jammed his thumb down hard upon its only button.

The incredible sound that the siren emitted had a profound effect on everyone present, including Mark. Its brief but ferociously screaming howl caused him to stagger backwards in shock. It felt as though the sound had overwhelmed his eardrums' capacity to hear and went instead to wreak havoc deep inside his brain. When he recovered a little and dazedly looked around, he caught a few fleeting glimpses of forms racing away from him. With the whole of his head still ringing and his eardrums ominously fizzing and clicking, he turned the *Ladybird* towards the open sea and made good his escape without further hindrance.

It had not been an auspicious start to his solo adventure, Kim admitted to Mark through his mobile, but she insisted on shouldering all the blame herself. Apparently, her 'new team' had picked up the heat-signatures of the dogs before Mark got close to the cave but, viewed at night from space, they were indistinguishable from the heat-signatures of the many goats that roamed the area.

Shortly after the abortive raid, he was sailing slowly southwest without any immediate purpose other than avoiding further encounters while Kim's new team selected another place for him to top up his now dangerously depleted supplies. The high spirits he felt during the first leg of the voyage were badly shaken. His earlier exhilaration seemed to have held his stomach problems at bay but they had not disappeared altogether, and his fright on the beach appeared to have triggered a particularly unpleasant bout of diarrhoea.

Feeling unsure as to whether he could safely bring his backside back into the boat, he decided to play safe and stay where he was for a while and look at the siren that had probably saved him from capture. Although there was only one button, there was also a small dial that he could not remember seeing before. He now saw that the dial controlled the direction of the blast and it was currently set at 360 degrees, which meant he had suffered needlessly and his assailers had probably got off lightly in comparison to a more focused blast in their direction. This, he thought, was a very powerful weapon, especially when used correctly against the unwary.

He also thought that his little debacle on the beach represented so much more than a painful failure to secure badly needed supplies and scaring a few people and dogs in the process. It had contravened the Gandhi Institute's noninterventionist policy to such an extent that it could create a ripple effect that might eventually cause the future of New Earth to sheer away from the history of his own Earth in ways that neither he nor Kim's new team could begin to calculate. Whether this was a good thing or a bad thing was impossible for him to judge, but he did wonder whether blundering around like this was any less irresponsible than deliberately intervening in the affairs of New Earth in accordance with some kind of prepared plan.

He was not quite naive enough to overlook where his thoughts were leading him. He knew he wanted to find reasons to justify any intervention in Spartacus' slave revolt that he dared to contemplate, and he knew he was fastening on recent events to bolster his courage to do so in defiance of Kim's wishes. Nonetheless, he could not think of any convincing reason why he should not abandon Kim's plan in favour of fulfilling his parting promises to Peter; apart from the little matter of being terrified of meeting an untimely and horrible death if he screwed up.

The aborted raid on the cave had made him much more aware of his force-field suit's limitations. Far from being able to boldly walk through ranks of hostile Roman soldiers, as he liked to fantasise, he could be pulled to the ground by a single soldier and pinned there until his captors figured out a way to kill him. He thought of several ways that were considerably more nightmarish than a quick death at the point of a sword, such as being caged until he died of hunger or thirst, or roasted over a fire, or buried alive, or tied to a rock and dropped into the sea. Still, he had not promised Peter that he would wade into battle or act like some kind of superhero. His parting words on the subject were that he would 'help Spartacus, *one way or another*, and as many slaves *as I can*.' These qualifications gave him quite a bit of wriggle room.

Instead of raiding coastal villages all the way to eastern India, he thought that he, Kim and her new team could be better employed devising ways of using their technological advantages to persuade the Romans that it was in their own interests to be a whole lot nicer to people. He decided he needed to get Kim and her team thinking along the same lines and, given that he was the only member of the expedition that could carry out Kim's plans on New Earth, he felt he needed to get himself in a position to negotiate with the leaders of Rome on her behalf. He did not know how he might accomplish either of these things, but he spent a pleasant half-hour fantasising about his part in an interplanetary diplomatic mission. He thought that these fantasies were much more agreeable than many of his earlier fantasies about helping Spartacus, which had too often involved mental images of death and destruction and increasingly involved horrible images of his own destruction.

He finally decided that his bowels were now just bluffing and that it was safe to withdraw his sea-rinsed backside back into the boat. When he was dressed again, he answered a call on his mobile. It was Kim, as expected. She had news of another target for him to raid for supplies the following night. He had difficulty concentrating on the details of what she was saying until she informed him that the proposed raid would mean a detour into Roman-held Spain about a hundred and fifty kilometres east of the Strait of Gibraltar. His stomach lurched dangerously when he heard this, partly because he was afraid of attempting another raid and partly because it would bring him a good deal closer to Italy.

When darkness fell the following evening, Mark turned east and sailed through the Strait, keeping as far as he could from the coasts and any other vessels that the *Ladybird's* radar detected. As the kilometres ticked by, he became increasingly aware of a very unwelcome change in the sea conditions. He had mostly enjoyed sailing over the long, large, regular and widely-spaced rollers of the Atlantic, but the waters of the Mediterranean were agitated into much smaller, closely-packed, steep-sided, confused waves that even his superbly engineered boat could not compensate for quickly enough to stop his stomach being troubled by its lurching movements. When added to his dietary problems and his anxiety about the coming raid, the erratic but distressingly persistent jolts brought on his first bout of seasickness and worsened his diarrhoea.

As he drew closer to the site of the proposed raid, a farm shed about half a kilometre up a small estuary, he became worried about putting on his force-field suit in case he soiled it from within. He tried stopping the boat for a while, but that just made things worse. After several difficult minutes of not knowing which end of himself to point overboard, he decided to steer the boat away from the estuary on full throttle in the hope that the sea spray would help his condition. It did help. He held onto straps either side of the bow as though he were riding a motorbike while his boat flew across the peaks of closely packed waves without pitching into any troughs. Feeling better surprisingly quickly, he turned back and slowed for another attempt at putting his suit on. No good. He managed to say 'can't do it' to Kim over his mobile before violently throwing up again.

Kim had heard him throwing up and she was very sympathetic when he got back to her. 'Not to worry,' she said, 'anyway, two other boats seem to be heading for the estuary now, so you might as well take off for a while.'

He did as he was told, entering a more or less random destination on the inboard computer and hanging on as the *Ladybird* rose to the moonlit wave crests again. He tore eastwards for as long as he had the strength to hold on. Although the waves had seemed confused when he traveled at slower speeds and lower in the water, now he looked down at the sea's serried ridges as though he were looking at ripples in the sand. The boat approached a few exceptionally high wave peaks, but it heeled round these at such a delightfully controlled pitch that some of his earlier excitement returned. It did plunge into the occasional broader trough, but then flew up from the trough's far bank like an off-road bike speeding over a hillock and landed with sufficient precision for him to keep hold without too much trouble.

For what might have been hours, he forgot about sickness, diarrhoea, raids, Kim, Spartacus and all else except riding the waves by moonlight. Ever on he went, ever eastwards, ever closer to Italy, until his strength finally threatened to fail him and he cut the throttle. His mobile was trilling out its chirpy little calling jingle.

He had expected Kim to ask him to return and carry out the raid, but she said that the two boats had anchored in the estuary, presumably to ride out an increasingly choppy sea in the western Mediterranean. 'Go further east,' she advised, 'if you want to find calmer water, and we will try to guide you to a more sheltered position where you can get some sleep.'

He did as he was told, but failed to find anywhere calm enough to catch any more than a few uneasy winks of sleep between bouts of sickness and bursts of acceleration over the waves. Throughout the following day and evening he moved further east and slightly north until he found more sheltered waters in a large bay off the southern coast of Sardinia. As the night deepened, he hung over the side in a miserable state of sickness and sleepless exhaustion. He could see three or four faint twinkles of light on the shore and jealously wondered how the people who had lit those lights were enjoying their evening.

Setting his mobile to vibrate silently if he had any more calls, he at last got some food to stay down and managed to catnap through the rest of the night. Even so, when the early morning light shone through the dome that he had forgotten to turn opaque, he felt as exhausted as ever, if not more so. At least his sickness and diarrhoea seemed to have dried up. Now he just felt empty, cold, weary, and without interest in anything other than warmth, comfort and rest.

No coherent plan had emerged in his numbed mind, but his urge to find the comforts he craved coalesced around thoughts of the one place in the Mediterranean that he had spent most time studying while on the Gandhi Institute's island base and which had fascinated him for most of his life: Rome. He knew that Rome was not a huge distance from where he was and he thought he could probably arrive off the river Tiber that day if he chose to, and then up the river to Rome if no one stopped him. He was also half aware that such thoughts were the dangerous product of exhaustion and the semi-delirious state he had been slipping into, but he could not summon up the will to think clearly or to care much about anything except finding sanctuary on dry land, preferably somewhere civilized. In this mood, he instructed the *Ladybird* to make for a point twenty kilometres from the mouth of the Tiber and promised himself that he would give some thought to what he proposed to do next when he had recovered a bit.

He arrived at the selected point off Tiber by late afternoon without incident. There he paused again and mentally rehearsed the rough plan he had been formulating and reformulating as he went. He was beginning to have severe doubts about his current mental capacity to make any kid of sensible plan, but he was too tired to think anymore. Having instructed the boat to stay at least ten kilometres from other vessels, he tried to get some sleep.

He could not sleep, partly because his body had been releasing adrenalin into his system to cope with his exhaustion, and partly because he felt his boat constantly change its position as it tried to comply with the impossible instructions he had given it. A small convoy of ships had come up behind him and were heading straight for the river's mouth. In trying to stay ten kilometres away from all vessels, the *Ladybird* had become sandwiched between the convoy and various coastal craft going in and out of the Tiber. Disturbed by the boat's zigzagging as it kept an equal distance from all other craft, Mark checked the inboard computer and found that four of them were now only seven kilometres away and that he was being squeezed closer to Rome by the convoy advancing behind him. 'I know all *roads* are supposed to lead to Rome,' he muttered to himself, 'but this is ridiculous.'

As he edged closer to the coast, Mark's body reacted to the dangerous lure of Rome by pumping an overdose of adrenalin into his system. Suddenly he felt unnaturally clear-headed and uncharacteristically decisive. Speaking aloud, he said, 'sod it, let's just do it!' Then he opened up the throttle and raced directly towards the river's mouth.

In keeping with the latest version of his 'plan', he stopped a few hundred metres from the Tiber's estuary and climbed into his force-field suit. He put his supposedly instant tranquilising pistol in one of the suit's pockets and his siren in another, set for a forty-five degree angle of blast, and switched on his mobile's verbal translation function, set for U.K. English / Latin / female voice, at full volume. The rest of his gear now fitted into one plastic sack, along with his remaining scraps of food after he had thrown some uneaten fish overboard in disgust.

Ignoring the silent vibrations of his mobile, he pulled out the telescopic manual tiller and A-frame from the boat's stern, practiced leaning nonchalantly against the hollow struts of the A-frame and then sailed boldly up the Tiber towards Rome.

The river's estuary was still busy with craft in the early evening light, especially along the southern bank where cargoes were being offloaded in the port city of Ostia, the main hub of Rome's overseas trade. People started to stare at him and he began to feel his earlier resolve slip away to be replaced by doubts about his flagrant disregard of the Gandhi Institute's 'noninterventionist raison d'être'. But he felt committed now and sailed sedately on.

Rome was about twenty-four kilometres, or fifteen miles, inland. No one challenged him until he was well past Ostia and had followed the river's meandering path east and then north through a semi-rural landscape. He eventually came to a rundown area of docklands and old wooden warehouses that marked the southern fringe of Rome.

A large wooden rowing boat powered by four oars angled towards him. A middle-aged man wearing a grubby toga standing in the bow of the boat with three other men called to Mark in Latin. Mark's mobile translated the man's words into: 'who are you, what is your business?' in the well-modulated accent of an English woman.

He called back: 'I am Mark Goodwin and I have important business to discuss with the Roman Senate.'

The man looked at Mark with an impassive seen-it-all-before expression as the two boats drew closer, and then a puzzled look came over his face when Mark's mobile translated his reply into Latin.

'How many are you?'

'I am alone,' Mark said.

'Then who is speaking?' said the man as the two boats drew level and slowed to a stop.

'My words are being translated by a telling-stone from the goddess Kim,' Mark replied, and pointed towards the sky.

One of the men grabbed at the *Ladybird* and two others clambered uncertainly on board. They stood in front of Mark and eyed him, his 'telling-stone' and his boat suspiciously. One of the two boarders, a tough-looking man with a goatee beard, said, 'the goddess who?' and took a step back when the telling-stone translated his words for Mark.

'The goddess Kim,' Mark repeated, and the telling-stone translated.

'Oh, her,' the man said doubtfully, 'that's alright then.' Then he held out his hand and said 'could I have a look at your telling-stone, please, it looks better than mine,' but he pulled his hand back when the woman's voice repeated his words in the funny language that Mark was using. 'That's a very clever trick, can it do anything else? Mine tells the time too.'

Mark saw the other man on his boat smile slightly through his confusion and decided to play along with the bearded joker. 'Sure it can', he said, putting his left hand in a pocket, 'can't all telling-stones? But I'm afraid I can't let you touch it, or the goddess Kim will scream out her displeasure.'

'Take it from him!' ordered the middle-aged man standing on the Roman boat.

The bearded man lunged forward and grabbed Mark's right wrist just as he whipped out his siren with his left hand, pointed it at the side of the man's face and jabbed at its button with his thumb. Mark had braced himself for the blast of the siren, but even outside its forty-five degree zone he was slightly shocked by how much of its echoing scream battered his eardrums. The effect on the already edgy two men on the *Ladybird* was instant and overwhelming. The bearded man threw himself back as though he had been shot and writhed on the floor with his hands clasped over his ears. The other man, who had just begun to advance on Mark when the siren went off, gave a convulsive leap backwards and toppled into the river.

No one could be seen on the other vessel until the echoes of the blast had finished bouncing off wharfs and warehouses. When Mark started up the *Ladybird* again the top half of the middle-aged man's face rose slowly into view to stare at Mark while the bearded man staggered back aboard the Roman vessel and someone helped the other man climb in from the river.

'Now,' said Mark in as casual a voice as he could manage, 'if you will excuse me, I have business with the Senate and the goddess Kim will become really angry if I am delayed any longer.'

He sailed off unchallenged and passed several moored ships whose decks were dotted with people staring at him, and others, who were emerging from buildings to find out what caused the horrible noise, watched him as he passed upriver. A few minutes later, two horsemen galloped passed him on the east bank. One of the horsemen dismounted at a river barrier ahead and spoke to some soldiers while the other rode on towards Rome.

Mark came up to the barrier, which consisted of boats chained together. On the other side of the barrier, he could see that the buildings on the eastern bank were packed more tightly together and were much taller than any he had seen downriver, which suggested that he was drawing close to the bustling heart of the city. He thought the *Ladybird* could glide over the chain where it dipped into the water, but he decided to talk to the soldiers first. He was regarded solemnly by two soldiers as he approached the boat they guarded and nudged it with the *Ladybird's* prow. One of them lowered a spear towards Mark's chest, and said, 'yes?' as more soldiers raced along a walkway to join them.

'In the name of the goddess Kim, I demand passage and escort to the Roman Senate,' Mark said with as much dignity as he could muster.

The soldiers looked at Mark's mobile with puzzled expressions as it translated his words, but made no move to take it from him. Instead, a newly arrived soldier said 'I think that could be arranged,' and ordered two other soldiers to climb aboard the *Ladybird*. When they were aboard they drew their swords while others hauled on a great spoked wheel. A floating wooden platform moved and a space in the barrier opened for the *Ladybird* to pass through. Mark steered through the gap with the tips of two swords pressed lightly against his force-field protected ribcage.

'Go to the right and tie up,' said one of his guards.

'Why?'

'Because I told you to,' the guard said, looking distractedly at Mark's mobile.

'Sorry, but I have business with the Roman Senate.'

Both guards pressed the points of their swords a little harder against his ribcage, and one said, 'do as you're bloody told.'

'Piss off,' said Mark, and he swallowed hard.

The guards looked at him and his mobile in surprise and doubt until one of them gave Mark a sharp but limited stab with his sword that seemed designed to inflict a shallow wound rather than death, but his suit adsorbed the thrust without him suffering any pain. The guard stepped back, looked at the unhurt Mark in alarm and stabbed harder, but again to no avail. The other guard looked on in consternation while his comrade made several more attempts to stab Mark, eventually using all his strength in what should have been lethal blows. One of Mark's hands gripped the boat's tiller, the other gripped a strut of the A-frame and his back was braced against its crossbeam to keep his balance against the blows, and he sailed on unharmed.

The guard who stood watching then had a go; first with a vicious blow to Mark's body, another to his face, and then swung a two-handed slashing blow with all his might upon the crown of his head and twice more across his face. Failing to make any obvious impression, the Roman let his arms and sword dangle at his sides and stared at Mark in amazement. Mark, internally shaken but physically unhurt, unpeeled his dry tongue from the dry roof of his mouth, and said, 'so, are you going to escort me to the Senate, or what?'

'I'll see what I can do,' the soldier said weakly, and they continued up the narrowing river in silence with crowds following them on both banks. They passed into the more densely built up area and came to a broad stone stairway that led down to the river. A fat, puffy-faced man wearing a snow-white toga stood at the top of the stairway behind a rank of soldiers.

One of Mark's guards pointed to the man in the toga and said, 'he's a senator, you could pull over there, if you want to.'

Mark pulled over. His boat was held by four soldiers while the senator came down the steps to take a look at this strange individual in his strange boat. Mark chose this moment to answer his mobile.

'Mark,' Kim said softly, 'what are you *doing?*'

'Are you watching?' he asked, feeling dizzied by what he had done and elated to have gotten away with it so far.

'Yes, we all are.'

Mark looked up, waved at the sky and said 'hello Kim, hi Rebecca, hi Sunita, hi Tarak, hi Tsang.'

His mobile loudly translated this and their return greetings into Latin. The senator and most of his soldiers looked up to see what Mark had waved at. They could not see anything, but a few of them gave little waves at the sky, just to be on the safe side.

'Please, Mark,' said Kim, 'I need to understand what you are doing.'

'I've stopped for some fresh supplies.'

'Right, I see,' she said, obviously not taking his reply at face value. 'Did you *really* need to make such an entrance?'

'I guess not, but all this nonintervention stuff is nonsense in the long run, and you know it.'

'Well, I just don't know what to say. I suppose you will do whatever it is you have decided to do, but do be careful and make sure you test any food and drink they give you for poison.'

He had forgotten about that, but he had his poison tester in his plastic sack. 'I will,' he said. 'Oh, and Kim, if anything does happen to me, you won't go destroying Rome or anything, will you?' he asked for the benefit of his audience while they waited politely for him finish his conversation with the goddess and step ashore.

'No, Mark, we have no plans to destroy Rome at the moment.'

'Okay then, I'll call you later. Bye,' he said as he cut the call and climbed out of the boat carrying his plastic sack.

When his guards had followed him ashore, the soldiers holding the *Ladybird* let go in alarm when the transparent dome closed and went opaque. Then everyone watched it sail itself into the middle of the river where it hovered and waited for Mark to return.

'Welcome, err, your Highness,' the senator said to Mark and bowed as low as his great belly allowed. 'You are very welcome to any supplies that may please you. Our humble stores would be honoured to provide you with the best food and wine in the known world, and we have gems and precious metals that may please the goddess Kim and their highnesses.'

'Food and wine will do nicely, thank you very much,' Mark replied while he was deferentially escorted to a large, ornately carved, open-topped carriage pulled by two pairs of silvery-white horses with plumes of scarlet ostrich feathers on their heads. 'Oh,' he added in hazy afterthought as his adrenalin surge began to subside, 'could you possibly ask some of your men to keep an eye on my boat until I get back, please?'

'Certainly, your Highness, certainly,' the senator agreed eagerly and bowed again. Turning his back towards Mark, he instructed one of his men to: 'take *very* good care of his Highness' most magnificent vessel while his illustrious graciousness permits us to offer refreshments for his delectation,' whilst aiming several conspiratorial winks at the puzzled-looking soldier.

When Mark had gone, the soldier charged with taking care of his boat knew that the senator's winks had been conspiratorial, but he did not know what kind of conspiracy the senator had in mind. Simply taking care of the boat would be to ignore the conspiratorial intent, but destroying it would be too irreversible if he found he had misread the senator's intention. Finally making up his mind, he instructed the occupant of a small fishing skiff to bring the boat ashore.

The man rowed his skiff towards the *Ladybird*, but it maneuvered itself away from him. Other people with boats joined in but they were also frustrated in their attempts to catch it. The chase became something of a game as the mellow evening sun turned into the warm amber glow of sunset. Eventually, a group of fishermen formed their boats in a circle around the *Ladybird* and closed in with nets stretched between them until they caught it. Pulling it to the steps that Mark and his escort had walked up, the soldiers had no trouble lifting the surprisingly light boat out of the water. Then they took it to a warehouse where their commander hoped that the prying eyes of strange gods and goddesses would not see what he was about to do to it.

6
GIVE UNTO CAESAR

Mark's plan had seemed sensible when he devised it in a high state of exhaustion, but he began to think it was a pretty feeble plan now that he sat in the senator's carriage in desperate need of a toilet. The essence of the plan was that he would tell Rome's senators the truth about what they were up against, or at least to expand upon parts of the truth that might convince them that having slaves would draw the wrath of abolitionists down upon their heads.

He had pictured himself giving an eloquent address from the floor of the Senate about how he came to their world from a technologically advanced other-Earth, about how others would follow with colossal resources and unimaginable destructive power at their fingertips, about flying machines that move faster than sound and could wipe out entire Roman armies in seconds, and about the power of nuclear weapons to incinerate cities like Rome in the twinkling of an eye. If they did not believe him, he could always shoot one or two of them with his tranquillising gun and go through his goddess Kim routine with his siren to make them afraid of her awful scream and, hopefully, tremble at his false but cataclysmic descriptions of the goddess' city-killing abilities.

However, one of the problems with this plan, the most pressing problem at this time, was that he had to take off his protective suit *very* soon if he were to avoid appearing at the Senate stinking of his own faeces and urine. Then there was his desperate weariness, now that the overdose of adrenaline was wearing off, and his hunger and thirst, and his rapidly returning timidity. What he really needed was a good few hours alone in a comfortable apartment or hotel with room service where he could rest and sort himself out, and then a few more hours to do a bit of work on his speech.

The idea of making any kind of speech now filled him with dread, and this dread seemed to pile still more pressure on his bladder and bowels. 'Excuse me, senator,' he said through a pained grimace, 'I'm afraid I need a toilet.'

'A toilet? Certainly, your Highness, we shall arrive at my humble dwelling before it is fully dark. Your graciousness would be doing me an inestimable honour if you would consider everything and everyone within it to be at your exclusive service. I shall have my servants arrange refreshments, baths, women, or boys if your honour would prefer, and any convenience or service, large or small, that you may require or desire and that I have the means or influence to make available.'

'Very kind of you, I'm sure,' said Mark, becoming a touch irritated with this senator's ingratiating long-windedness in the face of his more prosaic and pressing needs and desires, 'but I really need a toilet *right now.*'

The senator looked at his strange companion holding his stomach and leaning forward in his strange attire as though he were in pain. 'Ah,' he said, finally understanding the urgency, 'I see, of course!'

The senator told the carriage's driver to stop and ordered four of the ten horsed guards trotting beside them to dismount, enter what looked to Mark like a squalid residential apartment above a small clothes shop and to clear out its inhabitants. The guards barely hesitated. They barged into the apartment and unceremoniously ejected an elderly woman, a youngish couple and three sobbing children while the swelling crowds that had followed the carriage from the river murmured their disapproval.

Mark hated himself for causing such disruption, but nonetheless took the opportunity to relieve himself in a Spartan but reasonably commodious lavatory served by a communal water channel flushed by a constant stream of water. No one disturbed him while he sat upon wooded slats above the water channel with his siren pointed at the toilet door, and this left him feeling a little more secure regarding the effects of his goddess Kim bluff.

By the time he got back in the senator's carriage, he had decided to take advantage of the offer to refresh himself at the senator's home, although not in respect of the more licentious aspects of this offer. The senator beamed with pleasure, made a string of wordy comments about being deeply privileged by Mark's acceptance of his hospitality, and introduced himself as Quintus Aurelius Saturnalicus.

While Quintus was in full flow, the carriage clattered towards a structure that Mark recognised as the Porta Trigemina; a triple set of gated arches that led through a section of the Servian wall, Rome's main defensive bastion, dominated by two castellated towers. The Servian wall had stood for hundreds of years, but most of it had been periodically renovated, strengthened and enlarged. The section that Mark was admiring, which snaked around the western and southern edges of a dense residential area called the Aventine, looked brand new and capable of withstanding any siege weapons of the age. When they passed through the open gates of the central arch, Quintus politely asked whether Mark would 'wish to send any form of message to the Roman Senate whilst your Highness takes his pleasure and repose in my modest little home and gardens?'

Mark had to think about this, then decided that Quintus' latest offer might allow him a way out of nervously delivering a threatening ultimatum to a large and powerful audience that might think he was trying to humiliate them. So he said, 'thank you, Quintus, I would appreciate that. If it is possible to arrange, I am sure it would please the goddess Kim if I could make the acquaintance of a few members of the Senate in a small and private meeting. I think I have caused enough disturbance through my arrival, and neither the goddess nor I would wish to, err, disturb the peace of Rome any more than might prove necessary.' He hoped his words would convey a politely veiled threat that he could disturb the peace of Rome very badly indeed if he was mistreated in any way.

Whether Quintus picked up the implied threat was unclear, but he seemed pleased with the suggestion and offered his out-of-town villa as a place of meeting between Mark and some selected members of the Senate the following afternoon. Mark agreed, and then tried not to do or say anything else that would make him any more conspicuous among the huge throng that accompanied their stately progress.

Quintus sent two of his horsed guards ahead with orders for his villa to be made ready to receive his mysterious guest. The villa was just south of Rome in the middle of a walled estate of luxurious gardens. After their uninvited followers had been stopped at the estate's gates by Quintus' guards, the carriage went down a tree-lined avenue until they arrived at a wing of his enormous three-storied villa in the fading twilight. About forty household staff were arranged in two ranks either side of a lamp-lit vaulted entrance, and each inclined their heads in token of respect as Mark and Quintus dismounted from the carriage and went inside.

A man dressed in a turquoise robe and pale gold turban met them in the hallway with a deep bow. Quintus instructed the man to 'see to it that our esteemed guest's every wish and desire is anticipated or met without demur.' Then, apparently as an afterthought, he said, 'girls, I think,' and gave Mark a politely enquiring look.

Mark did not know what he was supposed to say or do next, so he just smiled politely back through his protective face mask.

The turbaned servant bowed and indicated an open door to his right. Mark moved towards the doorway and took one step into the room. Inside the room, three scantily dressed young women stood holding small piles of neatly folded linen in front of what looked like a small steaming spa. Beyond the spa, there was a sumptuous four-poster bed with curtains attached to each post. While Mark hesitated and gawped at the scene, several servants managed to slip past him to lay many dishes of food, decorative flagons of liquid and silver tableware upon a long table covered with white linen on one side of the room. He knew that some of the flagons contained wine and he had lost none of his taste for wine during his long enforced abstinence. Even though Quintus' lavish hospitality was beginning to seduce Mark's mind and body to crave many things, it was the smell of the wine that provoked his first temptation to yield to indulgence with less caution than the situation deserved.

Reasoning that a little wine might steady his quaking nerves, he easily convinced himself that a goblet or two would do him more good than harm. He walked to the table and shakily poured himself a large silver goblet full; without adding water, as Romans almost always did. He barely remembered to acknowledge his host, who had appeared in the open doorway and then left with a small bow and a small smile on his face immediately after Mark saluted him with his goblet, but he completely forgot to test the wine for poison.

He sipped at the wine, found it to be to his liking, drained the goblet and poured out another. He took a few more sips as he surveyed the room and his demurely smiling hostesses, and then realised that he had made a mistake.

Many people who are used to drinking relatively large quantities of wine on a daily basis, but then have a spell of abstinence followed by a sudden infusion of wine, will probably have experienced something similar, although considerably less violent, to the reaction that Mark's stomach now had. He had not noticed any such reaction to wine before, so he wondered if he had been poisoned. He had not been poisoned, at least not intentionally, but he suddenly found himself in desperate need of a toilet again. He quickly discovered a toilet attached to the room, and spent a miserable half-hour with explosive diarrhoea and wind. When he finally felt he was not going to die, he became acutely embarrassed by the sounds he had been making as his three would-be hostesses gathered outside the toilet door and anxiously enquired after his health.

Having recovered enough to dress himself, he felt too weary to face anyone and too embarrassed to even open the door. Devising a little plan to be left alone, he whispered into his mobile and let it translate his words loud enough to be heard through the door.

'This is the goddess Kim,' his mobile announced in Latin. 'My emissary is poorly, so I have come down to Earth to take care of him. Please leave now and inform your master that all will be well if my emissary is left in peace until the morning, thank you.' He heard the three women leave immediately.

Finally alone, he tested the food for poison and nibbled carefully at some of the delicacies, but left the wine alone. He then bathed for a full hour and ate more of the delightful food, especially the less exotic dishes of bread and chicken followed by perfectly ripe slices of melon; his favourite fruit. Feeling much better, he did his best to blockade the room's main entrance and a wooden slatted door at the other end of the room with furniture, and then flopped exhausted onto the sumptuous king-size bed and slept for about nine undisturbed hours.

When he awoke, he soon felt better than he had done since before the missile attack on the Institute's island base. After another bath, he ate a substantial breakfast of cold meats, bread, olives, grapes and melon. Then someone knocked gently at his door.

It was the turbaned servant carrying a tray of hot rolls, some glazed delicacies that he did not recognise or attempt to taste, and a large flagon filled with hot lemon tea. He would have ordered coffee if he had been in a hotel on his own world, but four glasses of tea seemed to put the final touch on his return to health and vigour. There was still the impending meeting with some of Rome's senators to worry about, and the nagging feeling of guilt that he felt over not contacting Kim or answering her calls, but he wanted to savour the comforts available to him in peace for a while.

Opening the wooden slatted door opposite the room's main entrance, he found a secluded veranda covered with vines that let in patches of dappled morning sunshine. Moving to the sunniest corner, he sat on a cool marble bench and gazed at a tapestry of lush statue-studded gardens, ornamental ponds and carefully manicured woodland walks. Gardeners worked in the foreground and tended a fire that blazed behind a neatly trimmed hedge. Listening contentedly to the birdsong and lulled by the homely smell of the garden fire, he dozed for a time. He woke up feeling hot, bathed again and dried off in the sun wearing only his shorts and defended by nothing else than the siren and tranquillising gun left beside his mobile on a marble table in front of him. He must have dozed off again, for the turbaned servant had suddenly appeared in front of the veranda's door, waiting patiently for Mark to notice him.

'Hello,' Mark said, and his mobile translated.

The servant did not bat an eyelid at the telling-stone's female voice, but bowed low, and said, 'your Highness' guests have arrived. Would you prefer to meet them in the theatre or should I show them to your room, your honour?'

Mark suppressed a smile at the way that Roman senators were suddenly at his beck and call, and tried to tell himself that this was a deadly serious business. Even so, he was feeling unusually at peace with himself and unaccustomedly relaxed at the prospect of meeting important people. He listened to people clearing his room's table of food and rearranging some furniture, and said, 'I would be very grateful if you could bring them to my room when I am dressed,' then rose from his chair and luxuriously stretched his limbs in the strong late-summer sunshine.

'Would there be anything else, sir?'

'No, thank you, I will get dressed immediately.'

When the servant left, Mark felt a little adrenalin return as he got into his force-field suit, filled its pockets with every gadget he had, except his mobile, which he set to interpret in a male English voice but not to take incoming calls, and waited for the senators to arrive. He did not have long to wait.

There was a knock at the room's main door. Mark opened it, and said, 'please come in,' with a gesture towards the room's dining table, which someone had cleared and placed ten chairs around while he was sitting on the veranda. Trying to bow in all directions at once, the nervous-looking Quintus led eight people into the room and introduced them all to Mark. Mark presumed they were all senators, but he failed to concentrate on the introductions after Quintus made his second introduction: to Gaius Julius Caesar.

When they were all seated, Mark sat opposite Caesar with his mobile on the table between them. Fearing that his shyness would return and redouble under the eyes of Caesar, Mark tried hard to suppress his awe of the man. He found it very difficult to return Caesar's level gaze, although it was equally difficult to avoid studying him for signs of his future greatness.

Caesar was about the same age as Mark, if one excludes the eighty-odd years that had flicked by while he had been in deep suspended animation without experiencing any signs of aging. However, aside from being younger than the others, having a slightly dandyish hairstyle and frilly cuffs on his long-sleeved toga while the others wore short sleeves with no frills, Mark did not think Caesar looked especially impressive or notably different from anyone else. He seemed genial enough and appeared to be more curious than daunted by Mark's attire, and fascinated by his telling-stone rather than frightened of it. Apart from his apparent concern for his appearance and relatively relaxed demeanour, Mark thought Caesar looked quite ordinary.

As Mark mused on these things, he became aware that a silence had fallen and that everyone was looking at him expectantly. He cleared his throat, and said, 'thank you all for coming today,' and then begun a preliminary explanation of why he had come to Rome in anticipation of a long discussion to follow.

'I am sorry to disturb you like this, but there is something you ought to know. You see, the world you live on is about to be invaded by people from another world, people with unimaginable powers. I am from this other world. I do not wish you any harm and neither will most of the people who come after me, but they have very different ideas about how people, ordinary people, should be treated than you currently do. The main problem for you is that a good many of my people will want to intervene in what you are doing, and you will be powerless to stop them.

'The few pieces of equipment that I have brought with me from this other world are nothing in comparison to the equipment and knowledge that will flow into this world when more of my people get here. The vast majority of these people will want to be at peace with the peoples of this world, but many of them will be appalled at some of the things that go on here.'

'What sort of things, your Highness?' asked Caesar quietly.

'Well, for one thing, slavery is not permitted on my world. In fact, many of my people find the idea of slavery so abhorrent that they would become angry with anyone who puts people into bondage and sells them or keeps them as slaves. I have no doubt that some of my people would be willing to resort to violence to free the slaves of this world, and some would wish to punish slave owners very severely, especially those who badly mistreat their slaves.'

'Would they be willing to destroy us for having slaves?' Caesar asked.

'Some would, I'm afraid.'

'How?'

'Err, well, there are many ways . . .'

The two-way conversation that was developing between Mark and Caesar was interrupted by a middle-aged man whose face had turned red in apparent anger at what he was hearing: 'so, it is you that has provoked this uprising, is it?'

'Uprising?' asked Mark.

'This filthy rabble led by the gladiator Spartacus!'

'Oh,' said Mark in surprise, 'has it started already?'

'WHAT!?' the red-faced man exploded and got to his feet, 'you knew of this in advance? I knew it, I just knew a bunch of stinking slaves couldn't wipe out Glaber's army of their own accord! Damn you, you filthy trouble maker!'

Mark was about to deny that he had had anything to do with the uprising when the man marched around the table towards him, clenching and unclenching his fists in a most aggressive manner. Mark stood up and made to put a hand in one of his suit's pockets, but Caesar was quicker.

In a flash, Caesar was round the table and had wrapped his sinewy limbs around Mark, forced him backwards to the floor, locked his arms behind his back and bound them tightly with a leather strap. While Caesar was doing this, several soldiers entered the room carrying nets. Turning Mark over several times, the soldiers wrapped him in their nets and bound him tightly in more leather straps.

Mark now lay on his back almost completely unable to move. Still feeling more shocked than scared by the sudden turn of events, he heard snippets of conversations via his mobile. Caesar mildly chastised the man who had caused the meeting to close before Mark was able to tell them more about himself, his world and his people. Then he tried to placate the slightly hysterical Quintus who was babbling about vengeance from the goddess Kim befalling the host of her roughly handled emissary.

'Nonsense,' said Caesar, 'there is no such goddess. I will show you.' With that, he picked up Mark's mobile, flung open the veranda door, strode to the far edge of the veranda, spread out his arms, stuck out his chest, and called: 'goddess Kim, I am Gaius Julius Caesar. I have taken your snivelling little emissary prisoner and I mean to kill him. If you do not like what I am about to do, then you can strike me dead right now. If you do nothing, then I command you to go and torment the Greeks with your pathetic little tricks!'

A minute or so passed in silence, and nothing happened.

'You see?' Caesar said when he came back into the room, 'it's all bluff and nonsense. Frankly, I am disappointed. Even I thought that some kind of response was in the offing, even if it was only another ridiculous conjuring trick or some absurd threat from this telling-stone. But no, it seems that his Highness, the great Mark Goodwin, is nothing more than a conjurer who has overreached himself, and that the goddess Kim is a frustrated mare that her emissary has dreamed up in the absence of a real, flesh and blood woman.'

Caesar gazed at Mark. 'You poor, sad miserable creature! Never mind, eh? After all, I suppose you and your party tricks might amuse us in the arena. Search him,' he told the soldiers, and sat calmly back in his seat to study Mark's telling-stone.

To everyone's surprise, including Mark's, the soldiers could not get any of his suit's pockets open, no matter how hard they tried to prise at the flaps with their swords. Mark had never had any such problems and it soon dawned on him that the seals of the suit's pockets must be controlled by DNA scanners, as so many things on his home world were, including his own mobile. That being the case, it probably meant that no one but he or other Gandhi Institute personnel would be able to use any of his gadgets.

This realisation gave Mark his first ray of hope, and allowed him to stave off some of the terror that was building within him and threatening to debilitate his capacity for rational thought. With that ability now returning, he caught the smell of smoke from the garden fire, and he thought he might have identified a second reason to hope.

'How does this thing work, master Mark Goodwin?' Caesar asked, holding the telling-stone in front of him.

'No one but I can use any of my possessions,' Mark replied, and silently steeled himself to rile Caesar in accordance with his newly-hatched plan.

'Oh? And what would happen if I tried, or pulled them apart?'

'You might manage to pull some of them apart, but you could never get them to work. They are programmed to respond to me and no one else.'

'Programmed?'

'Yes, but I'm not sure how to explain it, only the goddess Kim really knows how these things work.'

'Don't be foolish, Mark, there is no such goddess; you and I both know it.'

'Oh yes there is, damn you, and if you try to do anything to me she will send you to Hell to burn forever!'

Caesar's eyes narrowed and he came over to Mark. Bending down to eyeball him through his face screen, he said, 'you might scare children and the weak-minded with this goddess nonsense, but it will not work with me.'

'I am not trying to scare you,' Mark said in what he hoped was a haughty tone, 'I am *promising* you that you will burn before this day is out!'

'Oh, fighting talk, eh! Dear, dear, Mark, I really think you should be more careful of who you threaten.'

'Come off it, mister Julius snot-nosed Caesar. Let's face it, you're a pathetic little loser who hasn't got the guts to do anything to the likes of me!'

Caesar laughed out loud, and Mark realised that his plan was not working. Even so, he cannot have endeared himself to Caesar, so he had little option but to up the stakes or to give up. His increasing levels of adrenalin caused him to up the stakes.

'It's no good laughing to cover up your fear, Gaius the sheep-shagger, I've been watching you from the sky and I know what a perverted little shit you are. You'll burn alright, along with the rest of your vile family.'

This did rile Caesar. He did not lose control of himself, but his sideways looks betrayed his concern for what the others in the room would make of him if he tolerated such insults. He grabbed the straps that bound Mark and hauled him to his feet, put his face against his face shield, and in a low but menacing voice, he said, 'you go too far, you snivelling piece of arse-hatched frogspawn.'

Caesar looked around for inspiration, sniffed the air and smiled malevolently. 'So, I will burn, will I? Well, let us see who does and who does not burn, shall we?' He turned to the soldiers, pointed towards the veranda's open door, and said, 'you two, carry our big-mouthed friend into the garden. The rest of you can build up that garden fire and stoke it until it's nice and hot and ready to roast this turd of an emissary to the goddess lickspittle.' Turning to Quintus, he said, 'I want all your household staff gathered round that fire to witness what this goddess does to save her precious emissary, at once.'

Quintus scurried off to do Caesar's bidding and Mark was dragged through the villa's entrance hall, into the garden, and dumped near the fire. Soldiers commanded the gardeners to fetch all the dry wood they could find and then joined the work until a fine big fire was crackling up through the new fuel.

More than two hundred people were quickly rounded up to witness Mark's execution, and then a stillness descended in which only the gathering roar of the fire could be heard. Everyone was waiting for Caesar to join them in the garden, especially Mark. When Caesar did join them, the look on his face frightened Mark more than ever. It was not that Caesar looked angry; Mark would have tremulously welcomed that. Instead, Caesar seemed pensive as he walked towards him, and then he gently lifted Mark to his feet and regarded his captive's face thoughtfully.

The reason that Caesar's thoughtful look frightened Mark was that his plan hinged on the fact that his captors had not used chains to bind him. If Caesar decided to do so now, then Mark was doomed.

He was terribly frightened, and it must have shown to Caesar, although Caesar adopted a calm and conciliatory tone when he spoke. 'It doesn't have to be like this, you know. You could be useful to me. I would be willing to swear by any gods you choose that I will provide you with a life of absolute luxury in return for showing me how just one or two of your devices work.'

Caesar looked at the telling-stone in his hand as it translated his words into Mark's language. Mark knew that his mobile would not have spoken for Caesar while he brooded over it alone in the villa; its DNA scanner switched it off when Mark was more than twenty metres away from it, and so it had conveniently confirmed his claim that his gadgets would not work without him.

Trying to think through the implications of this, he was sorely tempted to agree to Caesar's offer, and he may well have done so if it had come before they had traded insults. But now, rightly or wrongly, he felt that Caesar was just trying to trick him into admitting defeat in front of the people watching them and that Caesar would kill him when he was no longer useful. Besides, Mark thought he would be acting in direct contradiction to everything he had dreamed of doing on New Earth if he entered into Caesar's service to save his own skin.

Instead of agreeing, he made the bravest decision of his life. Not only did he decide to refuse Caesar's offer, he did his best to do so in a way that Caesar was likely to find too humiliating to accept in front of so many witnesses.

Drawing a deep breath, he leaned his face towards Caesar's, and in a voice that carried as much scorn as he could manage to fake, he said, 'piss off, you sheep-shagging bastard of Rome's cheapest whore.'

He watched Caesar's nostrils flare and his jaw muscles tighten as the telling-stone translated this latest insult. Caesar stood rigidly still for a moment, only his eyes moved, flicking from side to side in response to the audibly shocked inhalations coming from their audience.

Caesar's fury finally overcame his reasoned approach to the odd character that confronted and defied him. Driving his hands between Mark's body and his tightly bound arms, he lifted him by his armpits, marched into the edge of the fire and hefted him into the centre of the blaze.

Mark crashed through brightly burning logs into middle of the fire's white-hot core. He managed to struggle into a squatting position and waited helplessly for the fire to eat through his force-field suit and devour him. Nothing much appeared to happen for several seconds other than the strands of netting across his face mask catching fire and melting away. The growing smell of burning was joined by a smell of singeing material and the temperature inside his suit started to climb. His terror increased when he found that the leather bonds still held tight, but there was nothing he could do except watch Caesar through the flames as he strutted in front of the fire with the telling-stone in his hand, lecturing the crowd about the absurd creature he had sent into the flames and the absence of any reaction from the so-called goddess Kim.

At last he felt his hands move as the burning leather straps that bound him were consumed. Now feeling the heat sting his skin, he was about to make his break from the fire when he saw Caesar wave the telling-stone at the crowd, and he paused for a second when Caesar made to fling it into the fire in a gesture of contempt for the goddess. Mark hoped to catch it, but Caesar caught Mark's eye through the flames and hesitated in mid throw.

Mark stood up and staggered out of the fire, silently willing the searing heat of his force-field suit to dissipate before he fainted. Caesar reacted quickly. Shrieking out a command for his soldiers to help him, he lobbed the telling-stone at one of them and launched himself at Mark for the second time that afternoon. Caesar tried to bind Mark's limbs again, but he was simply too quick. The heat that was threatening to overcome Mark within his suit was far, far less than the heat of its outer surface. Caesar's long sleeves slid up several inches as he grasped Mark and his face blanched when his exposed skin sizzled against the heat of the suit. Nevertheless, he managed to hold on long enough to drive Mark back into the edge of the fire, and then let go.

Mark saw soldiers advancing on him and Caesar readying himself for another painful encounter. The flames that lapped around him did not help his over-heated condition, but they were far less hot than the white-hot core of the fire that he had been squatting in, and they gave him a precious moment of respite from his hesitating assailants while he delved into his pockets. His right hand drew out his tranquillising gun and pointed it at Caesar, but Caesar was already running away in zigzags that defied Mark's ability to align his weapon upon him. So he turned on the soldier who had caught the telling-stone. When he fired the gun, a tiny projectile pinged off the soldier's metal breastplate, a second lodged itself harmlessly in his leather skirts, but the third hit the bare fleshy bit above the man's knee and he crumpled to the ground unconscious. With his left hand now holding the siren, he stepped out of the flames behind its hideous scream and fired tranquillising projectiles at anyone who came near him.

When he stopped firing and had taken his thumb off the siren's button, three tranquillised but very dead-looking soldiers lay sprawled at his feet, one of whom still held Mark's mobile in his lifeless hand. Caesar was nowhere to be seen. Almost everyone else had fled too. The only person to have stayed where he was, presumably to plead his innocence to his ill-treated guest and to the goddess, was Quintus, who had sank to his knees with his hands clasped over his ears.

Mark thought about taking off his force-field suit before it cooked him where he stood, but the filtered air-pump in its backpack was bringing in streams of blessedly cool air that saved his skin from crisping. He managed to stand still and bear the touch of his singed hair and clothes until they were merely very warm and still cooling. He was not conscious of his appearance as he stood triumphant on the field of his victory, but most of those who peeked from behind hedges or from the villa's upper windows were impressed by what they supposed was his heroic calmness. Not everyone was so easily impressed, however, and a spear suddenly arced towards him. The thrower was Caesar, who must have known that his parting shot was merely a gesture of defiance. It was a good throw, though, hitting Mark just above his heart and sending him staggering a couple paces backwards, albeit without doing any damage.

He was just congratulating himself for not taking off his suit when Caesar stepped from behind a hedge, and with characteristic aplomb, he said, 'I haven't finished with you yet. I will be back and I will personally slit your throat.' Mark felt inclined to believe his adversary's words as he watched him mount a horse and gallop purposefully away down the villa's private road.

Nonetheless, Mark was now high on adrenalin and feeling mightily pleased with himself. Rather than thinking about the consequences of his failure as an interplanetary diplomat, his buzzing brain reckoned that he had not only survived his open defiance of the great Julius Caesar, but that he had outwitted and outwilled him as well. For the time being, he felt himself to be the undisputed victor in a battle in which he did not hold all the cards. On the contrary, when he was trussed up like a turkey ready for the oven, the cards had seemed hugely stacked against him. This was heady stuff for an erstwhile reclusive academic to contemplate, and he felt his confidence soar with the exultation of still being alive and in one piece. 'At least I gave unto Caesar as good as he gave unto me,' he said to himself, 'better, in fact!'.

Feeling the need to strut his stuff in some way, he took his mobile from the soldier's lifeless hand and called Kim to see if she and her team had been watching. They had, and they all wanted to speak to him. 'Who was that man?' Rebecca asked.

'Oh, him? That was Julius Caesar.'

'Julius . . .!?'

'Yup, but he's gone now.'

They all seemed to be talking at once for a while, and Mark just listened with a big grin on his face.

'Mark!' said Kim, urgently, 'you have to get away from Rome immediately!'

'Why?'

'Well, for one thing, Caesar is a very powerful, very intelligent, very determined man who will not rest until he has killed or captured you. He has already sent riders in several directions and he is instructing others as we speak. He is clearly preparing for some sort of counter-strike. We might be able to give you some warning of attack *if you answer your bloody calls*, but you will still be vulnerable when you sleep, eat, wash, go to the toilet or generally bumble your way around in a daydream. For another, we have watched Roman soldiers take your boat away and hide it in a warehouse to do God knows what with it, so you cannot get out the way you came in. Is that enough reasons for now?'

'Yes, Kim, and sorry about the calls, but I have had quite a bit going on, you know?'

'Yes, Mark, we've noticed you've been busy. I am just trying to alert you to the urgency of your situation. Unless you find a horse or something and head away from Rome pretty damn quickly you will very probably find all roads blocked to you and that Caesar has cooked up some unexpected and very nasty surprises for you. Are you receiving me and do you understand?'

'Yes, Kim, I'll get going as soon as I can.' Mark hesitated for a moment, then added, 'but I may not always be in a position to answer your calls, or necessarily want to,' and made to switch his mobile off. Before he hit the relevant button, however, Kim suddenly snapped out the word: '*Spartacus!*'

'What?' said Mark.

'You were about to switch your mobile off again, weren't you?'

'What about Spartacus?'

'We can talk about it when you're on the road, but it's Spartacus' slave revolt that's driving you to do these things, isn't it?'

'What if it is, would you help me?'

'We've only just figured out what you're up to. Opinion appears to be divided up here, we need time to think this through before saying whether or not we'll help you.'

'Come off it Kim, you call the shots up there, it's your opinion that counts.'

'Alright, *I* need time to think it through. In the meantime, we will supply you with what information we have available *if* you keep your mobile switched on and answer your calls, okay?'

'Okay, will do. Oh, by the way, what year is it?'

'What year? Its seventy-three BC, why?'

'Oh, nothing, it doesn't matter now.'

'Right, well get a move on and we'll talk later,' said Kim, terminating the call.

'Damn!' he said aloud in irritation, 'I wanted to enjoy myself for a bit! Oh, well, hey ho, I suppose it wouldn't do to get too carried away.' As he stood there, ignoring the cringing, hand-wringing approach of Quintus, his thoughts turned again to what had just happened between him and Caesar. He now realised that he had not defeated Caesar all by himself; Caesar's own vanity had played a major part. Mark half-smiled and half-winced at some of the things that he had said to Caesar but, unlike Caesar, he would probably never get angry over colourful insults aimed at him, no matter how many people were listening. 'What did Caesar call me?' he said to himself, 'a "snivelling piece of arse-hatched frogspawn"; hey, that's good! I must use that sometime! Hopefully with Peter around to hear it.'

Mark knew that Caesar had many qualities that he lacked, but he had hit upon Caesar's Achilles heel. It was true that he had capitalised upon Caesar's weakness rather well but, given that he had just made some very determined enemies, he thought, 'I could do without that kind of vanity on top of all my other faults if I'm to survive against such people. I had better keep my feet firmly on the ground, just like Peter said beside Lake Geneva.' In the absence of Peter to talk him down from any adrenalin-inspired bouts of conceit, Mark silently thanked Caesar for providing him with what seemed like a suitably self-effacing phrase which he now promised to repeat whenever he caught himself getting too big for his force-field boots. Chuckling to himself, he tried to mimic Peter's voice and bobbing Adam's apple as he practiced his new feet-on-the-ground mantra: 'just you remember what the great Caesar said, Mark: you are a sniveling piece of arse-hatched frogspawn!'

Finally deciding to get a move on, he put a reassuring arm around his host's quivering shoulders, guided him back to the villa, and said, 'you know, one of the most famous – no, *the* most famous person ever to live just called me a sniveling piece of arse-hatched frogspawn. That would make a fine start to any collection of insults from famous historical figures, don't you think? Yes, a fine start!'

When they were back in the villa, Mark held the tranquilising pistol between Quintus' terrified eyes, and cheerfully said, 'right, I'm in a bit of a hurry and I need to know whether you would prefer to obey my every command, instantly and *without* any flowery speeches, or face immediate execution.' Quintus, who could not have known that the tranquillised soldiers lying on his lawn were not dead, quickly opted for the former option. With that agreed, Mark instructed him to have provisions put aboard his carriage, dismiss the driver and take him south as fast as his horses could go. He had made up his mind: using Quintus as his guide and hostage, he would make his way to Mount Vesuvius, where the Spartacus of Mark's world had made his stronghold in 73 BC.

7
RANI

Mark woke up amid fading mental images of screaming faces. He did not know what had prompted such dreams, so he just let them fade further and turned over to get more comfortable. As he turned he touched Rani with his knees. The feel of her ushered in a kaleidoscope of recent memories of someone like himself and yet so alien that he had to sit up to work out whether he, Mark Goodwin, could really have been the focus of so much violence, fear and hope.

Less than two days had passed since he escaped from the garden fire and seen Caesar ride off along the villa's tree-lined avenue. As he and Quintus clattered away from Rome in the senator's ornate carriage, he admitted to Kim that he intended to intervene in the slave revolt if he could find a way to do so effectively, and Kim said that she and her team were still discussing whether or not they should continue to support him. Then, on the second night of their journey, he had been wakened by a sudden chorus of warbling war cries.

Kim had informed him that a large detachment of Roman soldiers were waiting to ambush him in a ravine on his road south, so he and Quintus halted about two kilometres short of the ravine, hid in a wood and settled down for the night. Before he went to sleep in his force-field suit, he had turned his mobile's volume down, too far down as it turned out. He now pictured Kim's apoplectic frustration when she picked up the heat signatures of scores of people surrounding him only to find that the silly jingle on his mobile was set too low to wake him.

When the war cries woke him, he was looking at a circle of wooden spear tips. Knowing that Caesar would not forget to use chains if he caught him again, Mark immediately grabbed his two favourite weapons and let fly with them in every direction. With his heart pumping adrenalin-rich blood around his system for the third time in under a week, he had dropped several of his startled attackers before they backed off and several more as they moved in again and determinedly stabbed at him with their spears.

Of course, if he had really been attacked by Romans sent by Caesar, they would not have woken him with war cries or relied on spear thrusts to overcome his resistance, but would have had him trussed up again in a trice and secured with heavy duty chains. These new attackers had never heard of Mark and knew nothing of force-field suits. When they had backed off for a second time, torches were lit and multiplied until he could see that he was surrounded by warriors of a different kind to what he had expected: the vast majority of them were women.

A young woman strode forward holding the quivering Quintus by his hair with one hand and a knife at his throat with her other hand.

'Yield, Roman, or your master will die now and you will die soon after.'

'Err, I'm not a Roman, actually,' he replied.

After he had spoken his foreign language, Rani looked confused as she tried to identify the source of the disembodied voice that answered her in Latin from among the flickering shadows of the wood's floor. Although confused, she must have worked out that Mark and the Latin voice were in some way linked because she managed to say, 'then who are you and what are doing with this scum?'

Picking up his mobile, Mark said, 'my name is Mark Goodwin. Quintus is my hostage and guide. I am looking

139

for Spartacus' slave army so that I can do what I can to help them.'

'Well, you have found it,' she told him angrily, 'and already killed several of them!'

'Oh, I see,' he said, 'err, sorry about that.'

'*Sorry*! You are *sorry* about that, are you? Your sorrow will not bring them back to life, will it?' she said, gesturing with her knife at her fallen comrades.

Mark was about to tell her that they were not dead, but he stopped himself and reached instead for a small pocket on the arm of his suit. Quintus squealed as Rani pressed her knife against his throat, and the circle of torches and spears moved a little closer.

'It's alright', Mark said, drawing an innocuous-looking pen-sized implement from his pocket, 'I'm only going to bring your warriors back to life.' By the time he had injected an antidote to the tranquilliser into the arms of four 'dead' warriors, the first to be injected had woken up and was unsteadily getting to her feet. A few minutes after the last of the fallen warriors was given the antidote, everyone had made a full recovery, apart from the still ringing ears of those who had caught the siren's full blast, and the atmosphere lightened considerably.

Rani let go of Quintus' hair and told Mark that the distant sounds of battle, which he had been too preoccupied to notice before, were the sounds of Spartacus and his men attacking the Romans in the ravine. Mark was guiltily aware that this particular battle would almost certainly not have taken place if he had not angered Caesar into laying a trap for him. Whatever the outcome of the battle, many people were now being stabbed and hacked to death because he had decided to sail up the Tiber and show off his rinky-dinky bits of technological equipment.

While the distant sounds of death grew fainter, Rani asked him a few questions about his telling-stone and his intentions. He found himself telling her an embellished version of his goddess Kim story, saying that the goddess had sent him to help Spartacus because She abhorred slavery. Rani seemed to accept these explanations and eventually sheathed her knife. Mark decided he was now safe enough to climb out of his force-field suit and start acting like a human being again.

Several of the warriors set off in Quintus' carriage and led the others along a dirt track through the wood. Walking near the rear of the procession, Rani had been keen to find out all she could about this strange man who could single-handedly beat off massed attacks and then bring the fallen back to life.

As they talked, Mark gradually became aware of her excitement as she wove what he said into a vision of him and the slavery-hating goddess driving the Roman armies away like so many frightened chickens. He felt guilty at providing her and her comrades with false hopes. So, after making sure that Quintus was out of earshot, he confided to her that he had made up the goddess to scare the Romans and told her as much of the truth as he thought she could absorb in one go.

In return, she told him that she had always been a slave, that she had no idea who her parents were or where they came from, and that she had only adopted the name 'Rani' after stabbing her former owner's son to death when he tried to rape her, and then fled, alone, to join Spartacus' rebellion about two weeks earlier.

They followed the track for about two hours through woods and fields that were looking parched and lifeless after a long dry summer, arriving at a ramshackle encampment beside a dried-up river bed shortly before dawn. Rani led him to a small tent made of blankets held up by bendy sticks and which contained nothing but a bed made of odd bits of clothing and smelly sheepskins. She gestured at the bed, and said, 'we sleep here.' She took off her battered brown tunic and baggy brown trousers and climbed into bed still partially dressed. Feeling somewhat bemused by this matter-of-fact invitation, Mark took off his self-cleaning smart-fibre tee-shirt, trousers and socks and got into bed beside her. He tentatively tried to do what he thought was expected of him, but Rani immediately pushed him away from her and shouted 'NO!' Feeling mostly relief at having a good excuse for not exposing his sexual inexperience to this scary woman, he found himself apologising to her without knowing quite what he had done wrong. She seemed reassured by this and briefly apologised back. After that, Mark had taken care to stay as close to his edge of the bed as he could and eventually fell asleep.

Now, the morning after they first met, he looked sideways at her as she sat up in bed beside him and gave him one of her slightly crooked smiles from behind wisps of her long jet-black hair. At first, by the light of torches, he thought her lop-sided smile was mocking, but he had since realised it was the product of some past injury that all but the very poorest on his own world could easily get fixed with minor cosmetic surgery.

She looked considerably less fierce than she had done at night. In fact, he thought she seemed almost as surprised and awkward as he felt to be waking up beside a stranger, even though nothing had happened between them, and he wondered whether she was also prone to adrenaline-inspired bouts of uncharacteristic behaviour.

Rani got dressed and went outside. Mark was just stepping outside the tent when she returned with some unleavened bread, goat's cheese and a water skin full of purple liquid that tasted like a fruits-of-the-forest cordial drink. Not wishing to draw more attention to himself than necessary, he popped out his mobile's two earpieces, put one in his ear and guided Rani to do the same so that they could talk quietly together without anyone else hearing his telling-stone's translations.Once she had adjusted to this latest bit of wizardry, she outlined what had happened so far in the rebellion while they sat beside the riverbed eating their breakfast and watching small groups of raggedly-dressed people arrive to join their temporary encampment.

Aside from the battle in the ravine, Rani's account of the early stages of the rebellion was similar to most of those that Mark had read on his home planet. Having broken out of their compound in Capua, Spartacus and about seventy other gladiators set up their camp on the slopes of Mount Vesuvius. Other escaped slaves joined them until their numbers had grown to a few hundreds, perhaps a thousand at most. An army of three thousand Romans under Claudius Glaber was despatched to crush them before the rebellion spread any further. The over confident Glaber decided to use his numerical superiority to starve the small slave army out, but the ex-slaves made rope ladders out of wild vines to scale down a sheer precipice at night and launched a surprise attack on the Romans' unguarded camp. Glaber's army was annihilated. Every day since then, the slave army was joined by hundreds of others who had either fled from their former owners or killed them and started new offshoots of the rebellion in the surrounding region of Campania.

Many of these escaped slaves, men women and children from the more northerly sites of the revolt, were now filtering into the camp beside the river crossing where Mark and Rani sat and watched them gather for the trek through the ravine to link up with those in and around Vesuvius. By late morning, hundreds of poorly armed people had gathered around a few makeshift shelters and huddled together for reassurance in the absence of the slave army's main fighting forces. As he looked at the milling crowd, Mark wondered how, on his own Earth, it could have been that such motley collections of thoroughly ordinary-looking people could ever have defeated army after army of professional Roman soldiers before they were finally defeated themselves.

One of Rani's friends, a Germanic-looking woman with long golden-brown hair called Lili, joined them for a while and told Rani that Spartacus' army had destroyed the Romans in the ravine and then marched off to engage another Roman force threatening their road to the mountain. While those beside the river crossing waited and hoped to hear that their way was clear, Mark tried to explain to Rani that his world had shared the exact same history as hers, except that his world had moved many centuries ahead due to the time differential between them. Becoming unsure as to whether she understood what he was saying, he eventually fell silent while she sketched him an account of her life.

Rani thought she was probably twenty-four years old; the same age as Mark was when he first looked upon images of this world at the control centre in Geneva. He rifled through flickering memories of his life before that time while she spoke and found that their two existences had been completely incomparable.

As well as the scar on her mouth, Rani also had scars of ownership on her forearms and several narrow ridges of scar tissue that stretched across her back and upper arms. When she was a small child, one of her forearms was branded with the letters 'L M' with hot irons so as to denote her original owner. This was overlaid with a large 'X' when she was sold and her other forearm was branded with 'G S' to denote her new owner. The scars on her back were caused by whips when her current owner, or his wife or son, punished her for some supposed misdemeanour or simply because they wished to vent bouts of drunken frustration on someone who could not defend herself.

Roman law at this time was quite sophisticated in terms of protecting the property rights of Roman citizens, but Rani was a slave, not a citizen, and deemed to be a private possession with no more rights than a piece of furniture or a pair of shoes. This meant that it was perfectly legal for her owners to do whatever they wanted with her, including rape, torture or murder her on a whim if they so chose. Roman citizens could and did call upon the military might of Rome to help defend these property rights if anyone challenged them, as was now the case. However, Rani told him that most life-long slaves regarded

144

their lowly position as a natural reflection of their low value, and that their year-on-year compliance owed as much to this low sense of self-worth as it did to Roman might. She had spent most of her life thinking that she was worth very little, but a smouldering spark of rebelliousness within her was fanned by meeting Lili, who had been newly enslaved and bought by Rani's owners before her spirit was broken, and then by news of Spartacus' annihilation of Glaber's army.

She said her owners did not belong to the elite of Roman slave-owning aristocracy, as Quintus did, but to the dwindling number of 'middle Romans' who had not yet been bought out or forced from their land by big landowners and had to 'make do' with just a few slaves. Depending upon their owners' temperaments, this often meant that the slaves of middle Romans had a harder life because fewer of them had to perform more roles. Her original owners had her trained as a house slave, but it was soon made clear to her that her duties would not necessarily be limited to things like cooking, cleaning and waitressing.

She corrected her earlier version of how she came to join the rebellion, saying that her owner's son's fatal attempt to rape her was more than just an attempt. She had in fact been routinely raped by him, his father and their friends for years and had given birth to three children in this way, all of whom were taken from her after they had been weaned. She hung her head and hid her face behind her long black hair while she told him this, as though she were admitting some wrongdoing of her own. Mark was not wholly unaware that many people used to judge women for what had been inflicted upon them, and some people from his own Earth apparently still did this, although he could not recall encountering such gross ignorance in his own sheltered but relatively enlightened life and times in the leafy part of England he called home.

The scar on the corner of Rani's mouth had been caused by the slash of a knife when she tried to resist being gang raped.

The man she had since killed had done this immediately after the gang rape as a punishment for embarrassing him in front of his friends with her attempts at resistance. Her owner, thinking that the scar made her less attractive, switched her duties from that of a house slave to the more physically gruelling life of a field slave. Again, Mark was not unaware that such things went on and that the victims of violence often get blamed, but to actually meet someone who had routinely experienced such treatment brought home to him how hideous people can be to other people.

Aside from the minor indignities he suffered at school, life for him had been gentle and kind for most of his existence. He thought that was probably true for the vast majority of people living in peaceful and prosperous parts of his home world. But behind this peace and prosperity, he now thought, lay centuries of development in which uncounted millions were brutalised and shunned as inferior beings. While it was doubtless true that life had hugely improved for most people on his own Earth, and that this in itself was obviously a good thing, he had never before thought to wonder whether such progress was worth it if it had come at the cost of countless millions of lives destroyed or made deeply miserable for millennia. 'Was hunter-gathering really so terrible?' he asked himself pointlessly.

He did not know the answers to questions like these, but his quiet rage at how Rani and people like her had been treated, and at the likes of Quintus for his power over so many people, was mixed with a guilty feeling that he had been born into a world where the roots of his comfort and ease went deep into so much misery and injustice. Then he thought about how far he had come, partly in the hope of doing something meaningful on another Earth, and yet he had done precisely nothing to help any of the millions of people in other parts of his own world who still lived lives of poverty and degradation. 'So,' he thought to himself, 'what the hell am I doing here if I couldn't even be bothered to make a monthly donation to help people suffering on my own planet?' It was, of course, far too late for that, but as he looked at the still growing numbers of people around them, especially the 'warrior' sitting beside him and hiding her face in a very non-warrior-like manner, he felt he no longer had the option of not being bothered.

'We lose, don't we?' Rani asked suddenly.

'Unless something very different happens this time, yes, I'm afraid so.'

'Do we, I mean, did those others on your world, did they all get killed or did they become slaves again?'

'Most were killed, including over six thousand who were crucified, and most of the survivors became slaves again.'

'But some got away, didn't they?'

'I think a few did, very few.'

'Out of how many?'

'Most histories say it grew to about one hundred and twenty thousand at its peak.'

'All that; no, all *this*,' Rani said, gesturing to the people around them, 'is for nothing?'

'Well, I wouldn't say it was for nothing, exactly. I mean, I imagine it made many Romans and others think twice about mistreating their slaves,' Mark replied, feeling that his attempt to offer comfort to the doomed was woefully inadequate.

'Did it stop them replacing the slaves they killed with new slaves, and mistreating them too?'

'Err, no, it didn't.'

'Then we must stop them; forever!'

'How?'

'Is that not why you have come?'

'I do want to help, yes, but I have limited powers.'

'And what do you hope to achieve with your limited powers?' she asked with a hint of scorn.

'I'm not exactly sure, but I thought I might tell Spartacus and his generals what things went wrong on my world so that they can avoid the same mistakes.'

'What mistakes?'

'Well, for one thing, according to our history books, the slave army divided. Spartacus tried to escape to Gaul with the largest contingent while one of his generals, an ex-gladiator called Crixus, led thirty thousand followers to pillage southern Italy. Crixus' people were wiped out and then the Roman armies united to wipe out Spartacus' army.'

'I see, yes, this is interesting, they should know about this!' she said without any trace of scorn. 'But what about you, what will you do if they believe you and stay united?'

'I don't know yet. I guess I'll have to wait and see how things turn out,' he replied, looking thoughtfully at the ground.

Rani opened her mouth to say something, but closed it again without making a sound. Indeed, she hardly uttered a sound for hours, not even joining in the cheering when two riders brought news that another Roman force had been destroyed and the way was now open for them to join the main rebellion further south. Instead, she watched what was going on around her, especially the behaviour of her new companion, and did some thinking of her own; plenty of thinking, as Mark was later to find out.

While Mark helped Rani stow her tent, a rider weaved his horse through the crowds towards them and told Rani that Spartacus would like to meet Mark at the ravine as soon as possible, and then made off again on some other errand. They fetched a very tired and worried-looking Quintus from his spear-toting female guards and the three of them joined about a dozen small children, plus two gaunt young men who were still bearing their owner's heavy leg-irons, crammed onto Quintus' carriage. Leaving ahead of the main body, they entered the ravine and came to the place where Spartacus' men had slaughtered the Romans who had planned to ambush Mark. A man dressed in odd bits of Roman military gear and a bloody bandage around one of his hands told them that Spartacus had not been able to wait for them. Spartacus and his generals had gathered every able-bodied man they could to meet a large Roman army approaching the slave-held region from the east.

When they moved on again, Mark had to look away from the bits of limbs and stringy blobs of spilt innards that were left behind after their former owners had been dragged from the road and piled in grotesque heaps. He did not know whether he had the stomach to be involved in the gruesome conflicts that lay ahead, but his recent bouts of uncharacteristic boldness at least gave him hope of not wholly disgracing himself.

As a quiet academic, Mark's reaction to dire danger had never before been tested. He still felt amazed by his own behaviour when caught in a tight spot and hoped that this hitherto unknown and unguessed side to his character would see him through any more horrifying encounters. However, even his worst dreams of what he might find on New Earth had not featured the kind of human detritus that he was now trying his best not to look at.

Gulping back his rising bile, he thought again about his conversations with Peter beside Lake Geneva. 'Why are you assuming that you can do any good at all on the other Earth?' Peter had asked him, and he now asked himself the same question. He had no clear answer to this, but neither did he have an answer as to what effect his bumbling intervention had already had or would continue to have if he tried to stop intervening now. He was partly responsible for the many deaths in the ravine, which meant that he had inadvertently snuffed out countless generations of would-be descendents and therefore caused the future of this Earth to sheer away from the history of his own Earth in ways that were incalculable and permanent.

Looking back in the early evening light, he saw a column of hopeful but vulnerable and frightened humanity following Quintus' gaudy carriage through the ravine. He knew that the dye was cast for them, and he knew he could not go back. If he could not go back, then he had to go forward, and given that he had failed to negotiate with the Roman Senate, it very much looked as though he would have to go to war.

After missing his meeting with Spartacus, Mark found nothing he could usefully do other than give up his place on Quintus' carriage to two of the many tired children among the straggling lines of tired people trudging their way to the limited sanctuary of the mountain. Soon feeling very tired himself, he willed his soft body to keep pace with the leaner and much fitter Rani. Although they had not talked much while they walked beside Quintus' carriage together, she had spent some time listening to Quintus' account of what had happened between Mark and Caesar. Mark had been secretly pleased with her wide-eyed looks of admiration, but remained largely unaware of what she was thinking during her long periods of silence.

The procession stopped when darkness fell. Mark helped Rani put up her tent and then they sat beside a dry stream bed with Lili and several others to eat an evening meal of unleavened bread washed down with some of Rani's purple cordial. As Mark sat lost in his thoughts, Rani silently took his hand and led him back to her tent for their second night together. He felt he knew the drill now and curled up on his edge of the bed.He was not quite asleep when Rani broke her silence in untranslated Latin.

'Pardon?' he said, after he switched his mobile back on and they had put their earpieces in.

'I said, you do not want to kill Romans, do you?'

'Mmm, err, no, no I don't want to kill anyone,' he whispered.

'This is a war, people get killed in wars,' she whispered back as they both sat up in bed and looked at each other in the darkness.

'Yes, I know,' he said, 'but Romans are people too.'

'I know they are. I also know not all Romans are bad and not all slaves are good, but I dream of Roman armies being wiped out. But you, I have watched you and you are tormented. Not just because you do not know what to do to help us; you are tormented because you cannot see how to help us without causing many deaths. It is difficult for me to think like this, but I have been trying. If you find a way to help us beat the Romans, then many of our people will want to kill as many them as they can for what they have done to us.'

'Yes,' he agreed, 'I have been worrying about that.'

'But perhaps there is another way,' she said, 'not to avoid all battles and murders, but perhaps there is at least an end to aim for that is not all blood and death.'

'What sort of end? Escape to Gaul, like Spartacus wants?'

'That might be good for us,' she said uncertainly, 'but the Romans will replace us with more captured people.'

'Well, we can't be everywhere. Rome's slave trade stretches across three continents, and it is not just the Romans who capture people for the slave trade.'

'I know, but it is Roman money that drives many non-Romans to enslave people.'

'We can't stop that without defeating Rome, and then the vengeance would be terrible.'

'Maybe there is a way,' she whispered excitedly, 'if we can make the Romans *really* afraid of us, afraid that we will not only take vengeance on Romans outside of Rome but that we can destroy Rome itself, then I think they would prefer peace with Quintus ruling Rome instead of facing their own destruction.'

'Quintus?' he said in surprise, 'Quintus rule Rome?'.

'Why not? Quintus only wants what is good for Quintus, and he believes in the goddess Kim. He thought to use you to gain more power in Rome but now he is terrified of you and the goddess, and of Caesar too. He would like to return to Rome and live in comfort and safety again, but even if he gets away from us he thinks that the Roman authorities might never forgive him for helping you, even though he did so in fear of his life. With such worries, imagine how pleased he would be to find himself the ruler of Rome! If you could help him do this, you could make him stop Romans from having slaves through his fear of the goddess. Even if he stopped believing in Her, he would still want others to believe in Her and seek your help against his rivals in Rome. You and your people could give him this help in return for abolishing the slave trade throughout the Mediterranean lands!'

Mark had never considered that Quintus might prove useful after finding the slave army, but Rani had sown a seed of an idea that immediately appealed to him, however improbable it might be. Whispering together far into the night, they bounced ideas between them until they felt that her initial thought might not be so improbable after all. He did not think it constituted a coherent plan as yet but, as Rani said, it did at least give them something to aim for other than blood and death.

They finally decided to close their nocturnal planning session and wait to see if her ideas seemed credible in the light of day. As he lay down again, Mark thought he had found a very intelligent, very determined and very humane ally in Rani, and he felt sleepily excited by these thoughts. As he hovered on the edge of sleep, however, Rani sought a more active outlet for her feelings of excitement.

Their early morning coupling was nothing like Mark's only other sexual relationship. He did not know whether recent events had changed him or whether Rani's seduction had simply caught him off-guard and without any time to assemble his usual thoughts and feelings of inadequacy. Whatever the cause, they had rocked together in fluid union until they were both spent, and fell asleep as the pre-dawn light begun to filter through the material of the tent.

Mark woke, sat up in bed and remembered what he and Rani had talked about and done together in the night. She soon sat up beside him, and said 'are you hungry?' with a mischievous twinkle in her eye.

He was, but not for food. Feeling emboldened by their earlier love making, he suddenly felt that her lop-sided smile was a sexily endearing complement to her long black hair, big dark eyes and lithe olive-skinned body; and his hunger for her now felt like sheer greed. She appeared to be feeling the same way, for she slid on top of him where he sat and eased down upon him without further words.

It was some time before his main hunger really was for food. Rani's mood appeared to match his and she sprang out of bed and opened a bag of food that she had taken from Quintus' carriage. When they had eaten their fill of unleavened bread and cold meats, they squatted on the bed opposite each other and tucked into the flesh of a perfectly juicy melon.

Wiping melon juice from her chin, Rani looked at him, and said, 'you know, you are not completely unpleasant to look upon.'

'Why, thank you, your Highness, you do me great honour!' he replied, 'and if I may say so, I am also pleasantly surprised at how easy it is to keep my food down in your presence.'

She laughed at the translation and flicked melon juice from her fingers onto his face. He did likewise, and they started having a mini melon fight that soon developed into another bout of love making.

Shortly afterwards, two women, one of whom was Rani's friend Lili, poked their heads through the tent flap. 'Ah, there you are!' said Lili. 'We have just walked miles back looking for you two!

'Why,' Rani asked, 'where have you been?'

'Where have *we* been; we broke camp ages ago!' Lili replied while trying not to spoil her indignation with an indulgent smile. 'I only realised you weren't with us when a rider brought a message for Mark to meet Spartacus at Vesuvius as soon as the battle is over.'

Feeling like naughty truants, they leapt out of bed, packed their gear and raced to catch up with Lili and her genuinely annoyed companion as they resolutely resumed their march towards the mountain.

Mark willed his soft sweaty body to keep pace with his three much fitter women companions as they forced the pace under the blazing midday sun. He tried to put his legs into autopilot and think about the practicalities of Rani's idea of setting Quintus up as the ruler of Rome, but his mental horizons soon narrowed to making the next bend in the road or the top of the next rise, and choosing between enduring his thirst or sipping at Rani's cordial, which now tasted stale and brackish.

They came to the base of Mount Vesuvius in the late afternoon. Vesuvius was much steeper and more rugged before its many later eruptions, including the one that famously smothered Pompeii in 79AD, and they had to leave the much overweight Quintus and his carriage behind in a guarded camp at the base of the mountain, as well as the two gaunt young men while the camp's improvised smithy removed their leg-irons. Sometimes carrying children and sometimes hauling them up by their hands, they trudged and scrambled up the mountain amid rumours that Spartacus' army was crushing the Romans and counter rumours that it was being crushed by the Romans. Taking a much needed break, they sat on a large flat rock beside other weary walkers and shared oddments of food and gingerly sipped at the ever more brackish fluid in Rani's water skin. Then they sat for a while in silence and watched groups of people below them merge into a steady procession winding their way up and past them to the slave army's stronghold, which was hidden from their view above a steep rise not far above.

Mark thought how vulnerable they looked; just a stream of refugees with a few inadequate weapons or farm implements to protect themselves against the might of Rome if Spartacus and his men were beaten. Knowing how the first major battles had gone on his own Earth, he hoped that his meddling had not disturbed the course of this planet's future to such an extent that the slave army's initial victories were reversed, but he could not be sure. He felt so disturbed by the memory of Caesar's grim determination to avenge Mark's slight to his honour that he half expected to hear that Caesar had bullied his way into leading a Roman army to crush the rebellion in its infancy for the sake of his own injured vanity.

He now wished he had sailed as close as he could to Vesuvius instead of riling Caesar and the other senators with his pretensions as a self-styled interplanetary diplomat. Then he realised that a ripple of excitement was spreading through the weary host as galloping riders below them brought news of victory. With a surge of hope lifting their spirits, Mark, Rani and everyone around them scrabbled up the last stretch with barely a thought for their weary limbs.

Spartacus had led the slave army to their second major victory, this time effectively destroying two Roman legions led by Publius Varinius, just as the other Spartacus had done on Mark's home world. So far at least, Mark's meddling had not drastically altered the course of events. That much was a relief at this stage of the rebellion, but if the tens of thousands of slaves who had joined or were about to join the revolt were to survive, then he must find a way to drastically alter things at some point.

Feeling a good deal more secure, for the time being, Mark and Rani wandered round crowds of people while they waited to welcome Spartacus' victorious army back to their ever growing encampment. The atmosphere was a highly charged mix of excitement, pride, camaraderie and apprehension for the future. At the base of an almost sheer wall of the mountain, a small crowd was discussing what would be needed to carve a great figure upon the face of the wall. The statue would be similar to the carving of American presidents on the face of Mount Rushmore, except that this one would be in the likeness of a noble-looking slave standing with broken chains dangling from his wrists.

On more level pieces of ground, people were training to fight in groups while others were fashioning farm implements into more effective weapons or hardening wooden spear tips in fires, or making round shields out of animal hides stretched across a lattice of wild vine stems. Most of the gatherings upon the mountain seemed to be enthused with optimism and there were many discussions about a future without slavery; although a shadow came across Rani's face when she looked at one particular group.

'You must not think that everyone here is a friend,' she said darkly through his earpiece. 'I have just seen three vicious pieces of shit that I will never trust.'

'Were they slaves?'

'Yes. One of them was an overseer on a farm neighbouring my owner's farm and the other two were his thugs. I'm not sure what they're doing here but I *am* sure they would like nothing more than to have slaves of their own. Vicious pieces of shit!' she said again with feeling.

Mark wanted to know more but he did not press her. Instead, he said, 'then it is all the more important to find a way to end this peacefully, or else the oppressed will become oppressors and it will all start up again.'

'Yes,' she said in a tone of finality, 'we will do what we can to end this as quickly and as peacefully as we can.' While she spoke, she reached out and clasped his hand tightly with hers.

8
CAPUA

Kim called Mark while he and Rani were wandering around the slave army's mountain stronghold and told him that she and her team had reached a decision: they would provide him with information to help Spartacus lead his people to Gaul. Mark would have been delighted by this decision if it had arrived a day earlier, but now it presented him with a problem. Rani's idea to set Quintus up as the ruler of Rome on the condition that he abolish slavery in all Roman-held lands had taken root in his mind.

Although he had grown more confident in what he was doing, especially with Rani by his side, he still found it very difficult to tell Kim that he did not intend to do what she wanted him to do. However, given that Gaul and Rome both lay to the north, he reasoned that it was not yet necessary to tell her about his ambitious new plan. Instead of arguing, he said, 'that's great, Kim, I'll offer Spartacus our support for a march north as soon as I meet him.'

'I would like to talk with him as well,' she replied, 'and to Crixus, if that can be arranged. Now that you have made a mockery of our non-interventionist policy, one of our main reasons for intervening is to dissuade Crixus from carrying out his ill-fated plan to pillage southern Italy.'

'Yes, Kim, I want to dissuade him from that too. Do you want me to introduce you as the goddess Kim?'

'No, I think it would be better to tell the truth in a small private meeting. I do not like this goddess charade at all, but I suppose it might be worth using to scare Romans, if you absolutely must.'

'Okay, I'll do what I can,' he said, thinking that having the support of a reluctant goddess was better than no support at all.

It was well past midnight when a messenger approached Mark and offered to escort him to a meeting with Spartacus. He and Rani had been sitting on a slope with Lili watching people celebrate the victory around a large fire. The celebrations were not madly exuberant; there was still too much anxiety in the air for that, as well as sadness and concern for the hundreds of killed and wounded that they had suffered in their early string of victories, but they were quite jovial. There were jugglers, fire-eaters, various musicians, and a certain amount of drunken banter, but there was no apparent friction between people who might have had scores to settle from the divisive lives that their former masters had arranged for them as slaves. For now, the atmosphere in this multi-ethnic melting-pot was one in which a sense of common purpose and solidarity was being forged.

Mark knew that this sense of common purpose concealed differing aims between those who wanted to end slavery, those who wanted revenge, those who wanted to profit from the rebellion and dreamed of owning slaves themselves, and those who simply wanted to escape, but the predominant topic of the moment concerned their prospects for bringing about an end to slavery. If he and Rani were to attempt their new and ambitious plan, it seemed wise to start doing something about it soon, before this mood of solidarity started to fragment according to differing views of what the slave army can or should aim to achieve.

The bulk of the army had not returned to their largely barren and increasingly overcrowded mountain stronghold.

Instead, they had set up a fortified camp outside Capua, the main Roman city in the region and the place where the gladiators initially made their break for freedom. In the absence of siege weapons to breach Capua's defensive wall, it seemed that Spartacus was trying to pen the large Roman garrison within the city rather than attempt a siege, and to use the lull in fighting to rest his army after its series of forced marches and short, sharp, bitter battles.

Their escort handed flaming torches to Mark and Rani and they followed him down the steep upper section of the mountain path and then mounted a horse that a second escort held waiting for Mark. Rani had not been invited to the meeting with Spartacus, but no one objected to her presence. She had never ridden a horse either, but Mark had been on several pony trekking holidays and he was able to give her a rudimentary verbal horse riding lesson while their horse picked its way down the lower slopes by the light of a half-moon.

When they reached a well maintained road that led to Capua, twenty-odd Roman miles to the north, they and their two soldier-escorts stopped for a brief comfort break. Before setting off again, Rani took a long draught of the purple cordial from her water-skin and passed it to Mark. He took a small sip and spat the foul fluid out in disgust, despite the ever growing thirst that had been nagging at him for hours, and then grimaced as he watched her take another gulp. He decided to put up with his thirst until they found fresh water.

With a level surface beneath their horse's hooves, Rani wanted to sit up front and try riding it herself. Mark was a little nervous of this in the semi-dark, but he agreed and soon relaxed when she displayed an aptitude for horse riding that went way beyond his first hesitant efforts in the Brecon Beacons of mid-Wales. Indeed, as they clattered up to Capua shortly after sunrise, he ruefully admitted to himself that she had probably surpassed his horse riding abilities forever.

'What a woman you are!' he said in her ear in untranslated English as they slowed to speak to the guards waiting at the main entrance to Spartacus' new base.

Mark expected to have the opportunity to freshen up a little before the meeting, and he was now in desperate need of fresh water to drink, but he did not get the chance. They were shown to the army's tented headquarters without delay. It was only when he dismounted that he realised how incredibly fatigued and saddle-sore he was. It was not just his thirst and saddle-soreness that afflicted him, however. He had not slept all night, his leg muscles had grown stiff from his march to Vesuvius and up its steep slopes the previous day, and everything else that had happened to him since he sailed up the Tiber seemed to be making claims on the last of his physical and mental capacity to endure any more adventures without a respite.

Now that he was told he would meet his hero without delay, he suddenly found mental images of his timid past bubbling up to challenge his bold plans. Where he would once have baulked at the idea of even speaking to the likes of Spartacus, he was now about to stroll up to this great historical figure and tell him what he should do with his army to drastically alter the course of history for a whole planet against the express wishes of those who had brought Mark to this planet in the first place. This was not the kind of thing that reclusive academics anticipate doing, and certainly not when they are terribly tired and desperately thirsty.

As they approached the tent behind two armed guards, Mark tried his best to walk normally despite feeling that a hedgehog must have become wedged between the tops of his thighs, and every muscle below his neck seemed to protest at each movement. He also had the notion that his brain was dehydrated and had shrunk slightly, making him feel as though it rocked and tapped against the inside of his skull and the back of his eyes with every step.

He could see through the open tent flaps: four figures were bent over a trestle table. Finding himself beckoned forward by his guards without ceremony, he dazedly stepped over the tent's threshold and then stood stock still as a wave of strong perfume assailed his senses. He looked at the men in front of him, expecting to instantly recognise Spartacus, but none of them fit his mental image of gladiators and he wondered whether he had missed yet another opportunity to meet his hero.

He was fairly sure that one of the four men was not an escaped gladiator; he wore a clown-like gown of thick blue and green stripes with frilly white cuffs and collar, and he had thickly powdered white hair permed into tight curls that framed a bright blue face.

The other three looked much less bizarre, but they were still very different from what he had expected. Rather than the tall, muscle-bound, barrel-chested, sword-bearing, partially armoured gladiators-turned-generals of legend, two of them were quite short, one was a tall and slender black African, all three wore Roman togas – which Mark had expected them to see as the uniform of their oppressors – they appeared to be unarmed and they all looked as unwarlike as Caesar had initially done.

While he stood at the entrance and tried to take in the scene, Rani stepped forward and made some form of introduction before nodding a signal for him to switch on his mobile's translation function.

'We are very pleased to meet you both,' said one of the short men, and then paused and gazed at Mark's mobile in fascination as it repeated his words in a foreign language. 'I am called Spartacus; this is Julian,' he said, nodding towards the tall African, 'and Crixus, and this painted obscenity is Andy.'

'Andy?' Mark said in surprise; and it turned out to be the only word that he would utter at the meeting.

'Yes,' said Spartacus, indicating the clown-like figure, 'he is a conjuror and a failed bandit on the run from Sicily, so I should imagine the two of you will get along very well, as far as conjuring is concerned, I mean.'

Andy, who Mark now realised was the main source of perfume, held out a hand for Mark to shake over the maps on the table, and said, 'don't listen to them, my name is Andichios, but these miscreants show no respect!'

Still influenced by his preconceptions, Mark gave Andichios' hand an unnecessarily firm shake. 'Oo, aren't we strong!' Andichios said, withdrawing his hand with a theatrically effeminate flutter.

Mark stood in silence for a few moments while he tried to reorder his expectations. His hosts also stood silently, smiling benignly at him. No longer having a mental template with which to compare his new environment, he quickly rifled through his memory for some familiar image that might fit the bill. He knew the image he came up with was not really appropriate, but it was the best his tired mind could manage at that moment: it was of a group of office staff on a charity fundraising day who were unsure how they ought to welcome a new helper on their wacky office fun-day. Looking around the tent, he saw a plaque attached to a wooden strut inscribed with Latin words. He vaguely wondered if the words might translate to something like: *You don't have to be mad to work here, but it helps!*

Looking back at his hosts, he thought; 'why is nothing ever like I think it's going to be,' and gathered himself to speak again. No sound came out of his mouth; instead, he thought he saw a flicker of concern disturb his hosts' smiles before his vision glazed over and he collapsed to the floor.

When he opened his eyes he found himself looking at a white ceiling. For a moment he wondered if he was in his hotel room in Geneva and all this New Earth stuff was just a dream. Rani's voice and the modulated English male voice that translated her words made him realise it was no dream. In fact, he could now remember partially regaining consciousness as people bore him away from Spartacus' headquarters on some sort of stretcher, and Rani making him sit up in bed to drink fresh water.

'Are you alright?' she asked.

'Err, yeah, I think so. What happened?'

'You passed out.'

'In front of Spartacus!?'

'Yes, but you must not worry. You were very tired and thirsty, that's all. You had a long day walking to the camp at Vesuvius, then rode here without any sleep.'

'So did you.'

'True, but I think you are used to a much easier life than I am, and I took more care to drink.'

'Your drink turned foul.'

'Pig bladders do that, but they also help to prevent diseases.'

Mark did not know whether that was true and he preferred not to think about it. What he did think was that he had passed out at the worst imaginable moment; with the possible exception of when he was squatting in Quintus' garden fire.

'What happened, I mean after I passed out?'

'We brought you here,' she said as she tried on an expensive-looking calf-length black tunic and a velvety ankle-length black gown she found in the room's wardrobe.

'Where?'

'It's a captured Roman villa, just outside Capua.'

'What about the meeting?'

'I thought it went very well.'

'Without me?'

'Yes. You told me about Kim and what she wanted. I explained it all as best I could. Then I told them what *we* wanted.'

'What did they say?'

'They asked me to ask you whether you could demonstrate some of your powers to them, when you're fully rested, and they would make a decision then.'

'Oh, I see. What kind of demonstration?' he asked, thinking about office fun-days again.

'That's up to you.'

'Okay. Right. I suppose I'd better get up, then.'

'When you're ready,' she said matter-of-factly, and left the room.

While she was gone, Mark took a call from Kim. He explained what had happened up to the point when he had passed out and promised to seek another meeting with Spartacus and Crixus in which she could participate. Kim accepted this, and told him that the supply situation aboard her craft had become so critical that Tsang had volunteered to go into suspended animation two days earlier, that Rebecca and Sunita would go into suspended animation the following day and that Tarak would join them a few days later; leaving only Kim to guide Mark on his quest to help the slave army escape to Gaul. She then put Tarak on the line to answer any outstanding questions that Mark might have regarding his as yet unused gadgets.

When Rani came back bearing a platter of cold pork rashers, bread and the lemon tea he had drunk at Quintus' villa, he was toying with his gadgets and wondering what he might do to impress Spartacus and his followers. By the time they had eaten, he had put together the semblance of a plan.

'Anything I can do to help?' she asked.

'I am going to need an area of ground marked off so that no one gets too close to what I'm going to do,' he said, examining the four silver bomblets that Tarak had sent in the escape pod.

'What are they?'

'Holy hand-grenades,' he said, unhelpfully quoting a classic Monty Python film.

'And what do holy hand-grenades do?'

'They destroy things.'

'Do they destroy people?'

'They could do, but I don't plan to use them for that.'

'What then?'

'Tarak says that just one of these can destroy an entire Roman villa, like the one we're in now.'

'Really?' she said doubtfully.

'I'm going to need an empty building so that I can show Spartacus what these things can do, and a wide area around the building cleared of people so that no one gets hurt by bits of flying debris.'

'How big an area?'

'I'm not sure. Tarak hasn't actually seen one of these go off, so maybe he's exaggerating their effects just to be on the safe side.'

'Do you only have four of them?'

'Yes.'

'Mmm,' she mused, 'and you intend to use one of them to find out how powerful the other three are?'

'Yes, and to help Spartacus and the others decide what to do.'

'What about the other things?' she asked.

While he was trying to explain what his gadgets did, she picked up the chemical spray canister. He translated the words on it, which read: *EXTREMELY SEVERE IRRITANT*. However, it was the diagram below the warning sign that had attracted her attention. It was a silhouette of three people leaning forward in apparent anguish; one of whom was rubbing his/her eyes, one had hands clasped over his/her mouth and throat, and one was scratching his/her chest and stomach. As with the bomblets, Tarak had said that the spray was considerably more potent than might be supposed, although he had not witnessed the effects of this kind of weapon either. Rani was fascinated by all his gadgets, but she seemed to think that the chemical spray canister and its diagram was funny rather that fearsome.

'What did Crixus say about the Crixus of my world being defeated?' he asked, suddenly finding his little array of weaponry and his thoughts about their potential uses to be distressingly inadequate for the task they had set themselves.

'I didn't say anything about that in case he took offence. I thought I would leave that to you and Kim.'

'Fair enough.'

He then tried to bring Spartacus' face to mind, but could not do so, only that he had not seemed particularly impressive. He did not have a broken nose, as Mark had always pictured, or a square jaw, or a dimple on his chin, or any visible scars, or anything really noticeable. He vaguely remembered that Spartacus' eyes were set slightly wide apart in a roundish face, but not especially so.

'Spartacus didn't look like I thought he would,' he said.

'Why?'

'Well, for one thing, he's short; and I didn't see any bulging muscles or anything.'

'He might be short, but he is strong and quick and very intelligent. I also think he is a good man. A hard man by your standards, perhaps, but he would like to do something to help slaves generally, if he can. Not like Crixus. Crixus is not a bad man but he is bitter; he wants revenge, and he wants to profit from the war. I now understand more about why they divided their forces on your world. Crixus is becoming over confident as our army grows. He thinks that we can rouse hundreds of thousands of slaves to join us and beat all the armies that Rome sends against us. He is a Gaul and he wants his people in Gaul to hear of his victories and to pour into Italy to join him. I think he wants to turn Italy into a province of Gaul and to have the Romans as their slaves as a punishment for what they have done to us.'

'What do Spartacus and Julian think about that?'

'I don't know about Julian, he listens and thinks much more than he speaks. But Spartacus thinks the Roman armies will win in the end if we stay in Italy, and that the best that we can hope for is to escape to Gaul and then disperse to our homelands.'

'But you have no other home to go to.'

'This has been no home for me. I and many like me would have to find people to take us in and make their homelands our homelands.'

'Could you do that?'

'We could, I think, because we make friends with others who join the rebellion and who do have homelands to go to. But as I said before, our places as slaves would be filled by others, and Rome might invade our new homes and enslave any they don't kill.'

'That happened on my world. Caesar conquered Gaul and then he and others conquered many other lands and slavery flourished for hundreds of years.'

'So we must stop them, and stop Crixus from plundering southern Italy,' she said evenly, as though one might stop the Roman armies and Crixus' followers doing what they wanted to do as easily as one stops children fighting.

'Well,' he said, 'I'll do what I can to help, but I can't promise anything.'

Rani smiled brightly at him, and said, 'but you are not alone anymore. As well as Spartacus and his people, and Kim and her people, you have *me* now; and I have just had another idea!' As soon as she finished speaking she flew out of the room with her long glossy black, freshly washed hair swishing across the back of her fine new black outfit.

She came back about an hour later, found Mark relaxing in the captured villa's bath and excitedly told him what she had arranged. They were due to meet Spartacus, Crixus, Julian and Andichios in two hours time between the slave army's main encampment and the walls of Capua, with the bulk of the slave army drawn up behind them to witness Mark demonstrate his power. The essence of her plan was for him to blow a hole in the city's defensive wall with one of his four bomblets instead of 'wasting it on some silly villa or cow shed.' In return, she had got Spartacus and the others to agree to protect the inhabitants of the city with their best men against any elements of their army who might take the opportunity to take revenge on the Romans within. This, she thought, could then act as a dress rehearsal for the neutralisation of Rome itself.

Mark was initially horrified by Rani's plan, but his objections sounded feeble in his owns ears and her overwhelming enthusiasm was infectious. Now his misgivings were returning and multiplying, making his insides feel like eels sloshing around in a wet paper bag as they approached a long dense thicket of people who had gathered to witness the promised spectacle.

'I thought I was supposed to decide how I would demonstrate my powers,' he said unhappily from within his force-field suit as they walked through the space that the fascinated crowds were opening up for them to pass through.

'You already decided how, I just arranged a better target.'

'Oh, right, nice distinction!' he said sarcastically. 'Are you sure they won't pillage the place? Assuming I manage to knock a hole in the wall, that is, which I very much doubt.'

'As sure as I can be. If it does not work here then it will not work at Rome either, and then we'll know whether it can be done at all, or whether our people can be held back from taking their revenge. As for the wall, it was built to keep bandits out and keep slaves in, but it's old and crumbling. This is our best chance of doing something big. If one holy hand-grenade isn't enough, then use the other three together. If that fails, then it fails, but if you are not prepared to kill people with them, what other use can they be?'

'Mmm, I suppose so,' he said as he distractedly fiddled with one of the bomblets in his pocket, 'but I would have liked to have tested one of them first.'

'Tarak said they were very powerful, didn't he? And you only have four of them, so you can't afford to use any of them in a test!'

'I don't think Tarak really knows, he hasn't actually seen one go off or anything.'

'Yes, you said that, but now's his chance,' she said, glancing vaguely up at the sky, 'and your chance to do something useful instead of just talking!'

'Okay, okay, I get the picture. I'll do my best.'

'That's all I ask,' she said with the irritatingly contrite look of someone who knows they have utterly won an argument while pretending they have made major concessions.

They drew close to the slave generals, who stood in front of the main army at the head of a tight phalanx of two or three hundred soldiers wearing blue armbands, with a similar number of cavalry formed into six ranks close by. Mark felt the atmosphere was almost like that of a carnival. 'They're not taking this seriously, are they?' he said to Rani.

'Spartacus does not want to raise expectations, he has to think about morale if you fail; but you will not fail!'

'No? Well, we'll just have to see about that, won't we?' he said as he came up to the generals with his hand extended for Spartacus to shake.

Spartacus bowed his head slightly and shook Mark's hand. 'I hope you are fully recovered?'

'Yes, thank you.'

There was a moment of silence before Rani nudged Mark, and said, 'well, go on then. Julian's cavalry will come to your aid if the Romans try to grab you.'

'Oh, err, right,' he replied, and looked again at Spartacus, Crixus, Julian and Andichios, trying to judge their mood. 'If I can make a breach in the wall,' he addressed them as loudly as his current uncertainty and highly self-conscious mood allowed, 'do all of you absolutely promise not to pillage the city or allow anyone to harm anyone that poses no threat to them?'

Spartacus started to smile, then forced his features into a more sombre look when he heard the translation, and said, 'for my part, I absolutely promise to do my best to stop anyone pillaging or doing any harm to anyone who poses no threat to us on this day.' He turned to the others and raised his eyebrows to indicate that they should make similar pronouncements, which they all did in slightly doubtful voices. Then Crixus marched off to stand in front of another tight phalanx of soldiers a few hundred metres away and Julian mounted a horse in front of the cavalry. Most of the cavalry were black Africans wearing baggy brown tunics with round shields strapped to their left arms and holding spears against their right shoulders as though they were on parade.

'Are you sure that no one will take revenge?' Mark asked, looking at Capua's tall and strong-looking wall and feeling a rush of adrenalin kick in.

'My orders are *very* strict on this matter,' said Spartacus. 'If you can make a breach in the city's wall, I will lead the picked men behind me into the breach and demand that all the slaves in the city and the surrounding region be released. Crixus and Julian will follow up and help block the rest of our people from entering the city, and Andy will leap around like a demented monkey shouting curses at anyone who tries to disobey orders.'

'Unbelieving, puss-sucking bastards of cockroach infested cesspits,' Andichios muttered amiably, as though he were warming up for his part in the proceedings.

Ignoring Andichios' interjection, Spartacus shrugged and said, 'it's the best I can do, but I cannot predict how the Romans will behave.'

'Okay,' said Mark, 'but if this ends in a bloodbath, I will *never* help you again; do you understand?'

'I understand,' said Spartacus, looking slightly taken aback by the firmness of this strange individual's commitment to a non-violent approach to warfare.

'Alright then, I suppose I'd better get on with it,' said Mark. He straightened his back, took a deep breath and resolutely marched alone towards Capua while the watching army sent him on his way with a chorus of good natured whistles and cheers.

He stopped about twenty paces in front of the four or five-metre-high city wall within sight of the city's main gates and steeled himself to address the dozens of Roman soldiers who were looking down at him.

'Romans,' he began with his mobile's translation function set a little too low.

'What? Speak up, slave, we can't hear you,' said one of the Romans.

He cleared his throat and turned up the volume a bit. 'Romans, be warned . . .'

'Yes, looks like rain, doesn't it?' said another while others laughed at the absurd spectacle.

'ROMANS!' he shouted after turning the volume up full. 'Be warned that I am about to blow this section of your wall down! Move well away from this area or you will be killed!'

Two arrows bounced off his force-field suit.

'Right!' he said, putting his mobile in one of his suit's pockets. He marched up to the wall and stooped to place a bomblet at its base when he was knocked flat and winded by the impact of a large metal ingot striking his back, followed by several large rocks.

Although not seriously wounded, the ingot had hurt him and caused him to drop the bomblet, and the rain of rocks was now threatening to pin him down. In near panic, he scrabbled around for the bomblet, found it and pushed it against the wall between two rocks and then staggered off holding his aching ribs. More arrows were hitting him, but he regained his composure and turned to face the Romans on the wall from about the same distance that he had first addressed them.

Silence fell on the scene for a few moments while onlookers marveled at his survival.

'I have warned you,' he announced, 'leave this section of wall or you will be killed!'

'Bugger off, slave,' was the only reply.

Being unsure as to what would happen when he used his mobile to key the appropriate code that Tarak had given him for each bomblet, he thought he would try out his gas canister to see if it could drive the Romans away from the threatened piece of wall. Taking several paces back towards the wall amid a flurry of arrows, he held the canister up and pressed the button. A fine jet of liquid splashed near the top of the wall and let off small streamers of gas that immediately drove his Roman tormentors back with howls of pain and consternation. Lifting his aim, the jet of smoking liquid traced a wet line up to the top of the wall and then arced over it like a stream of steaming urine. He could hear anguished cries and angry curses as the gas caught numerous people in its embrace and they fled as fast as they could blindly stumble from the afflicted area.

Feeling guilty about the distress he had caused, and yet satisfied that the threatened section of wall had been cleared, he trotted away to what he thought was a safe distance, roughly halfway between the wall and the slave army, and quickly keyed the bomblet's code before the Romans recovered enough to return to their positions.

He pressed the 'send' button and looked up, hoping that the rocks would not block the signal and that the bomblet was powerful enough to blow some kind of hole in the wall. The signal was not blocked and the bomblet was powerful enough to blow a hole in the wall, although it took him some time to figure out what had actually happened as he gazed at all the pinkness.

'Pink?' he thought, 'why has everything gone pink?' It took him several seconds to realise that he was lying on his back, a few more seconds to realise that the pinkness was the afterimage of the bomblet's flash on his retinas, and then a few more to lift his dizzy head and see the last splinters of rock clatter down around him and a ragged twenty-odd metre gap in Capua's wall. Even then, he could only see around the pink blob still obscuring his view by using his peripheral vision.

Gingerly sitting up and looking back at the slave army, the pink blob forced him to swivel his head and eyes from side to side in order to get a full picture of the chaos that the explosion had caused among his new friends. Far from pouring into the city to exact revenge, the shockwave had knocked many of them over as well, and some appeared to be tending those who had been hurt by bits of flying debris. As for the cavalry, about thirty of them had managed to control their terrified animals, another twenty or so were scattered around the field where their horses had thrown them, and the rest were nowhere to be seen. Quite what had happened inside the parts of Capua nearest to the explosion, he dared not guess, but no one was to be seen near the wall's breach. Tarak had clearly not exaggerated the power of the bomblets.

Spartacus' phalanx of disciplined picked troops were the first to recover their composure and they began marching towards the breach. With the pink blob now clearing from his vision, Mark watched them pass while they turned to look at him in awe. Regaining his wits, he ran to join Spartacus at the head of his men. Spartacus welcomed him with a short but firm handshake and a wide-eyed expression of wonder, but no words. When they reached the breach, the only resistance they met was a few poorly aimed arrows. Spartacus directed some of his men to cordon off the breach from any would-be pillagers from his own army, some to scale the wall to either side of the breach, and the remainder to set up a curved defensive perimeter inside the breach. He then climbed onto a large chunk of broken wall at the deepest point of the defensive perimeter and bellowed: 'PARLEY, PARLEY, PARLEY.'

Mark scrambled over the debris behind Spartacus and stood beside him on the broken chunk of wall, thinking that he might be able to shield his hero with his force-field protected body if they were attacked. As he did so, he caught glimpses of blackened body parts in smoldering bits of clothing scattered among the ruins, and he knew that he had killed people after all. However, rather than feeling the crushing sense of guilt and shame that he would have expected, he merely felt numb and a little curious as to how many deaths he was now directly responsible for. He would have pondered upon his lack of emotional reaction to his multiple killings had it not been for around fifty Roman horse soldiers that cantered down a semi-ruined street towards them, and scores of runny-eyed, coughing, retching, spitting, scratching soldiers and armed inhabitants who came out of buildings into the street behind their cavalry now that the gas had largely dispersed.

When the lead soldier was well within bowshot, he raised a hand to halt his men, dismounted and strode to within three paces of where Spartacus and Mark stood.

Mark saw the Roman look towards the breach, and then looked for himself. He saw a sea of armed ex-slaves being held back from the breach by a line of Spartacus' men facing them and Andichios madly capering across the ruins of the wall screaming dire warnings that deadly diseases will infect anyone who disobeyed Spartacus' order to stay out of the city.

'What do you want, slave?' said the Roman commander.

'Peace,' Spartacus replied.

'At what price?'

'Release all slaves in this city and those that you still hold in the surrounding lands, to join us if they will or to go where they wish, even back to Capua if they choose to do so *after* leaving your city gates.'

'What else?'

'That is all.'

'And you will leave if I say this will be done?'

'We will leave if you give your word that this will be done immediately, but if you break your word we will come back and put every Roman within this city to the sword without a word of negotiation.'

Mark could see the commander flicking his gaze between Spartacus, Mark and the thousands of armed men waiting for the word to pour through the breach. While the Roman appeared to hesitate, more Roman soldiers were joining his men around the breach, and many among the slave army were becoming restive as they favourably weighed up their prospects for an attack on the suddenly exposed city before more Romans arrived to block them. With the first shouts for action being taken up by more and more voices, Mark looked back at the breach again and saw that many were starting to push forwards and jostle against Spartacus' picked men.

'I am sorry it has to be this way, Roman,' said Spartacus as he raised his right hand up and behind his head with his index finger extended in what could only be interpreted as preparing to signal a general attack.

'Wait!' said the Roman commander, 'I agree. I will begin releasing all slaves to you as soon as you pull your men back.'

Spartacus lowered his hand slowly with his open palm turned towards his army. 'Then let it be done,' he said, and turned back towards the breach with Mark and Spartacus' picked men falling back warily behind him.

Rani's black-clad figure ran up to Mark as soon as he walked outside the breach behind Spartacus and leapt up to scissor his body with her legs and arms and repeatedly kissed his face shield while many of her male comrades laughed, clapped and called out lewd comments concerning Mark's prospects for the night ahead. Andichios, looking very much like the demented monkey that Spartacus had spoken of, capered around the couple warning his teasing comrades that their private parts would rot and drop off if they dared to mock 'Mark the Great and Princess Rani', but no one paid him much attention.

'I wanted to join you in there,' she said when she unwrapped her arms and legs from him, 'but I wasn't allowed through! Stupid men!'

Mark could not think of anything to say, so he just held her hand and walked back towards the slave army's encampment while trying not to wince from the pain of his bruised ribs. As they walked, half of his mind wondered if and when he would react to the 'murders' he had just committed, albeit unintentionally and with what he felt were some pretty convincing reasons for thinking that he had done more good than harm in the wider scheme of things.

People started rushing forward to greet Spartacus and Mark before they got back to where they started, and the efforts of some of Spartacus' men to fend off the well wishers were not assertive enough to stop them being mobbed by relieved and cheerful people. They were not much discomforted, however, for the mobbing and well meaning jostling was soon replaced by a renewed surge of excitement and a generalised movement towards Capua's main gates as they were opened to allow a group of about fifty slaves to take their first uncertain steps to freedom in the mellow light of the late afternoon sun. Many hundreds soon followed, some of whom looked bemused and frightened while others raced towards their liberators in jubilation.

It had worked. As far as anyone could tell, all the slaves in Capua and the surrounding estates that still remained under Roman control were given their freedom, although not all of them chose to join the rebel army, far from it. Of the estimated fourteen thousand people who were either released from Capua or were unwillingly driven out of the city's gates during the rest of that day and night, only around three thousand joined the revolt. This was of course a welcome addition, but the other eleven thousand either scattered over the region or huddled fearfully together while they waited to be allowed back into the city as loyal slaves rather than risk Rome's terrible retribution.

While no one disputed that the assault had been a success, this success did not bring unanimity among the leaders of the rebellion regarding what advantage should have been taken of Capua's unexpected vulnerability, or what the ultimate aims of the slave army should be.

In the meantime, Kim was furious with Mark for not informing her of his intentions in advance and hugely frustrated to find that he was not answering her calls again. The normally shy, gentle, diffident Mark had clearly become a loose cannon. The consequences of his solo actions had already been utterly incalculable, and now she despaired of ever bringing him under control. To think that she had brought him to this world as a malleable backroom analyst would have been laughable had it not been so appallingly serious. Now, not only did she know that she could never undo this enormous error of judgment, the imminent arrival of an American expedition to New Earth must surely mean that she was about to be brought to account for her part in Mark's activities.

9
NO HALF MEASURES

Spartacus was quick to seize his opportunity. Within an hour of Capua's gates being opened, he had sent riders out to muster all available forces to join the main army as soon as possible. He then rode to where Mark and Rani stood watching the various responses of Capua's slaves as the rebels, most of whom had been agricultural slaves, greeted their city dwelling counterparts with food and encouragement. Mark assumed that he was about to be invited to a meeting with the generals where he would introduce Kim via his mobile, but Spartacus did not mention any meeting. Instead, he barely stopped his horse to say: 'we begin our march on Rome at dawn. I have despatched men to ride with Quintus until he joins us, and told them to treat him with all the respect due to an esteemed ally and future emperor of Rome,' and he rode off again without waiting for a response.

Mark was surprised by the suddenness of this announcement and uneasily aware that it meant cutting Kim out of the loop yet again, but Rani was impressed by Spartacus' decisiveness. 'There's no point discussing it,' she said, 'it would only waste time and cause confusion. What you did today has sent the army's spirits soaring and it will have frightened the Romans. Spartacus knows that now is the time to strike the decisive blow. Delay would just allow divisions to start creeping in on our side and give the Romans time to bring their legions back from their foreign conquests.'

This sounded sensible to Mark and he thought that Kim would understand the urgency of the situation, so he decided to call her and explain what was happening. As soon as he switched on his mobile's call function he found that Kim was waiting to speak to him, and she was in no mood to listen.

Her voice sounded outwardly calm as she berated him for not informing her in advance of his plan to attack Capua, but he had become sufficiently used to the changes in her intonation to realise that she was struggling to control herself. At first he thought she was merely angry with him, but then she dropped her bombshell: two pairs of American spacecraft had been detected as they hurtled through the outer solar system towards New Earth, one pair close behind the other. She said it was still about twelve days before they would arrive, although the relatively gentle rate of the craft's deceleration was consistent with crews who had emerged from suspended animation. This probably meant that they were already monitoring the Gandhi Institute's activities and would probably take a very dim view of Mark's blatant meddling. This was likely to be especially so for any fundamentalist Christians among their number who might feel that he was usurping God's plan for the planet more than seven decades before the birth of the second Jesus Christ.

Mark was badly shaken by this news. He had grown accustomed to being the only person from the home world left standing on New Earth, even though a part of his mind still wondered if Bernard had survived the American missile attack that he probably triggered in the first place, and might now be busily building an empire for himself in India. But even this notion had been fading in the absence of any news to that effect. It now seemed highly probable that Mark would be joined by an unknown number of people with weaponry that would make his piddling little gadgets look like children's toys and that they would be seriously pissed off by everything he had done so far, let alone the things he was still hoping to do. When Kim terminated the call he realised he had still not got round to telling her that the slave army was preparing to march on Rome rather than escaping to Gaul.

'Twelve days,' he thought, 'maybe I should stop intervening, but how can I let all these people down?' He looked again at the freed slaves leaving Capua and the excited people greeting those who were keen to join the revolt, encouraging the fearful or tearfully hugging loved ones with whom they were reunited. None of the historical archives on his own world said anything about the slaves of Capua being freed. This was his doing. The thousands of people that his activities had now directly affected would have millions of offspring over the centuries to come; or not, if they were killed in battle or crucified after Rome defeated them. Simply ceasing to intervene was therefore not an option given that what he had already done would reverberate throughout the future of this planet no matter what part he played from here on. He must therefore strive to make his interventions work out for the better rather than for the worse; and that, he decided, meant carrying out Rani's plan of breaching Rome's defensive wall and threatening to unleash the fury of the slave army upon them if they refused to accept Quintus as a puppet ruler.

On the other hand, for someone like Mark, who thought of himself as a shy and retiring man of peace, the idea of threatening the hundreds of thousands of people who lived in Rome with a storm of horrendous violence took some getting used to. To do this as an employee of the *Gandhi* Institute was a grotesque irony that would not be lost on the people watching him from space, nor on the billions of viewers who would probably end up watching everything he was now doing and the colossal carnage his meddling might cause before the Americans arrived to pick up the pieces. If it all went horribly wrong, saying 'sorry about that' was not going to be enough.

When they returned to the captured Roman villa where they were staying they found that most of the rooms now served as a hospital. Mark was greatly relieved when his earpiece translated the words of a nurse telling Rani that none of those present were injured by his 'lightning bolt' and that there were no reports that anyone among the slave army had been killed or seriously injured that day. The level of his relief made him think again about the unknown number of Romans he had killed. He still felt curiously unmoved by these deaths and wondered whether he was having trouble accepting his responsibility for them or if he had so completely taken sides that he was subconsciously dehumanising 'the enemy'. Either way, he found he could not summon up anything like the kind of guilt for causing their deaths that he would certainly have felt if he had caused the death of a single escaped slave. He was, however, uncomfortably aware that the Americans were unlikely to share his partisan view when they called him to account for his actions.

Finally alone in their room, Mark prepared himself for a night fretting about all his worries, but Rani had other ideas. While they ate a cold evening meal she talked incessantly and excitedly about an age of peace and freedom that would come when Quintus was their tame Roman emperor. After they had eaten she insisted that he lay on his front while she tenderly applied oil to his bruised ribs. As he relaxed and became sleepy, she gently worked oil into ever larger portions of his body. His mind skittered on the edge of sleep until the zones of her care brought him back to aroused wakefulness. Then he turned over and begun to massage oil into her body while she continued to rub oil into his, and they both became highly aroused. Once again, their coupling was fumble-free and like nothing that Mark had ever experienced on his own world.

They woke early. After hurriedly doing their ablutions, they walked around the encampment in the predawn light acknowledging well-wishers, accepting small gifts of food and listening to excited conversations through their earpieces while the army made ready for the march north.

Optimism in the camp had indeed soared after they witnessed Mark's power to break city walls, and rumour had it that this power was but a small token of the virtually inexhaustible abilities of friendly deities and foreign kings and queens. Mark was commonly hailed as the 'Mark the Great' who was sent to Earth by 'Kim, goddess of lightning'; and those who did not know Rani as a slave often spoke of her as 'Princess Rani, heir to the throne of Egypt'. All the talk was of marching on Rome and breaking open the city's walls with more bolts of lightning, but there were differing opinions of what they would do then. A majority of those they listened to thought that they were engaged in a grand campaign to force Rome to end slavery everywhere and forever, but a sizeable minority thought they were going to destroy Rome and make slaves of Romans.

Mark eventually plucked up the courage to call Kim and tell her what was going on. Tarak answered the call and said that Kim had retired to her sleeping cot looking exhausted and ill, leaving Tarak 'in charge of operations' until she returned. Mark felt a certain anticlimax at this, but also a sense of relief because he had always found Tarak easy to talk to. So he told Tarak what was planned and asked him what he thought about it all.

'What do I think about it? I think you're doing a fantastic job! I'm completely on your side. I just wish I could be down there with you, I would love to march on Rome with Spartacus and his army!'

'Really?'

'Absolutely!'

'You would be much more use to them than me.'

'Rubbish! I wouldn't have had the balls to sail up the Tiber like you did! I would have boarded a ship, took what I needed and continued on to India like I was told.'

'That would have been the sensible thing to do, I suppose.'

'Sensible? Yes, it probably would, but you've got more ambition than that, and I'm one hundred percent behind you!'

'Thanks, Tarak, I really appreciate that. What about Sunita and Rebecca, what do they think?'

'They went into suspended animation shortly before we picked up the American craft, but Sunita was behind you as much as I was. Rebecca was wavering, so was Kim, but mostly because they thought you would make a mess of things and get killed in the process.'

'You mean Kim isn't totally against intervening?'

'No, not totally, she's just doesn't want to do more harm than good, and she's a lot more cautious than you are.'

'You mean more sensible.'

'Maybe, but we are where we are, and Kim knows she can't just abandon you. My advice is to trust her, Mark, and let her and me help you as much as we can. I'll explain what's going on when she wakes up. In the meantime, I would suggest that you show Spartacus and his generals all your gadgets and let me and Kim talk to them about how they might be used to maximum effect while minimising casualties.'

'You mean that you and Kim will help us put Quintus in charge of Rome?'

'I didn't say that, but if that's what the generals decide to do then I can't see that we have any option other than trying to help them do it with the minimum loss of life.'

'Oh, thanks Tarak, I can't tell you how pleased I am to hear that. To tell you the truth, it has all been getting way too much for me.'

'Well, you have friends up here, Mark, if you will just let us help you.'

'I will, Tarak, I will. From now on I promise to do exactly what you and Kim tell me to do.'

'I'm not suggesting that you should have no say in what you do, just that you let us help you plan ahead and carry out your part as quickly and as peacefully as possible.'

'Gladly, Tarak, gladly!' said Mark, feeling as though a huge burden had been lifted from him.

As he put away his mobile, he realised that a horse rider was waiting patiently with two spare horses. When he heard the rider ask Rani if they would join Spartacus and his generals as they led the vanguard of the army out of the encampment, Mark grinned at her and she grinned back. With no words spoken between them, they leapt on their mounts and cantered off behind their guide as the sun began rising from behind distant hills. No longer feeling alone and afraid and responsible for everything, Mark allowed himself to be exhilarated by the moment and the sense of grand purpose that buzzed through the excited camp.

They were greeted by Spartacus in front of a host of horsemen and foot soldiers who held aloft swords and spears that glittered amber and gold in the sunrise, and cried: 'hail Mark the Great; hail Princess Rani.' They fell into step with the other generals at the head of a tightly regimented column of disciplined infantrymen wearing blue armbands, and the bulk of the army, including archers, slingers, and groups of women armed with fire-hardened wooden spears, began to uncoil itself from the sprawling encampment behind them.

There was a break in the middle of the disciplined infantry in which about thirty drummers tried to strike up an overly complicated marching rhythm on animal hides stretched across deep drums hung from their shoulders. At first it sounded as though they had not quite got used to their instruments and they suffered some good natured abuse before they silenced their discordant banging. Soon afterwards, a single drummer struck up a less ambitious rhythm and the rest followed suit. The *thrrrump, thrrrump, thrrrump-tump-tump; thrrrump, thrrrump, thrrrump-tump-tump* they settled on seemed to gradually synchronise the army's step and came to feel to Mark as though it were its heartbeat.

When they had marched three or four Roman miles, Mark looked back and saw that the column was still snaking out of the encampment. His mood of exhilaration remained undiminished until they approached six crucifixes, three on each side of the road, outside a walled farm complex. Four of the crucifixes held shrunken, blackened bodies while two stood empty and ready to receive their next victims. Several horsemen who were riding a few hundred metres ahead of the main army dismounted and hauled the bodies down before Mark got a good look, but he caught a disturbing glance of grinning teeth showing through what was left of their faces.

Rani saw him shudder, and said, 'they leave them up as a warning to other slaves who think about escaping.'

It was only then that it dawned on Mark that they were marching along the Appian Way, which linked Capua with Rome. On his own world, Marcus Licinius Crassus, the Roman general who finally defeated Spartacus, ordered six thousand of the defeated slave army to be crucified along this very road. This thought brought to mind the dream he had in his hotel room in Geneva when Spartacus had called him an arse with his dying breath. It was difficult to believe that he could really be here, about two years before the slave army of this world was due to be defeated and so many of them crucified along this now hateful-looking road.

Mark was not a great believer in mystical things, but he could not help wondering if the dream was some sort of premonition, or perhaps a sign that he really would have to choose between causing the deaths of thousands of Romans or letting the army that he now felt part of come to a tragic end. There were also the thousands of people, mostly women, children and old men, who were still camped upon the slopes of Mount Vesuvius to the south. How would they fare if their army never returned from its march north?

A few minutes after passing the crucifixes, he took the first of several calls that Kim would make to him that morning and into the early afternoon. Rather than sounding angry, her voice seemed weak and slightly shaky. She said that Tarak had briefed her about the march on Rome. Instead of objecting to this plan, she said they would provide him with what information they could from their remaining spy satellites to help the slave army avoid battle on its way north. However, her subsequent calls made it increasingly clear that avoiding battle was going to be extremely difficult.

Unlike the early piecemeal attempts to crush the rebellion on his home world, Mark's activities in Italy, including his little speech to the senators at Quintus' villa about more of his kind following him with deadly weapons and abolitionist views, appeared to have galvanised the Romans into pulling out all the stops.

Kim told him that strings of fire beacons were being lit on hilltops across the length and breadth of Italy, presumably to signal a general marshalling of forces; that a fleet of Roman troopships had put out from Ostia and turned south along the coast towards the rebel region, and that several unladen vessels built for speed had set off in directions that suggested they were heading for Roman armies stationed overseas, probably with the intention of recalling their legions to join the struggle in Italy. In her last call, she said that huge numbers of Roman troops were converging on Rome from the north and east while many of those already in the city had been gathered into what appeared to be the nucleus of two armies led by two generals, one of whom looked very much like Julius Caesar.

Mark's earlier mood of exhilaration ebbed further with each of these calls, and disappeared completely when she mentioned Julius Caesar. There were no more calls that afternoon, and little to dispel the feeling that he was drawing the thousands of people behind him into a giant Roman trap.

A halt was called in the late afternoon and the infantry plonked their weary bodies down upon whatever bit of ground they happened to stop at, or took a few paces to relieve themselves away from their comrades.

Spartacus indicated that their horse riding group should peel off the road to a large tent that was being erected under some trees. After Mark had relieved himself, he saw people handing out food to the army from baskets and wondered whether he should call Kim for a fresh bulletin or eat first when Andichios beckoned him into the tent as maps were being laid on the table within.

The scene inside the tent was much the same as their first meeting. However, although saddle sore again, this time Mark was not as tired or dehydrated or confused by the slave leaders' lack of resemblance to his preconceptions. Rani joined him and stood at his side while the generals faced them across the table and Spartacus got straight down to business.

'So,' he said, 'is Kim going to help us?'

Mark told them that she was and repeated all that he could remember of what she had told him during the day. Then he laid his gadgets on top of the maps and did his best to explain their uses and limitations and to answer their questions as honestly and as fully as he could. Finally thinking the time was right to involve Kim and Tarak in the meeting, he made to call them.

He had been looking forward to this moment, when he could finally hand over responsibility for the future to those who were better able to work out what should be done. But when he pressed the call button, his mobile said, 'call failed'. He tried again, and again, but the calls failed each time. Puzzled, he searched for a fault with his mobile and found that everything was working normally, except that he was unable to establish any kind of connection with his colleagues in space. After distractedly turning his mobile over in his hand a couple of times, he checked for messages. There was one unopened message from Kim, an hour-old email saying: 'Americans attempting to interfere with our connection. Stand by.' Nothing else.

'Stand by?' he said aloud, 'stand by for what?' and his mobile translated his words into Latin.

'Is there a problem?' Spartacus asked.

'I seem to have lost contact with Kim and the others,' Mark replied as he contemplated the idea of the Americans having the technology to cut all his links with the Gandhi Institute's spacecraft from such colossal distances. However they had managed it, he thought it probably meant they also had the technology to watch his every move, perhaps by hacking into the Institute's spy satellites, and that the support of Kim and Tarak would now be replaced by the judgement of furious Christian fundamentalists.

With nothing else to do or add to the meeting, he felt that his continued presence would distract the generals from piecing together what information they already had in order to plan their next move. After saying that he would keep trying to re-establish contact with Kim, he and Rani wished them good fortune and left them to it.

After grabbing some apples from a nearly empty basket, they rested under a tree and agreed that it was as good a place as any to pitch Rani's little tent, although neither made a move to do so. Mark was just beginning to refocus his thoughts on the implications of his communication problem when whistles were blown and the grunting and groaning soldiers got to their feet and set off again.

Mark spent long moments mesmerised by his horse's rhythmic movements and the thousands of leather-soled feet that thumped along the Roman road in time with the drums: *thrrrump, thrrrump, thrrrump-tump-tump; thrrrump, thrrrump, thrrrump-tump-tump.* When he forced himself to think it was as though his mind was in two worlds at once. Kim's last reports were extremely alarming, but part of his mind took comfort from the steady march of the slave army's disciplined core, even though it was probably taking him ever closer to a huge battle that is own activities had set in motion. Another part of his mind found no such comfort; he felt terribly alone and exposed under the hostile gaze of religious fundamentalists.

They carried on marching way after the sun had sunk. Eventually they came to a small town that had been deserted by most of its former inhabitants when they learned of the approach of the slave army. Mark and Rani stopped to pitch their tent under some tress before going into the town's large central square, which had been turned into one big dining area by forward elements of the army.

The town seemed faintly familiar to Mark, like one of the Tuscan towns he liked to holiday in back on his home planet. It was neatly cobbled and surrounded by prosperous-looking two and three storey buildings with small shops and cosy-looking restaurants on the ground floors. Lines of candle-lit tables and benches had been set up throughout the square. Lanterns were hung on lines stretched between regularly spaced trees. The overall effect was of a well-to-do tourist resort whose inhabitants and usual clientele had fled at the approach of a massive band of heavily armed football supporters.

When Spartacus caught sight of Mark and Rani he beckoned them to sit beside him, facing Crixus, Julian and Andichios at the centre of the square where they traded jokes and well meaning insults with the soldiers milling around them. Teams of men and women carrying baskets of food and watered-down wine brought some semblance of order as the tired and hungry foot soldiers set to their refreshments with gusto. Spartacus lowered his voice and asked Mark if he had heard anything from Kim.

'No, still out of contact I'm afraid.'

'Not to worry, you have already done us a great service at Capua. That lifted everyone's spirits and gained us a lot of recruits, not just those from Capua, but thousands of others who have been heartened by news of what we have achieved so far and are joining us as we march. We talked over some plans after you left our meeting and we think that it is still possible to carry out Rani's plan, although it looks like there will be a very big battle before we get to Rome. I know Kim wanted to avoid battles, but I don't think we can avoid this one, which I believe will take place the day after tomorrow. Would you be willing to help us win this battle?'

Feeling conscious of how any hesitation would appear to them and to Rani, Mark said 'yes, of course I would,' before he had time to give the matter any real thought.

'I'm glad to hear it,' said Spartacus. 'You see, we have not had time to develop into the kind of army needed to match big Roman armies in major pitched battles. I had hoped they would keep on underestimating us until we could develop that type of army, but something seems to have stirred them into a major effort and we badly need something to offset their advantages in numbers of trained soldiers, weapons, supplies, organisation, and perhaps most importantly, in cavalry.'

Mark was guiltily aware that he was the something that had stirred the Romans into making a far greater effort than they had at this stage of the rebellion on his own world. Given that Spartacus had pretty much depicted Rome as holding *all* the advantages, he was keen to find out what the battle plan was and what part he could play in redressing the balance. As they talked, Spartacus did not offer much detail, only that he hoped the Romans could be drawn into an impetuous attack against them and that Mark could use one or two of his three remaining 'lightning eggs' to drive off the Roman cavalry so that the slave army's much smaller numbers of cavalry could turn the Roman infantry's flank and fall on their rear. This sounded exceedingly bloody and not at all the kind of intervention he was hoping for. Although he nodded politely at what Spartacus said, he silently resolved to discuss his doubts with Rani when they were alone and see if they could come up with a less brutal way of doing things.

Having deferred any serious decision making, Mark found he was able to enjoy the evening. For the first time since his digestive system's violent reaction to wine at Quintus' villa, he allowed himself to drink a little of the wine that Spartacus poured in the goblet in front of him. He did so with care and moderation at first, but less carefully and moderately as the evening wore on and he soaked up the atmosphere of camaraderie that surrounded him. Had it not been for the initial foresight of watering the wine before it was brought to the tables, and then of Spartacus assertively insisting that everyone but selected guards turn in for the night, Mark and many hundreds of tipsy soldiers would have begun the following day's march with serious hangovers.

When they retired to their tent, which was now surrounded by hundreds of tents and thousands of people, Rani did her best to soothe the worried look that had crept back on his face as he repeatedly and unsuccessfully tried to contact Kim. Taking out the stopper from a small pot filled with the same oil that she had used the night before, she begun to oil his still bruised ribs again. For a moment Mark thought that his worries would not be so easily massaged away, but he soon found that he was not so preoccupied or so sozzled with wine that he could not rise to the occasion.

It was still dark when they were woken by the stirrings of the army and the smell of frying bacon. Men and women were distributing a surprisingly good breakfast of unleavened bread, several thick rashers of bacon, tender pieces of chicken, olives and a plentiful supply of apples. Spartacus and Crixus ambled over to their tent while they ate and enquired whether Mark had regained contact with Kim. He had not.

After the whistles blew and the march resumed, the morning hours passed much as they had the morning before. The drums beat, the soldiers marched, more escaped slaves swelled their ranks. In the afternoon, however, there were more periods of rest and the pace of the march was noticeably slower. The mood of the army seemed to grow edgy, as if the soldiers suspected that their slower advance betrayed uncertainty and indecision among their leaders. The generals were frequently approached by messengers and spent large portions of the day away from the head of the army on undisclosed errands while the column was halted and dawdled restlessly. When they stopped yet again in the late afternoon, Mark and Rani were invited to another meeting.

'Welcome!' said Spartacus brightly, 'are you still out of contact?'

'I'm afraid so.'

'Not to worry, we have news. I am told that one Marcus Licinius Crassus has been given overall command of Roman field forces in Italy and that he is now marching with a great army to crush us before we get to Rome. In addition, I hear that one Gaius Julius Caesar, who I understand you have met, has been put in charge of Rome's defences. Can you tell us anything about these men?'

Mark was not sure whether this was good or bad news. While he was relieved to hear that the Roman Senate had not chosen to put Caesar in charge of their field forces, they could hardly of made a better choice for their own defence. Crassus, who had defeated the slave army on Mark's world and crucified thousands of the survivors, was reputed to be a competent commander but without any of Caesar's military genius. He was also said to be prone to taking unnecessary risks in the hope of reaping the glory of victory rather than act in prudent coalition with other commanders. Indeed, although Crassus had won the final battle against the other Spartacus, he was widely accused of risking the destruction of his army just so that he could take all the credit before Pompey arrived with his army from Spain. Mark told Spartacus and the other generals all this, then gave a brief sketch of Caesar's brilliant later campaign to conquer Gaul and his subsequent rise to become emperor of Rome. He finished off his mini-lecture by saying that Caesar, along with Alexander the Great and Hannibal, was one of the three most revered military leaders ever to have lived on either of the worlds.

Having no real knowledge of their adversaries' abilities, Mark's audience was very attentive and appreciative of all he had to say. When it was clear that he had exhausted his knowledge, Spartacus thanked him and offered his hand for Mark and Rani to shake in a polite but obvious indication that their presence was no longer required. After they had taken several paces away from the tent, Mark turned and caught a glimpse of the generals bending over their map table listening to Spartacus speak as he swept his arms over the maps and made an expressive crushing gesture with his hands.

A few minutes later, the whistles blew and the army resumed its march while the sun hung low over the coastal plain. A double line of skirmishers was some way ahead on foot, lines of horse riders screened their immediate flanks and the silhouettes of distant outriders could be seen on low hills further out. Mark looked around at the people behind him. A slight curve in the normally straight Roman road allowed him to see a long way back, but not as far as the rear of the column. The army had grown to tens of thousands and was still growing as cheering groups of escaped slaves met them on the road or ran through fields to join them or pass them baskets of food to help them on their way. Others had gathered clusters of horses and carts, and the occasional opulent carriage, loaded with food or treasures looted from their former owners. At one point, Mark passed a field where three or four hundred fine-looking horses were corralled by a circle of men who were calling out for anyone who could ride to become 'cavalrymen'.

Mark did not know whether the Americans could see any of this in real-time, but he had little doubt that they would eventually have access to all the footage recorded by the Gandhi Institute's spy satellites, which would almost certainly be recording everything that he and those around him did in the open.

His mind then drifted to the impending battle. He could not fault Spartacus' logic for targeting the Roman cavalry with his bomblets. Even at six or seven hundred metres, the shock of the explosion at Capua had affected the slave army's cavalry much more than the foot soldiers. What is more, not one of them was killed. This certainly appealed to Mark's semi-pacifist approach to warfare, but there was likely to be a bloodbath if the Roman cavalry were chased off and their infantry were surrounded. A similar scenario had been played out at the battle of Cannae in 216 BC, when Hannibal's army of 54,000 men took on a Roman army of 87,000 men in what has often been held as an example of tactical perfection.

The bloodiest part of the battle occurred after Hannibal's cavalry had swept away the Roman cavalry from both flanks. While the cavalry battle was in full swing, Hannibal deliberately allowed his infantry lines to be bent into a C-shaped curve by the advance of the densely packed Roman infantry. Hannibal's cavalry then returned and hurled themselves against the open side of the C, thereby entirely encircling the Romans. Being pressed from all sides, the Roman infantry were compressed further until most of them were unable to wield their weapons. What followed was systematic butchery as 50,000 virtually helpless Roman foot soldiers were chopped to pieces.

Mark had read about Cannae with fascination and now wondered whether Crassus had the kind of temperament to march his army into such a trap. He also wondered whether Spartacus' sweeping arm movements over the map table represented the slave army surrounding the Roman infantry, and the crushing gesture of his hands had signified their extermination, much as Hannibal might have illustrated his plans before the battle of Cannae. Mark had no desire to replicate that kind of slaughter. On the other hand, he was having trouble thinking of an alternative that would not bring catastrophe for the slave army.

As he fretted over these two unacceptable alternatives, a rider approached and spoke to Spartacus. The rider tried to keep his voice down, but Mark's mobile was sensitive enough to pick the words up and translate them to him and Rani through their earpieces:

'Bad news, Spartacus. Hundreds of our people at Vesuvius joined the men you sent to fetch the fat Roman. They were trying to catch us up as you ordered but they were attacked by a large body of Roman horsemen who harried them towards the coast. There they were met by Roman soldiers who were landed by ships. It seems that they were then assailed from all sides and killed or captured.'

'Lili!' exclaimed Rani in horror.

'Quintus!' muttered Mark, feeling that their plans were falling to pieces. They looked at each other for a moment before returning to their own silent reflections. Neither could be sure exactly what this news might mean for all those still camped on or around Vesuvius, including most of the army's children, who were now cut off from their main army, or for the army that was now cut off from its stronghold. It was, however, fairly obvious that the Romans had closed off their retreat in preparation for a battle of annihilation.

10
BATTLE

It was not just the speed with which the messenger rode that made Mark, Rani and many others put aside the remains of their breakfasts and get to their feet. As he thundered towards the generals' tent from the north, he accentuated his urgency with a tight-lipped grimace that displayed a full set of tightly clenched teeth framed in a short but dense black beard. It seemed that everyone who saw him immediately knew that this was it; the battle that they had been expecting was about to burst upon them.

The bearded messenger had often reported to the generals since the army left Capua, and the two sentries posted outside their tent made no attempt to challenge him as he dismounted and strode inside to deliver his news. There was near silence for the two or three minutes that passed before the generals came out of the tent and calmly ordered their captains to get the army's foot soldiers up the hill that rose from the eastern side of the road, and the cavalry to gather on the road under Julian's command. Andichios then rode south along the road to hurry the tail end of the army to join them.

The sun had not yet risen, but the long sloping crest of the hill beside them was clearly visible against the lightening sky through gaps in the band of trees that grew between the road and the hill's craggy upper slopes. The army had reached this point in their march as the previous evening was turning into night, and it had seemed as though they had simply stopped at a random point because it was too dark to go on. However, when the infantry moved towards the wood's dense undergrowth they found they could easily file through the many passages that had been freshly cut through the brambles and wild vines. What initially appeared to be a knee-jerk reaction to news that the enemy was close at hand now looked very much like part of a prepared plan to do battle at a pre-selected time and place, and that the previous day's march had been deliberately slowed to fit in with the generals' schedule.

While the infantry were passing into the woods, Spartacus signalled Mark and Rani to join him in the command tent, which was now empty save for a large-scale map on its trestle table.

'We are strung along this section of the road,' he said, using his index finger to trace a section of the map that was roughly halfway between Rome than Capua. 'Crassus appears to have embarked on a headlong dash to engage and destroy us before Caesar gets a chance to take any glory for saving Rome. I dared to hope this might be the case after you told us what you knew about this man, and we have prepared accordingly. I only wish that we had anticipated his attack on our people who were bringing Quintus to us, but that cannot be helped now.'

'That could still have been Caesar's doing,' said Mark.

'Perhaps, but you said Crassus was a competent commander, and that he beat those like us in your home world, did you not?'

'Yes, he did, eventually,' said Mark, thinking that he really ought not to interrupt Spartacus again, especially when a Roman army was expected to arrive at any moment.

'Then I think we might make the double mistake of underestimating Crassus and becoming paralysed by fear of Caesar if we are too quick to think that all their best moves are Caesar's doing. Be that as it may, Crassus does seem very impatient. Most of his army has marched all day and all night, skirting around Rome from the north and covering more ground in one day than we have in two days. There are now around forty thousand men, including at least eight thousand cavalry, coming straight at us down this road. If they do not stop to rest, they will be here in under two hours. We are therefore in haste, and I have only called this meeting for one purpose: to ask you, Mark, if your conscience will allow you to accept what I am about to ask you to do. If not, then you are free to go where you want and do what you want.'

'What is it you want me to do?'

'I would like you to put two of your three lightning eggs in places that we have already selected, and then to watch what unfolds and make up your own mind as to whether or when you choose to use them to help us.'

'Could I just use them to scare their cavalry away?'

'That is up to you. My request is only that you place them in the positions that have already been chosen. After that, I cannot say for sure that any Romans will come near them, or if they do, whether you will decide to kill any of them or just frighten them. You may decide not to do anything at all. All I am asking is that you keep watch on the places where the eggs are placed and decide whether or not to set them off according to what your conscience tells you to do; that is all.'

This sounded eminently reasonably to Mark, and it did not actually commit him to harming anyone, so he agreed. Spartacus thanked him and asked them to follow him to the selected places while the two sentries began to dismantle the tent. The three of them were alone as they rode their horses through a neatly cut path through the wood.When they emerged from the trees they turned north along a track and then east over a shoulder of the hill. A grassy sheep-studded valley opened up before them. The ground dropped fairly steeply to a shallow dried-up streambed and then gently rose to another long sloping hill that was slightly taller but smoother than the one that the slave army was gathering on out of sight to their right. The distance between the crests of the two hills was about two kilometres.

Spartacus led them down into the valley to a point beside the streambed where a blackened tree stump stood on its own, and said that this was the first of the selected places. Mark got down from his horse and found a suitable tuft of grass to hide his bomblet. After fussing with it until he was satisfied that it could not be seen where it was cradled in the tuft a little above the ground, Spartacus led them at a fast canter alongside the dried-up stream under the gaze of the slave army, which was gathering on the craggy hillcrest to their right. They had been going slightly uphill, making the hillcrest appear lower as they went, and then it stepped down almost to the valley floor before rising again into another hill. They stopped short of a small stand of trees opposite the low point between the hills and Spartacus indicated that this was the second selected place. Mark found another suitable tuft of grass and hid the second bomblet.

When he finished fussing, they rode up a path that angled towards the centre of the army's position. As they did so, the silhouettes of four riders crested the hill on the opposite side of the valley with a sliver of the sun rising almost directly behind them, followed shortly afterwards by about twenty others who seemed to be pursuing them. The four being pursued rode hard for the safety of the slave army while their pursuers came to a stop on the crest and took in the presence of their foes until two of them rode back out of sight and the others split into two groups that rode in opposite directions across the hill's crest. The two groups each dropped off one rider at intervals until they were more or less regularly distributed and facing the entire slave army, and then they stopped and watched and waited.

Spartacus, Mark and Rani reached the centre of their army while this was going on. They dismounted and walked in silence to a small outcrop of rock from where they could see both of the places where the bomblets had been placed and all of the land between.

'Can you set the lightning eggs off at this distance?' Spartacus asked Mark.

'I think so, but I'm not sure.'

'Then I would suggest you keep hold of your horse in case you need to get closer to them,' said Spartacus as he turned and started to walk the hundred or so paces to where the headquarters tent had been re-erected in their absence. 'And you might want to put your suit on now,' he added over his shoulder.

'I meant to ask Spartacus why he was so sure that the Romans would attack us from that direction,' Mark said to Rani as he looked across the valley and absently checked his force-field suit's neck-seal.

'If they carry on down the road, then we could turn and attack them while they're strung out along the road. The Romans are not stupid, they know they have the advantage in open country like this,' she said, sweeping her arm at the valley before them.

As if waiting for her to invite them, a line of about three hundred horsemen topped the opposite hill and moved slowly downhill, fanning out as they went. Not far behind them, a dark mass started to appear and grow on the crest. As they focused on the mass, which wasn't an easy thing to do against the glare of the morning sun, it resolved itself into a column of men marching obliquely over the hill as though they were intending to bypass the slave army on their way somewhere else. The column was still emerging over the horizon when the head of another column appeared about a hundred metres beside it. Shortly after that, another column appeared, and another, until there were six columns crawling like centipedes at an angle across the hillside.

A distant chorus of orders floated across the valley, and the heads of all six columns turned abruptly to march straight for the slave army while rank after rank of those behind them turned at the same point so that the columns became dog-legged. When the two halves of the dog-legged columns were about equal lengths, another distant chorus of orders was heard and the back half of each column continued straight on rather than turning behind their comrades, thus separating the rear halves of the columns from the front halves. Shortly afterwards, another round of orders turned the rear ranks so that their line of march was aimed at the spaces between the forward ranks. There were now twelve shorter columns, six of whom were about fifty or sixty paces ahead of their nearest neighbours, when another shouted command froze them to the spot about halfway down their side of the valley.

At another series of shouted commands, rank after rank peeled sideways until the twelve columns had dissolved into streams of running men, half of whom moved to their right, half to their left. When the running stopped they had reformed themselves into squares. The result was a zigzag formation of twenty-four neat squares that could present a long block of infantry facing the slave army if the rearmost squares moved forward to fill the spaces between the foremost squares.

Mark could not help feeling stirred by the Roman army's display of discipline and precision, even though it was a killing machine aimed directly at him and thousands of people who had, he thought, quite reasonably and bravely decided to cast off their bonds of slavery and face killing machines such as this.

At this distance, however, the Romans looked like delicate little figurines. The sun's rays were now slanting down the hill and Mark gazed in rapture at the beautifully colourful fractures of light that sparkled off the Romans' shields, helmets, armoured shoulders and spear tips.

'Almost a shame to destroy them, isn't it?' said Rani in what Mark took to be an attempt at bravado rather than a genuine question, but it reminded him of a dream he had had in his hotel room in Geneva. In the dream he had a space-fighter to smash the pretty formations. He had no space-fighter now, although he could still smash a few of those squares if they walked over his bomblets.

Shutting the rest of the dream from his mind, he squinted against the sun's glare to work out the numbers of soldiers in each square and then used his mobile to work out the total size of the Roman army. There were twenty ranks of twenty to each square, giving four hundred per square. Multiplying this by twenty-four squares gave a total of nine thousand six hundred soldiers; 'no,' his conscience told him before he could stop it, 'nine thousand six hundred human beings'.

The small numbers of cavalry to show up so far plus the officers doing the commanding still only brought the total up to about ten thousand, or two Roman legions, although it looked to Mark to be a larger number than this when it was laid out before him. He was wondering where the rest of the Roman army had got to when the entire process of marching and forming squares began again with an equal number of men forming another twenty-four squares directly behind the first force, and then again by a third force directly behind them, giving an oblong checkerboard formation of seventy-two squares and a total of thirty thousand men. After a certain amount of shuffling, any spaces between the corners of each square were closed up, isolating four officers in each of the intervening spaces.

By then, several hundred others, presumably Crassus, his entourage and guards, had gathered upon the hilltop directly behind the Roman army, which more or less matched the slave army's frontage and was lightly screened by the six or seven hundred cavalrymen that had shown up so far. There were still no masses of cavalry on the Roman army's wings that Mark could frighten with his bomblets, but he supposed that they were being held out of sight, as the slave army's cavalry were, until they were needed.

He did not know how many fighters the slave army had and he could not see much of it over the folds of the hill behind and beside him, but he guessed it was around fifty or sixty thousand. Although it had reputedly risen to at least double this number during the course of the rebellion on his own world, it had only broken out a few weeks ago on this world and the army had not yet travelled far from its origin to gather recruits from many other parts of Italy as the other slave army had done so many centuries ago. Nonetheless, even allowing for the absent Roman cavalry, the slave army held a distinct numerical advantage on this day, although that advantage looked to be more than offset by the Romans' advantages in discipline, training, arms and organisation.

As he thought about these things, he suddenly realised that he had slipped into a feeling of unreality. Part of him felt like an uninvolved spectator while another part of him felt like a participant in a great game. He wondered if he was subconsciously blocking out the raw truth of what he was witnessing: it was the prelude to a monstrous orgy of violence. He shook his head in an effort to shake a bit of reality into himself, or at least to feel a bit of human compassion for those who were about to suffer horrible deaths, but he just could not register the enormity of what was about to happen. Giving up his vain attempts to summon up feelings of human empathy, he tried to focus logically on what he should do with his gadgets. As he did so, it came as a shock to find that he was in fact excited by what he was looking at, and hardly scared at all, either for himself or for those around him.

It seemed that Spartacus had chosen the places to put the bomblets rather well, although not perfectly. On Mark's right, the edge of the Roman army would just about walk over the bomblet near the stand of trees if they decided to advance straight forward, while those to his left would pass about five hundred metres short of the stump that marked the other bomblet; *if* they advanced. But they did not advance. Instead, after another chorus of commands the Roman infantry laid down their weapons, took off their helmets and body armour and then sat down on the grass and tucked into their pre-packed breakfasts.

The buzz of conversation and laughter drifted across the valley. More and more Roman soldiers finished eating and lay on the grass to doze in the morning sun. Horses dipped their heads and nibbled at the parched grass, scrawny sheep that had skittered away from their advance started to amble back again, and the whole scene on the Roman side of the valley looked and sounded like a massive, well organised club of hikers stopping for a picnic.

The atmosphere among the slave army was less relaxed. Having been keyed up by their adversary's advance towards them, they now began to question what they were doing in this place while other Roman armies might be coming at them from different directions. 'We should attack now while they're resting,' Mark heard one say through his earpiece, 'not let them decide when the battle starts.' 'We will be trapped if we stay here much longer,' said another.

This was beginning to worry Mark, and worry Rani too, judging by the questioning sidelong glances she gave him. He had suggested that Crassus was given to hasty and rash behaviour, but there was no sign of haste or rashness here. He was also aware that Crassus had deployed his forces in an innovative manner, not least in terms of the apparent lack of skirmishers, which were often used to goad Rome's enemies into battle. Crassus' novel deployments and his sudden lack of urgency might have been due to showy self-confidence, but Mark suspected they were actually a sign of a dangerously flexible mind.

An hour passed by, then another, and another, and still the Romans made no move. Indeed, some of them seemed to be lying in foetal positions on the ground, sound asleep and undisturbed by their officers. Meanwhile, the small signs of restiveness within the slave army appeared at first to grow a little before subsiding into pessimism. 'They've got us where they want us,' Mark heard, 'why would they hurry?'

This pessimism seemed all the more justified after a rumour rustled through the host that two other Roman armies were approaching them; one being landed by ships behind them, the other, formed from the garrisons of Capua and many other places, drawing close from the south. These rumours, and worse, were soon confirmed by Spartacus when he joined Mark and Rani on the rocky outcrop.

'The Romans have summoned all their forces from the regions to our south and east and are force-marching them here by the thousands,' he begun without preamble. 'Our scouts report that a fleet is disgorging troops along the coast a little to the south of us and an army is marching from Capua to met them.. Another large force of cavalry from Rome are linking up with units sent from the Apennines, and they are now closing on us. Crassus does not play his part as I hoped he would. It seems that he just wishes to hold us here for a day or two so that he can double his number, or perhaps to invite an ill-prepared attack from us.'

'What will you do?' asked Rani.

'We do not have much choice. We cannot stay here while the Romans collect all their strength and cut us off from reinforcements. We must attack today.'

'Can we get to them before they put their armour back on?' she asked.

'No, they are very well trained, they will be ready.'

'Can we beat them?'

'No, not if Crassus is patient. His legionaries can grind us to bloody ruin on their side of the valley. We might

205

hope to draw them to our side of the valley if Crassus sees an opportunity to crush us quickly, but that means exposing ourselves much more than I would like.' Then Spartacus turned to face Mark, who had so far remained silent and downcast by his misrepresentation of Crassus as an impetuous commander. 'If they can be drawn to attack, then you may be presented with a problem.'

'What?' asked Mark.

'I expect they will be close on our heels, cutting many of us down as we run. If that is the case, there will be no space between us and them in which you can use your lightning eggs to frighten them. You may have to choose between setting the eggs off below their feet or let them continue to cut us down.'

Mark could not think of anything to say, so he looked away from Spartacus' searching gaze and stared at the ground between them, until Spartacus said, 'I am sorry if you think I am trying to force your hand. I did not want this, any of it, and it is not your fight. May your conscience be your guide. Goodbye and good luck.' With that, he turned and strode off to do what he could to kick-start the battle.

The slave army begun to deploy in the heat of the early afternoon. Movements of men and horses within and behind the army alerted the rest that something was about to happen. Without being asked to, most of them picked up their weapons and pressed forward to get a better view over the valley. This alerted the Romans that something was afoot. No orders were heard from across the valley, but those still asleep were woken by their comrades and there was a generalised bustle as they put their armour back on.

A few minutes of expectant near-silence passed before a great deal of pushing and shoving rippled through the slave army as selected infantry captains wearing blue armbands bawled and pushed and bullied the army into separate segments, which the captains referred to as 'divisions', each of which consisted of around eight thousand largely untrained and poorly armed men and women. Six columns of disciplined infantry, about one thousand per column, then marched through the gaps in the divisions and picked their way down the steepest section of the hill. Commands rang out for the rest of the army to stay in their allotted divisions and only move when they were told to. The six columns formed into six widely spaced phalanxes below them and marched slowly forward while two streams of cavalry issued from each end of their hill and passed the flanks of the outermost phalanxes.

When the Romans saw this, the few hundred cavalry that screened the front of their army withdrew to either side like two curtains opening on a well rehearsed play and gathered into an oblong block at either flank. Two of the rearmost infantry squares on each Roman flank then dissolved as they ran towards their small cavalry wings and reformed into two lines behind them.

With no one to interfere with their movements, the slave army's cavalry, which Mark estimated at around one thousand five hundred on each flank, split into four roughly equal groups. One of the groups stopped three or four hundred metres beyond the tree stump where he had hidden one of his bomblets and one a similar distance beyond the stand of trees near to where the other bomblet was. The other two groups rode towards each other between the two hostile armies and spread themselves out in a line and wheeled to face their own phalanxes of marching infantry. When the phalanxes reached the horsemen, they halted.

After a minute of comparative quiet, the infantry captains on the hill led five of the big divisions down the slopes and into the large gaps between the six phalanxes. They stopped at the line of their own cavalry that faced them, and their captains shouted and pulled at them until they had shuffled themselves into an unbroken mass bristling with spear tips pointed at their enemies. When the captains were more or less satisfied, they distributed themselves in the front ranks of the infantry and the cavalry screen drew aside and joined their comrades on the flanks. While this was going on, another two larger columns of about two thousand men each moved forward from either side of the slave army's hill, marched inside their cavalry wings and joined the flanks of the main infantry line in two dense phalanxes that slightly overlapped both Roman flanks. The slave army's ability to send forth around ten thousand disciplined infantry in their phalanxes surprised Mark.

'I didn't know we had that many trained infantry,' he said to Rani.

'We haven't, they're paired up. Half of them had military experience before they were slaves or have fought or been trained since the rebellion started. When they go into battle, each experienced man is matched with one who has little or no military experience. That way they double their numbers and the old hands teach the newcomers their trade and stop them from panicking. They do the same with the cavalry.'

'Oh,' said Mark, not sure whether he was to blame for the need to send so many military novices to face a professional army because of their reckless dash on Rome that his presence had initiated.

While they had been speaking, two columns of about five hundred men each, all of whom carried bows, marched from each side of the hill behind fifty or sixty horsemen. The two groups of horsemen stopped a little way behind the cavalry wings and a few paces in front of where the two bomblets had been placed, and dismounted while the archers formed loose circles around them.

'That's Spartacus, in the middle of those archers' said Rani pointing to the circle on their right, 'and Crixus,' she said pointing to the left, 'I recognise their horses.'

She must have had better eyesight than Mark because he could not distinguish them at that distance, but he felt sure she was right when he saw several individual riders fan out from the circles to other parts of the army as though carrying orders. When these had reached their destinations, the sun beat down on the two stationary armies for several minutes and nothing happened. The entire slave army now seemed prepared and the Romans had not made the slightest attempt to interfere.

Mark and Rani and thousands of non-combatants, mostly children, their mothers and the very old, watched from the crest of their hill while the two static armies faced each other across about half a kilometre of knobbly grassland. The slave army did not look as impressive as the Romans did, but they outnumbered them by almost two to one, they were leavened with a few thousand experienced and disciplined fighters and their line slightly overlapped the Roman's on both flanks. However, although the slave army's three thousand cavalry could currently roam more or less at will over most of the valley, the missing seven or eight thousand Roman cavalry had yet to show their hand. Finally, whistles trilled from the circle where Rani had spotted Spartacus, then from where she had seen Crixus, and the battle began.

Other than the circles of archers who surrounded the two generals, the entire slave army moved forward at a steady pace. As the great block of infantry advanced a few arrows and stones thrown by slingers were loosed at the Romans from the big divisions but fell short. Just before they came within range, the second line of Roman squares moved forward by the fifty or sixty paces it took for them to slot neatly into the gaps between the first line of squares. They now presented a solid twenty-man deep line against their attackers, leaving the remaining forty-four squares where they were to deploy as need arose. Arrows and stones begun to move closer to the Romans' front line until they pattered off a wall of large oblong shields held together by their front rank and a roof of shields held up by those behind them.

All the arrows and stones came from the big divisions while the phalanxes and the Romans both sheltered behind their interlocking shields and held their fire. Mark did not see anyone fall until several ranks near the front of the Roman army momentarily lowered their shields and loosed a wave of spears and arrows. These did little damage to the phalanxes but felled dozens among the big divisions. This painfully one-sided process was repeated three times before the armies met, and several times more as the front ranks of the slave army hacked and prodded ineffectually at the Roman wall of shields. Many more among the big divisions were cut down by a flickering line of short double-edged swords jabbing through narrow gaps between the Roman shields which opened and closed again in an instant. The fighting between legionaries and the more cautious phalanxes of the slave army continued in virtually bloodless stalemate, but in the broad spaces between it was as though the Roman army was a giant chainsaw being attacked by tender saplings.

Meanwhile, the slave army's cavalry led the two larger phalanxes past the Roman flanks and clashed with the smaller numbers of Roman cavalry who gave way while their supporting legionaries took a steady toll of their mounted attackers with flights of spears and arrows. Although the slave army was now taking heavy casualties across most of it frontage, the Romans were being threatened with a double envelopment as the two large phalanxes turned behind their still advancing cavalry and made for the Roman flanks at the double and in good order. The Romans had seen this coming and reformed unengaged squares from the rear of their army into two deep lines with shield walls facing the double threat. But the men in these two phalanxes, many of whom had been selected for their strength, were fronted by ex-gladiators and ex-military men who knew how to work their short swords from behind their own shield walls, and they barrelled into the Romans with a dense mass of men pushing them from behind like a massive scrum of rugby players. The Roman lines shuddered under their impact and grudgingly gave ground on both flanks.

For a few moments, Mark thought that the slave army might just manage to scrunch the Romans up into a helpless mass, much as Hannibal's army had managed to do to such lethal effect at Cannae. However, this thought was soon overtaken by alarm as thousands of Roman cavalry appeared over the crest on their side of the valley and started to thunder downhill to outflank both wings of the slave army, threatening to reverse the outcome.

All the slave army's forward movements stalled as some of their best infantry and most of their cavalry reacted to the urgent trilling of whistles and cries for assistance. Hastily formed lines of infantry attempted to provide a protective screen for the main army's flanks, but found themselves largely uninvolved while their cavalry engaged in a running fight against their far more numerous foes. However, Crassus' cavalry were not aiming to break the slave army's forward flanks against stiff opposition; that would risk allowing the bulk of the ex-slaves to escape. Instead, they were set on riding over the very vulnerable-looking circles of archers that protected the rebellion's leaders, and then sweeping into the backs of the 'rabble' they led. Caught between the cavalry and the legionaries, the entire army could then be crushed like lice between fingernails.

The slave cavalry could not hope to stop the storm of Roman horsemen from completing their pincer movement, and so most of them eased up their efforts and waited to be joined by whatever infantry could be spared and gathered at haste from the main battle. As with all of the battle so far, what happened next on one flank was more or less repeated on the other flank.

At prearranged signals, the two circles of archers broke up and ran to their allotted positions. Half of them formed a thin line angled to face the horsed onslaught. The other half gathered in small regularly spaced groups directly behind the thin line, and each of these groups had a team of four horses that were faced away from the coming attack as though to offer the leaders a method of escape. It looked to Mark as if they were preparing to sacrifice the archers, perhaps with the intention of slowing the Roman cavalry down so that they rode over his bomblets in a dense mass. With a heavy sense of foreboding and anticipated guilt, he drew out his mobile and entered the first six digits of the seven digit code that would, if he was not out of range, wreck the Roman attack in a welter of bloody bits of human and horse flesh.

Much to his surprise, however, when he thought that the Roman cavalry were about to run down the scanty lines of archers that opposed them, no one mounted the teams of horses. Instead, the horses had been harnessed to ropes that lay hidden in the tufty grass and they were now lashed forward while the small groups of men also heaved on the ropes. There were ripples of movement running towards the Roman cavalry and the ropes pulled up a quadruple line of sharpened stakes that locked into position at a forty-five degree angle facing the Romans.

The stakes were not very close together and none of the Romans or their horses were impaled upon them, but when their front ranks tried to pass between them they were thrown from their tumbling mounts by the score. Mark could not make out the nets that were strung between the stakes, but there was no mistaking the carnage they caused as they tripped the horses by their legs and entangled their hooves. Others who either failed to pull up from their headlong charge or fell under volley after volley of arrows quickly added to the sprawling mess of writhing horses and men that was stacking up in front of the thin slave lines. Although the vast majority of the Roman cavalry had managed to stop short of the nets, all five hundred archers on each flank poured arrows on the milling mass of horsemen as they sought to go round the traps and fall upon their tormentors.

At that moment, two more of the slave army's big divisions, led by two colourful clown-like figures that both looked like Andichios, roared down the lower slopes at the ends of their hill screaming war cries behind a few dozen more of their horsemen and charged at the disorganised Roman cavalry. This was too much for the Romans and they turned back to the safety of their own army. But the mixed force of cavalry and infantry that had been gathered to protect the slave army's forward flanks had now deployed to bar the Roman cavalry's return. Bemused, demoralised and depleted, the surviving Roman horsemen baulked at the prospect of fighting the mixed force in front of them while thousands of screaming newcomers were advancing on their rear and lines of archers took turns to fire upon them while others moved in for a closer shot. After a brief moment of hesitation, a few Romans bolted along the valley floor away from the battle and the rest soon followed in disorder, leaving their dismounted comrades and crippled horses to be dispatched by swords, knives, clubs and arrows fired at close range.

Many of the slave horsemen chased them and hacked down stragglers with the kind of blood lust that often overtakes people when mortal fear is suddenly infused with the joy of victory, but most eventually responded to the whistles and shouts of their leaders who were trying to reform them to join the main battle.

Mark and Rani were both infected by some of this feeling as they watched with clenched fists thrust in front of them as though they were dealing blows to the enemy. With their mouths working gargled sounds of encouragement that none in the army below them could hear, they and thousands of others on the hill watched their horsemen being gathered into some kind of order behind their captains and then ride up the Romans' side of the valley to either side of the main battle. When they reached the crest of the hill they wheeled and headed straight for Crassus and his entourage from both flanks.

The leaders of the Roman army did not stay to witness the rest of the battle, but departed in haste on horseback before the slave cavalry could catch them. Their pursuers were again called with whistles and frantically shouted orders to break off the chase, and most of them again responded. With no one to stand in their way, the two wings of the slave cavalry rode along the crest until they met behind the Roman infantry squares.

More than half of the cavalry were still skirmishing with the Roman cavalry, who were beginning to rally after their flight along the valley floor, or had become casualties, or were chasing Crassus, or were simply too inexperienced to control their excited mounts. Even so, by the time the command to attack rang out, over a thousand horsemen had formed into a solid oblong mass with Julian and his disciplined core of African cavalrymen at their centre. Furiously jabbing their mount's flanks with their heels, they surged down the steepest part of the hill with blood-curdling shrieks just as the two clown-like figures, one of whom was Andichios and the other his trainee conjurer-cum-general, led their two divisions into the main battle line and the heavy phalanxes renewed their drive into the Roman flanks.

Roman infantry officers at the rear of their army managed to form several squares into a credible defensive line before the slave cavalry struck, but many of their foot soldiers cringed in fear and backed away from the horses and screaming riders that were about to pound into them at full tilt, leaving their wall of shields ragged and porous. A few of those who held their ground got in blows that felled a number of men and horses, but even dead and dying horses were lethal weapons as their downhill momentum kept them skidding, tumbling and flailing through several Roman ranks, scattering soldiers around like tenpins. Without a solid front to absorb the shock of the onslaught, the Roman formations quickly disintegrated into masses of fleeing men, many of whom were mercilessly cut down with swords, spitted in the back by spears or trampled under the ferocious cavalry charge.

Seeing the Roman army crumple at the rear, the slave phalanxes and divisions drove their attacks home with the fury of people who had seen many of their comrades go down from wave upon wave of spears and arrows or cut down by sword thrusts without being able to come to grips with their assailants. The Romans in the front ranks were still holding their ground and taking a steady toll of the novice foot soldiers who opposed them. However, those on the flanks, although they doggedly resisted, were subjected to such bone-crunching pressure from the shield walls of slave army's heavy phalanxes that their leather-soled feet were beginning to slide over the trampled grass as they were heaved backwards onto their struggling comrades.

Meanwhile, the slave cavalry's charge was losing some of its initial momentum, but their killing spree had sent swarms of panicking legionaries to seek shelter in unbroken squares, spreading ripples of will-sapping fear throughout the army as they went, including those on the hard-pressed flanks. When the flanks finally gave way, the entire Roman army started to collapse in on itself. The front ranks held their ground a while longer, but their lines were becoming compressed and concertinaed by those being driven onto them from behind and to each side.

Neat Roman squares in the middle of their army buckled under the weight of their own comrades from other disintegrating formations without ever having the chance to use their weapons, and found themselves being remorselessly pushed towards those still stoically fighting in the front ranks. The oblong shape of the Roman army soon shrunk into an oval-shaped ball that squeezed the spear throwers and archers within until they no longer had room to loose their missiles. Eventually, all their missile fire ceased and the stabbing thrusts of the Roman short swords grew fewer and more ineffectual as the floundering legionaries were pressed tight together under a rain of incoming missiles. Even their dead and dying could not sink to the ground. As their resistance dwindled on the outer edge of their ever smaller oval, many of the Roman foot soldiers were struggling to breathe against the mounting pressure on their chests.

It is a vile thing to have the life squeezed out of you by the press of thousands of people. Thankfully, a group of Romans near the left of their army used their wits while they still had space to move. Hoisting one of their officers up to stand on their shoulders, he called SURRENDER, SURRENDER, SURRENDER and kept calling until two more officers were raised up to join him and some of the slave army's captains began calling HOLD, HOLD, HOLD while those Roman soldiers that could still move a little began throwing their weapons at their adversaries feet.

Not everyone wanted to stop the killing and it took some time to stop it all, but it did eventually peter out with the ring of hundreds upon hundreds of Roman weapons being flung into the spaces that the slave army captains were bullying their comrades to open up. Those at the back of the slave army started to understand what was happening and stopped pushing forwards, and some of the frightened Roman infantry raised their hands and took their first tentative steps over piles of surrendered weapons towards their scowling captors.

Mark slowly let out a pent up breath as he watched the battle end, a battle in which he had, if necessary, been prepared to blow a large number of people and horses to pieces, but he had not been required to do so after all. He doubted whether this would appease his future accusers from his own world, although he was greatly relieved nonetheless; and just a little disappointed that he had not played an active part in the victory.

11
LADYBIRD

Mark would have thought the battle had lasted for many hours had it not been for the sun still riding high above the western side of the valley when it ended. There was still the horrendous aftermath to deal with, although he was spared these horrors by the chain of events that followed. After taking off his force-field suit, he and Rani fetched their horses and picked their way down to the valley amid hundreds of non-combatants who went to help the wounded, but his first task was to recover the unused bomblets. The fighting had not passed over the bomblet by the tree stump and Mark found it still nestling in its hiding place. As they were heading towards the other hiding place they were intercepted by Spartacus, who handed the second bomblet to Mark and asked them to follow him and three other horsemen. He did not say where he was taking them but he was clearly in a hurry. They made for the Appian Way and headed south at a good clip.

After riding two or three kilometres past an almost unbroken line of the slave army's supply carts that had been parked off the road during the battle, they turned down a track to their right and rode in single file until four armed but smiling men stepped out of the trees in front of them. The men wanted to congratulate Spartacus and talk to him about the battle but he had more pressing things in mind. As Mark listened to the men answer Spartacus' questions through his earpiece he understood why he had been summoned to this place in such a hurry. The sea was ahead of them and three Roman legions, about fifteen thousand men, had landed on the beach and moved cautiously inland some time ago, but had apparently begun to pull back again, presumably on hearing of Crassus' catastrophic defeat. In the meantime, a detachment of Roman soldiers had arrived from the south with Quintus and about four hundred recaptured slaves, and these captives had since been rowed out to the ships still anchored offshore.

'It seems we are too late,' Spartacus said to Mark. 'I hoped you might help us get our people back, but they are on the water now.'

Although they had arrived too late, Spartacus seemed reluctant to give up on his comrades, and most of those present looked at Mark in silence as if they still hoped he would perform some kind of miracle. Feeling powerless and slightly flustered by their expectant gaze, he said something about trying to contact Kim and checked his mobile for messages. He was still cut off from the Gandhi Institute's spacecraft, but a small automated dialogue box appeared for a few seconds at the bottom of the screen. It read: 'GI3653 detected in passive mode'.

'GI3653?' he muttered inaudibly and stared at the dialogue box until it winked out, and he continued to stare at the now blank space until he thought he remembered why the digits seemed familiar. The inboard computer on his boat, the *Ladybird*, always displayed GI3653, or something very like that, in the top right-hand corner of its screen for a few seconds after he switched it on. 'The *Ladybird*?' he said, loud enough for his mobile to translate his words into Latin. Still staring at his inert and uninformative mobile, he asked, 'how close are we to the sea?'

'About two miles,' said Spartacus.

'Can I have a look?' he asked, finally looking up.

'At the Romans?'

'No, at the sea, as far from the Romans as possible.'

The *Ladybird* had spent seven and a half days securely bound in chains that were attached to steel rings set into an old dry dock housed in a converted warehouse next to the Tiber. With help from the iron foundry next door, the boat's captors had finally managed to break through the top of its astonishingly resilient dome by softening it up with a steady stream of molten iron while a great metal ingot shaped into a razor sharp point on its underside was winched to the warehouse's ceiling five metres above the boat and dropped onto the dome's soft spot. This and earlier attempts to break in had left the *Ladybird* looking very sad and dishevelled, but they had not penetrated the hull and the inboard computer, the GI3653, was sealed in a chamber in the boat's extra-tough bow, which was designed to resist the best efforts of thieves who knew what they were looking for and had far more sophisticated methods at their disposal.

The GI3653 / *Ladybird's* circumstances only changed when Rome suddenly increased its naval activity. This put pressure on shipwrights and many other tradesmen to get every ship that happened to be in Rome or Ostia ready to carry troops and supplies south along the coast to help snuff out the slave rebellion. The old dry dock in which the *Ladybird* was kept was too small for such work, but the knock-on effects on private repair contracts made every dock all the more valuable.

The gruff old shipwright who owned the dock got up very early every morning and expected everyone else to do the same. First thing on this particular morning, he decided to pay the boat's tormenters a visit and ask them how long they were going to be with their foolish experiments. Finding no one there, he gave a snort of derision at the pathetic sight of the badly damaged little boat bound by enough chains to anchor a large ship in a gale-force wind.He uncoupled the chains from the metal rings, slid them off the boat and found he was easily able to pull the super-light boat up the ramp without calling for help. Dragging it to one side, he left it unchained on the stone floor while he went to organise a more sensible and profitable role for his misused facility.

As soon as he took his hands off the boat and started to walk away, it silently rose by about two centimetres and begun to roll forwards on three little wheels without the old shipwright noticing. When he pushed one of the warehouse's two big wooden doors open, he felt something brush past his arm and he leapt aside as fast as his gouty feet would allow. He was too slow or too afraid to react to the surprising sight of the boat gliding past him with its crippled dome opening like shattered beetle's wings and its still perfectly intact solar panels emerging from its stern. He simply watched it weave through the nautical junk in his riverside yard, drop lightly off the wharf and gently plop into the Tiber.

The shipwright was alarmed by the sight of a boat launching itself, but still more alarmed at the thought of what the soldiers might do to him if they found that he had let it go. Looking around, he could not see any other early risers about, so he quietly closed the warehouse door without locking it and padded off hoping that the soldiers would think the mysterious little craft had been stolen or had magically made its own escape, which in a sense it had.

Going with the seaward flow of the river, it was not long before the *Ladybird* reached the barrier of boats chained together. None of the bored and sleepy guards saw it approach them. It was not that they were completely neglecting their duty, just that the main point of them being there was to make sure that vessels coming into Rome had paid the appropriate tolls and taxes, not to guard against vessels heading away from Rome. By the time a guard saw it and nudged his comrade's arm, the little boat had glided through the few centimetres of water that flowed over the low point in the chain between two of the barrier's boats. From then on it would have taken some very swift and decisive action to catch the boat before it reached the sea, and no one on the river that morning showed much inclination to act swiftly or decisively.

The *Ladybird* sailed as quickly as its partially mutilated form could manage. Its goal, or rather the goal of the GI3653 onboard computer, was to position itself in a navigable stretch of water as close as possible to the living owner of a recognised DNA code. Having passively recorded electronic communications between the surface of the planet and space, it had identified the location of one living owner of a recognised DNA code and everything it now did was geared to getting near the owner of that code.

Having figured out what the GI3653 was, Mark hoped that the *Ladybird* had escaped and was tracking his movements, although if that was the case it might also mean that his presence so close to the Roman beachhead and their fleet was causing the boat to risk being recaptured.

When he asked to look at the sea, there was something about his expression and tone of voice that communicated his sense of urgency to Spartacus, who said 'this way' and spurred his horse back up the track. He paced his horse to allow Mark to catch up and ride beside him. Mark said it did not matter which bit of sea they went to so long as they found a bit away from the Romans.

Thirty-odd minutes later, Mark's companions watched as he jumped from his horse and raced into the surf while the *Ladybird* lowered its crippled wings and fluttered them as if it was excited by his return; although it was in fact trying to retract the two halves of its dome into its body but they were too misshapen. He stopped and tentatively reached out his fingers to touch the dome's shattered membrane and the fluttering ceased. As he tenderly traced his fingers around the edges of her wounds, their audience on the beach had no reason to think that the seemingly loyal little boat was not a living thing that had suffered greatly in its master's absence and was now being calmed and reassured by his gentle caresses.

Looking up from the emotional reunion, those on the beach saw the first of several small Roman galleys advance around a headland with nets droopily strung between them. For the chase to have become this determined probably meant that the *Ladybird* had been hovering in the area for some time while evading earlier attempts to capture her.

Rani called out a warning and Mark saw the ships. He raced back up the beach to collect the sack that held all his possessions from his horse and then ran back to the boat with Rani close behind him. He tried to stop her climbing aboard, fearing that she would merely provide Roman archers with an unprotected target, but she was plainly having none of it and he soon gave up protesting and let her aboard.

He managed to manually steer the boat past their pursuers out of bowshot range, then climbed into his force-field suit while the boat passed well behind the much slower Roman galleys. He was still trying to form some kind of coherent plan when the main Roman fleet and landing force hove into view.

Sailing in an arc around the back of the fleet while he considered his options, he saw that the Romans were starting to send empty landing vessels, which each of their fourteen large warships towed in a line behind them, back to their now vulnerable army waiting to disembark from the beach.

When they turned for another observation run Rani squeezed his arm tightly with her hand and pointed to one of the warships. Despite the still air, a piece of russet-brown cloth flapped from one of its oar portals. No hand appeared through the portal, but they had little doubt that the cloth was being waggled by some poor galley slave who was putting himself at risk of a lethal flogging with this small act of defiance.

'We have to help them escape,' she said, but in an uncertain tone that suggested her compassion for the ranks of chained slaves who rowed the warships' oars was vying with her fear. He had not paid her much attention after they set off from the shore, but now he looked at her face and guessed, rightly, that she had never been to sea and that she was feeling completely out of her element. For all her strong and determined character, it seemed that he would have to be the strong one in this environment.

'Yes,' he replied with uncharacteristic decisiveness and unfounded certainty, 'we will.'

Given that the thin membrane of the *Ladybird's* dome/wings had obviously required the Romans to resort to drastic measures to break into, Mark had at least worked out that it was resilient and there was enough of it left to shield a crouching person from all but the luckiest overhead arrow shot. He explained this to Rani and found her to be unusually compliant and eager to do what he asked, which essentially amounted to keeping out of harm's way while he did whatever needed doing from behind the protection of his force-field suit. He thought this was probably a good thing, given their circumstances and unequal knowledge of technology, although he secretly wondered whether his bold promise to help free the fleet's slaves owed more to his desire to impress her than to his ability to deliver. However, having made his promise, he found himself aiming the *Ladybird* at the waving russet-brown piece of cloth and simply hoping for the best.

Their progress was watched by more than twenty people on the ship's deck. By the time they got within a hundred metres, the number watching had dropped to seven or eight. Mark had expected more people to watch as they drew nearer, not fewer, and it was this that made him wary of what the missing Romans were up to.

With one hand gripping the boat's tiller and the other fidgeting with the gas canister in his pocket, he was as alert as he could be for any signs of danger. He did not want to use the gas, especially with all those slaves chained to their oars, but he figured that it was the best weapon he had for quickly disabling large numbers of attackers. He also hoped that the rowers in the lower deck would be protected from the worst effects of the gas by the upper deck. However, if the gas was heavier than air, some of it might swirl over the decking and drift back down to the *Ladybird*. The fumes were not a problem to him; his suit's air-filters had kept him from breathing them in at Capua, but he did not want Rani to suffer from them.

When he edged closer to talk to the ship's occupants, his suspicions about the missing Roman sailors proved to be amply justified. Immediately after calling out: 'Romans, in the name of the goddess Kim, I demand to speak with your captain' he heard the rattle of winding gear and the squeak of heavy timbers grinding against each other. A large wooden structure, standing above the deck of the Roman ship like a davit (ship's crane) with a great metal spike jutting from its upper end, quivered as it turned the spike towards the *Ladybird* and then toppled towards them. It was a clumsy weapon, called a 'corvus' (meaning *raven*, because of its stabbing beak), that Mark recognised from reading about Roman naval tactics. The corvus was heaviest at its outer end where the spike protruded. The aim was usually not to sink another ship but for the spike to pin it close to the Roman ship so that marines or legionaries could use the upper surface of the corvus as a walkway to board and capture their prey. In this case, the intention was almost certainly to sink the little *Ladybird*, but Mark had no difficulty steering his boat away and the would-be killer blow splashed harmlessly into the sea more than two metres from them. The Romans had made a serious error.

'Right!' said Mark as he steered back towards the partially submerged corvus and pointed his chemical spray canister in the direction of its winding gear aboard the ship. 'Take a deep breath, Rani, and hold it as long as you can.'

Rani took a deep breath and held it while a jet of liquefied gas flew over the edge of the ship. As happened at Capua, howls of pain and consternation immediately broke out around the afflicted area and quickly spread to either side; then a piteous clamour erupted from the lower deck. Mark winced at the cries and guiltily wondered if he had released a potentially lethal amount of the gas, especially if anyone aboard already suffered from a respiratory problem. On the other hand, he was pleased to find that there was no sign of arrows or other forms of resistance and, perhaps more importantly, the corvus still lay with its front end in the placid water and its rear end firmly attached to the ship, allowing him a relatively easy route aboard.

In fact, getting aboard was even easier than it looked. The upper side of the corvus had batons nailed across its surface to give Roman soldiers a firm footing and there was a handrail for them to cling onto when boarding ships in difficult sea conditions; and it worked just as well in the other direction. Clambering up the sixty-odd degree angle almost as easily as he would climb a steep set of stairs, Mark was able to spare one of his hands to hold his tranquilising gun. When he climbed aboard the ship he tranquillised two blinded, choking, retching marines who staggered towards him ineffectually waving their swords in his general direction. A few more semi-incapacitated soldiers and sailors dropped their weapons when he shouted: 'surrender or be destroyed by the goddess Kim!' He met no more resistance.

However, his hope that the slave rowers would be spared the worst effects of the gas was woefully ill-founded. This particular fleet had originally been designed to perform a specific role: to catch and board pirate ships lurking in bays, inlets, estuaries and other coastal hiding places. Corvuses, although very useful for boarding, were heavy, as indeed was their winding gear and the chunky decking needed to support them, making most ships that carried them draw too much draught to penetrate pirate havens. To reduce the draught, the architects of these pirate-catchers had gone for wide, shallow hulls with two ranks of sixteen big oars, each pulled by six men.

In addition, they had done away with as much woodwork as possible, including the tall central mast that most Roman ships used to support a large square or oblong sail for long journeys, and most of the upper deck. This meant that the rowers in the lower deck were not protected from the elements by the stout mezzanine that supported the corvus and covered the crew's quarters, or from the small upper deck at the ship's bow or the walkways that skirted the sides of the ship. Nor were they protected from Mark's gas.

On the contrary, being slightly heavier than air, the gas gently drifted towards the lowest parts of the ship: among the one hundred and ninety-two slave rowers. When Mark looked down upon them, their condition looked truly terrible as they clutched at their faces and writhed and choked and vomited and whimpered with agony.

Thankfully, the gas molecules were designed to become inert soon after coming into contact with water molecules, which meant that its effects were mercifully short-lived in the moist orifices of the human body. A few rowers grabbed buckets of water, which were kept beside them to sluice their faeces and vomit into the ship's scuppers, and doused their furiously itching skin. Those who did so made the quickest recovery and passed their new-found knowledge on to others. When one of the slaves had recovered enough to call out to Mark that keys to their chains were hanging on a wall in the captain's cabin, he had all the help he needed to sail the slave rebellion's first warship.

Once he had unlocked the chains of one rank of slaves they set about unlocking all the others. Some of them attached ropes to empty water buckets and dipped them into the sea so that they could wash off any active residue of gas that still lingered on their skin and ragged clothes. While they were doing this, Rani came on board and started to address them from the mezzanine deck. Still wearing the black outfit she had taken from the captured villa at Capua, Mark idly thought what an impressive figure she cut as she told them that they could banish their bonds of slavery forever if they joined Spartacus' great rebellion against their Roman oppressors, and he was evidently not the only person to think so.

Indeed, rather than clapping and cheering and baying for Roman blood, the bemused crowd that watched and listened to her grew silent until someone shouted: 'hail the goddess Kim, hail the goddess Kim!' Many of the freed slaves took up these words as a chant while others went down on their knees and bowed in supplication to her. Clearly taken aback by their response, Rani's oratory faltered and she gave Mark a 'help me!' look over the backs of her fast growing congregation of worshippers, followed shortly after by an expressive shrug that seemed to say something like: 'oh well, if that's what they want to think, I guess I can live with it.'

Unlike the many frightened city slaves released from Capua, only five of the ship's slaves took the opportunity to leave when Rani announced that anyone who wished could go with the Roman crew in one of the empty landing craft that were still attached to the ship's stern and make for the shore. All the others stayed to take part in the attack which Rani said that she and Mark would lead to free the rest of the slaves of the fleet. Still feeling high from his successful attack and shocked at how easy it had been, Mark simply nodded at her, climbed back down the corvus to the *Ladybird* and protectively circled their captured warship until the corvus had been winched back into position and they were ready to slip anchor, which they did just as the deep orange sun touched the horizon.

None of the other thirteen warships had thus far made any visible response to what was going on, and the next ship to be targeted was still at anchor when Mark swooped by on his gas attack run. Climbing a rope ladder thrown over the side of the slave-controlled ship, he rejoined Rani at the head of about eighty ex-slaves who were dripping from a fresh douse of sea water and the wet rags that swaddled their faces. All of them were armed with a variety of captured weapons or odd bits of lethal-looking seafaring equipment.

Having found a curved sword with a black hilt hanging on a wall in the captain's cabin, the completely black-clad, black-haired Rani had also managed to find some silky black material to wrap round her face and head, and she look no less impressive for being soaking wet. On the contrary, its effect was to enhance the litheness of her body and to imbue her with a dangerously sensual yet untouchable look of a middle-eastern warrior-goddess who had just performed some watery ritual in an expensive burka.

When they drew close to their quarry, the raised corvus crashed down and its spike thumped into the timbers of the other ship's mezzanine deck. Rani and Mark ran across the corvus's walkway at the head of their new comrades and jumped onto the pinned ship without meeting any resistance. Their wet rags were not wholly effective but they had got their timing roughly right, so that the gas had largely dissipated but the Romans aboard were still disabled by its effects. The ferocious-looking 'goddess' insisted that none of their captives should be mistreated, and none were. This attack set the pattern for subsequent attacks.

The next ship did slip anchor and tried to flee, but soon lost way when everyone aboard started choking from Mark's gas attack, and it was added to the growing slave fleet after a minimal show of resistance was ended by a few tranquilising pellets. So far there had been no bloodshed, although there may have been some drownings because many of the Roman sailors and marines had leapt overboard to escape the gas or the bloody acts of revenge that they might have expected but which never materialised.

Three more warships were caught in the fading light with little or no resistance while the other eight attempted to scatter under cover of the deepening night, mostly north towards the sanctuary of the Tiber. To the GI3653, of course, night made no difference. And crippled or not, the *Ladybird* was still the fastest thing on the sea. Using the torch that Tarak had sent him in the escape pod, Mark played its dazzling beam on the disabled ships to guide the ever growing rebel navy to each new victim, and only called it a night when his gas canister was empty.

By then, ten of the fleet's fourteen warships had been caught and were manned by nearly one thousand nine hundred ecstatically excited ex-slaves, plus almost all of the four hundred newly recaptured rebels who had been locked in storage holds aboard two of the captured ships. One of these was Rani's friend Lili, and they had also recaptured Quintus, who was now being held in a storage hold with scores of other captured Romans. After a brief but emotional reunion with Rani, Lili hurried off to arrange Quintus' release and to make sure that he was treated with the respect due to a potential ally and future ruler of Rome.

Aside from the four warships that had escaped them, the only notable blemishes on the night's work were that some of the crews aboard two of the ships captured in the night had put up a fight in the dark recesses of their vessels which resulted in a total of four deaths and thirteen injured among the ex-slaves' new navy and around twenty Roman deaths. Overall, it had been a breathtaking success that left Mark stunned at the enormity of what they had achieved. It was, he thought, the sea that made his gadgets so much more effective than they might have been on land, and this got him thinking about whether the sea could be the key to ending this war quickly.

Although they were tired after their long and eventful day, Mark and Rani both felt far too exhilarated to sleep and thought it was time to have a chat with Quintus. Using the *Ladybird*, they transferred to the ship he was on and met him in the captain's cabin. Not knowing whether he already knew what they were planning for him, they decided to begin by appealing to his vanity by saying that he would make a good Roman emperor, and then offer their help to make it happen if he promised to end slavery. They were surprised by his reaction.

When they entered the cabin, rather than greeting them with flowery language or blubbering with fear, Quintus eyed them coldly from the captain's chair and said, 'yes?' as though he were being disturbed by tiresome underlings. They looked at each other and Rani nodded at Mark to indicate that he should do the talking.

'Err, hello, are you well?' Mark asked.

'As well as can be expected when you keep showing up!'

'Oh, yes, right. I imagine you were looking forward to getting home.'

'I was and I still am, so get on with it please.'

'Ah, yes, err, well, we were kind of wondering if you had any plans? You know, after you put your feet up for a bit at home, if you have given any thought for the future, sort of thing,' Mark trailed off lamely.

'And?' Quintus pressed.

'And, err, well, we sort of wondered if you fancied becoming emperor of Rome?'

'No, I do not *fancy* becoming emperor of Rome.'

'Oh, right, I see. That's a shame. You see, we thought you would be really good at it.'

Quintus' frown deepened but he did not speak.

'We also thought you might be able to negotiate an end to this war before it gets even more out of hand. After all, if Spartacus brings his army to Rome I'm sure there would be an awful lot of slaves within Rome who would be willing to help him, and probably many poor Romans as well. I would hate to think what might happen if the slave army broke in and a revolution broke out within Rome. It could all turn *very* nasty, if you know what I mean,' said Mark, feeling uncomfortably like a gangster explaining the rules of his protection racket to a new victim. He was tempted to add 'cities can get broken, you know,' but decided that this would not be funny under the circumstances.

Still Quintus frowned and said nothing.

'Oh well,' Mark said resignedly, 'if you don't want to help, then we can't make you.'

'No, you can't, but I didn't say I wouldn't help.'

'Sorry?'

'You think I'm a bloated aristocrat who cares for nothing and no one but himself, don't you?'

'Err . . .'

'Well I am not! I know what you have in mind and I deplore it. For all its faults, I love Rome. I think it is a force for good in the world because it represents order and reason, even if it can lack justice in some areas.'

'I was one of those *areas*,' Rani said sternly.

'I do not want Rome brought to its knees,' Quintus continued, still addressing Mark as though Rani had not spoken, 'which is what I think would happen if all its slaves were suddenly released and abandoned their work. But that is what you want me to do, isn't it? You want me to be your puppet emperor so that you can free all the slaves. And then what? Will the ex-slaves disperse to other countries or roam around Italy taking their revenge on whoever they do not like the look of? What will happen to Roman citizens? Will they be enslaved by ex-slaves, or by the Gauls or whoever decides to take advantage of our weakened condition? Or perhaps by the people from this other world you speak of? No, I do not want to lead our great city and its people into slavery or destruction, or to the humiliation of becoming a quaint backwater ruled by others who wish to use me as their puppet emperor.

'However, I am a pragmatist. I will help you to achieve what you want for one reason and one reason only. I have now seen and heard enough to know that Rome cannot hope to survive as it is against the people from your world. We must adapt or die. I do not like either option, I just think that our best chance of survival lies in adapting, but I will not be your puppet. You shall not make me emperor of Rome. The word "empire" is in any case too grand and aggressive for what you and your people will allow us to be in the future. But if you bring me back to the Senate before Spartacus gets to Rome I shall do my best to negotiate some sort of phased end to slavery in favour of contracts of employment and the prospect of Roman citizenship.'

'Oh, right, I see,' said Mark, who had already had some vague thoughts along these lines. He caught Rani's eye and she silently nodded her agreement. 'I think that sounds very sensible,' he said, extending a hand that Quintus declined to shake.

'Not so fast,' said Quintus. 'If I am to be taken seriously as a negotiator then I will need to be treated with a certain amount of respect and dignity. To begin with, I will take this room while we are at sea and you will knock before you enter next time. I will need at least two servants to prepare my meals and so forth. In future, you will no longer refer to me by my first name. You will bow before you address me and prefix what you say with "senator Saturnalicus", is that understood?'

'Well, I'm not sure that we should be telling anyone to serve . . .' Mark began, but he was interrupted by Rani pulling at his arm while she said 'yes, senator Saturnalicus, of course we understand. If you will excuse us we shall do our best to arrange things to your satisfaction.' With that said, she gave Quintus a belated bow, guided Mark out the cabin by his elbow and gently closed the door behind them.

Pausing outside the door for a moment, they looked at each other until they saw amusement play across each other's faces and felt the tensions of their long and extraordinarily eventful day threaten to well up from their bellies in fits of convulsive laughter. Scurrying away before they angered Quintus with their undiplomatic sounds of merriment, they climbed onto the upper deck trying to restrain their slightly hysterical laughter. The six or seven ex-slaves who were gathered on the deck discreetly left their two strange deliverers of freedom alone to recover their composure with deep draughts of sea air.

Having recovered, they stood for a time at the bow, one of the few parts of the austere pirate-catcher that made any concessions to aesthetics. An intricately carved balustrade flowed up from the small upper deck until it blended into the ship's bow as it swept backwards in a graceful swan-necked arc above their heads. Discounting the ugly corvus behind him and the degrading accoutrements of slavery in the lower deck, Mark could imagine they were on a beautiful Elven ship bound for the Grey Havens in Tolkien's *Lord of the Rings*. Listening to the muted sounds of happy voices drifting across the sea from the fleet, now barely moving as it clustered together for mutual protection and comfort under the moonless but brilliantly starry night sky, it was hard to grasp all that had happened in just one day. At this time the previous night they were sleeping after a day of marching and wondering whether they were heading into a deadly trap. The trap appeared to be have been broken after an incredible day of battle on land and a running fight at sea, and now they felt they had taken an important step towards a negotiated peace.

'Why did we laugh like that?' Rani asked.

'For heart's ease rather than from jest,' said Mark, quoting Peter and wondering whether he would ever see his friend again and what he would make of all that Mark had done while he was in suspended animation.

'Was it really only this morning that Crassus' army showed up?'

'Yes, it was. Perhaps tomorrow will be a bit quieter,' he replied, yawning cavernously.

'I for one hope that *every* day will be quieter from now on.' Finding herself yawning too, she took his hand, and said, 'come on, it's time we got some sleep, in case tomorrow doesn't turn out to as quiet as we would like.'

12
DRIFTING OUT OF TIME

After a few hours of deep and surprisingly untroubled sleep, they were woken by shouts and the thumping of bare feet running on the mezzanine deck above them. Mark wondered if they were about to be attacked, although he was dimly aware that the voices did not sound as if they were expressing alarm. Leaping out of bed a couple of seconds after Rani, he dithered for a moment in sleepy confusion until he decided to pee in the basin under the absent captain's table before getting into his force-field suit. By the time he got to the upper deck, the slowly moving fleet of ten captured warships was bedecked with people waving and cheering at the sight of several hundred horsemen who were gathered on a beach waving and cheering back. Mark saw Spartacus and Julian standing by the gentle surf waiting to greet their new navy.

Rani threw a rope ladder over the side of the ship and followed Mark down to the doggedly loyal *Ladybird*, where Mark climbed out of his suit again. Spartacus met them in the surf with a broad smile and a vigorous handshake. 'So,' he said with feigned nonchalance, 'it went quite well then?'

'Nah, four of 'em got away!' said Mark with equally feigned nonchalance.

'What's next,' asked Julian, 'Rome?'

'Could do, if you're up for that.'

Julian simply smiled, but Spartacus said, 'oh, do you mean you might want some help?'

'You did alright against Crassus without my help, so I reckon you might have your uses.'

Spartacus laughed. 'So you thought you'd win a sea battle without our help, did you?'

'Something like that, but Rome might prove a bit awkward.'

Rani rolled her eyes at this, cleared her throat to attract their attention, and said, 'excuse me, when you've finished showing off you might remember that *I* was out there as well!'

'But of course, Rani' said Spartacus, 'I did not mean to downplay your part in all this.'

'Nor me,' said Mark, 'I mean, you made a magnificent goddess!'

'That's better!' she said, beaming at the three men. 'So, what's next?

'A rest?' ventured Julian.

Spartacus explained that he, Julian and most of their horsemen had been riding hither and tither all night and well into the morning. They had to gather sufficient forces to meet the three small Roman armies that had been closing upon them before Crassus' army was destroyed. In the event, the landing force was quick to march away from their vulnerable beachhead to join those moving up from the south, but found that their comrades had fled back to Capua, so they too hastened to Capua. Hearing of this and Crassus' defeat, those coming from the east marched back to their Apennine strongholds or to Rome. Even so, units of the slave army were sent to harass the retreating Romans, others were needed to guard Crassus' defeated legionaries, others to spread the rebellion, and still more to track the flickering light of Mark's torch as it played on the fleeing Roman warships. Finally losing sight of them, they took whatever cavalry they could spare northwards until they spotted the new navy just a few miles south of the Tiber. In so doing, they had led their men dangerously close to Rome and did not want to go any further until their main army caught up with them and they caught up with some sleep.

'Yes,' said Rani, looking around at the happy but gaunt faces around them, 'you all look like you need a good rest.'

And rest they did, for much of that day; except Mark and Rani, who had not long got out of bed and did not need to rest, at least not physically. What Mark wanted more than anything else was to have a mental respite from his helter-skelter series of adventures, but he figured he still had one task to perform before he could take advantage of any lull in the war. He thought he should make all haste to deliver Quintus to Rome so that he could present the Senate with a possible way out of the war while they still had time to think about it.

Rani was evidently thinking along similar lines, for she gave Spartacus a very quick sketch of what had happened in the sea-fight and their conversation with Quintus as if she were in a hurry to be going somewhere. When she finished speaking, Spartacus said that the slave army would march within sight of Rome the following day without attacking its walls and wait there until he had word of their negotiations or felt obliged to respond to any hostile Roman moves. After shaking hands again and swapping good wishes, Mark and Rani got back in the *Ladybird* and headed for the fleet while boatloads of newly-freed seagoing ex-slaves and re-released rebels rowed for the shore to mingle with those of Spartacus' land army.

Having taken Quintus and Lili aboard the *Ladybird*, it took just twenty minutes to sail within sight of Ostia. Lili tried to engage Quintus in conversation about a future without slavery but he was not very communicative. Although curious about the *Ladybird*, he seemed mostly concerned with recovering his dignity by standing at its bow and striking a noble pose as though he were in charge of the ramshackle little boat rather than a captive.

Delivering him to his people was a simple matter of letting him step ashore on a strip of unguarded beach within easy walking distance of a cluster of wealthy-looking seaside villas. They watched his progress from a little offshore until they saw him talking to a small group of women riding along the beach with servants riding in attendance. After a brief exchange and looks in their direction, the women instructed one of their servants to dismount and help the badly overweight Quintus onto his horse. Without a backward glance, Quintus trotted off to do whatever it was that he really planned to do now that he was free of his captors.

On their way back to the fleet and the army's encampment, Lili quizzed her old friend about their exploits since they parted at Mount Vesuvius and wanted to know all she could about Mark and his devices, especially the *ladybird*. Mark enjoyed listening to Rani tell her what had happened and he enjoyed showing off his equipment so much that he decided to spin out their little journey. Accompanied by his mini-lectures, the two women watched the inboard computer in awe as it showed them vivid three-dimensional images of their world from space, then of spacecraft, of cities on his world, of action-packed film sequences, of abstract state-of-the-art computer graphics, and a few short clips from classic Disney cartoons. Using the manual tiller, he got the boat to swoop around to show its agility, and then stunned a small shoal of fish before he realised that the boat's keep-net was missing. Of all these things, it was the boat's ability to disable fish that interested Rani most and prompted her to soberly suggest that it was time to return to their comrades and help feed them.

'Go fishing!' said Mark, 'just the thing to relax and be useful at the same time.' They all agreed that fishing would be a good way to spend the rest of the day.

Treating his two guests to an exhilarating ride that snaked through the placid water at full-throttle, they sailed back through the fleet three or four hours after they had set out for the Tiber. Approaching the shore at full speed, he brought the

Ladybird to a sudden curving stop that drenched Spartacus in a cascade of water as he waited at the edge of the surf to greet them. After holding out his soaking arms and inspecting his soaking body, Spartacus slowly raised his head to reveal a grim and foreboding expression. Fixing Mark with a steady glare, he said, 'is it my turn now?' and his features creased into a broad soppy grin that would not have looked out of place on Peter's face.

Nodding vigorously, Mark fussed about Spartacus while he stepped uncertainly aboard the *Ladybird*. Turning back out to sea, Mark indulged in a few cowboy whoops and yee-hahs as the boat made its first zigs and jinks around the fleet. When he thought that Spartacus was beginning to relax into the ride, he gradually upped the tempo until all four of them were whooping and yee-hahing whenever they came out of a steeply angled turn. Hundreds of onlookers vigorously clapped and cheered and whistled from the beach and the ships as though it was the best entertainment they had ever seen.

When they came out of a turn round one end of the fleet and approached the space between the ships and the shore, Mark suddenly realised that the main army had joined those on the beach and he became conscious of the huge numbers of people that were now watching them. He hesitantly slowed the boat to a crawl and an inexplicable moment of hush fell upon the crowds. Then someone on the beach raised a fist in the air and shouted: 'FREEDOM!' The gesture and the word were soon replicated by hundreds and then thousands of others in the army and navy, with the latter making up for their smaller numbers by rhythmically thumping their feet and banging their weapons against their ships' echoing timbers. Turning for another slow pass between the army and the fleet, the four people in the little *Ladybird* returned the fist salute and added what they could to the booming chant of *FREE-DOM, FREE-DOM, FREE-DOM, FREE-DOM, FREE-DOM, FREE-DOM* that rolled across the water from either side of them for several tearfully inspiring minutes.

It was, Mark thought, as though the sight of four people exercising their freedom to enjoy themselves had somehow crystallised into a symbol of what freedom could be, even for those, like Rani and her three lost children, who were born into slavery. Looking at her now, he could see tears welling up in her eyes, although she was not quite sobbing. She looked back at him as though she was about to say something poignant, and so he was not expecting her to blurt out the word 'fish'.

'Sorry?'

'Fish,' she repeated, with her quivering bottom lip slightly protruding as if to catch the tears that were now plopping from her cheekbones, 'catch fish!'

'Fish? Oh, right, I see,' he said, remembering their plan to help feed the army and navy.

He thought about turning on the *Ladybird's* fish-stunner and leaving others to work out how to haul the inert fish ashore, but decided against it. He was, he felt, in danger of making too much of his contribution if a stream of stunned fish miraculously appeared in their wake as though he were Jesus Christ feeding the five thousand. It was, after all, so very easy for him to press the right button and select the appropriate miracle, but tremendously difficult for these people to defy the might of Rome. It felt wrong to take advantage of such an emotionally charged moment by performing a cheap conjuring trick that would unduly impress those who had suffered so much and risked so much without such gadgets, so he decided to be a bit more discreet about his fishing.

'They'll think I'm some kind of god if I magically produce a mass of fish to feed them,' he said to Rani.

'Half the fleet already think Rani is a goddess,' said Spartacus.

'Yes,' Mark replied, 'but she didn't mean to make them think that, and it's not right to take advantage.' Looking back at Rani he saw her nod her assent and they set off to organise a fishing trip a kilometre or two offshore. This proved to be easy to arrange and carry out, although their abundant catch was not at all easy to be discreet about.

Having gathered about sixty volunteers from the fleet in four landing craft, all their helpers had to do was to scoop the stunned fish from the sea's calm surface in the fishing nets that all the Roman ships carried in case they needed to feed their sailors and slaves at sea. The *Ladybird* could not only stun whole shoals of fish, its inboard computer told Mark exactly where the shoals were, what type of fish they were, and instantly calculated the most efficient use of its power to produce the maximum effect from a cone-shaped electrical charge delivered to the appropriate depth. Even so, stunning fish at any depth was by far the most power-consuming activity that the boat was capable of, and its batteries were quickly depleted.

Nonetheless, three hours of hauling bulging nets into the landing craft were enough to fill them to capacity and literally thousands of fish were delivered to the shore. By then, the inboard computer informed Mark that the boat's batteries were low. In the absence of any wind or significant amounts of solar energy from the cloud-obscured late afternoon sun, he decided to call it a day and let the batteries recharge themselves in the morning.

Despite Mark's wish to avoid undue attention, the success of their fishing trip drew huge crowds of awed helpers and spectators to the shore and prompted a great deal of talk about the miracles performed by 'Mark Goodvictory' and 'goddess Kimrani'. Not being sure as to whether these muddled honorifics and worshipful tendencies might prove useful in terms of, say, averting an orgy of vengeful violence if the army broke into the streets of Rome, they both kept an awkward silence in the face of their unlooked-for elevation to the status of supreme beings.

As they were eating an early evening meal in the dunes, Rani realised that the body language of Spartacus and Lili meant that they were rapidly warming to each other, and she decided that they should have some time together without her and Mark drawing crowds around them. So she quietly hefted her sack of personal belongings over her shoulder and signalled that he should do the same and follow her back to the *Ladybird*. He did not resist, especially as he was finding all the attention oppressive.

When they had sailed away from the still growing encampment they used the four long bendy sticks that Rani used to erect her tent to prop the tent material against the gaping wound in the boat's dome, and then settled in for an evening and night alone together.

Having instructed the inboard computer to keep them at least two kilometres from land or ships, he showed Rani a few video clips until she decided what she wanted to watch. Finally feeling that a bit of normality had returned to his bizarre new life, he dozed contentedly while Rani sat transfixed in front of the latest remake of *Shrek* with the dialogue translated into Latin through her earpiece

All in all, they would have been hard put to devise a more effective way of recharging their psychological batteries on the evening before they and their comrades were due to arrive before the walls of Rome, or a more relaxed way of draining the last of the power from the *Ladybird's* batteries.

Mark woke up feeling anxious about something without knowing what was troubling him. Everything looked as it should. They were still aboard the *Ladybird* and Rani was snoring gently beside him in the bed of sheepskins that he could barely smell anymore, so they had obviously not been attacked or anything. There was, of course, plenty to feel anxious about on the day that the slave army was due to arrive before Rome, especially with Julius Caesar in command of the city's defences, but he felt that the source of his worry was much closer and more immediate. Rani stirred and opened her eyes.

'Is it morning?' she asked.

He could tell it was morning from the chink of grey light and the chill, damp air that drifted through places where flaps of the tent material had sagged away from the hole in the dome.

'Yes. I didn't notice you come to bed. Did you enjoy the film?'

'Yes, it was fantastic! Another one came on afterwards, it was called *Snow White and the Seven Dwarfs* and it was wonderful! But the picture box suddenly went dark, so I came to bed.'

Then it dawned on him; his semiconscious had prodded him into wakefulness because it was uneasy about draining the last of the *Ladybird's* power. This had obviously happened while Rani watched films because the inboard computer would not have switched itself off unless it had been forced to go into hibernation. Not that this was a major problem, the batteries would soon be charged up in the morning sun; unless, of course, there was no morning sun.

Getting onto his knees, he removed the tent sticks and material covering the irregular hole in the dome and stuck his head outside. He could see nothing but thick fog in every direction. The fog might have been a little lighter to one side of him, but not much. With a shiver, he withdrew his head and considered his options. He could switch the computer on to see where they had drifted to and if any land or ships were nearby, or wait for the sun to break through the fog before he risked draining even more power from the batteries' reserves. The thought of a Roman ship silently bearing down upon them prompted him to switch the computer on.

When the screen lit up it displayed a wide area of empty seascape around them and showed their fleet where they left it lying at anchor some fourteen kilometres north-east of their current position, but it also displayed a dialogue box in the bottom left corner which read 'critical battery'. Then the computer shut itself down again. He could not think of anything to do but wait for the weather to change. In the meantime, he knew they were going to have an anxious time wondering whether the weather would change in time for them to rejoin their comrades on the last leg of their journey to Rome.

After they had done their ablutions as best as they could, Rani rummaged around in her travel sack to find about a quarter of a loaf of stale unleavened bread, some strips of leftover pork fat and about half a litre of slightly brackish water in her animal skin. While they chewed disconsolately at their unappetising breakfast, Mark had to admit to himself that their position might have been a lot worse without her aversion to waste, for there was no other food aboard the *Ladybird* and the little plastic tap that dispensed desalinated water had been broken off by the Romans who had held the boat captive beside the Tiber. Even so, it was not an auspicious way of greeting the day; a day in which the slave army's war with Rome might reach a climax while they sat anxiously twiddling their thumbs in a becalmed boat.

For the umpteenth time, Mark put his head out of the hole in the boat's dome only to find that nothing much had changed. The day had grown somewhat lighter but there was no sign of the fog lifting, and the sunlight, such as it was, was too obscured and diffuse to give them any hope of charging the *Ladybird's* batteries before sunset, which was now little more than an hour away. For the fifth time that day, he used a bit more of the batteries' power reserves to check their situation on the inboard computer. As before, the dialogue box said 'critical battery', and the screen went blank again after showing him that nothing except their position had altered. The fleet had not moved, but water currents had carried the *Ladybird* almost forty kilometres away to the south. There was absolutely nothing he or Rani could do about that, and they had no way of knowing how the land army was faring on their march to Rome. In addition, with no food and very little water left, they were in danger of becoming physically weakened as well as psychologically distressed by their predicament.

Not wanting to spend the entire night and possibly another day becalmed, Mark decided to risk complete battery failure by switching the engine on and heading for the fleet. The *Ladybird* leapt obediently into action, but they covered no more than two kilometres before the engine cut out. On the next attempt, they barely covered a hundred metres. They now knew that they were indeed stuck for another night.

The next morning was no better; in fact it was a good deal worse in terms of their hunger, thirst and anxiety. After looking at the unyielding fog they finished the last of their water and then sat and looked at each other. Mark was feeling desperately unhappy with himself for letting them get into this state, but he also felt his heart ache with love for this woman who had trusted him and his presumed knowledge of the *Ladybird's* capabilities and limitations without uttering a word of complaint or showing any sign of feeling let down by him.

They had talked on and off during their long hours adrift, mostly about their past lives and what a future without slavery might be like for them and their comrades. In terms of her own future, Rani's greatest wish was to track down the three children who had been taken from her as so much 'stock' that her owner might do whatever he wanted with, regardless of her feelings or even any apparent recognition that she might be capable of any feelings. Now, with another day of fog threatening to derail all their plans, she looked at him with an expression of understanding and concern for his sense of guilt and frustration and showed no hint of blaming him for the difficult position they were in. As he looked back at her, he silently vowed to do everything in his power to help her find her children, but for the time being he was powerless to do anything at all to help anyone.

Neither of them seemed to have anything left to say, so they said nothing while they gazed unselfconsciously at each other's faces. After a while, she slowly reached out her hand and gently touched his lips with her fingertips, and then leant forward and softly kissed him. They gradually drew their bodies together and made love as slowly and as gently as the unnoticed breeze that was beginning to stir the fog outside.

When they were spent, they slept together for an hour or more in the warmth of each other's embrace and, had they but known it, in the steadily rising warmth of the air around them as the wind sighed and brushed away the last wisps of mist and the unhindered rays of the sun beat down upon the *Ladybird's* solar panels.

The boat turned slowly in the breeze until the sun shone through the hole in the dome onto their faces. Waking simultaneously, they both blinked at the sun, then at each other, and leapt out of bed without a word. Turning on the onboard computer, Mark saw that the dialogue box read 'low battery' rather than 'critical battery'. He hoped that was enough and switched the engine on. The *Ladybird* surged forward. He looked down at the screen to check that he was heading for the fleet, but the fleet was not where they had last seen it. Scrolling the image further north, he saw a line of ten dots near where they had dropped off Quintus. One end of the line was curved towards the Tiber. Holding his breath, he waited until he was sure they were moving and which way they were heading. They were moving; past Ostia and possibly on to Rome.

'They're heading up the Tiber!'

'Who?' Rani asked.

'The fleet.'

'Why?'

'God knows.'

'Perhaps they're looking for us.'

'What, the whole fleet?'

Rani did not answer.

'They must be attacking Rome!' he said aghast.

'Perhaps something has gone wrong with the army and the fleet is trying to help them.'

He felt it was useless to speculate any further, so he just kept the boat going at full throttle and hoped that the midday sun and the increasing breeze would provide enough power to keep them going.

The kilometres ticked by and the dialogue box still said 'low battery' when they turned into the bay where the slave army and fleet had gathered, hoping to find someone who could tell them what was going on. They made a pass beside the beach and saw that it was littered with discarded rubbish but no people. Mark started to make for the open sea again when Rani grabbed his shoulder and pointed towards the dunes. Four men were racing towards the beach waving frantically at them. Mark turned back towards the beach and one of the men waded out to meet them.

They both recognised the man as the same bearded messenger who had warned Spartacus of the approach of Crassus' army and had regularly reported to Spartacus ever since they left Capua, so they helped him climb aboard while the other three made off to fetch their horses from a fold of the dunes. When they set off again for the Tiber, the man introduced himself as Brennus, and Rani told him that they were hungry and thirsty. He gave them his meagre supply of cold fried fish, stale bread, apples and watered-down wine. Leaving the *Ladybird* to find its own way north, they ate hungrily and swilled down more wine than they really ought to have while Brennus explained what had happened.

After reinforcing the fleet with many of his best troops, Spartacus had been reluctant to march off to Rome with the rest of the army until the *Ladybird* had returned, so he put

Julian in command of the main forces and waited behind with the reinforced fleet and about a thousand horsemen for as long as he dared. Thinking that Mark and Rani must have got into some kind of trouble, he eventually sent his horsemen to rejoin the main army while he and Lili joined his men aboard the cramped ships and headed for the Tiber. Rethinking his plans, Spartacus decided on a show of force that, when added to the effect of the consistently victorious slave army appearing outside the walls of Rome, might persuade the Senate to agree peace terms. If that failed, he hoped that the fleet could blockade the river while their army spread the rebellion around Rome and completed its encirclement.

'They'll get slaughtered if Pompey's fleet arrives to bottle them up in the river,' said Mark, and his mobile translated.

'Not if you and the goddess get there first,' Brennus said matter-of-factly.

The confidence with which Brennus had spoken made Mark wonder if the entire army had become convinced that they were being aided by supernatural beings. With this unsettling thought, which he guessed Rani was also thinking, they ceased to question him further and fell to wondering how they were going to live up to such unrealistic expectations, especially now that the enormously effective gas cylinder was empty.

Mark got into his force-field suit as they were passing the place where they had last seen Quintus, then sailed into the mouth of the Tiber. The onboard computer told Mark that five ships at the rear of the fleet had turned and were heading slowly back for the sea while the other five were cruising slowly towards Rome.

'Oh,' said Brennus as an afterthought struck him, 'I forgot to tell you that Roman prisoners are rowing our ships now, mostly prisoners from Crassus' army.'

'What?' said Mark in surprise, 'not chained, I hope?'

'Well,' he replied, suddenly sounding uncertain, 'yes, they were chained.'

'Why?'

'So that they won't try to escape or attack our people, and so that the Romans will think twice before trying to sink our ships.'

'Jesus Christ!' said Mark in despair

'Who?' said Brennus.

'What?'

'You mentioned someone called Jesus Christ.'

'Eh? Oh, never mind that; Caesar won't hesitate to drown his own people if it means he can defeat us! I thought we were trying to end slavery, not make slaves of our captives!'

'We are trying to end slavery,' Rani said gently, 'and I'm sure they'll be released as soon as the war is over. In the meantime, it makes sense to have our people under arms rather than pulling oars.'

'And for Romans to drown instead of us if our ships are attacked,' Brennus said, as though he were stating an irrefutably clinching argument.

'Thank you,' said Rani impatiently, 'I'll handle this, if you don't mind.'

'Handle *me*, you mean,' said Mark unhappily.

'Mark, please try to understand,' she pleaded, 'this world is *much* harder than your world. We cannot hope to beat the Romans if we are not prepared to be as hard as them in a fight.'

'And how about in peace? Are we going to be as hard as the Romans after the war's over?'

'No, Mark, we are not, but the war is *not* over. I hope it soon will be, but we must use every advantage we have if we are to win. *Then* we can start building something better, much better, but not yet, Mark, not yet.'

13
CAESAR'S TRAP

Blue flags flew from the prows, sterns and the raised corvuses of the five ships heading back to the sea. Captured Roman shields, each of which was daubed with a large blue blotch, ringed the ships to protect those on board from spears and arrows. When the *Ladybird* drew close to the lead ship, someone threw down a rope ladder and they climbed through a narrow gap in the shields to a small but warm reception from a group of men dressed as gladiators.

Looking down at the Roman prisoners of war chained to their oars, Mark saw that they were packed tighter than the freed slaves had been, and he guessed there were at least three hundred of them. Several men, also dressed as gladiators, paced the aisle between the rowers menacingly holding their drawn swords as the rowers pulled to the slow beat of a drum banged by a muscle-bound gladiator standing on the mezzanine deck above them. There were no whips here, just the promise of instant death to anyone who showed any sign of rebelliousness. At first, Mark thought that the extra manpower was to make up for the Romans' lack of rowing abilities, but he soon wondered whether it might have been a way of making up for any that might be killed for disobedience. Not that there was any sign of disobedience, nor did disobedience look very likely under these threatening circumstances.

The thirty-odd male ex-slaves onboard were all dressed as gladiators and wore Roman helmets or other forms of military headgear. This, Mark guessed, was to impress onlookers with the kind of manhood that Roman society revered. There were also about a dozen women and two dozen boys aboard, whose main job was to scrabble along the upper walkway and jiggle the spears that leant against the wall of shields and bob their headgear above them so as to simulate a small army packed onboard. Listening to Rani speak with one of the 'gladiators', Mark leaned their role had been to give an illusion of great strength while the river was wide enough to fool those onshore, and then to retire to guard the river's entrance, leaving the other five ships heading for Rome with a genuine small army packed aboard each ship, but he did not know how close to Rome they proposed to go or what they were planning to do.

Having got as much information from this half of the fleet as they were likely to get, they took off again with Brennus in the *Ladybird* and caught up with the other five ships as they were nearing Rome. Spartacus and Lili waved to them from among yet more 'gladiators' at the bow of the lead ship. Climbing aboard the rope ladder, Mark saw that every shield in the wall of Roman shields around this ship had two heavily armed men behind it, most of whom were dressed in assorted bits of captured Roman armour or gladiator paraphernalia. With every piece of deck alive with armed men, there were in fact about eight hundred fighting men on each of the five ships. As long as the bulk of the Roman naval forces remained scattered around the Mediterranean, this seemed more than enough to repel any force of marines that might try and board them in Rome's backyard.

In addition to this formidable force, the ships carried chained Roman rowers that were packed just as tightly as the first ship they boarded. Mark tried not to think of the horrible fate that awaited them and their three thousand comrades distributed across both halves of the fleet if their ships were sunk, or, indeed, the fates that awaited any men, women and boys among the ex-slaves who might survive only to be blamed and horribly punished for the mass drownings.

Spartacus saw his look. 'I do not want this either, but it is difficult for us to take on the might of Rome as it is; how much more difficult would it be if so many of our people were rowing rather than fighting?'

'You know that Caesar will not hesitate to drown these men if it comes to a fight, don't you?' Mark asked.

'Yes, I do, but my purpose is to induce the Senate to agree to peace. An offer to release these and all other prisoners may act as some incentive for peace. Even if they only mean to get their men back and break the peace when they are ready, it may give us time to prepare, or perhaps to leave Italy altogether if it looks as though we will never have lasting peace.'

'Do you plan to attack Rome?'

'Not today, Mark. This is just a demonstration of our strength and determination, and we will turn back when I think it has served that purpose. I would have discussed this with you if you had not disappeared on your boat, and you are welcome to join any later discussions about what we should do next. In the meantime, I wanted to show the slaves within the city that they have much to hope for, and to show the Romans that they have much to fear. If we can demonstrate our ability to march a great army to the walls of Rome and sail a smaller army close to the heart of Rome, our enemies will need to divide their forces. Not just to protect themselves from our army and navy, but also from the thousands of slaves who might join us if we were to land inside the city's walls. Even then, I hope it will not be necessary to attack Rome itself, just to threaten to do so in order to strengthen Quintus' hand in negotiations.'

'Oh, I see. Has the main army arrived outside Rome?' Mark asked.

'It has. It is commanded by Julian, who I trust not to engage in unnecessary violence more than I would trust Crixus.

The latest reports I have had say that the Romans have not offered battle.'

'Well, I suppose that's something,' said Mark, feeling reassured about Spartacus' intentions but anxious to see the ships turn back before something bad happened. 'How close to Rome do you plan to go?'

Spartacus did not answer. Instead, he looked up the river and furrowed his brow.

Looking upriver himself, Mark saw that plumes of oily black smoke were beginning to rise from behind some buildings that blocked their view beyond a bend in the river about a kilometre away. Not sure whether the smoke was coming from the land or the river, they watched in silence for a few moments while the smoke increased and appeared to move in their direction. Already half expecting Caesar to spring a nasty surprise for them, he reacted swiftly when Spartacus asked him to take the *Ladybird* upriver to see what was going on.

Climbing down the rope ladder alone while the *Ladybird* obligingly positioned itself for him to step aboard, he was just setting off on his reconnaissance when he spotted the flight of stone steps where he had first met Quintus. This meant that they had passed the place where the barrier of boats ought to have been. Trying to work out what this could mean, his thoughts were interrupted by a deep rumbling that sounded like an earthquake. When he looked back up at the ship he saw that the group on the small upper deck were looking behind them, but he could not see what they were looking at.

He turned the *Ladybird* round and raced back down the line of ships until he caught a glimpse of two geysers of water as they were collapsing near the river's east bank, and the rumbling had stopped. He did not know what had caused the geysers or the rumbling, but he could see that the barrier of boats had reappeared about two hundred metres behind the cautiously advancing fleet. Then the rumbling started up again and he saw two small ships clattering down steep ramps from the open doors of warehouses on the west bank of the river. These small ships were rolling on great logs that bucked and bounced as if they were bearing great weights, then they ploughed into the sides of the river as though they were lifeboats being launched on an emergency; except that these were not lifeboats and they did not float.

As the ships burrowed into the river Mark realised what was happening. They were full of heavy material, probably stone, and they were being used as weights to pull chains that run round big metal pulleys to a second barrier of boats lying against the east bank. This barrier was hauled directly in front of the first barrier, and each of its boats contained two men who set fire to their boats before leaping onto the first barrier to make their escape.

While the flames were taking hold, thousands of Roman soldiers raced from between buildings to set up solid shield walls on either bank, and swarms of arrows arced towards the fleet from every available piece of wharf, roadway, windows and roofs of the buildings behind the soldiers.

No sooner had he taken in the fact that the fleet was hemmed in on three sides than the source of the plumes of smoke upriver started to appear round the bend; at least twenty burning ships were being led down the middle of the river by lines attached to four manned ships. As Mark watched, the manned ships severed their lines and veered aside to let the river take the fire-ships towards the trapped fleet.

Both upriver and downriver, the fires were growing rapidly as they eagerly fed on whatever flammable material had been stacked aboard, but the fleet of fire-ships in front of them held vastly more flammable material than the string of fire-boats behind them. Soon the boiling mixtures of red flames and black smoke coming from the fire-ships were merging into one seething mass of fire that no ship in their path could hope to survive. Even if the relatively shallow draught of the pirate-catchers allowed them to scrape over the shallows between the fire-fleet and the river banks, Mark's imagination was already hard at work conjuring up images of great underwater spikes and sunken block-ships that Caesar could easily have had placed at strategic points to tear their hulls open.

'Mark!' Rani's voice called through his earpiece, 'we're trapped, *do something!*'

He did not have much time to think. Moving with the flow of the river, the fire-ships would be upon them in a matter of minutes. He thought he might be able to blow a passage through the barrier of fire behind them with his three remaining bomblets, so he sailed up to a section of one boat that was not yet on fire only to find that the heavy chain that linked it to its neighbours was one continuous chain that linked them all. It seemed highly likely that the second barrier would be similarly secured, and highly unlikely that the blast of a single bomblet would be able to break both chains. After dithering for a moment, he took off in the opposite direction. As he passed the fleet again he hardly noticed the arrows that bounced of his force-field suit, but he winced at the sight of oars flailing uselessly in the air in testament to the agonies inflicted upon the unprotected Roman rowers by the streams of Roman arrows pouring over the ships' shield walls from both sides.

'*Mark!*' Rani pleaded again as her ship began a painfully slow turn away from the fire-ships, '*DO SOMETHING!*'

Mark desperately wanted to do something, he just didn't know what. He thought about throwing one of his bomblets at one of the banks and blowing the Romans away so that the fleet could pull over and disgorge its people before it was sandwiched between the fires, but he still had hopes of a negotiated end to the war and did not want to blow up hundreds of people, or unleash thousands of heavily armed ex-slaves to wreak their revenge on the citizens of Rome.

Coming to a snap decision, he said, 'throw me a bucket' into his mobile.

'What?' said Rani, 'a bucket? You can't put out . . .'

'Just throw me a bucket! No, three buckets.'

She did as he asked, and he raced towards the fire-ships, which were still a few hundred metres away. Putting a bomblet in one of the buckets, he went right up to the inferno meaning to place the bucket in front of the ships in the hope that the bomblet's explosion would consume most of the flammable material before it arrived to incinerate the fleet. If that was not enough, he would use his last two bomblets.

As he approached he saw that one of the ship's prows was still free of fire and that it had a triple-pointed battering ram, marking it as an old warship. The ram provided a convenient place to hang the bucket by its rope handle. Racing back to what he hoped was a safe distance, he entered the bomblet's code and then half turned and pressed the 'send' button with his eyes averted from the expected flash.

There certainly was a flash worth averting his eyes from. Not stopping the *Ladybird's* progress away from the fire-fleet also proved to be prudent, for the flash was followed by a slap of air pressure that rivalled the one that had overturned his boat near the Gandhi Institute's island base. In addition, a great deal of the already very hot but still largely unconsumed flammable material aboard the fire-ship was turned into an expanding ball of super-combustible molecules that ignited as they fanned outwards into the surrounding air, and which engulfed the rest of the fire-ships and their highly flammable cargoes. Within a second or two, an almost simultaneous chain reaction of ignitions threw out an uneven dome of burning oily material that grew white-hot as it expanded and fed on fresh oxygen. In other words, the bomblet's explosion had turned most of the fire-fleet into one big explosion, albeit a slightly flabby explosion that rumbled on after the sharp crack of the bomblet's explosion had died away.

Mark was pressed against the *Ladybird's* control panel and he felt the boat heel forwards under the pressure of the rumbling shockwave until it had passed him and dissipated to barely tolerable levels by the time it pummelled into the fleet, tearing away sections of the shield wall from the lead ship as it passed. Thankful not to have been caught amidships and capsized by the rolling blast, Mark looked around in horror at what he had done.

There was a pillar of fiery smoke rising several hundred metres from the river with what looked like the beginnings of a mushroom cloud opening up at its higher reaches; much like a small nuclear explosion. But that was not all. Buildings were bursting into flame on both banks of the river and the fiery bits of debris that were streaming out of the column of smoke and its mushroom-shaped cap would inevitably cause more fires as they slapped into densely built-up areas of Rome, especially the tall wooden tenements east of the river. And that was still not all.

Rather than saving his friends from the fire-ships, he saw what looked like a thick film of burning oil spread across the entire width of the river and continue advancing on the fleet as though the river itself was on fire, igniting more wooden structures on the banks as it went. When he got back to Rani's ship he barely noticed that the rain of arrows had all but stopped while the shocked Roman archers gawped at the inferno upriver. He grabbed the ship's rope ladder but stood rooted to the spot in shaky indecision watching their approaching doom.

'I think you're going to have to do something else,' said Rani with what sounded like unnatural calmness.

Wrenching his eyes from the fiercely burning river and the orangey-red fire-whirls that flickered and danced and twisted above it, he looked dumbly up the rope ladder and then at the nearest bank and tried to forced himself out of the shocked trance that had gripped him and thousands of others.

Racing back upriver, he tried making a few curving dashes with the *Ladybird* at the fierce wall of fire at full throttle in the hope of kicking enough of a wake to stir water into to the flaming oily material to deaden its combustibility. Not noticing the 'critical battery' message on the computer screen, he plied his boat from side to side until some of the intense heat of the roaring flames started to penetrate his force-field suit. His efforts had no discernible effect. Deciding to renew these attempts if all else failed, he placed another bomblet in another bucket, made a dash back to the barrier and hooked the handle of the bucket over the still unburned prow of a fire-boat. As soon as he turned back to the fleet, the *Ladybird's* engine cut out and he drifted into a particularly lively part of the blaze behind him

Repeatedly trying to restart the engine before it was ready to respond merely prolonged the agonising wait. It was probably less than thirty seconds before it did respond, but he spent most of that time with his head and torso wrapped in flame. His force-field suit was able to cope with the heat, although it must have looked like the end of him to those in the fleet and the Romans on the banks. The main problem for him, however, was that he had already left it very late to detonate the bomblet if he was to avoid destroying the fleet, and now the extra delay had taken the ships that much closer. By the time he got going again he despaired of their surviving the blast, so he gave up the idea and simply left the bomblet where it was.

Not knowing what else to do and not having much time or power left in the *Ladybird's* batteries to do it, he swallowed hard and made the decision he had been trying to avoid since Caesar sprung his trap. 'Rani', he said, in a high-pitched voice that betrayed some of the anxiety he felt over being forced to choose between the lives of his friends and the lives of many other people, 'get the fleet to follow me to the bank.'

Rani passed his order to the men at her ship's tiller and it begun to follow him as he angled towards the east bank, with the other four ships following suit soon after. Mark entered a code into his mobile.

Stopping near the stone wharf on the east bank, Mark stood up amid renewed flights of arrows, raised his right arm and threw a bomblet, the last he had aboard the *Ladybird*, as far as he could down a narrow passageway between some buildings behind the ranks of Romans guarding the bank. Allowing a moment for it to clatter as far along the passageway as it was likely to go, he ducked below the level of the wharf, raised his mobile above his head and pressed the 'send' button just as the rowers in Rani's ship were being ordered to back-paddle to avoid crushing him against the wharf.

The explosion was far less dramatic than the one that had engulfed the fire-ships because the buildings absorbed much of the blast and there were no secondary explosions. Even so, the force of the shockwave coming back down the passageway caught the tops of the *Ladybird's* extended solar panels and sent her spiralling back out into the river. Picking himself off the deck, he looked back at the bank to see what kind of mayhem he had caused.

What he saw looked like a Second World War newsreel of bombed-out facades of buildings with fire roaring from their widow frames as their dry wooden interiors burst into flame; except that these buildings had been festooned with archers a moment ago. One of the stone facades had already crashed down upon dozens of dazed Romans soldiers laying or crawling upon their hands and knees on the wharf below, and another façade folded forwards and collapsed in front of Mark's eyes. Dozens more Romans had been blown into the river or had jumped in to escape the falling masonry and burning beams of wood. Some of these were crushed by the slave-controlled ships as they bumped against the bank and many others would doubtless drown in their heavy armour or be consumed by the fiery river that was just behind the fleet. Mark did not stay to watch.

Making for the bank, he climbed onto the wharf and fought his way through a tide of armed men pouring out of the ships, followed by unarmed Roman rowers behind them. He had meant to try and free the rowers from their chains, but some caring souls had already done so. Ironically, a few of the Roman rowers who had survived the earlier swarms of Roman arrows now fell victim to sporadic arrow fire still coming from undamaged buildings, whereas most of the slave army wore body armour and helmets and defended themselves with shields.

Realising that he was no longer serving any useful purpose, he made his way along the wharf to look for Rani and saw her walking towards him carrying one of the oblong Roman shields above her head. They stopped for a moment and looked around. A few of the wounded were still being helped out of the ships as the river of fire started to take their fleet in its lethal embrace.

Mark did not want to look at the bodies entangled in the smoking drifts of rubble on the wharf, but he could not stop himself taking furtive, guilty glances. One pair of corpses caught his eye. Although his conscious mind baulked at absorbing any graphic images of their injuries, he quickly registered the fact that they were not dressed as the other Roman soldiers were. Rather than the moulded metal breastplates and overlapping plates of armour covering the shoulders, groin area and upper legs of the men of the city cohorts, these two men were dressed from head to foot with leather suits that gently steamed in the heat of the fires. And they both lay upon a crumpled net. The head of one of them was crushed under a great slab of fallen masonry; the other, whose lower half lay in a pool of blood under a burning beam, still wore a tightly bound facemask of what looked like wet brown towelling, and his leather headgear bulged at his ears.

It did not take a genius to work out that these men had been tasked to capture Mark with their net; that their leather suits were to protect them from his tranquilising gun; that their headgear concealed bulbous ear muffs to protect them from his siren, and that the wet material was to counter the effects of his now empty gas cylinder. Only the bomblets had been beyond their capacity to counter. Looking around again, he saw several men in similar attire mingled with the other corpses and among small knots of heavily guarded prisoners. 'That's probably all Quintus has done,' he thought as he considered the likelihood of Caesar hearing of the best means of defence against the gas from anyone else, 'just told Caesar everything he knew about Rome's enemies.'

Having escaped with fairly low numbers of casualties so far, Spartacus still led close to four thousand well-armed men, more than half of whom were disciplined, experienced fighters. Most of them charged into alleys and buildings to either side of those that were on fire. Meeting negligible resistance from the shocked and frightened Roman survivors, they quickly secured a narrow strip of territory to one side of a road that separated the predominantly commercial area they had landed in from the densely packed tenements of the Aventine residential area. Beyond the road, however, stood the heavily guarded buildings and barricades of Caesar's second line of defence. With those on either side of the road seemingly accepting a temporary stalemate, virtually everyone stood watching the burning buildings spreading fire to neighbouring buildings within the slave army's defensive perimeter or backed away from the wharf as the fiery river took their fleet in its lethal embrace.

Suddenly remembering the *Ladybird*, Mark ran to find it waiting for him in the rapidly diminishing stretch of fire-free river and dragged it ashore without much difficulty. Then he remembered the abandoned bomblet and, still thinking in terms of escape from Rome, he thought about the 'fake' fleet patrolling the estuary and wondered if they might come to rescue Spartacus and his men from their failed attempt to bluff the Senate into peace talks.

He joined Rani where she was taking cover behind the remains of a disused section of the Servian wall (which once defended the western end of the city before it expanded across the Tiber) and watched the fiercely burning fleet being swept towards the lesser fires of the river barrier. Thinking how foolish he had been to have left the last bomblet on New Earth unused in the middle of the barrier, he thought he might as well try to blow the barrier before the bomblet went to the bottom of the river. Having got Rani to call upon all those within earshot to take cover, he entered the bomblet's code on his mobile, shielded his eyes and pressed the 'send' button.

His doubts about the bomblet's ability to break both the chains proved well-founded. One of them broke, the other did not, but it made no difference. The explosion vaporised several of the boats and destroyed the rest. The shock of the explosion also caused the unbroken chain to thrash around and destroy the big pulleys that provided some of its tension and supported some of its weight on the banks, allowing it to sink to the bottom of the river. In addition, bits of flaming debris from the fire-boats were sent fanning outwards to set off yet more fires on either side of the river, and the slaves' fiercely burning fleet was slammed up against the bank at the edge of their small enclave.

The fallout from the explosion and the sudden inferno that their own shattered ships brought to the edge of their captured area killed at least half a dozen of Spartacus' men and burned or injured two or three dozen more. But it did something else too.

Caesar had deliberately sprung his trap between two of Rome's defence lines, one of which was the city's Servian wall, which had impressed Mark when he passed through it in Quintus' carriage the first time he came to Rome. The other, as Spartacus' men had already discovered, consisted of heavily guarded buildings and barricades thrown up by industrious legionaries a few hundred paces east of the Tiber. Caesar had selected this point partly because the river barrier linked the Servian wall's south-western terminus with a lesser defensive line that enclosed an area of suburbs (called 'Trans Tiberim', meaning 'across the Tiber') west of the river, and partly because the Servian wall would stop the main slave army joining Spartacus' men if they managed to land on the eastern bank. If Caesar's plan of entrapment went awry on the river, Spartacus' men would be sealed in a land trap.

Caesar's plan clearly had gone awry, but in a much more spectacular way than he could ever have imagined. After disgorging their occupants, the five burning ships were left to bump and scrape along the bank with the flow of the river until their starboard sides were shattered by the bomblet's explosion, which caused them to burst into a short-lived but utterly intolerable roar of flames and choking fumes that completely engulfed the end of the Servian wall. This not only inflicted death and injury among Spartacus' men, it also swept several Roman soldiers off the wall to their deaths and drove many others from their positions.

In addition, a small fortress, disguised as a stone warehouse, stood at the end of the wall and jutted nearly three metres into the river. This fortress was enveloped in flames and choking fumes, although its thick walls were not destroyed. The choked and scorched garrison within the fortress fled through whatever doorways they could before the heat and fumes roasted or asphyxiated them. While the fires were at their most intense, even the most stout-hearted of the wall's defenders were driven back at least three hundred paces from the river.

The first person to realise that this might present an unexpected opportunity was Spartacus' trusty scout and messenger, the black-bearded Brennus. Peering from behind the corner of a fire-free building beside Spartacus and Lili, he communicated his great faith in Mark's powers to his leader by suggesting that they should ask him to walk through the inferno to see what was on the other side. Having already seen Mark emerge unscathed after spending more than twenty seconds encased in fire, Spartacus decided it was worth a try. Collecting around twenty men as they went, they trotted up to Mark, who still squatted behind the remains of the old wall with his mouth hanging wide open, staring at the latest horror he had unleashed.

'Mark!' said Spartacus, 'come with me.'

Mark jerked to his feet in a nervous reaction to Spartacus' command and trotted obediently beside him with Rani and Lili following close behind.

When they got to the deserted area between their enclave and the deserted end of the wall, the intense blaze of the broken fleet was already beginning to lose some of its initial intensity as segments of the gutted ships toppled into the water with great hisses. What was left was also being dragged away by the seaward flow of the river, but flames still intermittently roared and spiralled around the disguised fortress as the flaming hulks bumped up against the three-metre section of the fortress that jutted into the river and scrunched up a mound of flaming debris in the angle between fortress and stone wharf. Pushing forward behind their shields as far as they could, Spartacus and a fast growing number of men behind him took stock of the deserted length of wall before them.

'Can you get onto that wall?' Spartacus called to Mark.

'I can get to the wall,' Mark replied, realising that they were looking at the Servian wall, 'but I'm not sure how I would get onto it.'

'If you could go up to it and take a look round, I would be very grateful.'

'Okay,' he said, feeling quite comfortable in the cool streams of filtered air flowing inside his force-field suit. Crossing the road that ran along this side of the wall, he came to a heavy iron door in the base of the wall, turned its big handle and pushed. It was locked. 'Probably a stairway,' he muttered to himself.

'Try that building on your right,' said Rani through his earpiece.

Looking to his right, he saw a shadowy recess. Moving through a billow of flames that swirled around the building, he saw that the recess was a porch that concealed an iron door which had been left wide open by the last of the fortress's occupants, who had been far too concerned about the searingly hot fumes in their lungs and their flaming hair and clothes to worry about closing doors behind them. Mark did not know why the door had been left open or what was inside, but he could see that the building was adjoined to the wall, so he reported his find to Rani and heard her relay his report to Spartacus.

'Could you see if there is a way from the building onto the wall?' Spartacus asked.

'Okay,' said Mark, hoping that no one could have managed to endure the heat and fumes within the building. Drawing out his siren and tranquilising gun, he stepped over the threshold into a world of lurid red smoke.

When he was inside he could see no more than a metre through the dense smoke, despite the diffused amber rays of the setting sun and the eerily flickering red glow of flames filtering through several small, heavily barred openings in the thick gable wall that abutted the river. Keeping Rani informed as he went, he came upon a stone staircase and made his way upwards hoping to find a way out of this spooky place before some macabre apparition leapt out of the smoke. He need not have worried about being attacked by someone lurking in the building; no living being could have survived without a force-field suit, but his sense of urgency was redoubled when Rani warned him that she could see Romans trying to get back to their positions on and below the wall.

On the first landing he came to a door made of iron bars. The door was locked and he could not see very far beyond the bars, but it looked like it led to a narrow, low-roofed passage inside the wall. On the second landing he found another metal door left open by the panicked garrison. He went through this door, into another narrow passage and saw a stone stairwell lit from above by daylight. He went up the stairwell and found that it led to a rampart along the top of the wall, and a hinged iron grate at the top of the stairwell had been left open. When he stuck his head into the open air, he saw a line of four Roman shields about twenty metres to his left moving gradually in his direction along the top of the rampart. While the soldiers behind the shields were protecting themselves against the diminishing but still intense heat, he padded up the few remaining stairs, crouched low and quietly made his way to within three or four paces of the shields without any sign of being noticed. Pointing his siren at the shields, he pressed his thumb on its button and held it there for two or three seconds.

The effect of the blast of sound was, as always, profound on the unwary. The shields were strapped to the forearms of the Roman soldiers, so they were not dropped, but they did buck and jump in time with their owners' shocked and fearful reaction to the hideous scream that seemed to burst into their heads from all directions. Tripping over each other in their haste to run away, they left Mark in control of a section of the Servian wall; Rome's main defensive structure. If he could defend it until the heat and acrid smoke in the building behind him had cleared enough for Spartacus and his men to join him, they could probably link up with the rest of the slave army.

However, looking down at his friends, he saw that they were facing a dense mass of Roman soldiers that had come along the roadway at the base of the wall, although both bodies of men appeared to have hesitated at the sound of his siren. Pointing the siren at the Romans, he treated them to a long and harrowing blast of terrifying noise. Ranks of shields quivered as if they were being struck by physical blows, but none of the soldiers ran away. Knowing that his tranquilising gun would be virtually useless against them, he kept his thumb on the siren's button until its sound suddenly dwindled to a sad little moan. It was empty, and still the Romans had not budged. Fishing around in his pockets, he drew out his torch. He could hardly imagine a more inoffensive gadget, but two of the Romans fled in panic and some of the others backed away in fear.

Realising that the power of his gadgets, especially his little silver bomblets, had communicated through the Roman ranks, he pointed his little silver torch at them and switched it on. Six or seven of the Romans broke ranks and fled when the bright beam played across their faces, and the whole force wavered in indecision. After performing an exaggerated mime of a cricket bowler preparing to deliver his throw, Mark sent the torch and its beam of light spinning through the smoky air towards the cowering mass of Romans as though he were throwing another devastating bomblet. Even Spartacus and his men, who were two or three hundred metres from where the torch would land, beat a hasty retreat to whatever protection they could find among the smoke and rubble behind them, but the Romans screamed and bolted as if the hounds of Hell were snapping at their heels.

With the fortress still too hot and full of fumes to occupy, Spartacus led several hundred men to block off any more Roman advances along the road below the wall. When they came to the area where the Roman soldiers had been before Mark's bluff had driven them off, Spartacus stooped to pick up the broken torch. As he straightened up, an iron door at the base of the wall opened and several Roman soldiers stumbled out coughing and spitting. These soldiers had been trying to make their way towards the fortress from within the wall, and might therefore have presented a threat to Mark, except that the enclosed passages they were moving through had trapped the choking, eye-stinging smoke and fumes inside. Seeking ventilation and communication with their comrades outside the wall, the half-blinded Roman soldiers could not understand why the men they met outside, most of whom held Roman shields and wore Roman helmets, suddenly started killing them.

When Spartacus and his men finished killing the soldiers he stepped through the doorway and signalled for Brennus to go left along the wall's ground floor passageway while he turned right towards the smouldering fortress, with men pouring in behind them both. Not knowing who was friend or foe in the near-darkness, most of the Romans who could flee did flee, while about a dozen who were trapped between the doorway and the fortress offered little resistance before they were put to the sword.

Racing up a stone stairway to the next level, Spartacus and his men charged along the first floor passageway stabbing at the backs of their semi-asphyxiated and terrified foes until an iron door was slammed shut and locked just ahead of them. Retreating back down the passage, they raced up another flight of steps to the second floor and found the stairwell that Mark had used to get to the top of the wall; with Mark waiting at the top of the steps to greet them.

In the meantime, word had spread through the slave army's enclave by the river and the entire force was now streaming towards the wall behind their wary rearguard and filing through the open door as quickly as they could. Having watched what they could of the action from across the road, Rani and Lili had nipped in front of the throng and joined their comrades on top of the wall before any interfering men said otherwise.

With the first and second floor passages now barred against them, Spartacus instructed some of his captains to stay behind with enough men to guard against counterattacks and to take possession of the fortress when the air within it had became cool and clear enough to breathe. He, Lili, Mark and Rani then led an ever lengthening column of men, four abreast, charging along the top of the wall to capture as much of it as they could before the Romans were able to organise a counter-attack.

Knowing that his force-field suit made him invulnerable to arrows, Mark pushed himself ahead of the column to draw as much fire as he could away from his friends, and was rewarded by the sight of dozens of Roman soldiers ahead wasting their arrows on him before vanishing down stairwells and slamming the heavy iron grates shut behind them. No one stood in their way, but their progress was soon barred by a square tower topped with castellated battlements about three metres above the main wall. Not realising that Spartacus had stopped the column a little way behind him to take stock of the obstacle, Mark went to within three or four paces of a closed iron door at the base of the tower, and stopped. He looked at the door, then up at the empty battlements above him, and with his heart pounding he waited for some new trap to be sprung upon him.

He heard sounds of clanking metal and leather-bound feet pounding on stone within the tower. Gulping nervously, he took a step or two backwards as faces appeared through the battlement's embrasures; and then one of them smiled through his blood-spattered beard, and said, 'what took you so long?' It was Brennus, looking like a ferret that had just emerged from a frenzied raid on a rabbit warren. Unlike Spartacus and his men, who had worked their way up through wall's first and second floor passageways, Brennus and his men had barrelled along the ground floor before the bemused Romans managed to slam any doors in their faces. Between them, they had captured several hundred metres of Rome's main defensive bastion.

A feeling of great relief swept over Mark as he fondly imagined that they had fought their way out of Caesar's trap. Even better, Spartacus seemed to have an ideal opportunity to unravel Rome's main defensive line and to position his disciplined men between the bulk of the slave army and the weakened and exposed city. Perhaps now the Roman Senate could be persuaded to talk peace.

However, given his extensive knowledge of Roman history, Mark's optimistic appraisal was strangely naïve. In fact, the wit and determination of Caesar, the resources of the Roman republic, the stubbornness of the Senate and the passionate hatred of slave owners for rebellious slaves was nowhere near played out.

As far as Caesar was concerned, the trap he had laid on the river was merely his opening gambit. He had of course hoped that this gambit would get lucky, but he was certainly not relying on it. While he thought of Mark as a sentimental fool, he had enormous respect for his devices, especially his explosive devices. Knowing that Mark had originally come to Rome with very little luggage, part of Caesar's aim had been to expend as much of Mark's other-worldly resources as possible. In terms of this aim, he had been extremely successful, much more successful than he realised. Caesar could not know it, but the only firepower left to Mark was thirty-four tiny tranquilising pellets, and he was about to use most of these in a very minor defensive duel while very major events were developing elsewhere.

14
FIRESTORM

The heavy iron door at the base of the tower was locked and Brennus' men could not open it from the inside. Not wishing to wait until the door's heavy hinges were dug out of the stone doorframe, Spartacus instructed sixteen of his men to use their shields to form a platform above their heads. Two men then braced a shield between them on their thighs to provide a step onto the platform. Eight other men bounded up the step and formed a platform of six shields and another step on top of the first platform, thus forming a human stairway between the wall and the battlements that topped the tower.

Mark tentatively followed Spartacus up this human stairway and Brennus helped him over the castellated battlements. The tower they had captured, Mark now realised, was one of a pair above the three gated arches of the Porta Trigemina, which he and Quintus had passed through after Mark's first brief visit to Rome. The gates were closed and the other tower was occupied by Romans who started shooting arrows at the invaders. Mark climbed onto the slave-held battlements to present himself as a tempting target and then carefully aimed his tranquilising gun at the Romans' bare forearms while their arrows bounced harmlessly off his force-field suit. He was not a good shot but the gun's sights were very accurate and he managed to tranquillise several before the rest gave up and took cover behind their battlements. Looking at the counter on his gun, he saw that he had just eight tranquilising projectiles left, and decided that these ought to be conserved for emergencies only, so he sat on the battlements and took in the scene around him.

Between their newly captured tower and the fortress by the river, which had now cooled enough for Spartacus' men to occupy, they held a solid defensive structure at each end of the stretch of rampart they controlled. With plenty of men to circle the iron grates at the top of stairwells leading to the Roman-held passages within the wall below their feet, a wary stalemate developed while everyone tried to work out what was happening elsewhere; and there seemed to be quite a lot happening elsewhere.

For one thing, Mark was taken aback at the number of fires there were in Rome. A significant portion of the city was blazing furiously, especially around the area where he had obliterated Caesar's fire-fleet, but he could also see many smaller fires much further off that he could not account for. Had his view not been obstructed by Rome's seven hills, he would have seen a great many more fires springing up across much of the city, but the sky was still too light for him to see the diffuse light of these fires and he was soon distracted by sounds of battle outside of the wall.

Spartacus' men had still not linked up with the main slave army, but they could hear and catch glimpses of fighting in the streets of the suburbs and commercial districts that had long since been built along the river outside the protection of the wall. This fighting was gradually drawing closer in the deepening twilight below them. Roman soldiers outside the wall were stubbornly and skilfully contesting the advance of the far more numerous slave army while the last of the Roman civilians living outside the Servian wall were passing through the Porta Trigemina into the main city. However, rather than the expected covering fire from their comrades on the wall, a merciless volley of spears and arrows suddenly struck many of the legionaries in their backs. The survivors promptly broke and fled in panic, leaving the exultant slave army to hew down scores of stragglers caught outside the wall when the gates slammed in their faces. About six hundred legionaries then surrendered when they found themselves caught in the angle between the river and the slave-controlled section of the Servian wall.

Spartacus' men had begun to chisel through the outer wall of the fortress by the river with their short but stout Roman swords, and this work was now taken up from the outside as well. When a large chunk of masonry was levered aside, Andichios stepped inside the fortress and thousands of men began filing through behind him, most of whom were expecting to join an all-out assault on Rome at first light.

Guessing what was afoot, Caesar had already ordered those of his troops inside the wall below Spartacus' men to evacuate their positions and join those defending an improvised series of linked strong points further inside the city. Now, with an ever growing host of his enemies gathering on the road on the inside of the Servian wall, Caesar ordered his troops to quietly abandon the entire south-facing stretch of the wall under the cover of night. Had he not ordered this withdrawal, a large portion of Rome's frontline forces would have been exposed to the kind of debacle that happened on Mark's world in 1940 after French frontline forces became trapped in the Maginot Line. In addition, Caesar was an aggressive commander who had every intention of taking the initiative as soon as he could. Defending two lines of defence would greatly reduce his options for offence, whereas abandoning the already breached wall in the south would enable him to increase the army he had already assembled in Trans Tiberim and an area just north of the main city, called Campus Martius, to over fifty thousand men, including twelve thousand cavalry and mounted infantry who had just arrived from Cisalpine Gaul.

Caesar was planning to lead this army along prepared routes through Rome to launch a blistering two-pronged attack upon the less disciplined mass of the slave army outside the Servian wall as soon as Spartacus moved on Rome's next line of defence.

Having swept away the 'rabble' from outside Rome, the slave army's best fighters would be bottled up and assailed from all sides, almost regardless of any devices that Mark might still be able to use in any one part of the battlefield. However, although this daring strategy suited Caesar's bold temperament, there was a problem developing in the areas of the city that his troops were preparing to pass through on their way to deliver their counter-stroke: Rome was rapidly catching fire.

The fires that Mark had set off were spreading to ever larger portions of southern and central Rome, and a huge number of other fires were taking hold in other parts of the city throughout the night. A few of the early fires had been caused by less disciplined elements among the slave army to the southeast of the city, many of whom took the conflagration caused by Mark's destruction of the fire-fleet as a conscious decision to burn Rome into submission, and they responded by shooting makeshift fire-arrows over the city walls. This had not been ordered by Julian, who Spartacus had left in overall control of the main army while he was with the fleet, but Crixus commanded several thousand infantry to the northeast of the city and he led them to the walls where they let loose volley after volley of fire arrows that they must have prepared for this very purpose. A large force of Roman cavalry and infantry sallied out and began driving Crixus' men off with heavy casualties, but this prompted the bulk of the slave army to move forward.

Hopelessly outnumbered, the Romans retreated behind their walls while most of the slave army set to making as many fire-arrows as they could using bits of cloth dipped in casks of lamp oil looted from Romans settlements. Now with Julian's consent, they sent these arrows winging over the walls like flocks of flaming starlings.

Seeing what appeared to be a concerted campaign to burn Rome down, hundreds of slaves within the city surreptitiously started fires by upsetting lamps or putting lighted candles under beds or next to curtain drapes or in wardrobes in their owners' homes, and others did the same in wooden workshops, theatres, stables, haylofts etc. Then thousands of slaves, destitute Romans, criminals seeking loot and assorted social misfits began to band together in large rebellious groups bent on large-scale arson. Roman soldiers scattered many of these groups, but they simply melted into the labyrinthine poorer districts to re-emerge elsewhere, leaving trails of fires behind them wherever they went.

Fear of being slain by these groups dissuaded most loyal Roman citizens from tackling any fires that were not directly threatening their own property, and even these limited efforts were coming to naught as hundreds of un-fought fires raged out of control and merged with each other. Before the night was over, order had broken down across much of the city to be replaced by the fire and fear that was spreading from district to district on this dry September morning at the end of a long dry summer. Even the port city of Ostia was not immune.

When the three hundred and forty men, women and boys aboard the five ships guarding the mouth of the Tiber saw the fiery mushroom cloud from the exploding fire-fleet, they thought they were witnessing the funeral pyre of Spartacus and his four thousand men. The sensible thing for them to do would have been to sail away from the estuary and rejoin their comrades on land as quickly as they could, but they dallied too long in their despair. When they finally made for the open sea they saw the silhouettes of a big Roman fleet coming at them out of the sunset, and promptly fled back towards the estuary. Thinking they were trapped and doomed, they did what they could to hit back at their enemies; and what they did said much about the bitter hatreds of this war.

Having transferred all of their people to one of their ships, they set the other four ships afire and cast them adrift with their helplessly screaming Roman prisoners still chained to their oars. Finding an unguarded wharf in Ostia, they did the same with their last ship and stormed ashore carrying torches and lanterns which they used to set fire to moored ships and any wooden structures they found, and killed any Romans who stood in their way. Their small efforts to set Ostia ablaze would have been contained and extinguished by Ostia's garrison and citizens, except that many of the port's already restive slaves took the opportunity to join what they took to be a planned campaign to liberate them. Some escaped slaves managed to link up with the desperate band of invaders and showed them where the port's galley slaves had been locked in their barracks for the night. Quickly overpowering their guards and releasing hundreds of tough and desperate men to join the rebellion, they set about a more systematic campaign to release all the slaves they could and set fire to as much of the city as they could while fighting running skirmishes against the Romans on their way to join the main slave army.

Meanwhile, the lack of activity on Roman-held sections of the Servian wall was noticed by Spartacus' men. Brennus led a stealthy reconnaissance party that found much of the wall had been abandoned, and the slave army's disciplined infantry then occupied it as quietly as Caesar's men had left it. Now having full contact with their main army, the four generals communicated through messengers and agreed to take advantage of Rome's problems by setting the impromptu campaign of arson on a more organised footing. Throwing open the wall's gates one at a time, dense phalanxes of heavily armed men shielded dense masses of archers as they moved towards Rome's second line of defence and poured waves of fire-arrows deeper into the city.

The Romans made sorties to drive them back but, as far as Mark was aware, none of these managed to break through the phalanxes before they retreated under covering fire from the captured wall. This pattern of incendiary attacks was repeated again and again across the southern flank of Rome, adding to the mounting conflagration in that part of the city and further stretching the disjointed Roman efforts to quell the fires elsewhere.

Mark spent an anxious and sleepless night watching all this develop from different parts of the captured wall and periodically arguing with Spartacus and Rani that the barrage of fire-arrows should be stopped. Neither Spartacus or Rani agreed with him. It was, they said, the right of the slaves within the city to rebel in whatever way they could and the duty of the ex-slaves outside Rome to help them. They did, however, concede that an all-out attempt to storm Rome might unleash a holocaust of unprecedented proportions, or else it might be defeated and allow many of the Romans facing them to be released to suppress the rebellion within the city.

The pragmatic solution, they argued, was to maintain the threat of an imminent all-out attack so as to pin Caesar's forces in their defensive positions, and for the Roman Senate to ponder over the ruination of their city until they agreed to end slavery. With nearly a third of Rome's main wall now securely occupied and all the regions to the south and east of Rome in the hands of the ever growing slave revolt, they were growing stronger while Rome was growing weaker. But they needed to keep up the pressure to bring the war to a conclusion before Roman field armies arrived from overseas. If this was not done by storming the city or by fire, then what else did he suggest they do? Mark had no answer to this, only his intense guilt that he had caused the slave army to come to Rome in the first place, and that he, the biggest arsonist of them all, had set the whole burn-down-Rome thing going in his desperate efforts to save his friends from Caesar's trap.

After yet another fruitless exchange of words with Spartacus and Rani, Mark wandered disconsolately through a door guarded by two sentries who respectfully bowed their heads in his direction, and trudged up the internal staircase to one of the wall's two towers overlooking this end of the Appian

Way. Despite his dislike of deference, he barely noticed the four men at the battlements as they turned towards him, bowed low and deferentially withdrew down the steps to leave him alone. Looking across the city, he thought the fires looked more extensive and brighter than they did when he last took a good look at them, just twenty or thirty minutes earlier. The scene reminded him of old newsreels of cities that had been carpet bombed during the Second World War, and it was getting worse rather than better.

'Oh my God!' he muttered to himself as he tried to take in what he had done to the 'eternal city' that had fascinated him for as long as he could remember. 'I can't believe I've actually set Rome on fire!' He had not done this alone, of course, but he knew that nothing like this had happened during the Third Servile War on his own planet Earth, so he felt entirely responsible for what was happing here. As he reflected on these things, his mobile rang.

'Mark?' said Kim's voice.

'Kim? How did you . . .'

'Never mind that; what on New Earth are you *doing*?'

'I, err, I . . .'

'Have you *any* idea what you've done?'

'Err, I guess I've, erm, I guess I've kind of made a mess of things, haven't I?'

'Kind of made a mess of things? For God's sake, Mark, you've TORCHED ROME!'

'Yes, yes, I know,' he said, feeling his eyes grow hot and heavy with tears. 'I didn't mean to.'

'You *didn't mean to*? Well, no, I dare say you didn't,' she said in an almost sympathetic tone, a tone that surprised Mark given the enormity of what he had done, 'but *bloody hell*, Mark, it's beginning to look as if the whole of Rome might go up in a firestorm!'

'A firestorm?'

'Yes, a firestorm! All those fires are sucking in the air; can't you feel the wind picking up?'

He could not feel the wind through his force-field suit, but there was something about the intensity of the fires that didn't seem quite right.

Kim did not say anything else for a while, and it occurred to him that she must be watching from the Institute's spy satellites without being concerned that the Americans might sever their communications at any moment.

'What happened, Kim?' he asked.

'Eh?' she replied in a distracted way that seemed to confirm that she was as transfixed by the sight of Rome burning as he was.

'I mean about our communications.'

'Oh, the Americans switched us back on.'

'Why?'

'Because they realised that you are a lethal loose cannon that someone has to try to control, and they're still too far away to stop you bringing murder and mayhem wherever you go.'

'Oh, right, I see.'

'Mmm.'

'So,' he said, 'what do you think I should do now?'

'Arrange for me to talk to Spartacus as a matter of the utmost urgency,' she said, becoming brisk again, 'but do absolutely nothing else until we get down there.'

'Here? You're coming down here?'

'Yes. We have come to, err, an understanding with the Americans.'

'What kind of understanding?'

'I'll tell you all about it when I get there. In the meantime, I *really* don't want you stirring things up any more, understood?'

'I'm not trying to stir things up,' he protested, but Kim had already cut the call.

'Right,' he said to himself without knowing why.

Before Mark went to find Spartacus, he spent several minutes watching the fires and pondering what he knew about ancient Rome before he came to New Earth, what he had seen of the city via the Gandhi Institute's spy satellites, what he knew about firestorms, and whether he might really be watching the genesis of a fully-fledged firestorm.

A great many Romans, not just the poor, lived in tenements built mainly of wood. Often six, seven or even eight stories high, many of these tenements faced each other across narrow streets and alleys. Some of them were so old and dilapidated or so poorly constructed by unscrupulous landlords that they were tipping towards each other, and may have met above the streets or collapsed into them had they not been braced apart by beams of wood. In terms of fire hazards, the narrow streets between the tenements could act almost as tunnels in which any flames escaping from the lower floors would lick the sides of the upper floors, and any draught of wind would fan the flames towards other tenements. If this process took hold over a wide area, the trapped flames could flow down a whole series of streets and draw in ever larger amounts of fire-fuelling air until the fires within them roared like jet engines. When burning tenements collapsed, they would send out billowing showers of burning debris and glowing sparks that the wind could waft into other districts.

On Mark's own world, the great fire of Rome in 64 AD, from which derived the legend of Nero fiddling while Rome burned, happened a hundred and thirty-five years after the Third Servile War ended. That fire had lasted six days and gradually spread from district to district. Estimates vary in respect of how much of the city was consumed, but most put the figure at between fifty and seventy percent. Mark did not know whether any kind of firestorm played a part in that catastrophe, but he did know that what was happening now was different, mostly because fires had sprung up in most districts of the city within hours rather than days. This contracted timeframe inevitably meant that the effects of the blaze would be far more intense, and therefore far more likely to set up the conditions that give rise to a self-sustaining firestorm.

A firestorm is essentially a miniature weather system created by rapidly rising hot air sucking in cooler air to replace it. The inflow of cooler air feeds the fire with oxygen, which creates more hot air that rises and pulls in more cooler air. As this process builds it can have a number of knock-on effects. Mark's gloomy mood focused on one of the gloomiest knock-on effects. That is, the mounting heat of the fire can penetrate below ground and expand pockets of trapped gas, such as methane from the accumulated refuse of cities that have stood for hundreds of years. For all of Rome's vaunted sewage systems, it nonetheless sat on top of centuries of refuse and human and animal effluent. The fires that he had initiated might now be expanding vast pockets of methane gas that had collected since the days of the Etruscan kings and earlier. If such pockets of gas started gushing through cracks in the ground into the fires, what would happen then? He shuddered at this thought and went to find Spartacus.

On his way, he tried to take a more optimistic perspective and his thoughts wandered to the oddly sympathetic tone in Kim's voice. He would have expected her to sound utterly enraged by all that he had done since they last spoke, especially if an all-consuming firestorm was really in the offing. She had been accusational, but her tone was not enraged, or even particularly angry, despite some harsh words. 'It's because the Americans have agreed to bring her here,' he thought, 'so she'll be taking an active role again instead of fretting in space.' Then he wondered if Rebecca, Tarak, Sunita and Tsang would be brought to the planet's surface too. And perhaps even Peter would be revived and fixed up by the suddenly obliging Americans!

But why? What were the Americans up to? The only thing he could think of just then was that Kim and the others would make useful witnesses for the Prosecution in Mark's trial for mass murder, or even for crimes against humanity. Perhaps they would all be put on trial, or at least Kim and Tarak for their part in Mark's trail of death and destruction. No, that couldn't be it, otherwise Kim would have been unambiguously furious. 'They must have agreed to blame me for everything. And why not? It was mostly my doing.' But that didn't seem enough either. 'They must have made a deal that benefits the Americans,' he decided, 'probably allowing Kim and the others to go free in return for rubber-stamping American claims to everything on New Earth, and put me in prison for the rest of my life,' he thought glumly.

Coming to where he had last spoken with Spartacus, he found only soldiers looking over the wall, so he asked one of them if he knew where Spartacus was.

'He's down there,' said the soldier, speaking softly and deferentially at the telling-stone in Mark's hand and pointing to the roadway on the inside of the wall, 'talking to Roman senators.'

'Really?' Mark said, looking down and seeing an indistinct gathering of people standing in shadows that were beginning to be penetrated by diffuse light from the flaming city and the equally diffuse ruddy light of a smoke-obscured sunrise. At least now there seemed to be some chance of a negotiated peace before it was too late. With this hopeful thought in mind, he looked again at the burning city and thought he saw a faint orangey-red flicker in the sky above one of the more intensely burning areas of Rome.

It flickered again, slightly more distinctly. Then again, and this time he thought the flicker moved up from the fire and spiralled as it rose. It happened several more times, and it seemed that the intervals between flickers were getting shorter and the flickers getting longer and brighter. Hardly daring to blink, he realised that he had seen this sort of effect before, very recently. It looked like a pale imitation of the fire-whirls that danced over the burning river of fire after he destroyed Caesar's fire-fleet; except that this fire-whirl was not a few metres high, it was a few *hundred* metres high. It was, he thought, now too late to save Rome from an all-consuming firestorm.

The massive orangey-red fire-whirl that he was watching develop was partly a result of gasses released from the fires above ground and partly from heated methane gas escaping through fissures in the city's sewage systems that the intense fires had opened up. South-central Rome, where the fires were at their hottest, was now drawing in huge quantities of gas and air. The flickering of the fire-whirl was the result of gases that had not quite caught fire until they were above the flames. When it ceased to flicker and stayed alight, it would diminish in height but grow in intensity as it merged with the main fire, and this would draw in yet more air and intensify the whole process.

Mark thought about shouting a warning to Spartacus but there was nothing he would be able to do about it now except make peace and hope for the best. So instead of interfering with the negotiations he ran back to the tall tower he had just left to get a better view. This time the four men on top of the tower, who had also been watching the strange flickering light, bent almost double bowing to him and hastened for the stairs and the reassuring company of their comrades on the wall below.

After watching the fire-whirl flicker a few more times, Mark saw it lose some of its height but become much more intense as it merged with the fire below. The whole roaring, dancing, high-peaked inferno began to look like some evil ethereal fortress thrusting its twisting central spire upwards as though it were intent on burning the heavens. The light from the fire illuminated a great spreading mushroom cloud above it with an eerie red glow. At the cloud's outer edges, the red light of the fire below it and the amber light of the sunrise behind it merged to illuminate the cooling curtains of falling ash with a ghoulish ruddy hue as they curled back towards the fire on the gathering wind. The overall effect was as if the mouth of some vast fiery monster was closing upon the entire city; which was not so very far from the truth.

If that was not enough to frighten the superstitious people of that age, a layer of moist air was drifting over the city from the sea on this early autumn morning. When this moist layer met the mushroom cloud it turned it into a 'pyrocumulus' cloud. Pyrocumulus clouds are not an uncommon feature of firestorms. The hot cloud that rises above a firestorm can become pyrocumulus when the cloud's agitated molecules generate static electricity. When there are enough water molecules present, the static electricity manifests itself in lightning flashes. In some cases the lightening can reach back to the ground and trigger other fires. The lightning flashes on this fateful morning were not violent enough to reach the ground or start new fires, but they were strong enough to send crackling traceries of light through the mushroom cloud and to give the illusion of diabolic life surging through the pulsating beast above.

Even Mark, who loosely understood the science of what was happening, felt his stomach contract with fear at the sight of the demonically glowing monster folding in upon him. For those who had no understanding of firestorms, the effect was generally one of maddening fear. From the southern, western, eastern and central districts of the main city, much of the populace was moving in panicked streams towards the northern gates of the Servian Wall or across the Tiber's bridges to the less afflicted areas of Trans Tiberim, and many were streaming out of the city altogether. Perhaps more importantly, from the slave army's point of view, the fifty thousand soldiers that Caesar had quietly gathered to the north and west of the main city could not be made to move under the monstrous apparition that hung over the routes of their planned counter-attack, despite the force of Caesar's character and his threats of mass executions. Even if they could be made to move, they would have been hard pressed to make much headway against the hordes of panicking refugees, and there was absolutely no chance of his cavalry and mounted infantry coaxing their terrified horses through the screaming throng or going anywhere near that hellish lightning-capped mountain of fire.

Many among the slave army and most of their horses were also streaming away from the city in fear, although most of the infantry just crouched in quivering awe or crowded into the shelter of the great wall. Or, as was the case for hundreds gathered in the shadow of the wall behind Mark, getting to their knees in supplication to the 'God of Fire' who stood alone on the high turret in his strange suit surveying the awesome beast that they believed he had summoned from the bowels of the Earth to smite their enemies.

With his back turned towards the growing mass of his uninvited and unnoticed worshipers, Mark's mind wandered back to his first visit to Rome. The contrast between what he was now looking at and his earlier worries about Quintus disturbing the peace of a Roman family so that Mark could use their toilet suddenly struck him as both macabre and funny. He thought his toiletry excursion was probably the closest he had come to the centre of the city that had fascinated him for so many years. He had not visited the Senate House or the Circus Maximus or any of the city's temples or famous landmarks or walked around its bustling market places; just a toilet above a clothes shop. Now it looked as though it was all going to be destroyed by the fires that he had initiated. He was letting out a slightly insane laugh at this thought when Spartacus, Lili and Rani approached him from behind.

'What are you doing?' asked Rani.

Snapping out of his morbid reverie, he turned and saw the gathering of prostrate worshipers behind him.

'Oh God,' he said, 'what are they doing?'

'They are worshiping their god of fire,' said Spartacus.

'What god of fire?'

'You.'

'What? I'm not a god!'

'They think you are.'

'I don't want them to think that! Say something to them, tell them I'm not a god.'

'They won't believe me,' said Spartacus, holding out a hand to catch flakes of ash that the wind was blowing back towards the inferno, 'not when you keep acting like one.'

'Nonsense, I haven't been acting like a god at all! It's just that things keep going wrong.'

'Going wrong? I'm not sure I would agree with that. Roman civilians are streaming away from their city. Their soldiers are being forced to leave their next line of defence in places where the fires are too fierce to stand. Some of our men have already taken abandoned sections of the line, although most of them are taking shelter until the fires subside.'

'You must stop them sacking Rome!'

'Sacking Rome? I don't think there will be much left to sack, at least not east of the Tiber. But many thousands of slaves are not fleeing with the Romans. Large numbers of them cannot get to us, so they are crowding into unburned parts of the city hoping that we will come to them. We must open routes around the fires to link up with them before they are burned alive or butchered by vengeful Romans.'

'Oh, I see, yes, yes of course,' Mark agreed, as he almost always did after speaking with Spartacus, or with Rani. 'What about the negotiations?'

'Negotiations?'

'I saw you speaking to Roman senators below the wall.'

'Oh yes, they said they would exchange ten slaves for every one of their soldiers and citizens returned to them, which I thought was very insulting to slaves. Nonetheless, I insisted on twenty slaves per Roman, and they agreed, although I expect they were just playing for time.'

'Nothing about ending slavery?'

'No, they would not discuss anything else. It seems they cannot stand the idea that we are as human as they are. They cannot cope with the thought of being beaten by us, and nor have they been as yet. I think they are now too frightened and demoralised to defend any of Rome east of the Tiber against a determined attack, but they may well try to hold out west of the river until Pompey and their other generals bring their armies back to Italy.'

'Oh God,' said Mark in despair, 'will it never end?'

'The Romans are a strangely determined people, Mark, but I do not think that they, or you, fully understand what has happened here. When we came here we were tens of thousands, and yet we were still far too few to take on the might of Rome. With the help of your god-like services, literally millions of slaves throughout Italy and Rome's overseas possessions will hear of what we have done to their once great city. Whatever the senators decide to do, I think it is too late for them to intimidate their slaves, as they still could after you broke the wall of Capua. I may be able to hold our people in check for a while, but if the Romans do not yield soon then I know of no way to end this that does not involve a final and massive wave of bloodletting, regardless of what you or Kim say or do to stop it.'

It was then that Mark remembered Kim's urgent request to speak to Spartacus.

Mark called Kim with Spartacus, Lili and Rani gathered around his mobile to listen to what was said. In what was effectively a monologue rather than a conversation, Kim explained how things stood in space. While she was talking and Mark's mobile was translating, thousands of slaves within the city, including hundreds of gladiators, took matters into their own hands by storming some of the fortified barriers that still separated them from the slave army. The few nervous Romans soldiers who had not already fled in fear from the cataclysmic turn of events that had left them sandwiched between two hostile forces while their city was consumed by fire, threw spears at the attackers and then bolted. One of the barriers successfully stormed was a sturdy barricade of dressed stone blocks behind a dense thicket of sharpened iron stakes that slanted towards the tower where the foursome stood watching and listening to Kim.

As relieved as they all were to see the mass of escaping slaves pouring over the barricade, tearing gaps in the stakes and joyfully mingling with the slave army, Mark was probably more relieved by what Kim had to say. It seemed that not all of the eighteen Americans were baying for his blood. Indeed, during a conference call in which she had been invited to take part in a free and open debate, three of the Americans had vociferously *supported* his efforts to help the slaves. Demands for a vigorous enquiry into all of Mark's actions and those of the other Gandhi Institute personnel were agreed by everyone involved in the conference call, including Kim. However, despite some furious tirades against the three 'Markists' among them, all of the Americans agreed that they had to deal with the situation as it currently stood by helping to end the war as quickly and as peacefully as possible. There was no consensus as to exactly how the war might be ended, but a clear majority had eventually agreed upon some interim objectives.

The essence of these interim objectives was that Spartacus' army should move into the ruins of the main city, which they were clearly going to do anyway, but leave the Romans in possession of the less extensively damaged suburbs west of the river. Both sides could then negotiate the exchange of all captives, whether they were slaves or prisoners of war. If it looked like the more aggressive elements from either side could not be adequately controlled, the bridges linking the two unequal parts of the city could be destroyed. If the two sides could not be brought together in the long term, then it behoved those who had access to sophisticated technologies to help them build two fine new cities; one on top of the ashes of the main city, the other built in and around Trans Tiberim and the Janiculum heights further to the west, and hope that these might one day unite into one. The analogy used to describe this eventuality was the twin cities of Buda and Pest that eventually amalgamated into Budapest on the other Earth. This was far from consistent with the Gandhi Institute's 'non-interventionist raison d'être', but Mark had effectively forced their hands with his wanton interference.

As for the Roman fleets and armies currently moving towards Rome from other countries, Kim's view was that their piecemeal arrival and the ever growing strength of the rebellion would force them to take refuge west of the Tiber or in fortified cities elsewhere in Italy. That being the case, she thought they could probably be contained without too much bloodshed by Spartacus' more disciplined troops aided, if necessary, by a newly *obedient* Mark and the judicious use of information technology, at least until the Americans and Gandhi Institute personnel got to the planet's surface.

Mark was hugely relieved. Rome was burning while they talked, but at least now they had a coherent plan to end all the death and destruction. It also seemed that they were about to be joined by at least three like-minded Americans who might be able to deflect some of the fury of the religious fundamentalists that he so feared. Given these positive developments, Mark silently resolved to be utterly obedient in all his dealings with Kim from now on.

However, he had some difficulty with the very first thing that she asked her newly obedient employee to do. She wanted him to play up to the 'God of Fire' nonsense in order to give him greater leverage over aggressive elements of the slave army; notably Crixus. Crixus was, she told him, currently leading several thousand men around the northern outskirts of Rome to attack the panicking Romans fleeing west from the city, and many thousands of agricultural slaves were streaming from their owners' estates to join Crixus' men. If Spartacus was willing, Kim wanted Mark to accompany him to Crixus' camp and back up Spartacus' authority over his men by claiming that he could intimidate the Romans into abolishing slavery without further bloodshed by threatening to conjure up another firestorm. Spartacus was willing.

Mark was not sure how much Spartacus had understood about the goings on in space, although he clearly understood that it was better to have these other-worldly beings helping the rebellion rather than using their powers against it. Enough horses were soon found for Spartacus, Lili, Mark, Rani, Brennus and about twenty other men to ride to Crixus' camp.

They rode from under the flickering pyrocumulus cloud until their horses became less skittish. When they emerged from the rain of ash they were greeted by a beautiful morning of mellow sunshine spilling over a well ordered pastoral landscape. Riding in an arc around the east and north of Rome with the ominous mushroom cloud to their left, the contrast between the hellish scene in the city and the peaceful countryside could hardly have been more stark. Had it not been for the insistent thumping of their horses hooves they would have been treated to a gentle cacophony of country sounds; birds were chirruping, cows were lowing, sheep were bleating and dogs were barking in the distance. Looking around at his grimy ash-covered companions, it struck Mark that they must look like ghostly harbingers of doom spawned by the carnage they had left behind them and bent on spreading death and destruction wherever they go. 'No,' he corrected himself, 'wherever *I* go.'

They came to Crixus' camp as his men were preparing to launch their attack, and found Crixus at the head of more than fifty horsemen blocking their entrance to his command tent. Just the look on his face told the newcomers that he was in no mood to postpone the attack, regardless of whatever Spartacus or anyone else had to say about it.

As it happened, Mark, who was still wearing his force-field suit, as he had throughout the long sleepless night, presented Crixus with one very persuasive argument. After having tried to mentally rehearse the God of Fire role that Kim wanted him to play if Crixus proved obdurate, he decided that he was just too tired and emotionally exhausted to pull it off. So, while Spartacus exchanged some very tense words with his old friend about who was in overall command of the troops in the camp, Mark took out his tranquillising gun and shot a pellet into Crixus' bare arm without uttering a word.

There was a moment of silence after Crixus flopped unconscious to the ground, which Spartacus broke by asking Mark: 'who's in charge here?'

'You are,' Mark replied, moving his gun from side to side to discourage any argument from Crixus' followers, none of whom appeared to know that Crixus was not dead.

Spartacus issued some terse orders at Crixus' men to carry his inert body into his command tent and then to await further instructions from their commander, while jabbing his index finger at his own chest to make it clear that the commander he was referring to himself, not Crixus. After barking out the word 'NOW!', some of Crixus' erstwhile followers dismounted and did as they were told. When they came out of the tent, Spartacus asked Mark, Rani and Lili to stand guard over Crixus while he and his trusted men went to assert their authority over the whole of the camp. And that was pretty much it as far as any proposed attack on the western suburbs of Rome was concerned.

Whether by accident or design, the moment that Spartacus and his men were gone, Mark got another call from Kim.

'Hi Kim. Job done, I think,' he said as he advanced on a freshly cooked chicken on the table in Crixus' tent.

'Mmm, not exactly what I had in mind, but I suppose it will do. Now, I've been talking with the Americans again and they want you on your boat as soon as possible.'

'The *Ladybird*?'

'The what?'

'Oh, that's what I call my boat.'

'Right. Well, they want you on the *Ladybird* as soon as possible.'

'Why?'

'They will be sending a team to revive Peter and treat his injuries shortly after they reach orbit. They should get there about the same time that you do if you leave within the next twenty-four hours, and they want you safely out of the way before you destroy any more cities.'

'Revive Peter?' said Mark, realising that his active involvement in the war was probably over, 'will I be able to speak to him?'

'You will need to ask permission from the Americans. But yes,' Kim said in a fairly friendly tone, 'I expect so.'

'What about the war? I thought you wanted me to help Spartacus to keep the Romans contained until it was over.'

'I said *if necessary*. Julian and Andichios seem to be acting in a restrained way. With Spartacus in control of Crixus' men, it looks as though things might calm down for a while. As for the Romans, the Senate appears to have put your friend Quintus in charge of things, which suggests that they are ready to talk peace.

'Really? That's fantastic!'

'Don't get too excited, it may all be some kind of bluff, and you might be recalled to Italy at any time if we or the Americans desperately need to speak to Spartacus, but I doubt it. I will keep you informed of all major developments on the ground. In the meantime, please, please, *please* promise me that you will do *exactly* as you are told: get on your boat and get out of Italy within the next twenty-four hours. Because if you don't, you risk losing any support you might have among the Americans and put anything you might have achieved in jeopardy.'

Mark could scarcely believe it; Kim used the word 'achieved', albeit in a qualified way, to described what he had done. But he had initiated the destruction of Rome and the deaths of thousands of people! How could such a senior figure in the Gandhi Institute possibly think of that in terms of an achievement?

'Yes, Kim, I promise!' he said, thinking he ought to have all sorts of questions to ask her but feeling too exhausted and light-headed to think of any. Besides, he was hardly able to contain his eagerness to hand over responsibility for any future interventions in the war or to work out what to do about the burnt-out ruins of Rome. Things might still go very badly for him personally, but he did not have the mental energy left to think about that either. For now, the prospect of seeing Peter's face when he heard about what Mark had done in his absence was as much as he wanted to think about; that and not being parted from Rani. So, finally, he was ready to do what Kim asked him to do: he would go back to where he had buried Peter in his suspended animation module. But not right away.

He had been meaning to ask Spartacus, Julian and Andichios about the kind of society they wanted to build to replace 'Roman order', and maybe suggest a few ideas of his own. But he badly needed to catch up on some sleep before he started discussing brave new worlds with people who were likely to take him seriously.

15
WORLDS APART

The firestorm and the loss of the city's southern defensive system had taken the fight out of the Roman soldiers, so Caesar ordered them to fall back to the Tiber and the northern stretch of the Servian Wall until he could launch his counter offensive. While Spartacus was reasserting his authority over Crixus' men, Andichios cautiously led several thousand men deeper into south-western Rome, skirting around the fiercely burning areas until they approached two heavily guarded bridges across the river. At the same time, Julian led many thousands more along and beside the abandoned eastern stretch of the Servian Wall until they came to a heavily guarded fortress on the wall's north-eastern corner. Both groups then stopped, built stout barricades just out of bowshot range of the Romans and waited for the firestorm to burn itself out. The ferocity of the fire in the centre of the city soon consumed all flammable materials, allowing tens of thousands of armed ex-slaves to pick their way northwards through the smouldering ruins without meeting any organised resistance.

Roman senators and generals vowed to pursue the war to ultimate victory, but they had lost confidence in Caesar. Given that he had had no military successes whatsoever against 'mere slaves', and knowing nothing about Caesar's reputation on Mark's world as being one of history's most brilliant military commanders, most senators deemed him to be an utter failure.

While it was true that the slave army had been aided by Mark, Caesar had repeatedly dismissed him as 'nothing more than a conjurer'. The reason he did this was to lessen Roman fears about Mark's powers. Caesar had been very successful in this. In fact, he had been far too successful for his own good. Now that the slave army and their 'conjuror' had managed to unite with the slaves of Rome to take possession of the ashes of the main city, including the fire-gutted Senate House, many senators concluded that Caesar must be one of history's *worst* military commanders. They therefore dismissed him from command, took possession of his property and ordered him to leave the remnants of their once great city in disgrace, alone and on foot.

Having found their scapegoat, the senators ordered the fortification of Trans Tiberim, the only piece of Rome which they felt they had any realistic prospect of defending in the face of the enormous number of jubilant ex-slaves now pouring into Rome and converging on the deeply demoralised legionaries in Campus Martius, which lay outside the northern stretch of the Servian Wall. When this was done, they could prepare for a long war. To do this, they decided that they must have a period of peace. Not a long period of peace, just a few weeks to gather all their field forces and to recruit a new citizen army from the hordes of refugees who had fled the main city. Although it pained them to do anything that their foes wanted them to do, they thought the slave army might be duped into allowing them a breathing space if they appointed Mark's 'friend', Quintus Aurelius Saturnalicus, their First Consul.

As soon as Quintus took over the reins of power he ordered his men in Campus Martius to retreat across the Tiber and all Romans in Trans Tiberim and elsewhere in Italy to start releasing their remaining slaves in return for their captured soldiers and citizens at the agreed ratio of twenty slaves for each Roman. So that is what they did, without any notion that what they were doing was broadly in line with the interim objectives agreed in space. The main difference was that the Americans apparently viewed these objectives as a prelude to ending the war, whereas most Roman senators and generals viewed them as a prelude to another round of war and the eventual annihilation of the ex-slaves.

In the meantime, Spartacus had split Crixus' men into detachments led by his trusted lieutenants and sent some to join their main army and others to spread the rebellion far to the north and east. He put Brennus in charge of the most reliable detachment and entrusted him with the task of intimidating the fleeing Romans back towards Rome without actually attacking them. Feeling less threatened by the subsiding fires in Rome than by the appearance of Brennus' men on the crests of low hills, most of those who had fled the city hastily turned back and made for the already overcrowded enclave of Trans Tiberim. To make room for some of the huge numbers of Roman citizens who had lost their homes, the relatively large communities of Jews, Syrians and other non-Romans who had long called this part of the city home were being hastily rounded up and herded across the Tiber's bridges into the ruins of the main city. When this bout of ethnic cleansing was more or less complete, Quintus would order the bridges to be destroyed and all Roman forces on the Italian mainland to go onto the defensive until help arrived from overseas and they were ready to retake the initiative. They would, however, have a long wait.

The rebellion was sweeping through rural Italy, isolating fortified Roman and allied cities from the food producing hinterlands of Italy and driving many thousands of Roman citizens to seek protection behind solid city walls. Fearing starvation if they allowed their troops to be bottled up in small overcrowded cities or in the Trans Tiberim enclave, the Roman commanders were also afraid that their overseas possessions might be overrun by their own restive slaves or others who were keen to take advantage of the Roman Republic's enfeebled condition. One by one, the generals and admirals would take it upon themselves to bring their men and ships back to the provinces from which they had come.

Spartacus had spent four or five hours exhorting and bullying some of Crixus' more stubborn men to turn their backs on the refugees streaming from the ruined city and march elsewhere, and he was now in a hurry to return to Rome. Having done what he set out to do, he came back to the command tent and found Mark snoozing in a chair while Crixus slept soundly on a couch. Mark had used another of his precious tranquilising pellets when Crixus started to wake up about fifteen minutes earlier, so he did not think he was neglecting his guard duties by snatching a few uneasy winks. Besides, Rani and Lili sat on chairs on the other side of Crixus, toying with wicked-looking daggers, which were still greasy from demolishing Crixus' cooked chicken, while they chatted about all that had happened since they left Mount Vesuvius.

'I must go back to Rome now,' said Spartacus, 'will you come with me?'

'Yes,' Mark replied immediately. Despite his tiredness, he very much wanted to placate the Americans by voluntarily presenting himself to them before they came to get him, and he didn't know if the *Ladybird* was still where he had left it on the wharf beside the Tiber. Going back to Rome now with Spartacus would give him a chance to talk to him about the future without delaying his departure. 'What about Crixus?'

'When will he wake up?'

'I've just given him another dose, so he should be out for at least another four hours, I think.'

'Then leave him. The camp is almost empty now, so I don't think he can do any harm.'

When they walked out of the tent, the cloud above Rome was no longer mushroom-shaped. There was no wind to speak of at ground level, but a slight breeze higher up had bent and stretched the cloud over the camp and a gentle rain of fine ash was obscuring the glow of the city's diminishing fires. The foursome mounted their horses and set off at a comfortable pace. Mark rode beside Spartacus while Rani and Lili rode together still locked in conversation.

'So,' said Mark, trying to strike up a conversation about the future, 'what do you think will happen now?'

'I don't know.'

'Do you think most of the slaves will stay together in Italy or go back to their homelands?'

'I don't know.'

'If they stay, what kind of society would you like to see come out of all this?'

'I don't know.'

'Oh. I thought you might have something in mind. You know, like setting up some kind of government, that sort of thing.'

'I don't know.'

'Oh, right, I see,' said Mark, feeling slightly snubbed. Silence descended over their party until Rani drew up beside Mark and Lili drew up beside Spartacus, and Rani said, 'get on with it, you two, we all know you both have dreams. Now's your chance to talk about them.'

Spartacus and Mark gave each other sidelong glances, but said nothing.

Lili was next to break the silence. 'Spartacus, you told me plenty about your dreams; about everyone being of equal worth, about how people will hold all things in common, about how there will be no rich or poor people, about a world where everyone shares all with all, about taking care of the weak and ill, and so on. Why won't you talk to Mark about your dreams?'

'Because I am waiting to be told what kind of society we will be allowed to build.'

'Allowed?' asked Mark.

'You come from a sophisticated world, I do not. Yes, I have dreams, but whatever I say will sound like the babblings of a child to you and your people.'

'Not to me! I want to hear about it.'

'And will your people take any notice of what I or our people say or think?'

'Well, yes, taking notice of what people think is called democracy, and my people like democracy.'

'That's what the Romans say, and the Greeks, but they do not mean it, not as far as slaves or poor people are concerned.'

'Ah,' said Mark, thinking he was beginning to understand, 'but in my world, democratic societies do not have slaves and everyone gets to vote on who should govern them, including women.'

'Fine,' said Spartacus, 'so you tell us how to make this democracy work and we will do what you say. What need is there for my dreams?'

This was not the kind of conversation that Mark had hoped for and he found it unsettling. What could he say? Would he explain how modern democracies work so that the ex-slaves could learn to replicate the kind of society that he grew up in, or was that the sort of cultural imperialism that the Gandhi Institute's 'non-interventionist raison d'être' was designed to avoid? He didn't know what to say, so he said nothing. After a prolonged and awkward silence, Rani made another attempt to bridge the enormous gap that separated their two worlds.

'There are many poor people on your world, Mark. I think Spartacus does not want this to be so on our world.'

'Yes,' Mark agreed, 'there are many poor people on my world, but there are many countries in which very few people are poor and virtually no one goes hungry.'

'Is that because of your democracy or because of your devices?' Rani asked. 'Or is it because there are many other countries where a great many other people are poor and do go hungry because the rich countries of your world take their resources?'

These were not easy questions to answer, but he did his best.

'Well, I think the wealth and comfort of some of my world's countries comes from a combination of democracy and technological devices. With regard to poor people in poor countries, I think one of the main problems is that they often do not have democracy, or if they do, then these democracies are often corrupt and their leaders turn their people into easy prey for the corrupt activities of others.'

'Do the people in the rich countries profit from the people in poor countries?' asked Lili.

'Yes, it is true that some of the wealth of rich countries comes from unequal trading relations with poor countries, although it doesn't have to be like that, not if you have good laws that prevent corruption and exploitation.'

'Which comes first,' asked Spartacus, 'poverty or corruption and exploitation?'

'Err, I think it varies, but the technology that my people have could be used to help you avoid poverty, and I hope that the goodwill and comradeship that has grown amongst the ex-slaves during the rebellion will help you avoid corruption and exploitation until you have constructed the kind of society you want, more or less.'

'Or the kind of society that your people want,' said Spartacus sceptically, 'more or less.'

'But you and your people can make your own laws. All I am saying is that you might want to learn from our experiences, good experiences as well as bad experiences, so that you can build a future without poverty or corruption or exploitation.'

'I believe you mean what you say, Mark, but will your people not want to control us for their own purposes?'

'Some will,' Mark admitted, 'and some will not, at least not consciously.'

'Then let them bring their laws to the new city they wish to build west of the Tiber. It seems to me that they have more need for laws against corruption and exploitation than we do, for their exploitation of slaves has corrupted them to the core. We may learn things from your people, and even learn things from the Romans, good things and bad things, but can we not choose how we live until we find out for ourselves what is good for us? Because what is good for us may not be the same as what your people think is good for us, or the same as what the Romans want.'

'Yes, of course, I'm sure you're right.'

'It's not that I distrust your people any more than anyone else, I just think we need time to discover what it means to be free before we become too influenced by others who want to decide our future.'

Two or three minutes of silence passed before Mark said: 'yes, Spartacus, yes, I think you are right. My people will want to help, mostly for what they think are good reasons, although they will see things through their own experiences, and so they might end up doing more harm than good. I have that urge to help too, but I rarely know if what I'm doing does more harm than good.'

'So far,' said Spartacus, 'you have done us a great deal of good. If you are willing, I would ask you to do one more thing for us.'

'What?'

'Will you speak to your people on our behalf and tell them to spend their energies helping the Romans rather than us?'

'Really? Won't you want any help at all?'

'Maybe, someday, I don't know, but it is the Romans who need help now that their corrupt old world is crumbling. Kim spoke of Rome uniting again, and yet we are not just separated by the width of the Tiber. Our dreams and their dreams are worlds apart. Their world is dying. Ours is just being born, and it is fresh and hopeful and full of energy. Can we not be left to shape it ourselves and pursue our own dreams?'

'Of course. I mean, I will say that to my people if that's what you want.'

'It is what I want, and I think it is what most of my people want. Is that what you mean by democracy?'

Once again, Mark was not sure what to say, so he said nothing else until one of Rome's gates appeared before them through a dense smog that had descended upon the city from the cooling pyrocumulus cloud while they were at Crixus' camp. When they dismounted, some eagerly helpful men took their horses and enthusiastically welcomed them back to 'Freedom City'.

'Freedom City?' said Mark to Spartacus, 'was that your idea?'

'No, it's the first time I've heard it said. I think I like it. What do you think we should call the rest of it?' Spartacus asked, gesturing beyond the gate.

'You mean Italy?'

'Yes, what we control of it. How about the "Democratic Republic of Italy", would that please your people?'

Mark felt that Spartacus' tone was a touch hostile, and he wondered if the Americans were not the only people who wanted him safely out of the way now that his part in the war appeared to be played out.

'Spartacus!' said Lili, 'why do you tease Mark when he has done so much to help us?'

The two men looked at each other for a moment, then Spartacus shrugged and said, 'you are right, Lili, I am being difficult and unfair to the one person that we owe most to.' Holding out his hand for Mark to shake, he said 'forgive me, Mark. It is not you that worries me, it is the thought of another set of masters replacing our Roman masters.'

Mark shook Spartacus' hand and said 'yes, I can fully understand that.'

'Before we began our rebellion, I might have wept for joy if I knew that well meaning people from your world were about to become our masters instead of the Romans, but now I don't want any masters at all.'

'Absolutely, quite right!' said Mark, feeling slightly ashamed of his presumption in thinking that he might have some kind of say in what these people do with their freedom.

'Am I right?' Spartacus pondered, 'I wonder. Perhaps I am just being obstinate and unrealistic. Perhaps it would be better for others to guide us into a good life rather than blunder our own way into a mess. I just don't know.' Then his face creased into a broad smile, and he said: 'on the other hand, Kim's guidance didn't stop you blundering your way into Rome, did it?'

'No, it probably should have, but I'm glad it didn't!'

'Me too!' said Spartacus.

'And me,' said Lili.

'And me,' said Rani, putting her arm through Mark's left arm while his right hand was pumped up and down by Spartacus'.

Then Mark's mobile rang.

'I take it you're saying your goodbyes down there,' said Kim, and her words were translated into Latin through Mark's mobile.

'You're going?' Spartacus asked in surprise.

'I'm afraid so.'

'And I'm going with you!' said Rani in a tone that suggested her decision was beyond debate.

'I am being called to account for my actions,' Mark said to Spartacus while looking at Rani and wondering whether he should argue with her, even though he badly wanted her to come with him.

'Not to be punished, I hope?' said Spartacus.

'I don't know yet.'

'Mmm,' Spartacus mused, 'how long have you got?'

'I need to sail today, or tomorrow morning at the latest.'

'Today would be best,' said Kim.

'Then we really *do* need to talk,' said Spartacus, putting his arm around Mark's shoulders like an old friend. 'Come, let us talk while we walk along the wall back the way we came into this cursed city, and we shall see if my men are looking after your boat as I told them to.' And so they did, after Kim had politely terminated her call and left them to it.

They walked in the smog that hid the ruined city from sight and passed back through the fortress by the river and onto the wharf where they had landed in Rome just a day earlier. Picking their way through the rubble, they came to where Mark had left the *Ladybird*. It was still there, guarded by ten of Spartacus' men and with more than enough packs of food and flagons of water and wine stacked beside it to last him and Rani for months at sea. Even so, the damaged, ash-covered boat looked sad and forlorn in the smog and among the smoking ash-covered wreckage of the now largely destroyed commercial district in which they had made their landing inside Rome. All the bodies had been removed, probably thrown into the river, and Mark was already finding it difficult to relate this desolate place to their wild and deadly struggle for survival and escape from Caesar's trap. It was not just the smog and the ruins or the lack of activity that made the area look and feel different; the river also seemed narrower and everything appeared smaller and more ordinary than it had when adrenalin was surging through his veins.

Their conversations on the wall and the wharf had been continually interrupted by messengers coming to and fro, although none of the messages were alarming. The rebellion was spreading throughout the surrounding regions with little resistance and an exhausted peace had descended upon Rome in the aftermath of the firestorm. However, between the giving and receiving of messages, Spartacus had managed to work out a plan that he thought might help Mark and further the interests of the ex-slaves. After they put the *Ladybird* back into the river and taken supplies aboard, Mark checked the inboard computer and found that the Roman fleet was no longer on the river and nothing stood between them and the open sea. Then Spartacus told them what was on his mind.

'I hope everything works out for both of you. I don't think anyone among your people will blame Rani for fighting for freedom in her own world, but it seems to me, Mark, that you could use some help from us now. I don't know much about governments and things like that, but I suppose I can make a few, err, *interim* decisions until we get ourselves organised. I will speak to Julian and Andichios later, but I am sure they will agree with what I propose to do. I would like to offer you two the posts of, umm, how would you put it, diplomats? Yes, I would like you to become diplomats for the new Democratic Republic of Italy, or whatever we end up calling ourselves, so that you can *officially* represent us when you speak to your people. If you agree, then I hope it will make it more difficult for your people to punish you for helping us. If they refuse to speak to you as our official representatives then we will refuse to speak to them at all. Would that matter to them?'

'Well, yes,' said Mark uncertainly, 'I'm sure it would, but I . . .'

'Good!' Spartacus interrupted, 'that's settled then.'

'But I . . .'

'You would also be doing us a great service in this,' Spartacus interrupted again, 'because between the two of you, you have more knowledge than anyone on this world about the differences and similarities between our peoples. If we are to have talks, then you two are the obvious choice as go-betweens between our peoples.'

'But . . .'

'If you say no, I will send Crixus so that he can threaten to cut their heads off if they don't do what he wants!'

They all laughed a little at this, and Rani squeezed Mark's hand several times to show that she thought they should accept Spartacus' offer. So they did, gratefully and without argument. As far as Mark's future was concerned, Spartacus had probably done the one thing that was most likely to help. Those among the Americans who supported him could now argue that he should have diplomatic immunity from prosecution, whereas his critics might find it difficult to offer counter arguments that could not be interpreted as being pro-slavery.

Otherwise, their departure from Rome was something of an anti-climax. There were no parades, no speeches, no long goodbyes; just a hug from Lili, a handshake from Spartacus and some mutual promises about meeting again soon. The late afternoon sun was now showing through the smog like a pale moon. Mark was well within the twenty-four hour deadline that Kim had set for his departure, but he was looking forward to a slowish journey in which he could catch up on some sleep and unwind with Rani and a flagon of wine in front of a few films, and just spend some time not worrying about anything major or being under the gaze of so many people. Having instructed the *Ladybird* to make for the open sea, they sailed off waving to their two friends as people do to those who they confidently expect to see again before very long.

As the waving forms of Spartacus and Lili were lost to view behind the end of the fortress that jutted into the river, they emerged out of the smog and back into the golden light of an early autumn pre-sunset. No arrows assailed them and no one approached them to ask their purpose. When they drew further from the cloud above the city it took on the shape of an hourglass. The top of the hourglass was in fact a long cloud that fanned out across the countryside, but that was not immediately apparent from where they stood. Although the cloud was an ugly reminder of the destruction he had brought to this once great city, it seemed to Mark that its hourglass shape was a fitting symbol for the demise of 'Roman order', i.e.

slavery. Soon after this thought struck him, he wondered if it might also be a fitting symbol for the demise of this world's independence.

For all that had happened, he still did not know whether his interventions would ultimately turn out for good or ill, nor would he ever know for sure. Even if scientists on his home planet got to grips with regeneration or retro-aging and he found himself living indefinitely, there would always be an unknown and unknowable future stretching ahead, and the full consequences of his actions, as with the consequences of everyone's actions, could never be laid bare and calculated for eternity.

When they approached Ostia, over which hung a thin haze of smoke from the port city's lesser fires, four or five arrows winged their way towards them from the Roman-held bank, but all of them fell short of the *Ladybird*. On the other bank, in Ostia itself, the Roman garrison and several thousand citizens had boarded whatever ships and boats they could find and fled their isolated city earlier in the day. All that side of the river, from Rome to the sea, was now in the hands of jubilant ex-slaves, many of whom began to gather on the waterfronts as word of Mark and Rani's departure spread before them.

Lines of people cheered wildly or chanted 'Mark Goodvictory, God of Fire' and 'Goddess Kimrani' as they sailed past. Hundreds of them ran beside the *Ladybird* waving and calling out the muddled-up names they had given them until they came to the mouth of the river estuary. Knowing that the setting sun would show their silhouettes against the horizon until they were well out to sea, Mark and Rani continued to wave after their well-wishers had merged into the landscape and the vast plume of smoke that was still drifting from Rome behind them.

'Well,' Mark said aloud to himself as he thought about the first time he had sailed up the Tiber and everything that had happened since then, 'all in all, I *think* that went quite well.'

307

COMING SOON:

BOOK II

FROM THE ASHES
(SEQUEL TO RELUCTANT GODS)

Printed in the United Kingdom
by Lightning Source UK Ltd.
135012UK00001B/36/P